Sexy Beast V

Sexy Beast V

KATE DOUGLAS
VONNA HARPER
CRYSTAL JORDAN

𝒜

APHRODISIA

KENSINGTON BOOKS

http://www.kensingtonbooks.com

APHRODISIA BOOKS are published by

Kensington Publishing Corp.
850 Third Avenue
New York, NY 10022

All Kensington Titles, Imprints, and Distributed Lines are available at special quantity discounts for bulk purchases for sales promotions, premiums, fund-raising, and educational or institutional use.

Special book excerpts or customized printings can also be created to fit specific needs. For details, write or phone the office of the Kensington special sales manager: Kensington Publishing Corp., 850 Third Avenue, New York, NY 10022, attn: Special Sales Department, Phone: 1-800-221-2647.

Aphrodisia and the A logo Reg. U.S. Pat & TM Off.

ISBN-13: 978-0-7582-1989-3
ISBN-10: 0-7582-1989-X

First Kensington Trade Paperback Printing: September 2008

10 9 8 7 6 5 4 3 2 1

Printed in the United States of America

CONTENTS

Chanku Wild

Kate Douglas

1

Tala Quinn buried her face in her hands and cried. Blood streamed down her left forearm from a shallow slash that ran from the base of her thumb to her elbow. The wolf beside her whined and butted her thigh with his nose. The wolf standing beside the body of the man he'd just killed growled, but his tail was tucked tightly between his legs, and his ears lay flat against his head.

The coroner ignored the bloody body of the dead man and carefully wrapped a tiny, lifeless bundle for transport. He shook his head in obvious dismay. "You and your team did everything you could, Ms. Quinn. This little one's been dead for hours. He probably killed her right after he snatched her." The man glanced at the body, then nodded toward the wolf. Blood spatters marred the animal's thick coat and matted the fur on his chest. "Those animals of yours seem amazingly calm, considering what they just did to that bastard."

Tala shuddered and tangled her fingers in Mik's thick coat. "I'm a professional. We do search and rescue. We don't kill. I shouldn't have lost control of them like that." She swept her one intact sleeve across her eyes and took a deep, calming breath. "Damn, I hate custody fights. Children should be protected, not used as weapons or pawns. Why . . . ?"

"Because they're selfish scum."

Tala glanced up as the sheriff stepped out from behind his car, carrying a first-aid kit in his meaty fist. He was a huge man, powerful, but even he looked shaken. He stared at the bloody gash on Tala's arm. "You okay, Ms. Quinn?"

Tala nodded. "It's very shallow." She looked at her arm, stared at the blood. She hadn't felt the blade when it sliced into her. He'd attacked so fast that he'd even caught the wolves off guard. At least her blood was congealing, the wound closing. "That's when AJ, my wolf, killed him. When the guy attacked me. It happened so fast. . . ." She was babbling. She knew it, but she couldn't seem to stop.

The sheriff opened his kit and pulled out some antiseptic cleanser and a roll of gauze. "Paramedic units all got called out on a big wreck over on the highway. Let me clean this up for you. It should be okay until you see a doctor."

Tala shut her mouth and held out her arm. The wolf near the body snarled. The one beside Tala leaned close to her side, watching intently. The sheriff glanced in his direction, then carefully cleansed Tala's wound and wrapped her arm with the sterile gauze.

He nodded toward a thick clump of trees. "His ex-wife's body's over there. I got a call from one of my deputies a few minutes ago. They found the new husband's body. It appears this prick murdered him one, maybe two days ago. That's when he took the woman and her baby. Killed 'em both. They probably died sometime last night. She fought him. Fought him really hard."

He stared for a long time at the tiny bundle in the coroner's arms, but he spoke to Tala. "Thank you, ma'am. For losing control. For turning these magnificent animals loose the way you did. Theirs was an honest justice. Better than this scum deserved." He turned and looked at Tala, at the fresh bandage he'd just applied to her wounded arm, and the grief poured off him in waves. Then he shook his head and sighed. "Sometimes I hate my job."

There were days when Tala hated her job as well. This was one of them. It was full dark by the time the sheriff got her statement and said she could leave. Numb and exhausted, she loaded her wolves into the SUV. They made it as far as the first decent body of water, a cold, clear river flowing not far from the site of the murders. She wondered what the guys in the back were thinking. Their silence was unusual, the lack of communication unnerving. Neither of them had shifted.

Generally, after a job, they'd shift back to their human form as soon as they were away from curious eyes. They'd talk about the job—what went wrong, what they'd done right.

Tonight, not a damned thing had gone right. Tala pulled off the road and found a secluded spot to park the SUV. She sensed the wolves' impatience, their guilt over her injury. Tonight had been a devastating experience for all of them. AJ was not a killer, but he'd ripped out the murderer's throat without hesitation. Mik had no problem with killing, but he'd done his best to protect Tala while AJ brought the bastard down.

It hadn't been enough.

Lunging at Tala Quinn with a knife was the last mistake the killer would ever make. As the sheriff had said, his death was better than he deserved.

Tala took a deep breath and swallowed back her tears. When a victim was killed or badly hurt, she felt as if they'd failed. When an innocent child died, there was no way to ignore the grief. Tala shivered. She couldn't let it go.

She reached for Mik and AJ, but their thoughts remained blocked. She stared at them a moment, unnerved when she realized neither set of amber eyes met hers. Did they blame her for the night's devastating conclusion?

The moment she opened the door, both huge animals jumped out and headed for the water. Moving on autopilot, Tala stripped out of her clothes and, naked and shivering, waded into the icy river.

She held her arm overhead to keep the bandage dry.

The water was so cold it stung, but she needed the numbing pain. Needed to feel clean again after such a terrible day and night. They'd tracked the killer and his kidnapped family from a small town east of Lake Coeur d'Alene in Idaho, where he'd headed into the forest.

When Tala and her Pack Dynamics team were called in, they knew from the beginning it might be a hopeless case, but she'd never been one to give up hope. AJ and Mik were realists, more pragmatic by nature, but they'd learned to trust her instincts.

Trust she obviously hadn't deserved on this job.

Right now, she needed to forget. Needed to cry. She loved her wolves, but she desperately desired the warmth of two strong men. Her men. The ones who loved her no matter what.

AJ Temple shifted first. Tall and lean, with the rangy body of a working man, his chin-length hair tangled wet and dark about his beautiful face, he lunged through the water toward her, determination and anger written in his glittering eyes. The night's ugliness still wrapped him in its steel grip, and she sensed his need to erase the pain, to expunge his own sense of guilt.

Grabbing Tala in his arms, he lifted her high, just above him, and held her there for a moment. "I am so sorry," he whispered. "So sorry." Then he plunged his cock into her, parting her sex with the pure force of his thrust. He was big and hard and it hurt—and it was exactly what she wanted. What he needed. Hot and angry at herself, furious with her failure, with the feeling that her mistakes had forced this man to kill, she wrapped her legs around his waist and sobbed her regret as he fucked her.

Even as she cried, her body responded. With each powerful thrust of his hips, AJ took her higher into pleasure, further from the ugliness of the past twenty-four hours.

His thoughts were blocked, but his love poured through Tala even as he ravaged her body. His cock plunged deep, banging against her womb hard enough to hurt. She welcomed the pain. Rolled with it, gloried in it. Her body tensed and her legs tightened around AJ's waist, and his thoughts flowered in her mind as her climax slammed through her.

She felt his anguish, his utter sense of failure. Not for killing. No, it was for failing to protect Tala. Her bandage was a sharp and ugly flag of dishonor, and the deaths of their targets left a stain on his soul. He had failed Tala, failed Mik, failed the young mother and her child. But most of all, he'd failed the team.

She understood. The same inadequacy defiled her own soul. AJ's big body shuddered. He filled her with the hot wash of his seed, and Tala's body responded. His guilt swirled around them both, shared and painful, growing instead of waning.

Suddenly the pain of failure was pushed aside. Mik Fuentes stood behind Tala and wrapped his arms around her, around AJ. The cold river swirled about their thighs; the night air had grown cold, but Tala was sandwiched between two fiery bodies, wrapped in heat and love.

Mik's voice soothed them. His steady heartbeat throbbed against her back, and the solid length of his cock pressed into the tight cleft between her buttocks. His words held power, carried a message that slowly swept away the guilt.

"AJ, you did more than anyone else. You destroyed a killer who needed to die. Tala, sweetie, you did not fail. We all did the best we could. They called us in too late. The baby and her mother were already dead by the time we got on the trail. You can't right every wrong, but you can learn and move on. Put this behind you."

Tala nodded and rested her head wearily against AJ's chest. His heart thudded beneath her ear, and he shivered, as much from the power of their orgasm as from the icy river. He listened intently to Mik's words, and Tala knew he took comfort in what their lover had to say.

She wished she could do the same. Even though she knew Mik was right, it didn't make the ugliness go away.

Mik's thoughts poured into her mind. *Shift. We need to run. You'll feel better when you're the wolf. This will all make more sense to you then.*

Tala shook her head. She unwrapped her legs from AJ's waist. His cock slid out of her tight channel. She lowered her legs into the icy water and gasped. It might only hit the guys at the middle of their thighs, but Tala was better than waist-deep. The shock to her body cleared her mind. She knew what she needed, and for once it had nothing to do with running through the forest or making love with her men. Her teeth chattered, but she refused to shift.

She tilted her head and looked over her shoulder at Mik. His dark amber eyes glowed almost green in the light of the waxing moon. His unusually long hair hung wet and straight, plastered to his chest and belly, blacker than black in the pale light. "I need something more, and for once you two can't give it to me. I need life. I'll feel better when I hold a healthy, living baby. One who is loved by both parents."

Suddenly it was all too much. Tala felt the tears flow in scalding trails down her cheeks. She wrapped her fingers around Mik's arm. "We're not far from Anton Cheval's home in Montana. Keisha and Xandi should be there. Please, Mik? AJ? I need to see their babies. I want to hold Lily and Alex. Please? I have to hold healthy, happy babies."

* * *

Padding on broad paws along the narrow trail, the snow leopard paused at a small creek, crouched low, and drank deeply. Her tail swished in a slow, hypnotic rhythm, and her whiskers sparkled with tiny droplets of water. Her pale coat, dappled with dark rosettes, provided perfect camouflage beneath the filtered moonlight.

She gazed skyward at the bulbous disk shimmering between the treetops, and her thoughts were anything but those of a wildcat. She was remembering a conversation held earlier in the evening, when she'd stood on two human legs on the back deck of Anton Cheval's lovely Montana home.

Oliver, the man she loved, had been on her left. Anton, her newest lover, on her right. The three of them had been watching the moon rise slowly above the tree line when Mei commented on its fat, imperfect shape.

Anton had laughed. Then he'd explained that the phase it was in now was called a *waxing gibbous moon*—almost, but not quite, full. She loved the way the words sounded, and she'd giggled like a silly kid when she repeated the phrase. *Waxing gibbous.* Even now it made her smile. She loved learning, and Anton was always willing to teach. He amazed her. There was very little Anton Cheval didn't know.

She only hoped he could help her fix what appeared, at this moment in time, totally unfixable.

A rabbit fed alongside the creek, unaware that a leopard crouched nearby. Mei raised her head and snarled. The rabbit stopped, nose twitching. Long ears swiveled, searching desperately for the source of the unfamiliar sound.

Mei chuffed and the rabbit scampered into the brush. She'd already fed, or he would not have been so lucky. It was time to go back. The others would want to run. Mei lifted her head, sniffed the night air, turned away from the creek, and padded quickly down the trail. Unlike the wolf, a snow leopard did not run for the sake of pleasure.

She'd merely needed to hunt. As always, she hunted alone, and her belly was full.

"There she is." Oliver Cheval spotted the leopard gliding out of the dark forest. Thank the goddess, she was safe, but he'd not been sure. He hated the fact that they couldn't communicate when she shifted, but their wolf and leopard brains had proved incapable of linking telepathically. If Oliver remained human, when she was in leopard form, Mei understood his verbal speech but not his mental words. He worried every time Mei hunted alone. Unfortunately, they'd discovered very quickly that wolf and leopard were not, by nature, compatible hunting partners.

At least they were entirely compatible in their human form. . . . but it wasn't enough. Not nearly enough. Oliver turned to the man next to him—his mentor, the one whose name he had taken with gratitude so many years ago. "Will it work? Will we ever be able to bond?"

"In theory . . ." Anton shrugged, a somewhat incongruous gesture, considering his patrician bearing and darkly handsome, aristocratic looks. "I've never tried this, transferring consciousness from one body to another. Other than my own, of course. The fact that Mei is a leopard and Eve a wolf begs the question, Will their basic nature prevent the switch? I don't know, Oliver. We can only try and hope for the best."

The big cat paused below them. Her powerful hindquarters bunched, and she exploded into the air. A lovely young Asian woman landed gracefully on the deck, her dark hair flowing about her nude body, her green eyes sparkling with the joy of the hunt and the sensual need throbbing in her veins.

Oliver responded, his body incapable of ignoring the woman he loved. Mei threw her arms around him. She was ripe with desire, and the thick wash of her pheromones was impossible to ignore. Oliver lifted her against his bare chest and glanced over his shoulder at Anton. "Go ahead and run. I'll catch up to you later."

Anton saluted Oliver with his glass of wine. "We'll wait. Keisha's trying to get Lily to sleep and Xandi's feeding Alex. Mei offered to babysit both the kids."

Oliver kissed Mei, a quick teasing taste of her lips. "We won't be long."

She pouted and rolled her eyes. "There are some things you rush, others you don't. This is one of those others."

Laughing, Oliver carried her into the house. "Yes, dear. As you say, dear." It was fun to tease her, but his heart was heavy even as desire raged through his body. One more week before Anton attempted the impossible—temporarily switching Mei's consciousness into Eve's wolven body.

Until then, they couldn't mate. Could not experience the truly deep bond that occurred only when Chanku mated as wolves. He'd already accepted the fact that they could never have children. Once a woman became Chanku, she could only be impregnated in her animal form. Most of the time this was not a problem. Not when both partners were both wolves.

But Mei Chen was unique among them. Perfect in every way. Beautiful, powerful, she was an unusual shapeshifter whose basic nature was far removed from the rest of the pack.

Far removed from Oliver, the man who loved her in spite of their differences.

When he and the others shifted, they became wolves. She alone became the cat, a snow leopard, descendant of those born in the same inhospitable slice of the world at the base of the Himalayas as the other Chanku ancestors.

One a wolf, the other a leopard.

Both shapeshifters.

Oliver carried Mei through the house, out the front door, and across the driveway to his private cottage. Once inside, he headed straight to their room. He gazed into Mei's eyes and recognized the feverish light in them, the overwhelming need for sexual release that was so much a part of their kind.

In that respect, they were entirely similar—creatures ruled by a powerful libido, made even more demanding after running in their animal form. After shifting, desire pulsed hot and deep through Mei's veins. Oliver smelled her arousal. His cock lengthened and swelled, pressing fiercely against his denim jeans. He needed her, every bit as desperately as Mei needed him.

In this, they were the perfect match.

His skin was dark chocolate to her creamy caramel, a perfect blend when Oliver lowered her to the bed. She arched into his touch, and he caught the small, breathy mewling deep in her throat. He kicked off his shoes, stripped off his pants, and knelt beside her on the bed.

She reached for him, but he moved quickly and settled himself between her legs. When he leaned close and touched his tongue to her swollen sex, she lifted her hips to his mouth and cried out.

This was how they connected, where their souls touched and minds linked. He felt her in his thoughts, her voice an incoherent plea for his lips and tongue, for the hard length of his cock. Wet and swollen after her shift, she needed no foreplay, nor did she want it.

Take me. Fill me. Please, Oliver! I need you.

You said there were some things I shouldn't rush. He lapped at her sleek folds and valleys, moving at a slow and leisurely pace that made his balls ache and his cock weep, but it was worth the pain to watch the myriad emotions flitting across her face.

Damn you! She cursed him with laughter in her mind, lifted her hips higher, and thrust herself against his mouth. He speared her with his tongue, suckled her hard little clit between his lips, and rubbed his fingers back and forth along the valley between her perfectly shaped buttocks.

She shivered beneath his touch. He licked with greedy abandon, lapping up her thick wash of sweet fluids. Nuzzling at her clit with the tip of his nose, Oliver settled in for a long, slow feast.

Mei's heart pounded in her chest. She fought for each breath of air as Oliver slowly but surely destroyed her self-control. His fingers traced the sensitive crease between her cheeks and lingered over her anus. She felt the muscle there flutter when he rubbed. She didn't know whether to press down against his finger or lift her hips higher to his mouth.

Moaning, gasping with the swirling sensations, Mei shivered. She knew he loved this, torturing her, keeping her on the edge of climax, making her wait for what felt like eons while he licked and teased, nibbled and stroked. Even now, Oliver kept her from coming, his thick middle finger pressing and retreating, his tongue lapping with long slow strokes that merely hinted at what he could do, what he would do . . . in his own sweet time.

Suddenly his finger breached her tight opening just as his lips wrapped tightly around her clit. Shocks coursed over Mei's nerves, pulsing bursts of power flowing throughout her body as he buried his finger deep inside her tight passage and compressed her clit with his lips and tongue. Screaming, Mei arched off the bed as her first orgasm slammed into her.

Oliver backed away, leaving her empty and still wanting. He knelt between her legs and rubbed the broad crown of his cock against her sex. Pulsing with the rhythmic spasms of her first release, Mei's body shuddered.

Slowly, he entered. She felt the throbbing tissues part and drew her knees up to give him better access. Stretching her sensitive channel to the point of pain, he moved forward, pushed deeper, filling her completely, not stopping until his balls pressed against her ass and the head of his cock was planted firmly against her cervix.

Opening her eyes, Mei watched Oliver's face. His eyes were closed. His arms trembled, and he held perfectly still. She opened her thoughts to his, called to him with the soft voice in her mind.

He was there, his thoughts open to Mei, a beautiful sharing they were denied in their animal forms. Tears filled her eyes. It hurt, knowing she was incapable of truly bonding with the man she loved. In answer to her bittersweet thoughts, Oliver shared the sense of her, the soft undulations of feminine muscles clasping his shaft, the slick moisture spilling out of her, covering his cock and balls so that each movement he made followed a smooth, wet slide of warm, giving flesh.

Her flesh, his . . . for this moment, they were one creature, irrevocably linked. One single mind, one heart beating. Now, when they loved as man and woman, connected in the only way they could. Even so, the sense of isolation each felt when they roamed in their bestial counterpart waited in the shadows.

Oliver slowly withdrew, thrust forward again. Mei cried out and clasped him tightly with arms and legs, clinging to him. Unlike the other men in the pack, Oliver was slightly built, almost exactly her size. They fit perfectly. Mouths together, her breasts to his muscled chest, his powerful cock to her warm and willing sex. His slim hips pumped slowly back and forth as he rocked her to his rhythm.

She felt her climax building once again, sensed Oliver's struggle to maintain the slow, steady torture. Mei ran her hands along his smooth flanks, squeezed the taut muscles and trailed one finger along the damp crease between his buttocks. She rubbed gently over the puckered muscle, circling the sensitive flesh until she felt his muscles shuddering, sensed the desperation in his mind.

Smiling against his mouth, she teased his sensitive anus, pressing and then releasing in time with each deep thrust as he filled her. His balls had drawn up tight, the sac hard and wrinkled between his legs, and she took a moment to stroke that as well.

Oliver moaned and plowed into her harder, faster. Heat spiraled through Mei. Shocks of sensation raced from breasts to womb to clit, growing more powerful with each thrust. She speared him with her finger, driving deep inside his tight, moist passage, her long finger heading unerringly for the small, round gland he probably wished she'd never discovered.

Oliver cried out when she found it, cursed her, laughing, as he arched his back with the depth of powerful penetration. The hot spurts of his seed bathed her sensitive tissues, the final sensation taking her tumbling into the abyss with the one she loved.

Panting, almost sobbing in relief, she cradled Oliver as he slumped across her chest. Her hands stroked his sweat-slick back, her thighs held him close, and the muscles in her pulsing channel milked him even harder, squeezing every last drop they could wring from him.

Mei's thoughts spun with the combined sensation. His climax, hers. The blending of their bodies, the pounding of their hearts, even now beating almost frantically in sync. But it wasn't enough. Not nearly enough.

There was a sharp rap on the door. Stefan Aragat's voice slipped into both their minds.

Ten-minute warning, he said, and it was obvious he was laughing. *The babies are almost asleep, and we don't want to miss our window of opportunity.*

Oliver pushed himself up and over, flopping onto his back beside Mei. *We'll be there. Mei's going to take a quick shower.*

Oliver leaned over and kissed her. "We'll know next week at this time if it's going to work. There's no reason to worry. Anton knows what he's doing."

Mei nodded, but she turned away and sat up without looking at Oliver. Even Anton wondered if the switch would work. She felt it in him whenever he glanced her way. He didn't realize how she read him now. Didn't know that the one time they'd made love, the one time they'd linked so closely when he tried to learn more about her true nature, she'd learned more about Anton than even she had first realized.

He might project a sense of confidence, a self-assurance that was hard to deny, but he was every bit as nervous as any of them. Mei turned around and smiled at Oliver. He grinned back at her and winked.

She would keep her fears to herself. If it didn't work and she didn't survive, it didn't really matter. Without the full bond, without the ability to love this man completely, life really meant nothing to her at all.

2

Moonlight filtered through the open window and cast a soft glow over both babies. Mei ran the back of her fingers along Alex's satiny cheek. Just over two months old, he slept soundly at his end of the crib, arms and legs stretched wide in contented abandon.

There was a peaceful smile on his perfect, bow-shaped mouth, and a thick tuft of dark hair in front showed evidence of a definite widow's peak. He was going to be every bit as handsome as his father, but the general consensus was he'd have his mother's stubborn streak.

Three-month-old Lily might have started out at the opposite end of the crib, but already she'd managed to scoot around in her sleep and was working her way toward Alex. Mei carefully shifted Lily back to her end without waking her, but she knew it wouldn't be long before Lily was on the move again in search of her buddy Alex.

The link between the two was already evident—perfectly understandable, considering the bond among their parents. Stefan,

Xandi, Keisha, and Anton might as well have been a bonded *foursome*, from what Mei could tell. She'd never seen such unconditional love among adults in her life.

Sometimes it frightened her, the way her life had changed so quickly. She'd always been alone and honestly couldn't remember ever loving anyone. She'd spent years in Florida's foster-care system, then lived on the streets until her old friend Eve Reynolds had caught her shoplifting, of all things.

With Eve had come Oliver and the others in their unusual extended family—Adam, Anton, Stefan, Keisha, and Xandi—all so willing to accept her, to want her as a part of their pack. Unconditional love from people who had been complete strangers just a few short weeks ago, yet they actually *wanted* her as one of them.

Even though she didn't really fit.

Mei raised her head and gazed out the window. They were running even now, seven glorious wolves racing the moonlight.

Snow leopards hunted alone.

Wolves ran with the pack.

She turned and gazed at Lily. Moonlight caressed her perfect little form. The baby was a blend of both Anton and Keisha, her silky skin almost the same color as Mei's, a rich, dark caramel. Her thick, sleek cap of hair was black as night.

Mei's eyes clouded with tears, but she held them back. She loved Keisha and Xandi. They didn't know how difficult it was for her to watch their beautiful babies, the living proof of their parents' love, of their commitment.

She might shift into a snow leopard, not a wolf, but Mei knew she shared the most important traits with other Chanku females. The good thing, of course, was the immunity. She couldn't catch human diseases. The ability to release an egg for fertilization only when she wanted to get pregnant had been the most empowering feeling. When she'd first perceived that part of her physiology, she'd been absolutely amazed by the sense of strength she'd felt.

Until she realized what it actually meant. She was Chanku. She could no longer get pregnant in her human form.

She was fertile only when she shifted.

When she became a snow leopard.

Oliver would forever be a wolf. She ran her finger along Lily's silky cheek and thought of babies with Oliver. The babies they'd never be able to have. If Anton's plan worked, they'd finally do the mating bond as wolves, but she wouldn't actually be a wolf. She'd be Mei, in Eve's body.

"Yeah," she whispered, stroking Lily's hair. "Like Eve's gonna let Oliver get her pregnant. I imagine Adam would have something to say about that." As much as Adam loved Oliver, Mei could guess what his reaction would be about sharing his mate for breeding. He was worried enough about the mind swap.

Of course, that wasn't what Mei wanted, either. She wanted what the others had. Wanted her man beside her. Wanted to hunt with the one she loved beneath the dark Montana sky.

She wanted Oliver's babies. It was simple, really. She merely wanted the impossible.

Swallowing back a quiet sob, Mei checked the babies' blankets and quickly slipped out of her clothes. She stood there a moment in the darkened room and listened to the silence of the house, felt the familiar yet comforting sense of isolation she'd known all her life. Then she shifted. The leopard sniffed the air, implanting the scent of the babies on her feline mind. Then she slipped through the open doorway and padded down the long hallway.

While the others ran through the night answering the call of their wolven souls, she would keep watch. No harm would come to the children. Not while the snow leopard guarded them.

* * *

"Poor little thing's out like a light." Mik carefully lifted Tala out of her nest of blankets and sleeping bags in the back of the SUV. She grumbled something unintelligible, then snuggled against his chest and relaxed. Tears stained her cheeks, and her long, dark hair tangled about her shoulders in total disarray. She looked about twelve years old.

Mik could hold her like this all night long, but she needed her rest. They'd been on the road for over four hours, making the run from Idaho to Montana. It was almost three in the morning. Not a time for visitors to come calling, but Anton and his pack often hunted through the night.

Mik followed AJ up the steps to the house.

AJ stopped in front of the heavily carved door. "I wonder if they're even home?"

Mik shook his head and switched to mindtalking so he wouldn't wake Tala. *It's late. They're probably hunting.*

Frowning, AJ glanced at him. *I doubt they'd all leave with babies here, and I can't imagine them taking little ones into the woods.*

Mik shrugged. *Hell, what do we know about babies? They might figure it's safe to leave them for a little bit out here. There are cars out front, so someone's probably around. They've probably just gone for a short run.*

AJ tapped lightly on the massive, intricately carved door. No one answered. He glanced at Mik and tried the knob. The big door swung open without a sound. *Do you think they're asleep?*

Are you kidding? We wouldn't have made it up the steps if anyone was home. Holding Tala against his chest, Mik brushed past AJ and stepped over the threshold, into the dark foyer.

AJ turned toward a long hallway and gestured for Mik to follow. *Head for the guest wing. Keisha always puts us in the same room when we're here. Maybe it's empty. We can at least put Tala to bed. She's had a rough night.*

Mik nodded. Silently he turned, prepared to follow AJ. Then he stopped. *AJ. Hold up. I sense . . .*
What?
I don't know. But it's not a wolf.

Mei heard the crunch of gravel as the big SUV pulled into the driveway. Still in leopard form, she watched through the big front window as two unfamiliar men got out. The biggest one, his long, black hair falling unbound past his waist, reached into the back of the vehicle. He lifted what appeared to be a sleeping child out of the back.

Ears laid back against her broad skull, Mei slipped through the dark room and hid behind a doorway leading to the entry. She sensed their telepathic conversation but couldn't understand them.

Chanku? They must be, but Anton hadn't said anything about guests arriving. Damn, she wished she could communicate with Oliver and the others, but there was no way. Even if she shifted to human, Mei doubted they could understand her mental voice while in their wolven forms.

One of the visitors knocked on the door. She waited, muscles tense, eyes narrowed. It was her job to protect the babies. If these fools persisted . . . Mei snarled. Let them. She crouched low, her muscles bunched.

They stepped through the doorway and paused in the dark foyer. The big one held the child. No way could she attack someone with a little girl in their arms, but she couldn't let them in, either. Not until she knew who they were, what they wanted.

Snarling, Mei stepped out from the shadows. She crouched in front of the two men, tail whipping back and forth, ears pressed tightly against her skull. She curled her lips back from sharp canines and snarled once again.

Both men stopped midstep.

"What the hell?"

"Don't shift!" The big one carrying the girl shook his head. He stared directly at Mei. *Unbelievable!*

His thought speared her brain. She understood him.

"Shit, man. That is one mean-looking cat." The other guy took a step backward.

The big one held his place with the girl sleeping soundly in his arms. He studied Mei a moment. She lashed her tail and snarled again, a low sound that thundered deep in her chest. He grinned at her and nodded his head.

Are you Chanku? Who are you? We mean no harm. We're friends of Anton's.

She understood! It was like listening to someone with a thick accent, but she knew what he asked. *I hear you,* she sent. *I understand. How?* Mei relaxed her posture only slightly.

"Mik, what's going on?" The second man kept his eyes on Mei.

"Don't you hear it?"

"No. A weird buzzing in my head. Can you talk to it?"

She snarled and felt the hair along her spine stand up. *I am not an it. I am Mei Chen, and I live here. Who are you?*

The big one grinned at her. Damn, but he was gorgeous. Were there any ugly Chanku men . . . or women? He adjusted the sleeping female in his arms. This close, Mei realized she was older than she'd first thought. The big guy's mate?

I'm Mik Fuentes. This is my partner and bonded mate, AJ Temple. I need a bed for our woman. Tala's exhausted. She needs to rest. He glanced at the sleeping woman in his arms and then back at Mei, chastising her with his dark gaze. *Anton and the others would welcome us.*

Mei sat back on her haunches, shocked. He understood her. She understood him! His partner—his bonded mate? Now, that was different. Whatever. That one apparently lacked the ability to communicate with her, but to actually converse with this big guy was absolutely amazing. She looked closely and realized he was staring at her. Probably waiting for an answer.

I'm sure they would welcome you, but they're not here, and I don't know you. She thought of shifting, but as a woman, she was barely half his size. At least in her leopard form, Mei had teeth and claws and speed. She sensed no threat from these people, but for now, she felt more confident holding them at bay.

Do you mind if we sit in the den and wait for their return? Mik continued to smile. The other guy looked impatient, but apparently he had no idea what they were talking about.

Mei stepped out of their way. *That would be best.*

They headed directly toward the study, which meant they knew the house. Mei followed, more comfortable now about this group, and wondered once again if she should shift.

Alex made the decision for her. She heard his indignant wail coming from the nursery. *Wait in the study,* she commanded. Then she turned and padded down the long hallway.

She shifted the moment she reached the babies, wrapped her sarong around herself, and reached for Alex. Lily had managed to scoot the length of the crib and had her fingers tangled in his dark hair.

"No wonder you're crying, sweetie." Mei lifted him out of the crib and rocked him in her arms until he stopped crying. Then she changed his diaper and wondered how she'd get Lily changed without Alex starting to wail all over again.

"Please? May I hold Lily?"

Mei spun around. The woman standing behind her was no child. She might be a tiny little thing, but she was rounded in all the right places and was absolutely beautiful. Her dark hair hung in tangles to her waist, but the sadness in her catlike eyes caught Mei right in the heart. There was no threat from her, no sense of anything other than a very deep need. Mei nodded. "She's awake. I'm Mei Chen. Who are you guys?"

The woman was already at the crib, gently lifting Lily and placing her against her shoulder. She patted the baby's diaper-clad bottom. "Oh, Lily. How you've grown. Good. You're dry." She turned and smiled shyly at Mei. "My name is Tala Quinn. That was you, wasn't it, who met the guys? They told me there was a leopard at the door to greet them. AJ and Mik, my mates. Mik's the big scary one."

"Not all that scary. He's gorgeous." Mei sat in one of the matching rockers with Alex. "They both are."

Tala took the chair beside her. "They are, aren't they?" She cooed over Lily, but Mei felt her sadness and wondered what caused it.

"Are you Chanku?"

Tala nodded. "We are. You are, too, aren't you? I've never heard of anyone becoming a leopard." She raised her head. "Mik said he could mindtalk with you, but AJ didn't understand a word. I guess I missed all the fun. I didn't wake up until a few minutes ago, and Mik told me what happened. Are you always a leopard? Can you be a wolf, too?"

Mei cuddled Alex against her shoulder. He snuggled his legs up and immediately fell back to sleep. She shook her head. Felt tears threatening and held them back as best she could. "No. I'm a snow leopard." She raised her head and smiled at Tala. "The man I love is a wolf. Go figure . . ."

Tala turned and gazed steadily at Mei. "You can't mate . . . you can't bond." She glanced at the beautiful baby in her arms and kissed the top of Lily's head. "You can't have babies."

"I know." Mei's voice cracked on her whispered reply. "All of the above."

Tala raised her head. Tears glistened in her amber eyes. Eyes shaped much like Mei's. "I'm sorry. Really, truly sorry."

Anton ran his long wolven tongue across his mate's muzzle, thankful for this short break from reality. Tonight had been special, a chance for the four of them to run as they had before babies. Oliver, Eve, and Adam had chosen to hunt, but Stefan, Xandi, Anton, and Keisha had followed their familiar trails, racing the night and making love in the quiet, moonlit meadows.

Suddenly Keisha raised her head. Her ears pricked forward and she snarled. *Do you feel anything different about home? I sense Mei is no longer alone with the babies.*

Xandi trotted across the damp grass and touched her muzzle to Keisha's shoulder. *I don't feel anything. Is there a threat?*

No. No sense of threat. Just a feeling. Anton?

He raised his head and sniffed. *I'm not sure. It's time to return, anyway. Mei's been alone with the babies for almost three hours.*

Stefan took the lead. His gray-tipped coat glistened and rippled in the pale light. Anton took up the rear, with the females between them. Running like this, they should reach the house within ten minutes or so.

Anton cast about for the other three. Oliver's familiar voice answered in his mind.

Is there a problem?

I don't know. How far are you from the house? Keisha senses something. She's not sure what.

I'm already headed back. Should arrive in a couple minutes. Adam and Eve took a . . . um . . . detour.

Anton opened his thoughts to include the others in his group. *We know how that goes. We're right behind you. Be careful. Keisha has a feeling Mei's not alone.*

Heart pounding, Oliver raced the last mile to the house. He hated leaving Mei alone. He shouldn't have let Anton talk him into going tonight, not when it meant being out of touch with her. She should be in his head, a part of his thoughts, not separated by that damned leopard brain of hers.

If she was in danger, if the babies were at risk . . . terrified, Oliver skidded around the corner of the driveway at the front of the house. He paused, panting, and stared at the big SUV in the driveway. He recognized it as belonging to the San Francisco pack. Forcing his racing heart to calm, Oliver raised his nose and sniffed the air.

Mik and AJ. And Tala, of course.

He exhaled and dropped his muzzle almost to the ground. Relief weakened him. He realized he was trembling. Instead of racing into the house, Oliver trotted over to his cottage, where he shifted and grabbed a pair of sweatpants. He sent a silent message to the others. *All okay. Only friends are here.*

Then he entered the house.

Both Mik and AJ rose to their feet when Oliver walked into the study. Mik stepped forward. "I hope we aren't out of line, coming in like this."

"Not at all, though I imagine you startled Mei." Oliver sent his thoughts her way. He had a good idea where the women were.

Her one-word reply confirmed it. *Babies.*

"The snow leopard." Mik shook his head. "Now, that's an unexpected twist."

"She and Tala are with the babies." AJ waved his hand in the direction of the nursery. "The job we did yesterday was tough. A guy killed his ex-wife's new baby, her and her husband. We couldn't save any of them. Tala took it hard."

"Said she needed to hold a live, healthy baby. One who was loved." Mik had turned away and stared out the dark window, but now he looked back to Oliver and shrugged. "I think we all do."

"Understandable." Oliver went to Anton's liquor cabinet and pulled out the ever-present bottle of cognac. He held the bottle up and both men nodded, so he poured glasses for all of them. "Anton and the others will be back shortly. Mei stayed to watch the babies so we could run."

"You?" Mik grinned at Oliver. "I didn't realize you were Chanku. I thought you just worked for Cheval."

Oliver took a sip of his cognac. He had no idea how much, if any, of his story had gotten out to the other packs. He doubted any of them knew he'd been castrated as a child, then completely restored with a little help from Adam Wolf, the one among them who claimed his talent was "*to fix things.*"

He'd definitely managed to fix Oliver.

"It's a long story," Oliver said, "but, yes, I'm Chanku. I've served Anton Cheval for many years."

"Interesting." Mik glanced toward AJ and then narrowed his gaze, studying Oliver over the top of his glass. "Do you have a mate?"

Such a loaded question. Did Mik have any idea? "Hopefully, the snow leopard. Once we work out the logistics." He took a sip of cognac. *If only it were that simple.*

Mik nodded. "She's very brave, and she's beautiful. Just what a man wants in his mate. I've still not seen her as a human, but she's got one hell of a sexy leopard voice."

Oliver set his glass down very slowly. "You could mindtalk? With Mei in leopard form?"

Mik nodded. "It took a minute to get past the accent, but yeah, we could communicate. I was human. Not sure if I could do it as wolf, but maybe."

Oliver felt an unwelcome chill and realized it was jealousy, pure and simple. He looked at Mik, trying to see him as Mei would. Miguel Fuentes was a mountain of a man, well over six five with broad shoulders and thick, straight, coal-black hair that flowed to his waist. A perfect meld of Hispanic and Native American features gave him a look that was both beautiful and cruel. His nose was long and straight, his cheekbones sharply defined, his mouth wide, his lips full.

Tonight he wore scuffed cowboy boots that added to his already impressive height, faded denims, and a worn cotton vest over a sleek, muscular chest nearly twice as wide as Oliver's. His skin was dark, a combination of sunlight and heritage, and the look he returned Oliver was fierce yet filled with understanding and a surprising depth of compassion.

AJ, however, was the one to put words to the roiling emotions Oliver felt. He stepped forward and wrapped an arm possessively around Mik's waist. "That's got to be tough, man, to love someone you can't bond with. We worried about that. First Mik and me, because we didn't know if it would work with two men. It did."

Mik nodded. "It was just the two of us for years. Then we met Tala. We knew we couldn't let her go, but we were afraid a three-way bond was asking too much." He shrugged his massive shoulders, then turned and grinned at AJ. The love between the two men shimmered between them. "Turned out, we didn't have anything to worry about. Where there's a will, there's a way."

Anton led Keisha into the den where the two Chanku waited with Oliver. He thought back to the first time he'd met Mik and AJ, to the posturing and male displays of aggression they'd all performed, members of two separate packs meeting on Anton's home turf. Now, though, he knew them as valued friends, men with whom he could trust both his mate and his daughter.

"Anton, it's good to see you." Mik stepped forward and clasped his hand. AJ gave Keisha a hug, then held her at arm's length with a long, low whistle.

"You're even more gorgeous than usual," he said. "Motherhood definitely agrees with you."

"Thank you." Keisha glanced around the room. "Where's Tala?"

Mik hugged Keisha tightly. "With your daughter. Where else? She really needed to hold that baby girl of yours."

Keisha looked into his amber eyes, then glanced at Anton. *They're all suffering right now. Their pain is barely under control.*

Anton nodded. He'd felt the same misery when he and Mik shook hands. Something raw and bleeding, an open wound far from healed.

Keisha smiled and took AJ's hand. "C'mon. You have to see how she's grown, and it's time to relieve Mei. Have you met our resident snow leopard yet?"

AJ laughed. "Oh, yeah. Or, rather, you might say she met us. Your leopard takes her babysitting duties seriously. If Mik hadn't been able to mindtalk with her, she might have taken my leg off."

Anton paused in midstep and glanced at Oliver before turning back to look at the big guy. "Mik, you could mindtalk? You understood Mei in her leopard form?"

Mik nodded. "Yeah. AJ couldn't, but I could."

Anton nodded, but his thoughts were spinning. "Any idea why?" What about Mik was different than all the rest? He glanced at Oliver, who turned toward him at just that moment. The pain in Oliver's eyes was almost palpable.

Mik paused, and though Anton was the one who questioned him, he directed his answer to Oliver. "I've been thinking about it. Obviously, I didn't realize my understanding Mei was an issue, because it just happened when I saw the leopard, but my grandfather was Sioux. He raised me after my mother died, and the old ways were important to him. His spirit guide was *Igmutaka*, the mountain lion."

A shiver crossed Anton's shoulders. He merely nodded, acknowledging Mik's answer. Was there a connection? Something between the ancient peoples of Tibet and the Lakota Sioux? He would find out, all in good time.

Anton slung an arm around Oliver's shoulders and steered him toward the nursery. "Fascinating, Mik. The crazy thing is, I honestly think it makes perfectly good sense." He gave Oliver's tense shoulders a squeeze. "One more piece to the puzzle, eh, Oliver? Don't worry, my friend. We'll find a way."

3

"You looked adorable, holding that baby, Mik." Tala yawned and then crawled into the big bed next to him. She snuggled close. He wrapped an arm around her tiny waist and drew her even tighter against his chest.

"I am not adorable, little one. I am a warrior. Big. Mean. Scary."

"Yeah, right." AJ wandered out of the bathroom with a towel looped lightly around his waist. He leaned over and kissed Mik full on the mouth. "You scared the crap out of me tonight, talking to the leopard."

"I like Mei. How sad for them, though." Tala held the blankets up for AJ. He turned out the light and crawled in next to her.

Mik sighed. "Oliver's jealous of me. He doesn't want to be, but I can feel it. Such a pointless emotion, really. Mei has eyes only for Oliver."

Tala tilted her head back for Mik's kiss. "There's something with Anton. A connection between them. They have some sort of history. I sensed it."

"Who knows what goes on in Anton's mind?" Mik felt his tension slowly ebb as Tala and AJ snuggled closely against each other. The pain of the past hours had begun to fade the moment they'd gathered in the nursery. Tala had been right. Holding healthy, much-loved babies was exactly what the three of them needed.

Crawling into bed together, gossiping about normal stuff, people they loved, events that had nothing to do with death or dying . . . it felt good. The strain began to melt away.

Tala wriggled her round bottom against Mik's groin. The lemon scent from her shampoo filled his nostrils, and the damp warmth of her fresh-from-the-shower skin aroused the beast he'd thought tamed for the night. Mik cupped her mound in his big hand and held her close.

He heard a small sound, barely audible, the lightest whisper of need escaping from between her lips. Felt her laughter in the soft tremor where her back touched his chest. "I thought I was too tired, but you might be able to change my mind."

AJ chuckled. "Mine's already changed." He cupped Tala's face in his hands and kissed her. She groaned and pressed her buttocks even closer to Mik.

He slid his middle finger between her pouty nether lips. Her clit already felt hot and swollen, as if she'd been waiting for his touch. He slipped between the damp folds of her sex, dipped inside her wet heat. The heel of his palm dragged across her mound, pressing her clit as he filled her. One finger, then two.

AJ threw the covers back and crawled over the two of them until he lay against Mik's back. A dark coil of heat pierced Mik's gut, a sense of anticipation that had him rising hot and hard against Tala's buttocks.

It wasn't often that AJ took the top, but when he did . . .

Tala turned in Mik's embrace. For a little thing, she had an amazing chest on her. He never thought a woman's breasts could turn him on so much, but that was before Tala. Before he'd discovered that love knew no gender, that he could find as much completion buried in this woman's heat as he'd ever known with a man.

With AJ Temple. His first love.

Someday it might make sense, but Mik had long ago quit trying to figure it out. They were Chanku. Creatures of the forest, beings ruled as much by the strength of their powerful libido as by the wolf within.

Tala slipped low and kissed her way along the line of his belly. His muscles quivered beneath the damp brush of lips, the sharp nip of teeth. Her small hand cupped his sac just as AJ's finger reamed his ass. The dual sensations caught Mik by surprise, and he jerked his hips.

Tala laughed. Then she dipped lower and circled the smooth, flared crown of his penis with her lips. Mik groaned. For some reason, he was on the edge tonight, so ready to blow he knew he wouldn't last if she took him in her mouth.

Shrugging away from AJ, Mik rolled to his knees and pulled Tala beneath him. His hair draped over his shoulders, enshrouding her in a black curtain. She stared at him with her moist lips and eyes filled with love, and he knew he'd never find another like her.

She accepted his love and loved him in return. She loved AJ just as fiercely and would defend either man, no matter the risk. She directed their team as if she'd been born to the job. Tala was everything Mik could dream of, more than he'd ever believed possible. Now she was raising those perfect legs and wrapping them around his waist, baring herself to him without fear of his massive size, of his criminal past, of his convoluted sexuality.

He pressed the head of his cock against her tight passage, pushed forward and filled her. It never ceased to amaze him, as big as he was, that he could pierce this tiny woman, fill her until his balls slapped her firm ass, and she took him, all of him, with a look of pure bliss.

So caught up in the sensation of Tala's tightly contracting muscles holding on to his cock, he'd missed the fact that AJ knelt behind him, missed the first touch of lube against his ass. But no way in hell could he miss the hard thrust of his lover's cock, piercing him every bit as powerfully as he'd just taken Tala.

There was pain. The burning pain of tight muscles stretching to accommodate AJ's thick cock, the pressure of that shaft surging deep within his bowel. He groaned with the sense of fullness, the dark pleasure when AJ finally pressed his hard belly against Mik's ass and ground his hips against him. Their balls pressed tightly, almost painfully, together before AJ withdrew, slowly dragging against sensitive tissues, pulling almost all the way out before plunging deep inside again.

Mik copied the rhythm AJ set, pressing deep within Tala with each powerful thrust his lover made. He leaned over and sucked her left nipple between his lips, tonguing the sensitive tip and drawing it hard against the roof of his mouth.

He pinched her right nipple between thumb and forefinger and felt an answering blast of pleasure in his mind. Tala's lust, her powerful needs, her frustration with the failed rescue, her gut-wrenching pleasure when she finally got to hold those beautiful babies, all coalesced into pure, blinding passion, an arousal so pure, so complete, it brought tears to Mik's eyes.

AJ clasped Mik's slim waist, pressed deep with each long thrust and opened his mind to the love of both his mates. Mik's impressions spilled powerfully into his mind, the myriad sensations he felt sandwiched between AJ and Tala almost overwhelming. Heat and pressure, pain and pleasure, the pure wonder of his woman's slick hot channel, and of thick, driving cocks, his inside Tala, AJ's deep in him, so wound up within Mik's thoughts he'd lost track of where his body ended and where AJ's and Tala's began.

AJ absorbed and accepted the pleasure, the pain, the anguish the three of them shared. This was right and good, the way it should be for three who loved as they did. Dawn was only an hour or so away, a new day with the potential of driving out the pain of the past. Their failure had affected all of them, each in a different way.

Tala hated to lose a life, any life. AJ hated to kill. Mik hated to lose. Period. AJ sensed his mate's frustration with yesterday's job and poured his healing thoughts into Mik.

We did our best. You said it well—they called us too late. It's over. We move on. We still have each other.

We could have lost Tala.

You didn't. And I'm still here. Tala's quiet laughter swept over both of them. *We're alive and we've got each other. Quit blaming yourselves. Mik, I listened to your advice. Now you do the same and cut it out. Fuck me harder. I want you deep inside screwing, not worrying about where you screwed up.*

Yes, ma'am.

AJ threw his head back and laughed. Only Tala had the balls to keep the big guy in line. He reached down between Mik's legs and wrapped his fingers lightly around his lover's sac. Squeezing gently, he ramped up the pace of his thrusts and poured all his love into Tala's and Mik's minds. Bad things might happen, but in the end, it was good. He had Mik. He had Tala. They had each other. It was all so damned good.

Mik's lips tightened forcefully around Tala's left nipple. He grunted as AJ slammed into him, forcing him against her. His thick fall of ebony hair swept forward like a silken curtain, covering her. Tala had no time to prepare, no warning as the powerful shock of pure, unbridled pleasure engulfed her body, and she tumbled, free-falling over the edge into orgasm. She couldn't have stopped the scream that ripped past her throat if she'd wanted to. Her body spasmed as she arched her back and lifted her hips to Mik's powerful thrust, to his sweet mouth. Lights flashed and burned behind her closed lids, and Mik's mental touch slammed into her. She felt AJ plowing deep inside Mik, felt the heat of AJ's fingers wrapped tightly around clenched testicles, felt the coil of pain and pleasure as Mik's body threw itself off the same abyss and followed her into climax.

Gasping, sobbing for each breath, Tala felt it all, every clench and spasm as each of them experienced the same climax, the same orgasmic rush of pleasure, defined individually, shared exponentially. She loved it all, the burning pain, the addictive rapture of bodies finding ultimate satisfaction. She breathed in the scents of her men, their touch, their taste. Lungs heaving, pussy rippling in sensual spasms, her body slick with sweat, Tala lay beneath Mik's weight, her legs trapped by AJ's heavy thigh, and once again felt whole.

This mattered. This joining, this complete sharing of hearts and souls and bodies. She trailed her fingers through Mik's tangled hair and clasped her other hand with AJ's. Though the men rested on her much-smaller frame, they didn't crush her. Instead, Tala felt protected, comforted by the weight of the men she loved, by the sound of three hearts beating as one.

They'd not pulled apart. AJ still pulsed in slow, measured beats inside Mik. Tala's vaginal muscles continued the same, steady rhythm, holding Mik's quiescent penis in their velvet grasp. His lips still circled her nipple, nursing quietly at her breast as if he were a newborn, finding the same natural rhythm. Without consciously deciding, Tala realized the three of them had chosen to immerse themselves in the joining, to let their sated bodies connect beyond the burst of sensation that was the height of climax.

This link was so special, so amazingly intimate. A sharing beyond mere sex, beyond love, a true immersion of self, a joining of consciousness and desire. Three minds as one, three bodies, one entity.

She thought of Mei and Oliver. Of the wall separating them and their hope for at least a partial joining through the mating bond. Would it work? Was Mik's ability to communicate with the leopard something that might help Oliver find his way to Mei?

They'd have to ask Anton. If anyone had the answers, it would be the wizard. He was an amazing man, Anton Cheval.

We're off to see the wizard. . . . Tala smiled as her body relaxed into sleep. Mik's lips parted and a soft snore sent a gentle breath of warm air across her damp nipple. AJ's fingers loosed their grasp on hers. She closed her eyes, content, picturing in her sleep-stilled mind a wide yellow brick road stretching into her dreams.

"Good morning."

Anton glanced up from his laptop. "Good morning, Mei. Or should I say, good afternoon?"

Mei dipped her head and blushed, but she bumped her hip against Oliver, which gave Anton a clear picture of what had made them late to what was more brunch than breakfast.

"Sorry we're late. Blame Oliver."

Anton nodded. "Of course. We always blame Oliver."

"Thanks, loads." Oliver grinned as he grabbed a plate and scooped eggs and sausages out of the warming pan. "Looks like we get dish duty, Mei. Next time, *you* need to get up earlier."

The banter might be lighthearted, but Anton couldn't ignore the underlying tension, the sense of desperation he felt in both Oliver and Mei. Time was growing close for their grand experiment. He wished he felt more confident of the outcome.

He glanced at Mei and caught her looking back at him. Anton had the strangest feeling that she knew more than she let on, that she read him better than he'd been willing to admit. Did she pick up his lack of confidence, his fear of something going wrong?

Mei nodded. Just once, but it was enough. Then she went back to filling her plate. Anton felt an unfamiliar chill course the length of his spine.

This was not good. Not good at all. He needed their complete faith in him if there was any chance the attempt to trade consciousness between Eve and Mei was to work.

He turned his attention back to his laptop and the less-than-stellar financial reports that had come in this morning. He and Stefan really needed to make a trip into Seattle as soon as they could get away. One of their investments looked as if it needed a visit from two of the major stockholders.

Thinking of Stefan, Anton glanced out the large picture window at the end of the dining hall. Adam and Stefan were out in the garden, checking on a problem with the irrigation. Xandi and Keisha nursed their babies, sitting in the sunlight near the window. Tala and her men sat out on the deck quietly sipping coffee.

Now that was an unusual ménage. Their bonding amazed Anton, that two men and one tiny woman could find such a perfect balance. There was no competition between AJ and Mik. Both powerful alphas, their love for each other was apparent to all who knew them. That they loved Tala completely, without reservation, was a given.

And Tala, all five foot nothing of her, ruled them both. The ultimate alpha bitch, she was the head of their search team, the one they deferred to in all matters, the one they protected and respected. Most amazing of all, they had all been souls more lost than most. Not everyone knew of Mik's and AJ's pasts, nor did they know of Tala's.

Two ex-cons and a retired whore, sitting out on his deck, enjoying the warm sunlight and the towering trees. Three powerful Chanku, with abilities he'd still not totally discerned. Would they stay? At least until the full moon? That was five days away, but with Mik's unique ability to communicate with the leopard, his addition would be a valuable resource for what Anton hoped to achieve. He'd have to ask them, maybe check with Luc Stone. Their team was one of the mainstays of Pack Dynamics, but from the condition they'd been in when they arrived last night, Anton had a feeling they might be ready for a break.

But would they even consider it a vacation once they learned the details? He turned his attention back to the screen, tapped a couple keys, checked another page online, and wondered how long he could get his people to go without any sex at all.

Anton figured his packmates would have no problem, once they realized Oliver's happiness depended upon their sacrifice. The San Francisco pack was another question altogether. They had no ingrained loyalty toward any of the Montana pack. It didn't work that way.

He could only hope they had enough compassion for a man they considered a friend. Compassion for a young woman who had lived her life on the fringe, who even now was prevented from becoming a part of the whole. He glanced their way again. Mik, Tala, and AJ were a sexually powerful package, something he needed for sex magic to work. Their cooperation might be the critical key to Mei and Oliver's happiness, but it would have to be their decision. This was something he couldn't control.

Damn. He hated *anything* he couldn't control, and one of them was joining him now.

Mei carried her plate to the table and sat down next to Anton. She glanced shyly at him and smiled.

And what are you thinking this fine morning? He narrowed his thoughts directly to Mei.

She raised her chin and stared at him a moment, as if daring him. Anton couldn't help but admire her bravado, especially when he knew she was terrified of so much and on so many levels. *I'm thinking you're not as confident as you want everyone to believe. That this could be dangerous, for Eve and for me.*

Mei glanced sharply away from him and stared at her plate, but Anton saw how she gnawed at her lower lip.

I'm never as confident as I want everyone to think, but appearance is everything. Please don't give away my secret. He smiled and lifted her chin with his fingers. *I will attempt nothing that will put anyone in danger. I promise you.*

Mei nodded. At that moment, Oliver pulled up the chair across from her. "The full moon's in five days. Is there anything we should be doing? Any preparation?"

Anton carefully closed his laptop. "I've been thinking about it and trying to come up with a time frame to request abstinence from everyone. Too long and the power gives way to angry frustration, not something easy to work with or control. Too short a time and there's not enough power built up. I'm thinking three days with this crowd should just about do it."

Oliver chuckled. "I think you're right. I checked online. The moon is full in the afternoon, around quarter after three on the sixteenth. Will that affect anything? I always associate stuff like this with night and darkness."

"No." Anton shook his head. "Daylight merely makes the woo-woo factor a bit less."

Mei grinned at him, the first relaxed expression he'd seen on her face in days. "Woo-woo factor?"

"Stefan's description of my messing with things he doesn't understand." Anton glanced up and grinned.

"Someone talking about me?" Stefan poured a cup of coffee and joined them at the table.

"Only when we can't avoid it." Oliver's dry answer made even Anton laugh.

"Since we're all here at the same time for once, I would like to call a meeting." Anton glanced at everyone in the room. Keisha and Xandi raised their heads and watched him. He stood up and tucked his laptop under his arm. "I think at three this afternoon, on the front deck. The babies should be napping then. I want Keisha and Xandi there, definitely Eve and Adam. Also Mik, AJ, and Tala." He stacked his plates and gathered them up in one hand. "Make certain everyone knows." He carried his dishes into the kitchen, then continued down the hall to the suite of rooms he shared with Keisha, Xandi, and Stefan.

Confident. Self-assured. Even Mei wouldn't see the strain he felt deep inside. He hoped he could hide it from Keisha as well, but it wouldn't be easy. Three days without Keisha's body tied to his, without Stefan and Xandi's powerful connection. Damn. He might be able to provide enough power to not only switch Mei into Eve's body, but he could also probably turn her into a damned wolf by then!

"It's entirely up to Mik and AJ. And Luc Stone, of course, since he's our boss. I'm not sure we can stay away from Pack Dynamics for a full week." Tala smiled at Mei and shrugged. "If Luc agrees, and the guys, of course, my vote is to stay. Anything we can do to help you . . ."

"I agree." Mik turned and looked at AJ, who nodded in agreement. "Possibly my affinity with the cat will help. Who's to say?"

AJ threw his arm around Mik's broad shoulders and laughed. "Of course, keeping Mik celibate for three days is asking a lot. He might just explode."

"Thar she blows!" Mik clapped his hands, and the tension in the room fled.

"Then it's settled. I'll contact Luc. We had some other things to discuss, anyway." Anton looked around the small group sprawled about the back deck—some sitting at the picnic table, some on the porch swing, and some on the deck railing—and felt their powerful sense of unity, of shared purpose. "The moon reaches its fullest point a little after three in the afternoon. After much thought, I've decided to wait until nightfall before we attempt the switch." He tipped an imaginary hat toward Stefan.

"My partner prefers the dark for magical events. Is that all right with you, Eve?"

Eve nodded. "Whatever you decide." She reached across the hand-hewn cedar table and took Mei's hand. "I know this will work. Don't look so nervous, Mei."

Mei glanced toward Anton, then squeezed Eve's hand. "I don't want anything to happen to you. There's always a risk."

"It's okay. Look at it this way—I get to be a snow leopard for a few hours. I can't wait!"

"That's all it'll be, right, Anton?" Adam, Eve's mate, leaned forward and stared at him. There was no animosity in his steady gaze, but Anton felt his concern, his fear for Eve. He nodded.

"Two hours at the most. Time enough for Oliver and Mei to bond as wolves. I don't think we can sustain it any longer. It will take our combined mental strength to hold the link steady, to keep Eve within the leopard's body and Mei's consciousness in Eve's wolf."

He sighed and leaned back. Keisha sat on the railing directly behind him, and Anton rested his head against her legs. "There is one other thing, somewhat unexpected. Stefan and I need to make a trip to Seattle. The fact that Mik and AJ will be here makes us more comfortable leaving all of you. Hopefully it will just be an overnight trip, but we've got some investments we need to check into before they go sour on us."

Xandi grasped Stefan's hand. Anton felt Keisha's fingers tangling gently in his hair. "We'll fly out in the morning and be home by midday on Friday." He sighed. "Which, as you know, is the first day of the three days of abstinence I've requested from all of you." He leaned back and glanced at Keisha. She had a rather resigned look on her lovely face. "I'm sorry, sweetheart. I promise to make this up to you."

She laughed. He loved the sound of her laughter. He could live a thousand years and never hear it enough. "Oh, I have no doubt you'll make it up to me. You, my love, are going to owe me big time."

"What she said." Xandi tugged Stefan's hair. "I can't believe you guys would choose now for a business trip, of all times."

Anton grimaced and caught Stefan's eye. "For what it's worth, the trip has chosen us." He waved his hand, encompassing the land and home they all enjoyed. "Those irksome investments you complain about pay for our creature comforts."

Xandi nodded, laughing. "And you know how we love our creature comforts." She sighed dramatically. "Well, poor Oliver and Adam—we're going to wear those boys out."

Anton flashed her a resigned grin. "I was afraid of that."

"You should be." Xandi leaned over and kissed Anton on the cheek. Chastely. "You should be very afraid."

"And if Tala doesn't mind, there's always Mik and AJ." Keisha leaned over and high-fived Xandi.

The meeting broke up amid laughter, which was exactly what Anton had hoped for. The next few days were going to be little short of an orgy. He was sorry to miss it, but then he'd be with Stefan. There was no other man he'd rather have in his bed.

AJ and Mik flirted outrageously with Keisha and Xandi. Adam and Oliver teased Mei. Tala and Eve wandered into the kitchen to figure out something simple for dinner. The babies slept on, and all felt right. The way it should be.

Which always makes me nervous as hell. Anton stood up and brushed imaginary lint off his dark pants. He caught Stefan's eye and cocked one brow.

Relax, bro. Everything will be fine.

Yeah. Right. I think you said the same thing right before we left for Luc and Tia's wedding. At least he could joke about it now. The plane crash had almost cost them their lives.

Laughing, Stefan flipped him a perfectly executed bird, grabbed Xandi's hand, and led her down the hall to their room.

4

Mik grabbed Stefan's and Anton's bags and set them on the curb at the airport just northeast of Kalispell. The sun had not yet risen over the mountains, and the air felt crisp and fresh.

"Thanks for the ride, Mik." Anton shook his hand. "I always hate to drag Keisha out of bed to haul our butts down here, but if we don't get an early flight, half the day's a waste."

"No problem. I enjoyed the ride. I don't get to drive much. AJ thinks that's his territory."

Stefan laughed and slapped Mik on the back. "It's nice to know you guys occasionally disagree about something."

Mik shook his head, grinning. "Actually, we don't. I'm the one who hangs on to the keys. He drives. It's a control thing. You guys have a safe trip."

Anton grabbed his bag and turned to walk away. Then he paused and looked back at Mik. His eyes glittered, the amber lights in them shimmering beneath the lamps illuminating the unloading zone. Mik sensed a level of power in Anton he'd felt only a few times before.

"Mik, I want to thank you and your mates for choosing to

stay. Now I have another favor to ask of you—see if you can reach your grandfather's spirit guide. It may reside in your soul as well. Find the wildcat before Sunday, if you can."

Mik nodded. "I'll do my best. Oliver is as special to us as he is to you. His leopard will be a fitting mate."

"If we can work out the logistics." Anton shrugged.

"No doubt in my mind." Mik saluted both men.

Anton and Stefan headed for the terminal. Mik stood on the curb long after they'd gone. Then he climbed into the SUV and headed back to the house. Tala would be crawling out of bed by the time he got back. If anyone could help him find the beast, it would be his own little hellcat.

Adam Wolf poured himself a cup of coffee, then walked outside to the back deck. Eve still slept, curled up in bed with both Mei and Oliver. He'd not wanted to disturb them. Not after the amazing night the four of them had spent making love. He'd lost track of how many times he'd come, lost track of the various places he'd found to put his more-than-obliging cock. He'd been Chanku for such a short time, but Adam figured he'd had more sex in the past couple months than in all his years before.

Not that he was complaining. Nor could he stop grinning. He'd never in his wildest dreams imagined the kind of life he led now. Adam closed the door quietly behind him before he realized he wasn't alone. AJ Temple sat by himself in a chair at the deck's far end, watching the rising sun. The golden rays glistened off his dark hair and framed him in a corona of shimmering light.

Adam paused, caught by the pure, masculine beauty of the man. AJ somehow paled beside the darker, larger Mik Fuentes, but seeing him out here on his own reminded Adam what a perfect male specimen he truly was. Long and lean, dark hair curling around his collar, his strong profile in the morning light a contrast in angles and shadows. Adam's cock twitched and swelled against the zipper of his jeans, and he almost laughed aloud. When Oliver said the Chanku had an overactive libido, he hadn't been kidding. How could that damned body part even think of getting hard?

Of course, with a man like AJ Temple right there within reach, how could he help it?

AJ raised his head and glanced in Adam's direction, then waved him over. "Another early riser, eh? Good morning."

Adam took the chair next to him. "Too pretty out here to stay in bed. Where're Mik and Tala?"

"Mik left before sunup. He took Anton and Stefan to the airport. They've got a plane chartered for an early flight to Seattle. Tala's still sleeping. This past week's been tough, and I didn't want to wake her."

"I figured as much. I'm glad you've decided to stay." Adam sipped his coffee, almost preternaturally aware of AJ. He'd not noticed the attraction so much the night before, but then he'd never seen AJ without Mik's hulking presence. Mik was scary enough to give anyone a reason to stay clear.

"He's not, you know." AJ grinned at him. His eyes twinkled, full of good humor. "Scary, that is. Sorry. You were broadcasting."

"Shit." Adam laughed. "I'm still getting the hang of all this. I shifted for the first time only a few weeks ago."

AJ nodded. "I figured as much. It's cool, though. Finding more Chanku. Adding to our numbers. I'm glad they found you. At first, the packs were really tight. There was a lot of territorial stuff, raised hackles, pissing on trees, that sort of thing, but it's not that way now. We've learned we have to work together. It's better when we all get along without the pack rivalry."

Adam studied AJ's eyes. There was definitely something else

going on behind his statement. "Get along? Does that include sex?"

AJ's lip curled in a grin. "Occasionally."

Adam's heart rate jacked up, and his lungs had a hard time finding enough air. "How occasionally?"

AJ set his cup down and reached for Adam, his hand open, his fingers spread wide. Adam pictured those same fingers grasping the weight of his cock, holding his balls. So often he sensed something wrong in a person. His need to fix things definitely got in the way, but not with this man. AJ was whole. Healthy. Complete . . . and definitely interested.

Adam took AJ's hand in his. They stood together, looked at each other, measured one against the other. Then they walked down the steps, hand in hand. Both men disrobed. When AJ shifted, Adam followed. When AJ raced toward the dark forest, Adam as wolf was right behind him. It all seemed very calm, very adult, but his wolven heart pounded in expectation; his mouth was dry, his cock already growing harder.

They didn't go far. The meadow just beyond the band of forest was sunlit and small, the thick green grass surrounded in tangled blackberry vines and twisted willows. The sound of a creek burbled in the background. AJ shifted first, standing tall and aroused. Adam joined him. Two powerful men, both of them naked. Both with thick, veined shafts rising against taut bellies.

Adam swallowed, imagining the taste and texture of that perfect cock between his lips. He licked his lips, caught in his fantasies, sensing the blood rushing through engorged veins, the flavor of AJ's semen. He didn't normally choose male partners, but AJ's beauty, seductive smile, and perfect body called to him.

"I've wanted you since the first time I saw you. Wanted to touch you." AJ shrugged. He looked embarrassed, suddenly uneasy. "I've not wanted anyone since Mik and Tala. Why you? Why now?"

Adam shook his head. "I don't know. I felt the same thing when I came out on the deck and saw you this morning. Weird thing is, I'm not gay. Never actively sought out men as sexual partners until Oliver, though he wasn't my first. But you . . ." He shrugged as well. "I don't know. Makes no sense."

"Makes a lot of sense." AJ stepped closer. "I thought I was gay, until Tala. Now I don't know anymore. Now I'm just Chanku. I think that's all it takes." He laughed.

Adam liked the sound as much as he admired the look of the man. AJ was tall and lean, his muscles sharply defined. Pectorals. Abs. Thighs. His cock rose out of a silky nest of dark hair, thick and solid, curving up against his belly.

A perfect match to Adam's erection. He stepped forward and touched AJ's shoulders, pressed his hips forward. The thick length of his penis rubbed against AJ's. Their balls connected, and the pressure of his sac rubbing against another man's sent a thick, hot coil of need from spine to cock.

AJ's arms came around him and he held Adam close. They stood there, nipples touching, cocks rubbing back and forth, balls connecting. Adam groaned. He rubbed slowly, moving his hips in rhythm with AJ. Their shafts pressed against their bellies, rubbing crown to crown. Adam's testicles swung back and forth against AJ's heavy sac. He closed his eyes and bit back a groan. What was it about this man?

AJ's hands were on his shoulders, pushing, slowly forcing Adam to his knees. He knew then what AJ wanted. His lips, his tongue, the heat and pressure of his mouth. Adam went willingly, accepting AJ's domination more easily than he'd accepted any other man's. Adam took AJ's heavy phallus in his hands and stroked him. AJ grew even more, the veins standing out in stark relief along the length of his shaft, and the crown turning a dark and dangerous shade of purple.

Adam grasped AJ's taut buttocks in his palms to hold him steady. He licked the tortured map of veins, found the weeping slit at the apex of AJ's crown, and delved into it with the tip of his tongue. He forced entrance, knowing he caused as much pain as pleasure, aware on some unexplored level of consciousness that this was part of AJ's journey.

He sucked the thick cock deep into his mouth and reveled in the taste, the foreign flavors of a man he hardly knew. Obviously fresh from his shower, AJ's damp pubic hair carried the faint scent of soap and male musk. AJ spread his legs wider, tangled his fingers through Adam's hair, grasped his shoulders. He held on lightly, balancing himself.

Adam wrapped his lips around AJ's cock and stroked the underside with his tongue, holding AJ's hips steady with a firm grip on his perfect ass. Adam's cock, sadly neglected for now, twitched against his belly.

After a few moments, AJ pulled free. He brushed Adam's hair back from his eyes and smiled with a look of wonder on his face. Then he slowly bent his knees and lowered himself to the ground. There was nothing at all submissive in the action, especially when he wrapped his big hand around Adam's sac and squeezed lightly.

Still holding on to Adam's balls, AJ stretched out in the soft, green grass and motioned Adam to come over him. Adam straddled his face, leaned down, and once again took AJ's cock between his lips.

This time, though, the connection was complete. Adam felt the same pressure against his cock, the hot, wet suction of a man's mouth, the scrape of fingernails over his perineum. Groaning, Adam took AJ even deeper inside his mouth, using teeth and tongue and lips to mimic exactly what AJ did to him.

He wrapped his fingers around AJ's sac, massaging the solid orbs inside the wrinkled flesh. Trailing a fingertip down the damp crease between his cheeks, he pressed against the puckered ring of muscle and felt the same pressure against his own ass. He pressed harder, sucked deeper, fighting the growing need to come as AJ's tongue and lips and fingers brought him to a fevered pitch.

AJ's rapid heartbeat echoed in Adam's skull. It took a moment, but he realized their hearts beat together, in perfect sync. Startled by the reality of their growing link, Adam licked the tiny white bubble at the end of AJ's cock and tasted the bitter tang of precum. Stretching his lips wide, he slipped his mouth completely over the thick shaft, moaning at the erotic slide of a saliva-slick cock down his throat.

In and out, sucking and swallowing, feeling the heavy thrust of his own cock past the tight stricture of Adam's throat; he felt the spasm of muscles rippling along his hard length, the pressure of tongue, the scrape of teeth.

He fought to contain the thrust of his hips, aware AJ did the same. Finally he pulled away until only the crown of AJ's penis rested between his lips. As if they'd choreographed the move, AJ did the same thing, withdrawing until barely the tip of Adam's crown was in his mouth.

Adam stroked AJ's lean flanks and pressed once again into the dark cleft between his buttocks. Slipping his middle finger through the tiny, puckered ring of muscle, he felt the tight ripple and clench around his fingertip. He pushed harder, probed deeper, and finally pressed through, going beyond the tight spasm of muscle into AJ's damp heat. Felt the same pressure and burn as AJ pierced his own sphincter and slid deep, all the way to his knuckle.

Adam added a second finger. So did AJ. Then a third, both men stretching, forcing their way through burning muscles, abrading nerve endings already screaming in the familiar pain so closely linked to this dark pleasure. Body trembling, hovering closer yet to orgasm, Adam opened himself to the purity of sensation, the amazing sense of AJ as an extension of himself.

There was a subtle blossoming in his mind, a joining of desire and sensation as AJ's thoughts melded with his own. This was a unique sharing, of sensation and need, desire and arousal, beyond anything Adam had known.

Beyond his link with Eve, beyond even the healing he'd accomplished when he'd entered her injured mind just a few weeks ago, when he'd become an actual physical presence within the brain of the woman he loved.

Adam tightened his lips around AJ's cock, slipped his fingers back and forth inside the other man's ass, and recognized the sense of connection, the knowledge he'd slipped just as deeply into AJ's awareness. The link intensified, sensations expanded, and he became AJ, became the length of his cock, the fullness of his balls. He pulsed with the powerful meter of two hearts beating as one, two bodies responding in perfect unison.

Not the bond of mating. Not the intense link of life partners. Something else. Something new, an awareness beyond all understanding. His thoughts floated, separated entirely from Adam Wolf, from AJ Temple. Joined, then, with AJ's equally disengaged reality, until the two connected, existing as a single experience, somehow apart from the bodies of two men fucking in the damp grass in the misty morning light.

There was a sense of power, a shift of reality and a single, pulsing entity hovered in the morning mist, watching, observing, aware of the purity of the moment, the beauty of two male bodies reaching for the ultimate satisfaction, the perfect orgasm.

Both bodies stiffened, groaned, clasped lips tightly around straining phalluses, probed deep with searching fingers thrusting through clenching tissues. Light covered them, a pulsing, glowing incandescence barely visible in the sunlight.

AJ's mouth tightened around Adam's cock, and he caught each drop of the thick ejaculate shooting down his throat. Adam's tongue formed a tight suction around AJ's pulsing shaft, and his mouth filled with hot jets of seed. The moment expanded, lengthened, until it seemed to Adam as if he climaxed forever, as if his body hung suspended in time and sensation.

Slowly, the powerful sense of joining eased, the light faded, the entity the two had become left the space above their bodies and found their respective minds once again.

Adam collapsed to one side. AJ's flaccid penis slipped from between his lips, but his fingers remained buried between AJ's clenched buttocks. He lay there a moment, stunned, aware of the fingers still buried inside his own ass, feeling the rhythm of clenching muscles, the intimate joining that somehow transcended anything he'd known before.

How? He'd watched himself. Stared down at his back and watched as AJ fucked his ass with his thick fingers. The same fingers still buried inside him. It made no sense.

It was its own sense.

"What the fuck was that?" AJ slipped his fingers free of Adam's body and raised up on one elbow.

Adam merely shook his head. His ears buzzed. His eyes refused to focus. "I have no idea. I hope like hell Anton will have an answer."

AJ laughed, but there was a breathless quality to the sound. A sense of disbelief. "Anton's gone until late tomorrow. I wonder if we can do that again?" He flopped back down in the beaten grass, still chuckling. "Shit, man. I don't know if I can handle it again, but I want that feeling. I want to know what happened. Have you done that before? That out-of-body-glowing thing? Do you do that with Eve?"

Adam shook his head. "Never. I've done some weird shit with Eve, but that was spooky. Damn." He glanced down at his cock. He was hard again. Rolling his head to one side, he grinned at AJ. "Wanna try it again?"

This time Adam took AJ from behind. After the finger-fucking they'd both done, it was easy enough to part AJ's perfect ass cheeks, press his broad crown against that tiny puck-ered hole and slip inside the relaxed muscle. Thrusting forward, Adam buried himself to the hilt. AJ groaned and braced him-self.

"Shit. You're as big as Mik, and he's huge."

"Am I hurting you?"

AJ's strangled laugh wasn't much of an answer, but he pushed back against Adam, forcing him even deeper.

Adam slapped his butt, then grabbed AJ's cock with one hand and cupped his sac with the other. He fucked him hard and fast, driving as deep as he could on every forward thrust, fisting his cock and fondling his balls until AJ was groaning and sweat slicked his back and thighs.

Linking minds with AJ was easier this time. Sharing sensa-tions took Adam over the top when AJ climaxed, but as good as it was, it was just a fuck.

Exhausted, fully sated for the first time in days, Adam slowly withdrew from AJ's body. Neither man spoke. The two of them bathed in the nearby creek, as comfortable now as lovers who have experienced a powerful connection.

Lovers, but not mates. Not in the same sense as AJ and Mik or Adam and Eve. Still, even after they shifted back to their wolven form, the sense remained that something unusual had occurred this morning.

Adam led the way back to the house, his paws beating a powerful tattoo on the hard-packed earth, his thoughts a tangle of emotions and sensations. When they reached the stairs lead-ing up to the back deck, he shifted. AJ stood beside him, his amber eyes filled with confusion, with questions Adam knew he couldn't answer.

He grasped Adam's forearm, holding him back. "Thank you. I'm not sure what happened out there, but it's still with me. You're still with me. Somehow, you've shared a part of yourself like I've never experienced. What happened this morning came from you, not me, and I will be forever grateful."

Stunned by AJ's heartfelt words, Adam could only nod. Then he leaned close and kissed AJ. Parted his lips with his tongue, held the back of his head in his palm, and for the first time today, actually kissed the man. He wasn't sure why. He only knew there was a reason, a powerful reason, for whatever they'd shared.

AJ touched the side of Adam's face. There were tears in his eyes when he turned away and walked slowly up the stairs. The deck was empty. Their coffee cups sat cooling on the table where they'd left them. They'd been gone less than an hour, but in that brief time, Adam knew he'd been forever changed.

AJ headed straight for their room and Tala. He met Mik in the hallway. "You just getting back?"

Mik nodded. "Yeah. I dropped Anton and Stefan at the airport." He stopped with his hand on the bedroom door. "You okay? You look . . . I dunno. Different?"

AJ took a deep breath. "Check and see if Tala's awake. If not, I need to talk to you."

Mik nodded. He opened the door quietly and looked inside, then shut it just as carefully. "She's out like a light. What's up?"

AJ led the way to Anton's study with a quick stop in the kitchen for more coffee. Both he and Mik grabbed a cup. The house was still quiet, most of the residents sleeping, but AJ wanted privacy with Mik. A chance to work through his feelings about the morning with Adam.

He followed Mik into the study and closed the door behind them. Mik sat in one of the big leather armchairs. AJ paced. "What do you know about Adam Wolf?"

Mik cocked an eyebrow. "He's new. Sexy as hell. Anton said he's got an uncanny ability to repair things that break, and it appears to extend to bodies. He's got some healing skills. What gives?"

"He showed up on the deck this morning, real early. I got up when you left and was just sitting out there enjoying the sunrise. I felt an amazing connection to him. Purely sexual. We shifted, went into the woods, and fucked like we'd come off six months of celibacy. I don't usually do that. Well, at least not on my own." He grinned and sipped his coffee when Mik cocked an eyebrow and snickered.

"So how was it?"

AJ took a deep breath. "It was amazing. Scary. Something happened. We weren't doing anything special, just lying in the grass blowing each other when our bodies started to glow. All of a sudden, it was like we connected outside and above ourselves. Scared the shit out of me, but I'd give anything for it to happen again. I've never felt anything like that before."

"Did you really glow, or are you using that as a metaphor of sorts?"

AJ laughed. "We glowed. We, as in Adam and I, also hovered as physical thought above two guys sucking each other's cocks, and those guys were me and Adam. It was literally an out-of-body experience. Freaky. Absolutely freaky, but damn, I have never experienced an orgasm like that—present company excepted."

Mik sipped his coffee and seemed to think about what AJ had said. "I believe you. I can feel your disbelief and can sense the experience at the same time. Amazing. I wonder . . . I don't know Adam all that well. How do you think he'd feel about sex with me? Anton wants me to search for my grandfather's spirit guide. Maybe this thing Adam does would help, whatever it is."

"He thinks you're scary." AJ grinned.

Mik shook his head, laughing. "Hell, everyone thinks I'm scary."

"I don't."

AJ and Mik both looked up as Tala wandered into the study wearing one of Mik's T-shirts. It slipped off one shoulder and hung below her knees. "I think you're cute." She wrapped her slim arms around Mik's neck and hugged him, then crawled into his lap like a sleepy child.

"I am not cute." Mik kissed her. "I'm big and scary and intimidating. Just ask Adam."

AJ leaned over and kissed Tala as well, then planted one on Mik for good measure. "I think we should. Ask Adam, that is. I imagine if it'll help Mei and Eve, he'll be willing to try anything."

Mik nodded. "I like Oliver. Always have. If linking with my grandfather's totem makes a difference in what Anton is hoping to do, I'm all for it."

AJ slapped his shoulder. "Hell, you just want a chance to fuck the cute guy."

Tala yawned and Mik hugged her close. "Well, there is that." He kissed the top of her head. "Maybe we all need to fuck the cute guy."

Adam threw a load of clothes in the washer, set the temperature, and checked the stuff in the dryer. The jeans and sweatshirts were still damp, so he reset the dial. He didn't hear anyone until Tala, AJ, and Mik were all in the laundry room, standing quietly and managing to block his exit at the same time.

Were they angry about his sex with AJ? Adam still wasn't quite sure what had happened this morning, but their coupling had been entirely by mutual agreement. He straightened up as he turned slowly around and stared at the group from San Francisco. AJ leaned against the doorjamb, Tala stood in front of him, and Mik filled the doorway.

"Should I call this meeting to order?" He leaned back

against the washer, folded his arms across his chest, and made eye contact with each one. If he'd been wolf, his hackles would have risen along his spine.

Mik shook his head. "Actually, we're here to ask you a favor."

"A favor? What?" Adam's tension ebbed and he relaxed. There was no threat here.

AJ stepped forward. "This morning. What happened to us was unusual, to say the least. I keep thinking of it as an out-of-body event."

Adam nodded. "It was, actually. New for me, too. I didn't plan it, AJ." He shrugged. "I saw you, thought you were damned hot, and wanted to fuck. Nothing out of the ordinary there."

AJ laughed. "I appreciate an honest man. Thing is, Anton wants Mik to try connecting with his grandfather's spirit guide, his totem. *Igmutaka* is a panther. We think it allowed Mik to talk to Mei in her leopard form. Maybe what happened to you and me this morning . . ."

"Would happen with Mik and allow him to find the cat." Adam straightened up. "Damn. It sounds almost convoluted enough to work. We'd have to try it today or tomorrow. Anton wants us to start the celibacy thing on Friday."

Mik nodded. "I would like to include my packmates."

Adam cocked his head and grinned at Mik. "Afraid?"

"Never. But I watched AJ's face today when he described what the two of you shared, and I want the two people I love most to be part of this, should it work." He took a couple steps forward and placed his huge hand on Adam's shoulder. "For what it's worth, my friend, I only look scary. Tala says I'm harmless."

Considering he had to look up to meet the humor in Mik's amber eyes, Adam figured he'd withhold judgment on that one. "I would like to include Eve, then, as well. Maybe with all of us together . . ."

Mik nodded. "I would like that." He tugged Tala close and wrapped his arm around her shoulders. "How about you, little one? Are you willing?"

Tala looked up at Mik, and the adoration in her eyes was so obvious it made Adam's heart ache. "You know I'm willing to do anything you ask. I love you." She glanced toward Adam. "Mik really wants to help Mei. So do I, and AJ feels the same. Whatever we need to do . . ."

"How's the line go? Show up naked. Bring beer?" Adam couldn't have wiped the grin off his face if he'd tried. Sometimes it felt as if his entire life had taken a surrealistic slant. He shrugged. "I'll admit it feels weird to make an appointment for sex, but that's what we're going to do."

Tala laughed and wrapped her arms around both AJ and Mik. "Doesn't bother me at all. I was a prostitute before I met these two. I used to make appointments for sex all the time."

She grinned up at the dark-haired giant beside her. Then she bumped Mik's thigh with her perfectly rounded hip. His fingers tangled in her thick fall of dark hair. Adam realized Tala was right. Mik Fuentes wasn't nearly as scary as he'd originally thought. Just big and fierce and totally in love with the little woman beside him.

Adam cleared his throat. "There's one more thing. I would ask that everyone abstain until we get together. Maybe it will make the glowing thing happen again."

"You really have no control over it?" Mik frowned and hugged Tala close. Protecting her? Adam wasn't sure.

"None that I knew of. What happened this morning with AJ was a first, but that's not to say it won't happen again. I've had the sense, ever since my first shift, that we're all a work in progress, all constantly evolving. Who knows, if it does happen, it might help you call on your grandfather's totem. Anything I can do . . ."

"Thank you." Mik took Tala's hand in his. "How about

tonight after dinner? We can gather in the meadow behind the deck at sundown. I wouldn't feel right, calling Grandfather's spirit guide indoors."

"That's a good point. Outside in the meadow it is." Adam glanced toward AJ. He solemnly nodded in agreement, pushed himself away from the wall, and followed his packmates out the door. Adam watched them go and wondered what the hell he'd just agreed to.

5

Anton tossed his coat over the chair and took the cold can of beer Stefan handed him. He loosened his tie as he finished up his call with Keisha, set his cell phone on the bedside table, and took a long, welcome swallow of the cold brew. Then he kicked off his shoes and stretched out on the bed.

Stefan took a drink of his beer and sat on the arm of one of the overstuffed chairs in their suite. "How're things at home? Was that Keisha?"

Anton nodded. "Looks like Mik took my request seriously. Keisha said he's planning to call on his grandfather's spirit guide tonight with help from the others."

Stefan loosened his necktie and pulled it off. "Really? I wish I could be there. Do they have a plan?"

"Something to do with a power Adam appears to have discovered within himself. An out-of-body experience during sex with AJ this morning." Anton traced his finger through the condensation on the side of the can. "I've suspected all along Adam has more to him than we've realized. It's probably better we're not there. Too often the others defer to me and miss their own capabilities."

"I'm willing to defer to you tonight." Stefan unbuttoned his shirt and slipped it over his shoulders, well aware of his affect on Anton.

Strong and muscular, his lean chest was powerfully sculpted with a mat of silver-tipped hair stretching between flat, copper-colored nipples. More muscles rippled across his abdomen, and a line of hair trailed down beneath his waistband, a trail Anton's fingers itched to follow. His nostrils flared. His cock pulsed and engorged as he admired Stefan's body. So perfectly formed, even at forty-five, Stefan had the physique of an athlete in his prime.

Obviously aware of, but just as obviously ignoring, Anton's perusal, Stefan rubbed one hand across his chest. "It's been a long day, and that abstinence decree of yours is weighing quite heavily on my mind." He laughed and flopped down on the bed next to Anton. "Besides, it'd be nice to let you take control."

Anton cocked am eyebrow and grinned at his packmate. "*Let* me take control? As if you have a choice?"

"Never hurts to try." Stefan rolled over and propped himself up on one elbow. He took a long, slow breath and released it. "I know today was tough on you. I'm sorry."

Anton shrugged as if it was no big deal, but Stefan's sympathy touched him deeply. "He was embezzling from the company. I knew there was something more behind the loss than a slow economy. The guy had to go."

"He's lucky you didn't have him arrested." Stefan bridged the small gap between them, slipped his fingers beneath Anton's starched cotton shirt, and gently traced the line of his collarbone.

Anton leaned back against the stack of pillows. "I wish I

could have had him arrested, but there would have been a lot of negative publicity that could hurt the company more. This way he'll pay back the money and be gone. It sets an example for others. You can't get away with theft."

"Especially when the head of the board of directors can read your mind."

Anton grinned and relaxed for the first time all day. "There is that. The look on his face was priceless when we called him on it, especially when you listed the offshore banks where you knew he'd stashed the cash."

"Well, the lawyers can handle everything now. At least we'll get home early tomorrow. I miss Xandi and Alex."

"I know. I feel the same about Keisha and Lily. Amazing, isn't it, how our lives have changed in such a short time?" Anton rolled over and cupped Stefan's jaw in the palm of his hand. He gazed into the amber eyes of the man he loved more than any other, remembering all that had passed between them. "All for the better. Every bit of it." He leaned close to kiss Stefan and reached for the zipper on his slacks at the same time.

"Since you're so generously allowing me control," he said, whispering against Stefan's mouth, "I've decided to take it." Anton slipped his fingers inside the loosened waist of Stefan's pants, found the thick weight of his straining cock, and palmed him through the soft cotton knit of his boxers.

Stefan groaned and lay back against the pillows. Anton knelt between his legs and tugged gently on his pants. Within seconds, he had Stefan naked, his body fully aroused and waiting for whatever Anton had in mind.

It was early yet. The long night stretched before them, and it felt like old times. Rising up on his knees, Anton grinned down at Stefan, imagining all the things he wanted to do with this man. He slipped his shirt off his shoulders, unbuttoned his slacks, and slowly lowered the zipper. Freeing his fully erect cock while opening his thoughts, Anton drew Stefan into the erotic images filling his mind. Then he finished disrobing and proceeded to take control.

Oliver wrapped Mei in his arms and pushed at the deck with his left foot. The old porch swing squealed in protest, then jerked and fell back into a steady, calming rhythm. They'd been out here for over an hour enjoying the quiet evening.

Oliver heard movement in the house behind him, and his breath caught in his throat. Eve, Adam, Mik, AJ, and Tala were heading out to the meadow to call down Mik's grandfather's spirit guide, *Igmutaka,* and they were doing it for Mei. Keisha and Xandi remained with the babies. Oliver and Mei had taken a spot on the opposite side of the house, out of sight of their friends so as not to interfere.

Mei shivered in Oliver's arms. "You don't have to go through with it, sweetie. I know you're scared." Oliver nuzzled her dark hair and inhaled her scent. Shampoo, fresh air, woman. Goddess, how he loved her. "I will always love you whether we bond or not. Whether we ever hunt together or not, whether or not we can have children. The leopard isn't all you are."

Mei rubbed her cheek against Oliver's arm. "That's where you're wrong, Oliver. It is who I am. I am the leopard. It's my nature, the woman I was long before I knew I could shift. I've always been a loner, always gone my own way. You're the first man I've ever had a relationship with."

"I'm also the last." He kissed the edge of her ear, trailed a line of small kisses along the line of her jaw. "We'll make it work. I just don't want you to think I'm pushing you to do the mind thing with Eve. Not if you're at all frightened. There will be other full moons if you decide to try later."

Mei snuggled close. "Thank you. I don't think I'd be as nervous if Anton was a little more confident, but he's worried, too."

"Are you sure? He doesn't act like it." Oliver tipped her

chin up with his fingers. With her lips so close, he had to kiss her.

"Since he and I . . ." Mei turned away from his kiss, dipping her head and blushing.

Oliver sighed. Mei still had trouble with the fact she'd had sex with Anton, just the two of them. The wizard had wanted to link with as deep a bond as possible in order to learn what he could about Mei's leopard side. She'd admitted the sex was fantastic, the link amazing, but she still blushed when the subject was raised.

"Mei, don't be embarrassed. Hell, I've had sex with Anton, too. We're Chanku. All of us. Human morality flies out the window once we shift. We have no choice."

Mei raised her head and looked Oliver in the eye. "That's where we're different. You accept that side of your nature—the powerful libido, the drive to hunt, to run as a member of the pack—and have sex with any of them. Because I'm a leopard, I'm not part of your pack. It feels unnatural for me to sleep with so many others. I like sex with Eve and Adam, because I love them, but what they're planning tonight? All of them together when they hardly know each other? I couldn't do it."

Oliver slipped his hand beneath her loose shirt and raked his fingertips over her nipple. Mei drew in a sharp breath, and her nipple puckered.

"How about sex with me? It'll take your mind off what's happening in the meadow. They're doing it for you, sweetheart, but they're enjoying it, a lot. I can guarantee you they're going to love every minute and probably want more." He brushed another kiss across her lips. She kissed him back, then put a hand against his chest and shoved.

"You'd like to be there with them, wouldn't you?" Mei sat back and glared at him.

"I'd rather be with you. But if you weren't here? Yes. I'd be with them. Is that what you want to hear?" He shrugged. "Discussion's over. No more arguments." Oliver stood up with Mei in his arms. She was almost as tall as he was, but she still felt light. Her lean body was muscular, without an extra ounce of fat. With Mei still glaring at him, Oliver carried her down the steps and across the drive to his cottage.

"I've told you I don't like it when you go all caveman on me, Oliver. Put me down." She didn't struggle, but she wasn't smiling yet, either.

Oliver pressed his lips together to keep from laughing. She was so damned independent, but she was hot and ready whenever they came together. After so many years of a totally asexual existence, the fact that he had a woman who loved him, who wanted to make love with him, absolutely amazed Oliver.

And "going caveman," as Mei so sweetly put it, turned him on more than he liked to admit. He nudged the door open with his shoulder and kicked his shoes off in the entry. Mei remained stiff and unyielding in his arms.

Someday he would make love to her in the forest, both of them in their animal form. She would be a wolf or he would be a leopard. He wasn't sure, but he had no doubt.

For now, Mei was getting Oliver as he was. An average-sized man in a world of giants, the one who loved her, who would be her mate. And, for whatever reason, he knew she loved him back every bit as much. With that thought in mind, he carried Mei down the hallway to their bedroom and dumped her unceremoniously in the middle of the king-sized bed.

"Just what do you think you're doing?" She sat up in the middle of the bed and folded her arms across her chest. Though her stance was aggressive, her eyes twinkled. They'd played out this scene before. It always ended well.

In fact, it usually ended with the most mind-blowing climax imaginable. Oliver leaned over and caged Mei between his arms. "What do you think I'm doing?" He kissed her. She pressed her lips together. He kissed her again, slowly this time, and his tongue traced the tight seam of her mouth.

She groaned and parted her lips to the quick thrust of his tongue. Her hands clutched his shoulders, and her tongue twirled around his. Then she pushed him away and scrambled across the bed, laughing.

"I am not going to make this easy for you, Oliver Cheval. You think you can get your way all the time, don't you?"

He stalked her, circling the bed and coming around on the other side. Mei slipped out of his grasp. Oliver lunged for her, but she twisted away, her moves catlike and quick. He managed to catch one slim ankle and pull her back toward him.

She grabbed the edge of the mattress and flailed her legs. Oliver caught her thigh and the waistband of her pants and locked her legs in a scissors grip between his. They were both panting, both of them laughing when she managed to flip him over and hold his hands above his head. Her strong thighs clasped his chest, and she sat on his bare belly.

"I've got you right where I want you," he said, bucking his hips and trying to throw Mei off.

"Oh, you think so, eh?" She leaned close and kissed him. Her soft lips worked their magic across his mouth, and her tongue parted his lips, driving deep inside to lick the roof of his mouth, the sensitive ridge behind his teeth.

Oliver lost himself in her kiss. His cock swelled beneath her round bottom, and he groaned with the absolute pleasure of Mei's sensual touch. He didn't realize she'd reached under the mattress until she came up with something shiny and hard. He heard the rattle of chains and the solid click of a lock at the same moment it registered that she had just handcuffed him to the iron headboard.

He broke away from her wet, clinging kiss. "What the fuck?" Frowning, he jerked at the chains.

Mei stood beside the bed now, grinning broadly. "I have told you not to manhandle me. You don't listen. Now you have to listen, okay?"

Oliver didn't answer, but he watched her. Very closely. She slipped her loose shirt over her head. He knew she wasn't wearing a bra, and the sight of those perfect round globes made his mouth go dry. When she slipped out of her pants and ran her fingers across her smooth mound, he almost choked.

She walked to the end of the bed and grabbed the cuffs of his loose sweatpants and tugged them off. Oliver watched her every move. She walked over to the closet, found the hanger with his neckties, and selected two of them. She tied slipknots in both ties. When she tried slipping one over his left ankle, he jerked his foot out of her grasp.

Laughing, she finally threw herself across his legs and managed to slip the knotted ties over both his feet. Within moments, she had him securely bound to the foot of the bed. In spite of himself, Oliver felt his arousal grow. "Okay," he said. "You've got me where I want me," he teased. "Now what?"

"Now I show you what it's like to be tortured. Remember what you did to me last week?" She stood at the foot of the bed with her hands on her hips while he tried to remember something he'd done that was remotely close to tying her down.

"Nope. Can't recall a thing." He tugged at the cuffs and succeeded only in bruising his wrists.

"Maybe this will help remind you." Mei reached into a drawer in the bedside table and drew out a large phallic-shaped vibrator. The plastic was soft, the shape lifelike despite its bright blue color.

Oliver felt a chill race down his spine, and his cock twitched. He'd used that on Mei one night. Had kept her on the edge of climax for over an hour, teasing her clit, her anus, her breasts. She'd been a quivering mass of nerves when he'd finally taken her over the top. Her comment about torture started to make very graphic sense.

She rummaged around in the drawer and brought out a few more things. Nipple clamps. A fairly involved cock ring with leather straps. Lubricant.

Oliver swallowed. Mei put everything down on top of the cabinet. She grabbed two thick pillows and slipped them beneath his hips. He struggled, more as a matter of principle than from any hope of breaking free. She had him well and truly restrained.

He couldn't call the others for help. They would be starting their project in the meadow about now, but he opened his mind to their thoughts.

A full blast of lust in its most primal and basic form swept into his mind. Yep. They were definitely busy in the meadow. He tamped down their passionate mental link and forced his attention back to Mei. She picked up the nipple clamps first, then leaned over and licked his left nipple. The damned thing sprang to life, poking up from his chest just enough for Mei to fasten the first clamp.

He'd put them on her, but he had no idea how much they hurt. "Ouch. Shit."

"Hurts, doesn't it?" Mei smiled sweetly and flicked the clamp with one finger. A streak of pure lightning flew from his nipple to his balls. He grunted but pressed his lips tightly together. He had to admit, there was a definite sexual thrill behind the pain, but he wasn't going to admit that to Mei.

She leaned over and rubbed her breasts along his belly, licked his right nipple, affixed the clamp, and stood back to admire her handiwork. Twin bolts of lightning burned, and he felt his nipples swell against the tight clamps.

His balls were beginning to ache, and if his cock got any harder, he figured he'd come all over his belly. The way it curved against his stomach meant he'd probably shoot himself between the eyes. Now, that would be embarrassing.

Mei ended that worry with the soft touch of her fingers

when she slipped a series of tight bands down his cock and fastened them at the base. A strip of leather rode along the top of his shaft, and she did something that tightened all the rings. The pressure increased when she added a leather loop to the base that wrapped around his balls, separating his testicles and holding the entire sac up close against his tightly restrained shaft.

Oliver raised his head to see what she'd done, but his cock stood in the way. The tight metal bands and leather straps held it straight up instead of curving against his belly. No way could he ejaculate with that contraption fastened to him. He practically growled when he asked, "Where the hell did that come from?"

"Mail order," Mei said. "I ordered everything online." Her voice sounded husky and deep.

Oliver jerked his head around to get a better look at her. Tying him up like this was getting her totally hot. Her nipples jutted out like twin pencil erasers, and her inner thighs were slick with her juices. He'd never considered bondage, but obviously Mei had given it a lot of thought. She must to have taken the time to order toys just for him.

She held up a feather and he shuddered. Damn, she knew he was ticklish. *Payback.* He'd tickled Mei until she'd begged him to stop.

No way in hell was he going to beg. Oliver closed his eyes when she dragged the feather lightly along his chest, but that made it worse. He couldn't see where she was going next, so he opened his eyes just in time to watch her swirl it around his tightly restrained balls. His entire body twitched and jerked. He wrapped his fingers around the chains to his cuffs and pulled until he thought his wrists might break.

At least it helped mask the tantalizing path of the long, white feather against his dark chocolate skin. When she finally set the feather aside, he was panting. Maybe now she'd turn him loose. All he wanted was to fuck!

When she reached for the tube of lubricant, Oliver groaned. Mei smiled. She'd found the stuff that heated and almost burned, a slick oil he'd rubbed between her legs and over her ass until she'd whimpered with the need to climax.

Oliver Cheval did not whimper.

She coated his ass with the stuff. Heat spread over his sensitive tissues. Then she smeared it over the vibrator and pressed its broad head against his asshole. He hadn't realized how big the damned thing was. No wonder Mei had squirmed and grunted when he'd used it on her.

Biting his lips, he swallowed back a groan when she rubbed the smooth, gelled head against his ass. She shoved the pillows back and changed the angle so that his butt tilted up higher. He tried drawing his legs together, but the ties kept him spread wide.

Mei held the head of the phallus against his ass and pushed. She rubbed it back and forth and pushed harder, but she couldn't get the angle right. Next she crawled up on the bed between his legs and used her fingers to spread him.

His nipples reacted to her intimate touch. The pain was sweet and all-consuming, shooting down his spine to settle in his sac. His cock twitched and his balls ached, but he couldn't come, not all trussed up in metal rings and leather. Her finger breached his sphincter. She added a second, then a third. In and out, her slim fingers opened him, aroused him until he knew he couldn't take anymore without blowing that damned contraption right off his cock.

Then she slipped the plastic phallus inside his ass, buried it all the way to the base . . . and turned it on.

The thing vibrated like it wanted to take off. She'd placed it perfectly against his prostate, and that little gland was doing its best to make him come. Within seconds, he was arching his hips and thrashing against his restraints, but he couldn't escape the overwhelming sensation, the pleasure so tightly linked with pain he knew he'd never be the same again.

It seemed unbelievable that, until a few short weeks ago, he'd lived his entire life without knowing sexual arousal at all—he'd been literally asexual until his first shift. This experience, what Mei was doing to him right now, pushed boundaries beyond anything Oliver could have imagined. He'd never been so aroused, never realized how painful it could be, how addictive, this desire for release denied.

Frantic with need, he no longer thought of control. No longer wanted it. He was pain linked with desire, a body frenzied beyond thought, an entity of pure carnal cravings.

Cool fingers stroked his chest. Oliver stilled his thrashing, stopped struggling against his restraints. He blinked as Mei, smiling sweetly and taking all the time in the world, straddled his hips. She teased the end of his cock with her slick, hot sex. Her fingers traced the smooth edges of the rings along his shaft. Then she rose up on her knees, paused at the apex, and slid all the way down on his tightly caged penis.

He squeezed his eyes shut and cried out. She sat back with him buried inside her, and the smooth globes of her ass surrounded his tethered balls. He no longer felt his nipples. No, his entire being centered on his cock and the powerful vibrations rolling from his ass through his tightly restrained testicles. Mei's hot, wet vaginal muscles stretched to accommodate his metal-and-leather-clad cock. She rocked forward, rising and falling in slow motion. Even with his eyes shut and her thoughts closed to him, Oliver knew she dragged her clit over the series of smooth metal rings.

The intensity was blinding, the pleasure as Mei raised and lowered herself over his straining shaft totally indescribable. He heard a strange, rough noise and realized he was grunting with each lift and stroke. He opened his eyes just enough to see

Mei and would have come if he could have, merely from the ferocious pleasure etched on her face.

Time ceased to have meaning. His cock had become an instrument of pleasure for the woman who mounted him. The vibrating phallus seemed to reach a crescendo and remain there, holding his quivering body in stasis, unable to climax. Never would he beg for relief.

Mei leaned forward and removed both nipple clamps at once. The rush of blood to his tits brought a cry to his lips and a fresh surge of sensation to his cock. Next she reached beneath herself and somehow released the pressure on the cock restraint. She raised up, removed the rings and the leather straps from his genitals, and carefully slipped back down over his aching cock.

He should have come, but he could only lie there with the vibrator in his ass and her warm pussy clamped around his cock. He'd thought his ejaculation would be immediate, but the pressure continued to build, pleasure spreading until his entire body trembled. Mei suddenly went still, arched her back, and drove down hard on his shaft. She cried out as her body spasmed around him.

Watching Mei climax shoved Oliver over the edge. Arms and legs jerking against his restraints, he surged up into her. His balls contracted, and his cock pulsed with the force of orgasm. She convulsed again and fell forward. Oliver bucked his hips, driving into her as much as his tightly restrained hands and feet would allow. The vibrator seemed to swell inside him, and his cock continued pumping more seed deep inside Mei.

Finally there was no more. Her pussy clenched and rippled around him; his nipples burned with returning blood flow. His balls no longer hurt but still felt sensitive to the sweep of Mei's soft bottom. She reached behind her and finally turned the damned vibrator off, but she left it in place, deep inside his rhythmically clenching body.

"Shit." He struggled to catch his breath. "That was amazing. You ever done this before?"

Mei sat up and glared at him. "Of course not."

Oliver started to laugh. Once started, he couldn't stop. Mei stared at him like he was nuts, but her lips trembled and she giggled. He felt her laughter in the tight contractions around his cock. He couldn't believe it when the damned thing started getting hard again.

Mei finally got her giggles under control enough to ask him, "Why would you think I'd done this before?"

"Untie me and I'll tell you."

"Oh. I forgot." She kissed him hard and fast and reached for the handcuffs. The key was tied to the left cuff, so she released that arm first, untangled the chain from the headboard, and loosed his right arm as well.

Oliver reached up and cupped her face in his hands. "I asked because I have never, not in my wildest fantasies, experienced anything remotely as intense as the past hour with you. I just wanted to say, if this was a practice run, I doubt I could survive the real thing."

"You're not angry?" She leaned down and kissed him.

"You're kidding, right?" He kissed her back. "I've never come so hard in my life. However, if you don't mind, would you please pull that damned vibrator out of my ass?"

The giggles got her again, but she managed to untie his legs and remove the dildo as requested. Oliver lay there beside her. His heart still pounded, his blood rushed, and his penis was once again engorged. Red lines, the marks from the metal rings, ran its length. He hoped she would do that again. He never would have guessed how her domination would turn him on.

After so many years as Anton's assistant, as the one who kept the house clean, the meals prepared, and everyone's life in order, he never would have guessed that submission might be so sexually arousing to him. Just the opposite.

What a wonderful gift Mei had given him! He'd taken control from the very beginning of his relationship with her. In many ways, he'd neglected her needs in favor of his own, but tonight Mei reminded him just how important she was. He couldn't imagine any other woman taking the time to explore his darker side, to force him to acknowledge desires he'd never suspected.

He wrapped his hand around Mei's and squeezed. Her mind, blocked throughout the evening, flowered open. He felt her love, her need for him, even though a shadow remained. Mei's powerful sense of isolation, the disconnect from the rest of the pack. Still there. Still a powerful part of who she was. She still feared Anton's solution, but she feared, just as much, the loss of her own nature. She was the leopard, just as she'd tried to explain to Oliver. It wasn't merely the creature she became when she shifted; it was the woman who lay beside him as well.

She didn't want to lose that sense of herself.

Filled with a new respect for her unique yet perfect nature, Oliver reached for Mei. He thought of the others, even now calling on the ancient Sioux spirit guide. Would *Igmutaka* be able to help, should they make contact? Would he want to?

Suddenly Mei's fingers found his erect shaft. They wrapped around his length and stroked him. All thoughts of the spirit guide fled. He had a bigger problem right now—the horrible fear that Anton's decree of abstinence was going to kill him.

6

_____

The moon was almost full when they gathered in the meadow.
Tala and Eve walked out together. Mik, AJ, and Adam waited,
all three men gloriously naked and already aroused.

Tala elbowed Eve and whispered, "What is it with these
guys? Are they ever *not* horny?"

"No. I think it's a permanent condition." Eve chuckled.
"I'm still trying to figure out how you handle two of them."

"She handles them very well, thank you." AJ leaned over
and kissed Tala.

"I do my best." She put her hands on her hips and looked
from one to the other. "Okay. What now?"

"We decided to run, first, if that's okay with you," Adam
said. "Not for too long. Just enough . . ."

"For everyone to be really ready for sex," Mik finished.

Tala stroked the length of his erection and thumbed the tiny
bead of precum off the tip. She grinned up at him. "You mean
you're not ready now?"

"Getting there." He shifted before she could cup his balls,

which was going to be her next move, and Eve and Tala were suddenly surrounded by wolves.

Eve untied her multihued sarong and dropped it on the grass where she stood. Tala did the same, shifting as she pulled the fabric away from her body. She raced ahead of Eve, right on Mik's heels. She might be barely five feet tall in her human form, but as a wolf, Tala loved that she was every bit as big and powerful as any other female.

The night was warm, the air filled with the scent of small living creatures; damp humus, and the heady resinous perfume of cedar, spruce, and fir. Another scent tickled her nostrils, and she glanced at Eve, racing beside her.

You've come into heat, haven't you?

Yes.

Well, shit, so have I. The guys are going to go nuts when they pick up the scent.

We want them turned on for this, don't we?

Tala didn't answer. She didn't need to. Once the males scented them, things were going to get very interesting.

Mik reached the small meadow first. He sniffed the air, confirmed they were alone, and shifted. Adam arrived next, then AJ, Eve, and Tala. Mik recognized Tala's rich odor the moment she entered the meadow. Heat flooded his cock. The same seductive scent surrounded Eve. His heart pounded. He glanced toward AJ and Adam.

AJ, Tala, and Eve shifted, but Adam remained in his wolven form. He stuck his nose between Eve's thighs and inhaled. Mik heard his low growl, saw Adam's wolven tongue snake out and reach deep inside Eve.

"Adam. No. Not now." Eve backed away. The wolf followed. Eve glanced helplessly at the others. "I didn't think this would be a problem."

"It's not." Mik reached out, grabbed Adam by the scruff of

his neck, and hauled him away from Eve. Adam turned, snarling, his teeth bared. Mik tightened his hold and forced the wolf to meet his eyes.

"The woman said not now. She meant it."

Adam shifted. Mik backed away. Adam shook his head, two sharp jerks, then blinked and looked sheepishly at Mik. "Sorry, man. I lost it."

"Save it for the spirit guide."

"Yeah. Right." He turned to Eve, his mate. "I'm really sorry, honey. But damn . . ."

"Well, you said you wanted everyone horny." She looped her arms over Adam's shoulders and kissed him. "What do we do now?"

"Mik, AJ, and I have been talking." He smiled at Eve and brushed his palm over her long hair. "As much as I hate to say this, because I want you so badly I ache, I think you and Mik need to fuck. You're the designated receptacle for Mei's leopard consciousness; Mik's the one with possible access to the feline guide. The rest of us will join you but not until you're very close to climax." He glanced at the others. "That okay with you?"

Mik glanced at Tala. She stood beside AJ, but she was grinning broadly at Mik. She knew he was more attracted to men than women. Tala was the only exception. Thank goodness Eve was in heat, because her scent inflamed him even when her gender didn't.

It was strange, approaching a woman he hardly knew, especially with an audience, but Eve made it easy. She moved into his arms as if they'd known each other forever. Kissed his mouth and rubbed her hips against his. Then, instead of getting in position to fuck, she slipped to her knees and took his cock between her lips.

With a soft sigh of relief, Mik accepted her mouth with gratitude. Her tongue traced his smooth crown, dipped into the small hole, and licked like a cat after cream. Her teeth scraped the broad head as she took him deeper, sucking him into the hot recess of her mouth, and then even deeper, into her throat.

He groaned and his knees almost buckled. A mouth was, after all, a mouth, and Eve's was spectacular. Mik groaned again when her fingers found his sac. He tried to remember what Adam had told him, to think of the spirit guide, not the woman doing her best to turn him on, but it wasn't easy. Not with her scent flowering around them and her slim fingers wrapped around his balls, but he raised his head and called out to his grandfather's spirit guide, amazed when the ancient language returned to him.

Chanting in the once-familiar song of the Lakota, Mik channeled his rising arousal into his plea for Grandfather's guide. He was barely aware when Tala moved close. Then her scent, similar to yet even more powerful than Eve's, enveloped him. Small and agile, she slipped down between his widely spread legs and nuzzled Eve's fingers aside. He felt Tala's tongue caress his sac, felt her lips wrap around his testicles, and his legs trembled.

AJ stepped behind him, knelt, and parted Mik's buttocks. With his mouth and tongue, he managed to thoroughly moisten Mik's ass before standing once again and kissing Mik's shoulder. Then he placed the head of his penis against Mik's anus and entered him in a single, powerful thrust. Mik's song to the spirit guide faltered, and he cried out with the dark pain of entry. Then AJ slowly withdrew, taking the pain with him. He thrust forward, pulled back, sliding in and out easily now in his own rhythm.

Mik's rhythm.

Mik lowered his head, accepting one more level of sensation, and resumed his plea to *Igmutaka*.

He sensed Adam's nearness. Without halting his chant, he glanced down and watched as Adam knelt behind Eve, took his engorged penis in his fist, and entered her sex from behind. She groaned. The vibration traveled the length of Mik's cock.

Adam's thoughts entered Mik's first. He shared the damp grass beneath his knees, the slick heat of his mate's tight sex. Then Eve's experience filled Mik's mind, and he realized how much she loved his taste, the way his thick shaft filled her mouth and yet slipped so easily down her throat.

Tala's mental signature, so sweet and familiar, almost took him over the edge. She suckled Mik's balls, but her right hand was wrapped carefully around AJ's sac and her left was buried three fingers deep inside his ass.

AJ fucked him, slowly and carefully, and the song poured forth, rising in tempo as Mik's climax neared. Their minds seemed to merge, and the link grew in power. Chills raced over Mik's skin, and the damp suction of mouths, the piercing pleasure with each powerful thrust from his lover, gave over to the pure carnal bliss of five bodies moving in perfect synchronization, five powerful sexual creatures joined as one.

He'd not believed it when AJ described the morning's experience, but Mik knew he would never forget this moment. Passion consumed him, thoughts and sensations overwhelmed him, and he was suddenly more than himself. So much more— a melding of souls, a joining of minds totally merged and floating, watching the lush tableau in the meadow, five writhing, twisting bodies with the same intent, the same purpose, all of them bathed in golden fire.

Only one voice filled the night—the powerful words of Mik's chant. His voice grew in strength, ringing out in the darkness as he called on *Igmutaka*, called forth the spirit of the wildcat. Glowing brighter now, his body alone shimmered with an incandescence so otherworldly, so beautiful, that the merged mind watching was caught in a moment of wonder.

A sense of something *other* appeared. Powerful. Older than time, it hovered, invisible yet omnipotent. The melded mind acknowledged its strength, welcomed it. Cold light flashed. Mik's body bucked with a surge of power, the long strands of his hair spread out about his head as orgasm rocked him. Eve twisted with her own climax and clamped her lips down tight, catching the burst of Mik's ejaculate. Adam threw his head back and howled, his hips forcing Eve against Mik. AJ and Tala both groaned as the shared orgasm spilled over onto them, and the fire glowed brighter, encompassing all of them in one brief flash of cold light.

Mik's legs buckled. The others helped lower him to the ground. He sprawled on his back, panting. His big body still glowed with cold, golden fire. AJ, Tala, Eve, and Adam lay beside him in the damp grass, hearts pounding, lungs heaving.

Tala was the first to reach for Mik. She stretched her hand through the glow shimmering over his body and touched his chest above his heart. "Are you okay, Mik? What is this?"

Mik raised his head in time to see the glow race along Tala's arm and surround her. Her lips parted in surprise. Her long hair sparkled with static electricity. Then with an audible *pop,* the fire disappeared, leaving them all in the pale silver light of the fat, gibbous moon.

The silence was broken only by the harsh rasp of breathing, as if they'd all just run a marathon.

"What the fuck happened?" Adam raised his head and stared at AJ. "That was ten times weirder than this morning."

AJ rolled to one side and shook his head. "Did you ever consider we might be fiddling with things better left to Anton? I think cold fire and glowing bodies is more in his realm of experience."

Eve slowly sat up. "I tend to agree, but wow! That was the most amazing orgasm I've ever had in my life."

"Me, too." Adam scooted over beside his mate and wrapped his arm around her shoulders. "You okay?"

"Definitely. Tala? How about you?"

Tala sat up and reached for Mik's hand. "I'm fine. Mik?" He nodded and looked down where their fingers were linked and smiled. Then he turned her hand over. "Look." A single black rosette, similar to those that covered Mei's leopard coat, marked the back of Tala's left hand. "Grandfather had the same mark." He looked at his own hands. Nothing. "The spirit guide has chosen you, Tala. He resides within you." She raised her head, and her beautiful catlike eyes were troubled when she looked at Mik. Then she stood up and backed away from all of them. Mik held his breath when she shifted.

He let it out on a long sigh of relief when the familiar wolf stood before him. They shifted and trotted slowly back to the house. Mik followed close behind Tala, with AJ beside him. Stefan and Anton would be home in the morning. They had three days of abstinence ahead before Anton attempted the switch. He wasn't looking forward to that at all—neither the abstinence nor the switch.

They'd all assumed it would be Eve who took on Mei's consciousness. Mik wondered just how much Anton's plans might have to change, now that Tala harbored the soul of the cat.

"You don't need to look at me like that. I'm not any different, you know." She'd been getting those weird looks ever since last night's event, and it was beginning to freak her out. They'd spent the day cleaning house and working in the yard, but no matter how busy everyone had been, Tala knew she'd remained the center of their curiosity, and she'd had enough of it. She sipped her wine and glared at Adam.

He grinned and shook his head. "I keep seeing you with that golden glow around you and your hair all frizzed and sparkling. Sorry, Tala, but that was probably the most amazing thing I've ever witnessed."

Mik wandered out with a cold beer grasped in one big fist. "What? I wasn't amazing?"

Adam laughed. "Nope. You were just plain freaky. Covered in gold fire, your hair standing out all over your head. Then when your spirit guide decided to show up . . ." Adam shook his head. "If I hadn't been in that weird meld with all of you, I probably would have run for the hills."

AJ scooted Tala over and made room on the swing for Mik. "It was pretty amazing, that's for sure. Ten times more intense than what Adam and I experienced. Not sure if I want to try that again."

Anton walked across the deck and sat across from Tala. "Are you okay?" When she smiled and nodded, he added, "I wish I'd been here. I hope you'll be willing to attempt such a meld again, Adam."

"Maybe without calling the spirit guide. That added a level of power I'm still not sure of. Believe me, AJ and I were both wishing you were there."

Anton raised one dark brow, and his lip curled in a sardonic grin. "The rest of you weren't?"

"All of us were, Anton." Mik took a long swallow of his beer and glanced at Tala. Of them all, he was the only one who seemed to be taking the conversation seriously. "We've given you the details as well as we can recall, but I'm still worried about Tala. I'd hoped to call the spirit guide into my own body. For whatever reason, it chose hers. I'd like to know why."

Anton studied her so closely, Tala felt like squirming in her seat. "Do you by chance have Asian blood?" He reached out and touched the side of her face, next to her left eye. "You have that beautiful catlike tilt to your eyes. Neither Lisa nor Baylor have your eyes."

Tala pictured her brother and sister; they'd been estranged for so long but were now Chanku, just as she was, and once again they were family. None of them looked anything alike. "For all we know, the three of us may have different fathers. Our mother wasn't the most monogamous of women. My biological father could have been anyone. I don't really know." Tala looked at the glass of wine in her hands. She'd tried so hard to put memories of her parents out of her mind. Knowing her father had murdered her mother and her lover wasn't an easy thing to live with.

Anton merely nodded. "I ask because I'm wondering if the Asian members of our race lean more toward the leopard. It's the only link that would tie you to the spirit guide—which we assume is feline—and Mei's leopard."

By now, everyone had wandered out to the deck and joined them. Keisha and Xandi with their babies, and Stefan, Mei, and Oliver. All of them were curious as to how last night's event would affect Mei's and Oliver's chance to bond.

At this point, Tala didn't care. She merely wanted to fade into the shadows, find a quiet corner with her two men, and let the world go away.

Of course, with Anton's abstinence edict now in force, even that wouldn't be as satisfying as usual. "Why is it," she asked no one in particular, "that the minute someone tells you not to have sex, you're immediately horny?"

"Go figure." Stefan sat next to Xandi and took baby Alex in his arms. "Those weeks after this runt was born just about killed me."

Xandi leaned over and kissed his cheek. "Sweetheart, going without for more than a day just about kills you."

After the laughter died, Tala glanced around at the others. She felt edgy and out of sorts, so unlike her usual disposition. She knew she was generally pretty even-tempered. "Any of you plan to run tonight?"

Most of them shook their heads. It had been a long day, and there were more projects slated for tomorrow. Anton had decided the best way to avoid sex was to keep everyone busy.

"I'd like to." Mei shrugged. "I'll probably just go alone."

Oliver covered her hand. "I'd rather you didn't. I'll go with you."

"Let me." Tala stood up and stretched. "I really feel a need to stretch my legs."

"It's obvious our attempts to stretch them haven't worked." AJ patted the top of her head, and Tala stuck out her tongue.

Mei, thank goodness, ignored AJ's short-person quip as she stood up as well. "Thanks, Tala. Oliver worries when I go alone, but he's bored going out with a leopard—all he wants to do is run." She leaned over and kissed Oliver before he could object. "Don't worry. We'll be fine."

"I know." He touched her hand and watched her go.

Tala followed Mei out to the meadow. They stripped out of their clothing, but before she shifted, Mei touched Tala's arm. "We may not be able to communicate. If we get separated, don't worry about me. I'll meet you back here in an hour or so."

"Okay. Works for me. I'm heading out toward the mill pond. It's not far and is really pretty in the moonlight." Tala stood aside as Mei shifted. The snow leopard, as gorgeous as it was, had intimidated the hell out of her for some reason.

But not tonight. *Mei. Do you understand me?*

The leopard raised her head and growled. *I do. Like Mik, you have an accent, but I understand.*

I'm going to let Oliver know so he doesn't worry. She turned and waved at the group on the deck. "The spirit guide must be working. I understand Mei." Before anyone could question her, Tala shifted. As a wolf standing so close to a leopard, she had an odd sense of danger, a feeling that these two animals should not be sharing the same space. Then the feeling passed and she sniffed Mei's face. *Do you understand me now?*

The leopard nodded. A very human gesture. *I do. Amazing.*

Let's go. Tala took off at a slow trot, well aware of Mei's dislike of running long distances. The leopard followed on silent paws. They crossed the meadow and glided through the trees.

This was a totally new experience for Tala. So often she ran with her guys, two huge, powerful wolves who raced the wind. Now, though, she trotted along at a slow yet steady pace, keeping to the familiar trail. The leopard slipped on and off the beaten track, slinking through thick grass and winding among the trees. Her spotted coat provided perfect camouflage, and she actually seemed to disappear as she wove in and out of the shadows.

For Tala, merely going off with a female was unique, but then so was this amazing life she now led. From abused prostitute in a small high-desert town to head of a shapeshifting rescue team with two sexy guys as her bonded mates . . . well, it didn't get any stranger than that.

She glanced to her left and saw Mei sliding in and out of shadows and felt a sudden jolt in her mind, a sense of someone or something else hovering just beyond her consciousness.

Maybe it did get stranger. She had a feeling her spirit guide was making his presence known. Nose down, ears alert to any sound beyond the ordinary, Tala headed toward the shallow pond with Mei slipping through the woods beside her.

Oliver leaned on the railing and stared at the woods. Anton sensed the loneliness, the feelings of exclusion his old friend was dealing with. Sometimes Anton felt as if things were slipping out of his control, and this situation with Oliver, Mei, and now Tala, didn't help.

He walked over and slipped an arm around Oliver's shoulders. "She'll be fine."

Oliver nodded. "That's what Mei keeps telling me. Will it work, Anton? She's afraid."

"I know. We have a better chance now than before. Instead of Eve, I imagine Tala is the one Mei will switch with. Are you okay with that?"

Oliver's harsh bark of laughter shook him. "Me? I think we should wonder if Tala's okay with it. Or Mik and AJ. They didn't sign on for this when they offered to stay. They merely agreed to lend their mental power."

Anton shrugged. "Things changed. They haven't mentioned leaving."

"They wouldn't. They're too honorable for that. They've got a hell of a lot more integrity than we do."

"How can you say that?" Oliver's comments made him uneasy. Had he lost sight of what was right? Stefan often teased Anton about his single-minded quest for answers to questions no one really cared about, but in this case, they did care. Oliver and Mei cared . . . didn't they?

"You were willing to risk Eve, and now Tala, to help me bond with Mei. Is this because you really want to help, or because you want to see if you can actually do it? You're risking trading one life for another if things don't work the way they're supposed to, and you have only the slightest chance of any of this working. Why, Anton? Is it something so important as the quest for information, or is it just plain old guilt? Do you feel bad enough to take risks because you couldn't help me for all those years? Are you concerned about your power, your status within the pack? Adam's doing stuff you never imagined. Hell, Adam fixed me when you couldn't. Does that bother you?"

Anton stared at Oliver, his thoughts whirling and spiking. Oliver had never spoken to him like this, but dear Goddess, was he right? Was this about guilt? Was he jealous of Adam? Oliver nailed one thing for sure—Anton could be so damned single-minded in his quest for knowledge, he wouldn't hesitate to take risks. Was it honorable to ask others to take those risks as well?

Anton stared out over the meadow, thinking long before answering. "In my own defense, I've never consciously felt jealous of what Adam is capable of. I feel only pride and amazement in his abilities. As for you, Oliver, yes, I will always feel guilty that I was unable to help you, that I didn't recognize the depth of your needs and desires. Blame me for that if you will. It's a burden I will always carry. As far as risking Mei and Eve, and now possibly Tala . . . you may be right. I prefer to think I'm attempting this because I love you and want your happiness, but my subconscious motives might not be all that altruistic. I'll have to think more about our plan. If it's too risky, we may have to rethink our options."

Oliver rubbed his forehead with his palm in a gesture of absolute frustration. "I'm sorry. I had no right to say those things. I know you too well, Anton. I admire you too much. I'm just so damned scared. What if something goes wrong? What if . . . ?"

Anton touched Oliver's shoulder and felt the tension thrumming beneath his skin. "You have every right to question me. This should not be my decision alone, not when it affects so many others. There are no guarantees, Oliver, and there is definitely a lot of risk. We'll call everyone together tomorrow to talk about our options. I don't want anyone doing anything they're uncomfortable with."

Oliver nodded. "Mei's afraid, but she's afraid not to try, too. She doesn't think we can hold a relationship together if we don't bond. I know she wants children, and that's obviously out, so the bond is all we have left."

Anton wrapped his arms around Oliver and held him close. "Actually, you have much more than that. You have love. You have each other. We'll make it work, my friend. Somehow we will make it work."

Mei floated on her back beside Tala in the sun-warmed water of the shallow mill pond. Moonlight sparkled off the surface, and she felt a sense of peace she'd not had for many days. Not since her first shift. "It's beautiful out here. How did you know about this place?"

"Stefan brought us here one time when we visited. It's so peaceful. The guys and I always try to swim here at least once. I'm surprised Mik and AJ didn't come."

"I think they wanted to give us a chance to get to know each other." Mei lowered her feet and stood up. The water lapped at her waist.

Tala stood as well, but she was so much smaller that the water reached her breasts. She circled her arms lazily, treading water. "I wondered about that. I imagine Anton hopes to use me for the host, now that I've managed to catch Mik's spirit guide."

"How do you feel about that? Eve volunteered." Except Tala was the more perfect host. If she didn't want to take the risk . . . Tala stared at Mei for so long she shivered under her intense scrutiny.

"I believe things happen for a reason, but I also believe we're in control, to a certain extent, of our own fate. Last night when we melded, the spirit guide spoke to me. At first I didn't understand the words. I think they were in the Lakota language, the same as the chant Mik was singing. Later, they started to make sense to me, just as mindtalking with you now makes sense. *Igmutaka* is in me, for better or worse. I think he chose me for a reason. I prefer to think that reason is to help you, so my choice is simple. If your consciousness chooses me, I will welcome it. Just as I will welcome the chance to be a leopard, if only for a very short time."

"Long enough for me to mate with Oliver. To achieve the mating link that will bind us." Mei touched Tala's shoulder. She needed the connection, a physical link. "Thank you. I've been so afraid of this since Anton first mentioned the idea. You give me hope. I think we might actually be able to do it."

"I sure hope so. I hate to even think what could go wrong." Tala flashed Mei a cheeky grin and headed back to shore.

7

They gathered in the darkness, all of them unclothed, standing behind matching chairs set in a circle here in the meadow. Only Xandi and Keisha were absent. Anton knew the women watched from the deck, but he'd worried for their safety should anything go wrong. Mothers were the heart of the pack, their babies the pack's future, and neither one had argued against his request. Still, Anton felt Keisha's presence. Knew she supported him with every fiber of her being, and he accepted her mental caress with an almost frightening sense of gratitude.

He couldn't imagine how empty his life would be without the bond that linked them. The same bond Oliver and Mei wanted so badly. He could not fail. Oliver trusted him. Mei feared him but loved Oliver enough to risk anything for the chance to bond. And Tala . . . Anton glanced at the tiny woman standing between Mik and AJ and knew he'd never been in the presence of such bravery in his life.

She knew the risks, accepted them, and offered her body as a living sacrifice in spite of everything he'd warned her could happen.

And he'd only been able to warn her of the things he knew.

The moon was full, though it had set at dusk, and the darkness was absolute. Anton stepped to the center of the circle and scraped a match across the rough edge of a small stone brazier. Flames leapt up, burned brightly, then settled back to a flickering glow that cast living shadows across each one of them.

He noticed that every man among them was aroused, himself included. Chanku did not take well to celibacy, but the sexual energy contained within the circle formed a palpable vibration—power he fully intended to use.

"The flame is for focus. It gives you something to watch while the transfer occurs. All of us except for Mei, Oliver, and Tala need to sit and grasp hands. Oliver, I want you to wait outside the circle. Tala and Mei will be next to the fire."

Mik leaned close and kissed Tala. AJ did the same. Then he shot a glance at Anton that spoke volumes. Mik trusted in the strength of the spirit guide, but it was obvious AJ wasn't all that comfortable with their plans.

There was a shuffling of chairs and bodies. Oliver moved outside the circle and shifted. The wolf sat quietly in the thick grass and waited.

Mei and Tala clasped hands and stood close together at the circle's center. Tala suddenly turned and hugged Mei and kissed her cheek. "Don't worry. It's going to work. I feel it."

She might be the little one, but her heart was huge.

"Thank you." Mei's voice shook. She took a deep breath and slowly let it out.

Anton sat between Mik and Adam. He'd chosen this spot for Mik's link to *Igmutaka* and for Adam's mental strength. Both men grasped the hand he extended. He felt their power. Absorbed their pure sexual energy.

It coursed through him. Made the hairs on his body stand up, made his cock even harder than it was. It was going to work.

He felt it. Anton took a deep breath, found his center, and looked at the expectant faces around him.

"Here's how we're going to do this. Mei, I'll go into your mind first and guide your consciousness to Tala. Tala, you'll feel my presence and Mei's the moment we enter your thoughts. You'll need to reach for me then. Mei will remain behind, and I'll lead you back to the leopard. After the transfer is complete, do not shift. You must remain in your animal form. Tala, you'll need to control the leopard. Don't leave the circle. Oliver, I know it's asking a lot, but if you can, please stay within the area of the meadow to bond with Mei. I want to know where you are at all times, and we can't break the circle. Okay, Mei? Tala? I want both of you to shift now. Power should surge and peak in a few minutes."

The leopard and wolf sat side by side. Anton glanced briefly at both of them and then made eye contact with each person in the circle. Eve. Stefan. Mik and AJ. Adam. Beautiful, powerful Chanku. Linked not by their humanity but by their shared heritage as shapeshifters, by their desire to help two of their own. The circle was small, their arms stretched wide, the power growing with each passing second. Anton sent a brief prayer to the goddess and buried any misgivings he might have.

"In order to accomplish this, I need your power, the energy each of you holds for me tonight. Open your minds to me. Imagine a golden cord linking us, and send your strength along that line. Do not break the circle. Do not cut the power. I'll need it to hold the transfer in place."

The shining energy was visible, something he'd not expected. Golden threads linking each of them to Anton. He glowed with their light, swelled with the power they shared.

It was a simple thing, really, to enter Mei's mind. They'd had sex, after all, and their link was already established. She left her leopard body and entered Tala's waiting wolf, where Anton left her to find her own way. He accompanied Tala back to the leopard lying quietly in the grass. She slipped from his mind and entered the big cat.

Anton shivered. He had the oddest feeling she hadn't traveled alone.

Mei looked out at the world through the eyes of a wolf, and the first one she saw was Oliver. He waited outside the circle. She took a moment to get a feel for this body, recognized she was strong and healthy and also in heat. Oliver was going to love this. She leapt over the linked hands and joined him.

He sniffed her body and stuck his nose between her hind legs, sniffing and nuzzling. Then he licked her muzzle and pawed her shoulder, already prepared to mate.

Not here. Anton wanted them to stay close, but the far side of the meadow would give them more privacy. She raced ahead, eluding his paws and sharp teeth, pausing at the edge of the forest. There she waited.

Oliver raced past her, snapped his teeth and pivoted. She met him with fangs bared. He dipped and twirled past once more, raking her shoulder with his claws and blocking her before she could turn again. This wolven body wasn't as supple as the leopard, and Oliver was a determined wolf.

When he mounted her, Mei snarled, even as she accepted his dominance. When he grasped her with his forelegs and pierced her with his wolven cock, she acquiesced, but only because this was as it should be. When the huge knot in his penis locked them together, she bowed her head, submissive for once, and opened her thoughts to her mate.

The link, when it happened, went miles beyond anything Mei had expected. A melding of souls, a joining of spirits so complete, so fulfilling, she lost herself in the memories, the powerful needs, the thoughts and aspirations of the man and wolf who claimed her for his own.

It was over too quickly. It lasted a lifetime, both their life-times, and when it was time to separate, to sever the bond and rejoin her leopard body, she hesitated. This was the man she loved. This body, this wolf, was a part of him.

She raised her head and saw the leopard. Far across the meadow, it watched her. Waiting. With an overwhelming sense of regret, Mei slipped away from Oliver. She turned to him and licked his muzzle, then slowly trotted across the meadow to return to her own body.

Outraged, Tala watched the Mei wolf as it turned away from the Oliver wolf. She wanted this body back? How dare she. Snarling, Tala twisted around within the circle and studied the humans surrounding her. They sat as if under a spell, linked by golden lines of power to the one who called himself wizard.

The wolf drew closer. Tala glanced to the keeper of the spirit guide. Mik. His name was Mik, and he, like the others, was caught by the link of power, growing weaker with each second that passed. Only the wizard remained strong, but his strength would wane.

Once the wolf arrived, before the switch could be made, that was the time to make her break for the forest and freedom. She looked down at the spotted coat, the broad paws with their sharp, retractable claws, and would have smiled were she human. It was a good body. A strong body. The perfect vessel for *Igmutaka.*

She'd waited so long, so patiently, guiding her needy hu-mans, but now it was time. The wolf drew close. The wizard raised his head and welcomed the wolf within the circle. He touched the wolf's head, stared into the eyes of the leopard.

Igmutaka averted her eyes and leapt over the arms of the two closest humans. She raced across the dark meadow and slipped beyond the first line of trees, into the forest.

* * *

"Don't break the circle." Anton grabbed for Adam's and Mik's hands.

"What the hell happened?" Mik jerked Anton's arm. "I sensed the spirit guide. There was no sense of Tala. None."

"I think he's taken control. Shit." Anton placed his hands on the wolf's head. Mei waited, patiently, fully aware of what had happened.

Oliver joined them, still in wolf form, but he shifted the moment he reached the circle. "I felt it all. We need to find her. Tala's under *Igmutaka*'s control, but she's fighting him. She's just not strong enough."

Anton grabbed his arm. "How do you know this?"

Oliver shook his head. "I understand their speech. When Mei and I bonded, it all came clear for me." He looked at his mate with eyes full of concern. "Don't shift, Mei. It could lock you into Tala's form. We need to get her back."

The wolf nodded. So human, yet terribly confused.

Oliver stood beside the wolf. "I'll stay with her. Mik, you need to go after Tala. You're the only other one who can communicate with her in this form. Get her before *Igmutaka* takes over completely."

Anton found himself willingly taking orders from his manservant. He shifted and followed the others into the woods. The trail was easy enough to find. The spirit guide had been ethereal spirit longer than it had been leopard, and Tala thought like a wolf. They ran her to ground near the mill pond. Lungs heaving from the run, she paced the edge of the water, confused and frightened.

"Tala?" Mik was the first to shift. He held out his hand to the leopard. She snarled but didn't attack or run. *Tala? Am I talking to you or to Grandfather's spirit guide?*

Tala. He's here, but I think I've got him cornered.

Good girl. Mik glanced at the others waiting behind him.

"Tala's in control, at least for now." *Can you come back to the meadow so we can transfer you back to your body?*

I can try. This guy's a real son of a bitch. He wants the leopard for himself. He's been trying to kick me out.

Mik felt a chill pass through his body. *Hang on, sweetie. You know you're tougher than he is.*

Of course I am, but he caught me by surprise. I didn't even know he was there.

Are you ready to go back?

The leopard growled. *Well, part of me is. Start back, Mik. I'll follow you.*

Trusting Tala, Mik turned and headed back along the trail. The leopard followed, snarling and growling all the way. The light from the brazier marked their destination. Oliver and Mei waited beside the small flame.

The leopard stalked past the humans and waited beside the wolf. Everyone rejoined the circle, including Oliver this time. The golden cables appeared, and Anton drew the strength that flowed along their length.

When he entered Mei's mind, she was waiting for him. He sensed her joy, and it was an easy thing to traverse the small distance between the wolf and the leopard. Tala was another experience altogether.

The spirit guide waited beside her. Confused, angry, it was a dark cloud on Tala's consciousness. Anton reached for Tala. *Igmutaka* held on. Mei's consciousness flowed around them and found its place within her leopard mind, but the spirit guide blocked Anton's attempts to hold Tala. Suddenly she seemed to leap through space at the same time Mei's thoughts blossomed into light. Anton attempted to catch Tala, but the swirl of consciousness was too fast, too powerful.

He searched, but only the dark shadow of the spirit guide remained, held fast by Mei's mind. Anton felt the power feeding his search growing weaker. He'd taken everything the others had to give, but where the hell was Tala? Dear Goddess. Somehow he'd lost her. With a final, desperate look, Anton winked out of Mei's mind.

He reentered his body and crumpled helplessly to the ground, sobbing uncontrollably. His mind whirled with a sense of loss, with a powerful condemnation ringing in his head. *Hubris.* He'd once, so long ago, accused Stefan of hubris, of arrogance and pride, but he was worse. So much worse, thinking he could play God with the minds of people who trusted him.

Tala had trusted him, and where had it gotten her? Lost, her mind floating without an anchor, and he had no idea how to get her back. Anton curled into the fetal position, shoulders shaking, his mind totally blotting out all he'd done wrong. Darkness enveloped him.

He welcomed the void, the sense of nothingness, but Keisha's soft voice drew him back. Ordered him to return. Stefan's strong grip on his arm centered him. Slowly Anton opened his eyes. All of them—Mik, AJ, Adam, Eve, and Oliver . . . Mei and Tala? Blinking, unaccountably confused, Anton rolled to his back. Stefan helped him sit up. "Tala? You made it back?"

Smiling through her own tears, she nodded. "I did. I followed your link. It was hard, shaking off *Igmutaka*. He's a persistent bastard, but I did it."

Anton slowly turned his head. Saw Mei smiling at him.

"Yep. *Igmutaka.* I've got him now, but he's happy. He's found a leopard host, and he's willing to share. It's either that or I boot his sorry ass out and he goes back to the spirit world. I'm okay with that. But you, Anton, are you all right?"

He wasn't sure. Anton brushed his hand across his eyes. He looked up and caught Stefan smiling at him, encouraging him. He'd never lost it like that. It unsettled him, to think he'd lost control . . . in front of witnesses no less. "I think so. Is everyone . . . ?"

"We're fine." Oliver touched his shoulder, then dragged him into a hard embrace. "Damn it all, Anton. You scared the shit out of all of us."

"I'm sorry. Did you and Mei . . . ?"

Oliver nodded. "And more. I haven't tried it yet, but I think I got more out of the mating link than we intended. More than a spirit guide. A lot more." He stepped back.

Anton rose to his feet. The world seemed to spin, and he flopped back down in one of the chairs by the brazier. Stefan stood protectively beside him. Keisha grabbed his hand and held on. He patted her hand and raised his eyebrows when he looked at Oliver. "I'm almost afraid to ask."

Mei snorted. "Me, too. He told me, in great detail, all about the barbs on a leopard's penis."

"What?" Anton swung his head around to stare at Mei. He almost missed it when Oliver shifted. Almost, but not quite.

The male snow leopard snarled and arched his back. Mei shifted. She snarled, then rubbed her head against Oliver's. Together, two leopards raced into the forest.

Stefan handed a fresh cup of coffee to Anton. Morning sunlight brushed the tips of the pines, and there was a chilly nip to the air. The two of them were the only ones up so far, but Anton hadn't quite made it to bed.

Stefan sat next to him on the porch swing. Both men sipped their coffee in silence until Stefan said, "Oliver and Mei got back a few minutes ago."

"Good. I was worried. I'm still not sure of *Igmutaka*'s power, or Mei's ability to control him."

Stefan nodded. "Yeah. Well, I think Mei's tougher than she looks. Oliver wanted me to tell you he can shift to both—wolf or leopard. So can Mei."

Anton smiled and took another sip of his coffee. He'd wondered, ever since the two had raced off into the night. This was better than he'd dreamed. "The questions are endless, you know. Is it something all of us are capable of? Are there beasts besides the leopard and the wolf? And what of *Igmutaka*? There's something irresistibly amazing about a Lakotan Sioux spirit guide residing in a shapeshifting snow leopard."

"From Tibet, no less."

"By way of Florida." Anton took another swallow. "Did you talk to Mei?" He turned and cocked one eyebrow at Stefan.

Stefan grinned and nodded enthusiastically. "Yep. That sucker's got barbs. Better than a wolf's knot. She couldn't get away. Mei's not too crazy about it. Oliver thinks it's great."

Anton laughed. "He would, wouldn't he?" He tapped his mug to Stefan's in a toast. "Well, it's only fair. If anyone deserves a barbed cock, it's Oliver."

"Agreed." Stefan pushed against the deck with one foot. The swing went into motion, and the two of them watched the sun rise over the forest.

Night Scream

Vonna Harper

1

You don't belong here.

A harsh but muffled drumbeat accompanied Amy Patterson's comment to herself. Perhaps the drumming was responsible for the way the words kept repeating inside her. Perhaps.

You don't belong here.

Squaring her shoulders under her hundred-dollar silk blouse, she continued down the street that had been roped off for the yearly Flagstaff, Arizona, powwow. All around her were groups, families, friends, neighbors, and people who worked together. They laughed and shouted, pointed and watched, none of them paying any attention to the lone woman tiptoeing around a small storm of debris blowing over the asphalt. If someone had, that person might have wondered at her tailored slacks and impractical heels in contrast to the predominance of jeans and boots.

Didn't matter. She wasn't one of them.

Wasn't one of anything.

Angered by her moment of self-pity, Amy gritted her teeth and focused on her surroundings. The powwow had been billed as one of Flagstaff's premier events, and it was certainly living up to its billing, thanks in part to a mix of carnival atmosphere and reconstructed Western days. Mixed in with trinket and fast-food booths were displays of Native American crafts ranging from blankets to baskets to jewelry. Maybe she'd buy a bracelet or necklace to remember . . .

To remember what? That her career as an independent small business auditor had just happened to bring her to Flagstaff?

She'd been going with the flow, so to speak, letting the crowds propel her along, but now she made her way onto the sidewalk and stopped so she could turn in a slow circle. Thanks to the large number of merrymakers, she could barely see beyond the end of her nose—a nose currently overdosing on the smell of fried food—but eventually she spotted a large graveled area where a number of tepees had been set up. The tepees were larger than her perception of tepees and were predominately white but colorfully decorated. She hoped the *village* represented one of the Southwest's Native American tribes, because if she did buy a memento, it should be authentic.

For reasons rooted deep in her reserved nature, she approached slowly. A number of Native American children wearing long, colorful dresses or leather loincloths over jeans ran from tepee to tepee, their laughter filling her heart and infusing her with a longing she knew better than to explore. Still, she loved laughter, carefree and total! Loved and envied the ability to let loose, something that had long eluded her.

Adults, mostly women, were watching the children with the eyes of mothers and grandmothers well experienced in the responsibilities and joys of watching the younger generation. Like their children, the women were dressed in ceremony finery that bore pioneer as well as Native American elements.

She might have ventured closer if she hadn't noted movement to her right. Turning in that direction, she caught sight of a group of five or six Native American men who were all watching as another man approached them. The newcomer was leading a string of haltered horses kept together with a lead rope. The horses were stocky and not particularly tall, their coats rough and thick as if they spent their lives outdoors. As fascinated as she was by the livestock, the handler truly held her attention.

He resembled the horses. All right, so he stood upright, maybe going a couple of inches over six feet, but there was something strong and rugged about him, something not quite tame. He held the thick rope in the sure way of a master horseman, his attention divided between his charges and those waiting for him. Clad in a blue and white flannel shirt rolled up to his elbows, molded-to-muscles jeans, and boots that looked as if they'd married his feet, he didn't walk so much as glide.

No, not glide. As if he had no use for gravity, leaving thigh and calf muscles free to dominate his turf, his world. He could run, leap, pounce, attack—

Lordy! What was she thinking? Damn it, she was logic, all logic, devoted to the science and predictability of math. Waxing erotic about a hunk of man-flesh was hardly her style. As for lusting after a member of that sex, not going to happen!

Unsure in ways she couldn't list or sort, she tried to slide her hands into her back pockets, but of course the damn professional slacks didn't have any. Instead of dropping her arms to her sides, she ran her fingers over her rump, feeling her femininity, her soft roundness. Experience had taught her that touching herself in certain areas and ways in certain circumstances was unwise, because it set off feelings and emotions she had to struggle to contain.

Just the same, her fingers stayed put as she ogled the cowpoke or whatever he was. His shoulder-length hair wasn't just dark but capital letter jet black, glossy and wind-tossed at the same time, and sweeping across his forehead above deep-set eyes. What color were they? She hoped they were black. And the mouth—sigh—strong and firm, a man's mouth. No puny little nose but proud and broad. Wonderfully high cheekbones and a squared chin she'd give a month's pay to run her fingertips and lips over.

Get a grip, damn you! What is your problem?

Okay, so she knew the answer to that: too many nights, and days, alone. But she'd deliberately carved out that life for herself. She craved independence and solitude, the peace that came from lack of emotional entanglements.

The safety and security.

He'd come close enough to the other men that they should have no trouble carrying on a conversation, but instead of the mutter of deep voices she expected, they did little more than nod and step back as the newcomer approached. She told herself they were putting distance between themselves and the horses, but something about the way they kept their attention on the handler made her doubt that. It was as if they didn't want him intruding on their space.

Her curiosity now on high, she folded her arms over her breasts. After the better part of a minute, the oldest man stepped forward and hooked his fingers around one horse's halter. Then the old man leaned his head against the horse's neck, his free hand scratching between two pointed ears, his long thin silver hair obscuring his features. His movement seemed to galvanize the others into action, because each chose a mount and untied it from the lead rope until the loner was left with a pinto. Except for the silver-haired man, the group turned and walked away with their charges following close behind. The hunky handler and the old man started talking, making her wish she could hear what they were saying or read their expressions. Then the old man stuck out his hand, and the hunk took it, their shake saying a great deal about mutual respect and reservation.

When the man who she decided must be an elder or a chief took off after his companions, her attention went back to the loner. The way he studied not just the horses but also the other people reminded her too much of how she'd watched the various groups earlier.

And not just today.

She and Black Hair were set apart, she in part because she didn't know anyone in town, but why him? He'd apparently just provided a service for those men. Didn't they owe him something—money, at least a thank-you?

Although the men were already starting to paint designs or symbols on the horses' flanks and necks, probably in preparation for some ceremony they'd be involved in during the pow-wow, they didn't hold her interest.

How could they when Black Hair was looking at her?

Heat lashed through her, much of it centered in her spine but an alarming amount concentrated between her legs. The unexpected realization that his study went far deeper than a man checking out a woman's physical attributes made her want to turn and run. And yet she stood her ground, shoulders squared and head back, challenging him in the only way she could think of. Where was his damnable study taking him, and even more important, why? He was so damn bold, tearing at her defenses and peeling off the layers. And was that puzzlement in his expression, as if he wasn't sure what about her had caught his attention?

Oh, shit, he was walking toward her!

His every move mesmerized her even though she was unnerved. She might have seen a more fluid glide in her life, maybe on a gymnast or dancer, but his bone-marrow-deep confidence in what his body was capable of left her in awe. A casual runner, she took a measure of pride in her strong leg muscles. Next to him, however, she felt awkward and unsure and far from graceful.

Of course, it wasn't just his stride that riveted her to the spot. There was also his pure, clean maleness, a raw confidence perhaps designed to disarm every female he came in contact with. As the seconds ticked on, she drew an uneasy comparison between him and, of all things, a male cougar, jaguar, or puma approaching the female he'd chosen as his mate. Whether the female wanted to have sex with the male predator didn't concern him. He had decided, his strength and size adding to his supremacy. His mate might submit or fight, but either way the outcome would be the same. They'd mate. And when he'd spilled his seed inside her—

"You don't belong here," he said, his voice a silken rumble.

Shocked, she gaped up at him, her arms pressing against her suddenly hard nipples. "What?"

He nodded, indicating their surroundings. "This is Apache. You aren't Apache."

And you are. "I . . . I didn't mean to . . . if you want me to . . . I'm sorry if I've—"

He stopped her with the barest jerk of his head. "It doesn't matter."

"What?" Oh, yes, his eyes were as dark as his hair, all right, deep as a midnight pool, quiet and yet reaching out for something—maybe her soul?

"You're here, doing things to me and taking me in directions no one ever has," he said. "That's what we have to deal with."

What was he talking about? He could simply order her to leave, no harm done. Fighting the urge to run her damp palms on her slacks, she concentrated on letting her arms slide to her sides in what hopefully came across as a casual gesture. As soon as she did so, she regretted her decision; her nipples couldn't have been more exposed if she'd been naked. And between her legs—where had this hot energy come from? Surely not because he was so close she could feel his male heat.

Maybe because he'd said she was taking him in new directions, whatever that meant.

Her head throbbed, and her lips were somewhere between

numb and alive with the need to press them against whatever part of his anatomy she could reach. She wished she could call what she felt a buzzing sensation, but it had more layers than that. It was as if everything she'd ever been and felt had been stripped away, leaving her born anew, turned on, hungry. Hungry for this stranger.

"What are you feeling?" he asked in that same rough-satin tone.

"What?"

He answered, if she could call it that, by raking her with his eyes from neck to toes. He took his time, a sculptor examining something that had spoken to his creativity, a photographer deciding on the best angle for the perfect shot, a predator at the moment when prey becomes possession. In his eyes she found question and hunger, determination and disbelief. Most of all, she read an inescapable message. This moment would forever change both of them.

"You asked me something," she blurted, because otherwise she might explode. "About what I'm feeling. What makes you think you have the right to?"

"I might not yet, but I will. Soon." With that, he held out his hand, palm up.

Legs trembling and hot between her breasts and along her throat and in her temples, she stared at the offered flesh. His hand was broad with deep calluses, the fine lines standing out against the dark background. This was an Apache hand, fashioned equally by genetics and a physical lifestyle. She couldn't imagine he'd ever submit to a manicure. Creams were unknown. Those fingers, that palm, the broad wrist served him well when he did whatever he did with his horses. Any and all wild broncs he might capture would soon understand that they were under a master's control, but the master could be gentle and understanding, capable of mixing domination and love.

Was that what she'd face if she didn't turn and run? He'd

dominate her because that was his way. But what if beneath the hard surface lay a hot-beating heart? Under him she'd quiver and quake, not in fear but in anticipation. He'd stroke her until she'd forgotten that she'd ever been touched by another man or cried tears she thought would never end, and when he buried his cock in her weeping tissues, she'd turn herself over to him. Completely.

Careful, Amy, careful.

"Don't be afraid of me," he said. "Please."

Please? What a strange thing to say, but his eyes were telling her he meant it with every fiber. Maybe that's why she placed her palm against his and again looked up into those remarkable eyes. In her mind, and maybe her heart, she became small and young, innocent, on the brink of womanhood. The touch resonated all the way up her arm and from there to her already swollen breasts. She felt capable of floating.

"I'm not afraid of you." Did she mean it? Was she in touch enough with herself to know anything? "I just don't understand what's happening." She swallowed, perhaps gathering courage to continue, perhaps waiting for him to close his fingers around hers. "What you said about my not belonging here, I'm surprised you're not telling me to leave. After all, you and the others—"

"I'm not part of them, not really. I've been set apart."

More mystery, more depth in those endless eyes.

"Why?"

For the first time, he appeared less than supremely confident, but maybe she was reading something into his expression that wasn't there. He took so long to respond that she wondered if he'd dismissed her question. Either that or he was deciding whether to say anything.

Finally he broke the electric silence. "Give me your other hand," he ordered.

The command should have been a simple one to respond to.

She'd tell him there'd already been more than enough intimacy, and she'd decided to pack it in and return to her motel room for a long solitary weekend before getting back to work, but damn it, she wanted to place her hands in his, to turn something of herself over to him. To have him explain what he meant about her taking him in new directions.

Shaking a little more, she obeyed. As he'd done before, he simply wrapped his fingers around hers.

Let him do his thing. Count to ten or whatever it takes. Don't move, don't think, don't feel.

Not moving was possible as long as she put her mind to it, but she couldn't begin to shut down her nerve endings. His legs and hips were scant inches from hers and were giving off male vibes no breathing woman could ignore. His sexuality seeped into her, spreading, spreading. Her lips buzzed again.

She might have collapsed against him if not for the shadow growing over his features. He seemed to be aging slightly, becoming deeper and more complex, going someplace emotionally she couldn't begin to comprehend. He'd been studying her hands, but now he lifted his head, his eyes insisting she return his stare.

"What?" she demanded.

"I knew." He spoke in a whisper. "The moment I saw you, I knew."

"What do you know? That I'm a year overdue for a manicure?"

Her sad attempt at a joke died without a response from him. Instead, his gaze became even more intense. For a moment, she could have sworn his eyes were changing from black to yellow. His muscles seemed to be loosening and elongating, his features shifting into something no longer human. Alarmed, she attempted a backward step, only to have his fingers close around her wrists and hold her in place.

"Don't be afraid," he said. "I won't hurt you."

"Let me go. Damn it, I'm not some—"

"What you are is lonely," he whispered. "Your loneliness seeps out of you and coats the air around you. Crying inside and trying to deal with your pain by closing down. You're afraid of your emotions, so you deny them. But it isn't working, because as long as you do, you're only half alive."

Her knees threatened to buckle, and for only the second time in her life, she nearly passed out. Not a single rational thought or word broke free of the swirling mess inside her mind. There was nothing but this mysterious and mystical man with his hard body and knowing eyes, his own loneliness.

"Break free. Put the past behind you and embrace life."

Bury the past. Embrace the future.

"How?" she whimpered, swaying. "Please tell me how."

2

Amy had no idea what she was doing in the man's pickup, and if asked where they were going, she'd be forced to respond with a blank look. All she knew was that his essence filled the less-than-plush cab, and although she was sitting a respectful distance from him, it wasn't nearly enough to blunt his impact.

That was something she'd have to get used to, his hit on her senses, emotions, nerve endings, even the tips of her toes.

At the moment, he was concentrating on the narrow road beyond the city limits that headed toward Humphreys Peak, an awe-inspiring mountain waiting for winter snow. She'd asked—no, she'd insanely and impulsively begged—this stranger to show her how to put the past behind her, and when he'd nodded, she'd agreed to get into his truck and sit passively while he put distance between them and the city's celebration.

It would be dark soon. Already, the horizon was closing down and becoming more blur than reality. She wasn't sure how she felt about no longer having traffic and streetlights to define her surroundings but couldn't put her mind to that because *he* was beside her.

And she'd never felt more alive.

"What's your name?" she asked, speaking loud enough for him to hear despite the dusty work truck's rattles.

He glanced at her, nothing more than a quick look, the shadowed interior seeming to close down around his features. "Tohon."

Tohon. A word seeped in tradition beyond her comprehension and reach, letters and syllables reaching deep into the past. "It's Apache, right?"

"Yes."

"What does it mean? Is there a translation?"

"Several."

Something about his tone caused her to look at him again. "Can I ask what they are? Maybe it's a—"

"Big cat, cougar, puma."

Her mind snagged on *puma.* As a child, she'd been fascinated by wild animals, particularly predators, and had read everything she could find on them, undoubtedly boring her parents with her endless chatter. The various names given the predators were pretty much interchangeable, with most people calling every four-legged hunter with a powerful body and long thick tail a cougar. Perhaps in a bit of rebellion, perhaps because *puma* sounded more exotic, she'd refused to copy everyone else.

As she recalled, pumas had short, coarse fur that was either slate gray or reddish brown. Rarely a male weighed two hundred pounds. Two hundred pounds? Didn't Tohon weigh around that? Suddenly light-headed, she fought the urge to lower her head so the blood would rush back into it. Talk about insane thinking!

How many pictures had she collected during her wild-animal phase? Her mother, not surprisingly, had been appalled by clippings of deadly-eyed killers and had tried to force her to get rid of them. But as he'd always done, her father had defended her collection, insisting that as long as she didn't have nightmares, he supported her interest, although for a while it had been more an obsession than a hobby.

She'd never dreamed of being pursued by sharp-toothed killers; her nightmares, when they'd come, had been triggered by something from her own life, something she'd spent years battling.

Enough, damn you. Bury the past!

Back to the present and the man called Tohon.

And his words about moving forward and no longer looking back.

Pumas, yes, pumas. They were solitary hunters, coming together only to mate. Most of their hunting was done at dawn, dusk, or night, and they used their powerful legs to lunge with long, running jumps that easily landed them on their prey's back. A single bite usually broke the hapless creature's neck.

"Any particular reason?" she blurted, trying not to imagine those long and strong Apache fingers of his turning into claws. "I mean, maybe it's a family name."

"It is."

He didn't want to continue this conversation; she knew that as she'd seldom known anything in her life. Silenced by what she'd just learned, she tried to quiet her thoughts by studying her surroundings, but before long, she was staring at his hands again. Going by his calluses and the way he'd handled the horses, she had no doubt that whatever he did for a living was physical. Maybe he was taking her to where he worked? That made sense only if he believed his career would help her put her past behind her.

Oh, damn, what was she doing here? An only child, she hadn't been overprotected so much as well parented, particularly by her father. In addition, she wasn't an idiot. Bad things happened to people who didn't watch their backs. She knew to watch her back.

Except today.

Fragments of questions piled up in her mind, but instead of voicing them, she slid her hands between her thighs and stared ahead. There was *something* about Tohon. Hell, yes, he was sexy, and her reaction, well, what could she say except that she was hot for the man's body. But she was also cold sober and not about to jump his bones.

Yet.

Where had that come from? Just because he made her skin sing and filled her lungs with heat didn't mean the day would end with a roll in the hay. She might want that. Oh, all right, deep in the quiet place where fantasy continued to live despite her attempts to walk the path of logic, libido pulsed.

The road they were on must have been newly paved. Either that or she was no longer capable of hearing the grind and bump of tires and metal, just a deep hum. The hum fed the fantasy-flame buried in her core, giving rise to thoughts of tearing clothes off, exposing bodies, touching intimately, and spreading her legs as a full, hard cock pistoned inside her.

She'd slept alone since—since when? Without thinking about it too much, mostly because she couldn't get her mind to go in that direction, she recalled that her last lover must have been Jim, the neighbor who'd helped her buy her current car. He'd wanted casual to become serious, but she hadn't, so things had ended. Consequently, she'd been forced to rely on her sex toys and an admittedly faulty imagination when it came to scratching her itches until they stopped bugging her.

If Tohon had sensed or could sense how horny she was . . . oh shit, maybe that's what this trip to hell knows where was about. Nothing to do with some damn promise to set her free of something without a name and everything to do with him getting his.

Was that so bad?

Yeah, if he turned out to be a bully or a creep or, even worse, a rapist, it could turn out capital letter Bad.

Squeezing her thighs together trapped her hands, but at least the move kept her from reaching out and touching him, not that she would, of course. "I'm not going to regret this, am I?" she asked when she could trust her voice to be calm. "For your information, I know self-defense."

He smiled, a brief but real smile that melted something in her and made her ache to slide her hands closer to her pussy in answer to a certain harsh need.

"You won't need it," he said.

"I'm just supposed to take your word for it?"

"No." He drew out the word. And was she imagining it or did his jaw muscles clench as if keeping something locked inside? "But I'm enough of a human to hold the beast at bay."

Something—not quite fear—sped throughout her veins. What beast? she needed to ask for her own self-preservation, but she didn't because maybe she longed to see glimpses of the animal beneath the surface, anything to break her out of the cocoon she'd worked so hard to place around herself and that now threatened to strangle her. "That doesn't exactly fill me with confidence."

"What does?"

"Interesting question," she said after a moment. "Knowing my job, knowing I do it well."

"Do you like it?"

Not going to go there. "It's Friday night. I'm not much into talking about how I pay the bills." Then, although she had absolutely no idea she was going to do so, she slid her left hand out from the prison and shelter she'd created for it and ran her nails over his knuckles. Although his forearm muscle bunched, he didn't let go of the steering wheel. "You make your living with your hands, don't you?"

"Yeah."

She continued lightly stroking him, watching the taut knot beneath his dark skin. "Doing what?"

"Gentling broncs."

She thought she'd have to prod him for more information, but after a moment, he nodded and continued. "I contract with federal agencies to round up, tame, and train wild horses who run on public land. Then when they have value to the public, I turn them over to be sold."

Damn, a throwback, an Apache doing what the prairie tribe had done since horses were first brought to this country. It fit this solitary and physical man. She could almost smell the prairie scents on him, hear pounding hoofbeats as he raced after a stallion or mare. "Then, the horses I saw you give to those men—they were wild?"

"They used to be."

Before you took that out of them.

"How do you do it? Ropes, corrals, whips if necessary?"

"That's never necessary, Amy. These hands"—he turned his right palm toward her—"know to be gentle."

Instead of focusing on what he'd said about being gentle, her mind snagged on something else. "How do you know my name? I didn't tell you."

For too long he didn't respond, maybe deliberately drawing things out as he slowed and turned onto a dirt road stretching out over gently rolling land untouched by man's creations or barriers. "I know things, Amy. Things I'll probably never be able to explain. Things I don't always want to know. That's part of why I approached you, because the moment I looked at you, I experienced something I never have."

"You—you're not making any sense."

"Hopefully I will before we're done. It's too late for it to be any other way. No, don't say anything. Look around. Let the land speak to you; it'll explain a great deal."

She'd done as he'd suggested. Yes, she'd studied the land, albeit with tension evident in her shoulders and her eyes wide, but he knew he'd broken through at least some of her layers. Somehow he'd been able to reach her where he suspected she hadn't realized it was possible to be reached.

He didn't want this, damn it! Oh, hell, yes, he wanted her with a fire and power he seldom felt, and that frightened him when he didn't believe himself capable of being afraid. But fucking the slight, gray-eyed woman with the short, too-businesslike haircut and sexless clothes was only part of what this was about.

Hard or easy—and it was going to be damn hard on both of them—he owed it to her to break her free of the chains she'd placed around her heart. If he didn't, her spark would die, and she'd spend the rest of her life not truly living.

So why was that his problem?

Because it is; because you are who you are, his father's and grandfather's and great-grandfather's spirits responded.

But it's never been like this, he told them. *I look forward, like you. The past belongs there. I can't change it.*

No, he couldn't, he admitted. But maybe he could change the past's impact on her. If that was true, it explained why she'd been surrounded by a cool, almost cold light when he first spotted her and why he'd been relentlessly drawn to the light.

Yes, he acknowledged as the hundred-year-old farmhouse he'd been born in came into view. He and Amy had been sucked into something that went far beyond male and female, flesh and blood. The moment he'd laid eyes on her, he'd sensed more than what had always been both familiar and inescapable. First had come the *hit,* the opening up of the world beyond the here and now. Being given the briefest glimpse into the past, her past, instead of someone's future, had shaken him, but he'd been unable to examine the how and why of that for one simple reason: She turned him on.

More than turned him on. Captured him. Connected him in ways he'd never felt before.

Hearing the baying howl of Lobo, the hundred-twenty-pound mutt who'd adopted him a couple of years ago, distracted him from what he'd experienced back in town. In true Lobo way, the big-bodied dog with the oversized head was letting the pickup know it wasn't welcome. Fortunately, he'd resigned himself to Lobo's disgust for anything with tires and no longer laughed at him. Instead, he studied Amy's reaction as Lobo ran on her side of the truck. She showed no sign of being afraid of a creature that probably outweighed her by several pounds and had much sharper teeth. Not that he often brought women here, but those he had invariably asked if they were safe from *his* dog. So far, Amy hadn't done anything except lean out the open window, muttering something he couldn't understand, her tone low and gentle.

No, Amy Patterson had nothing to fear from a dog. As for whether she'd regret getting close to him—

There it was again, a repeat of sensations as old as his great-great-grandfather and new as earlier this evening when his and Amy's eyes had met. His joints and connecting tissues felt as if they were lengthening, loosening, becoming something other than human.

The change wouldn't come yet; he could still hold himself together. But sooner or later, it would take place, maybe before the night was over. Once the *energy* burst free, there'd be no stopping it. And if she was like those who were his people and yet not, the transformation would terrify and confuse her and he'd lose her.

Unless he'd managed to connect with her in other ways. Physical ways. Man to woman. Heat to heat.

Foot on the brake and right hand over the floor-shift knob, he stopped. Turning off the engine, he leaned back and stared at Amy's profile. She'd gone back to cradling her hands between her legs, and there wasn't a way in hell he didn't want to be the one doing that. Only, once he had his hands on her, he wouldn't be content exploring just her inner thighs.

She was soft and warm and wet in that place all men wanted to be. Maybe she'd let him into her core; maybe she wouldn't. Either way, he'd think about her cunt and breasts and the hollow at the base of her throat and the small of her back until his thoughts drove him crazy.

Weakness, damn it! Despite the strength that allowed him to earn a living working with wild horses, powerful muscles and strong bones meant nothing in her presence. Not just any attractive woman, but *her*.

"This is your place?" she asked, her attention still on Lobo, who'd lost interest in the truck now that it was silent and had sat down waiting to see who would exit. "Who all lives here?"

"Just me."

Her spine straightened just a fraction, but because his senses were already sharpening, he didn't miss the subtle sign. He also didn't waste his breath telling her she was safe, because he might have lied earlier. To her credit, she turned and met his eyes. A quick flash of something akin to lightning sped between them; she was the first to pull it under control. Just the same, enough of the electrical charge remained to tell him she didn't trust her self-control around him.

Maybe he'd have to exploit that.

And if he did, would the lightning burn both of them?

"It's better if I live alone," he told her.

"Why?"

Tell her. Damn it, at least warn her. "You wouldn't understand if I explained," he said instead, hating himself for the words. Then he concentrated on his decision to exploit the hot woman beneath the cool surface. Once the exploitation had begun, if he wasn't too far gone, he'd bring her into his world.

And then?

"There isn't much about this I understand." Still meeting his gaze, she reached for the door handle. "One thing before I get out. When I say no, to anything, I expect you to hear and heed."

The only thing he obeyed was his heritage. Because he had no choice. "I'll try," he said.

"That's all you can promise me, an attempt?"

"Yeah." Then, feeling as if someone else was in charge, he watched as his arm reached for her and his fingers trailed over her neck. Her pulse jumped and then raced.

So did his.

3

The house's interior smelled of leather and wood. There were also hints of earth and vegetation, probably because he'd left the windows open. Semi-sheer drapes were pulled back to let in what remained of the daylight. Tohon hadn't locked his front door, which told Amy something about his sense of security.

Lair. That's what the room put her in mind of, a lair.

Wood-framed oil paintings of nature scenes covered the living room walls, and much of the furniture appeared to be handmade. She imagined Tohon turning slabs of wood into chests and tables, then wondered how he had time for such pursuits if he wanted to be around other people, specifically women?

Women would want him. Hell, she wanted him, and she hadn't so much as glimpsed his naked chest. Not that she'd made a study of such things, but she was fairly certain the majority of women longed for the touch of a man born and bred for the outdoors, a man whose muscles and bones had been carved by physical work.

He appeared to be in his midthirties, although the fine lines around his eyes and mouth could be the result of countless hours in the sun and not years. Not seeing so much as a hint of a paunch was a welcome change from most of the men she came in contact with. She was glad her longtime love affair with running had kept her trim.

He was rough and raw, quick-moving and fluid, as evidenced by the way he wove around the leather and dark-wood furnishings on his way to a desk with a telephone on it. She decided he must be checking his answering machine, but either he didn't have any messages or had no intention of sharing them with the stranger he'd brought into his home.

Damn, but he was sexy. And she wanted him. Wanted his flesh against hers, the smell of him flowing into her, her smaller body blanketed by him and her pussy full and vulnerable and satisfied all at the same time.

What am I doing here? Where is this going to take us and why?

"I have to ask it again," she said from her side of the masculine space. "You promise I'm not in over my head? You won't do anything I'll regret?"

A slow and smooth turning of his hips brought them face-to-face again. Shadows eased around him as if determined to keep his thoughts hidden from her. "You might regret some of what happens between us," he said, "but I hope that in the end you'll know you've done the right thing. That we both have."

The man spoke in riddles when she insisted on direct answers to direct questions. He hadn't said anything about being a gentleman, but *gentleman* wasn't what he was about, was he? She'd never expect a wild animal to be anything except what it was, a creature ruled by instinct. And despite his clothes and house and pickup, this dark, intense man was steeped in instinct. She sensed that in the way he moved and the look in his eyes.

But instead of wanting to run away, she needed to stay. Needed to feel alive and female in ways she never had, to fuck.

Yes, to fuck, to take and give, sweat and scream, barriers gone, reservations abandoned, the question of regret ignored in the wake of the electricity searing her nerves and senses.

Despite the peace she'd just made with herself, she wrapped her arms around her middle and dragged her gaze off him for the relative safety of their surroundings. In addition to paintings and furniture that had nothing to do with modern style and everything to do with the kind of man who lived here, there were several hand-carved figurines on the coffee table and end tables. The largest one anchored the right side of the stone and wood mantel she'd just now noticed. Drawn to the figurine, she found herself staring up at the masterful carving of a wild cat. The maybe two-foot-tall, three-foot-long puma was positioned in such a way that intense and intelligent eyes ringed with black returned her gaze. The head was small in contrast to the solid body, but although she admired the accurate proportions and message of fierce strength, the eyes made it impossible for her to concentrate on anything else.

I'm a killer, the puma seemed to be saying. *Nature designed me as the perfect hunter, and if I'm to live, that's what I must be. I regret nothing about what I am and feel nothing toward my prey. I inspire fear, but I didn't intend it that way. Accept me; you have no choice.*

"Incredible," she heard herself whisper. Her voice shook a little. "Masterful. I can see every muscle, the power beneath the deceptively calm exterior. Did you—"

"Not me, my father."

"He's unbelievably talented." Unnerved by the relentlessly staring eyes, she backed up a few feet. "Is that how he earns his living, by creating—"

"This is the only thing he's ever carved."

Impossible! she wanted to throw at Tohon. No novice could have gotten everything from the size of the puma's feet to the small, perked ears so right or been able to bring a chunk of wood to life this way. But something she didn't understand or maybe didn't want to understand kept her silent. With every fiber in her, she ached to caress the predominantly gray figure, but she didn't dare.

"This is what we're about," Tohon said, startling her because he'd killed most of the distance between them without her knowing it. "The men in my family. My father's heart ruled his hands while he worked on it. I hope that someday I can do the same thing."

Tohon was more than mortal, more than male, even. How she knew that she couldn't say, but as she looked up at him, she accepted that she'd stepped into a realm or space she'd never known existed. The truth lay in the way his surroundings embraced him, the gray now glinting in his previously all-black eyes, the way his nostrils flared as if he was memorizing her scent. *Who are you? What are you?*

Instead of asking those vital questions, she dug her fingers into her sides until pain pulled her out of whatever spell she'd slid into. Not losing the connection in their shared gaze, she nevertheless concentrated on how to put more distance between them. He was too much, too intense.

Maybe he knew what she had in mind, her fears and frailty, because instead of backing away, he ran his knuckles from the base of her right ear to her collarbone, causing her to shiver and sigh. To lean into him. When she did, for the barest of moments, he leaned back as if needing his own space, but then he closed his hands over her upper arms and turned her toward him.

Being in his grip unnerved her more and not just because of the strength in his fingers. Something darker than midnight lived in his eyes and on his lips, cloaking his features and making her wonder if the human was sloughing off, leaving what? Animal?

"I'm not ready for this." She tried to shrug out of his grip. "You're taking things too fast."

His hold tightened. He pulled her so close she felt his breath. "It has to be fast, because there might only be this one time."

One time for what? she nearly threw back at him, but his damnable hold seemed to encompass more than her arms. Somehow he'd touched her from the top of her head to her feet, phantom fingers tracing every inch of skin, sliding over her hips and between her legs, melting her there.

He had her where he wanted her, controlled and contained, for this moment at least. Despite the hot desire coursing through her, her thoughts settled on the look in an antelope's eyes the instant a predator attacks. The creature might continue running, but somewhere deep where nothing except instinct lives, the antelope knows that its life has come to an end. The killer has won.

Tohon had won whatever existed between them. And she wanted victory to be his.

A shiver rolled through her, slight but making her wonder if it might never end. Her awareness of her surroundings dimmed until she noted only the thin line of his mouth and powerful legs now bracketing hers. She'd never felt this alive, not even on the night when the life she'd always known had ended in blood. Tohon had become her world, her existence, and because he had, he maybe understood as she couldn't that sex was only the beginning of what flowed between them.

But she was at the beginning.

Suddenly starved for oxygen, she filled her lungs. As she did, his scent and more spread even deeper into her. She found his essence in her belly and breasts and between her legs. There was no hiding her awareness, her desire, from either of them, so she widened her stance and arched her upper body toward him.

A touch, a simple brushing of her already hard nipples against his shirt and then he was gone, leaning away while still holding her in place.

"What?" she managed, staring down at her breasts. "Don't you want—"

"Don't ask!" He shook her. "Damn it, don't even ask. You know the answer."

She did because his body spoke the truth about the heat in his veins and the swollen cock struggling against its confinement. Sex was supposed to be simple for men, wasn't it? They wanted it all the time, and if it was offered, they took, no questions or doubt or quarter given.

She was offering, damn it. Maybe simply and solely because she was on his turf and he was the most primal male she'd ever met and she was starving as she'd never known it was possible to starve. Didn't he know not to give her time to regain her senses and sanity? Strike while everything was hot, take advantage.

"I'm not—I've never done this."

"I know."

"But you must have, right? All you have to do is look at a woman and she—"

"You aren't other women; you're you."

And that makes you special to me, she needed him to add, but he didn't. Despite the grip on her arms, she managed to touch her fingertips to his hip bones, causing him to start and push her back but still without freeing her. Caught by his strength, she willed her legs to hold her and her cunt to be patient. If they didn't have sex, she wasn't sure she'd survive, but if they did, would she be alive at the end?

And why, for the first time in her life, did she have this overwhelming need?

"I've never had this happen before," he muttered, making her wonder if he was experiencing the same incredible turmoil.

"It's always been about looking into the future, not stepping into the past."

Don't talk! Throw me to the floor or carry me into your bedroom and make that everything! "My arms. They're going numb." They weren't, but she needed more than what was taking place.

Grunting, he loosened his grip. And when he worked her arms back so her hands touched behind her, she nearly told him she wasn't going to try running, and he didn't have to treat her like a captive. Being in charge had always been vital when it came to her relationships with men; that was something she'd never compromised on. But here she was with her arms useless while she looked up at this man who maybe didn't have a last name while fire flickered over her thighs and pelvis, and she couldn't find enough air.

He stepped toward her, his legs sliding around hers and trapping her. Effortlessly pitting his size and strength against her, he loomed over her, forcing her even more off balance. Just when she was certain she'd fall backward, his forearm pressed against the small of her back to hold her in place. Although he'd freed one of her arms, she left it where it was, waiting for his next move. Waiting for the next wash of desire.

Ah shit, ah shit, stupid as hell, trapped in need, feeling as if she were floating, burning up.

"How did this happen?" a female voice she barely recognized asked. "To go from spotting a man leading some horses to—"

"It's taking place because you need it to." His mouth was inches from hers, closing in.

Tipping into insanity, she struggled for words. "What was it? You somehow figured I was horny by the way I was walking?"

"Both of us are horny."

No denying that. There was also no denying her body's response to the demanding lump now grinding into her belly. Maybe that's why his impact on her was so overwhelming. Unlike the restrained civilized men who peopled her world, Tohon had a primal animal nature that demanded life be lived on its most basic level. Like the beast he'd been named after, his instincts were simple and carnal. And for reasons that evaded her, he'd chosen her as his mate.

Not a life-mate, she quickly amended. Nothing that encumbering or frightening. Hormones had drawn them together, and once need had been fulfilled, they'd go their separate ways, occasionally remembering this day but able to distance themselves emotionally from the purely sexual act because their hearts hadn't been involved.

Clinging to the liberating thought, she willed herself to relax and let him show her the way. She brought her hungry body with its already wet pussy to this affair, but the dance steps were his to command.

His mouth came closer, his features blurring, and her senses filled with him. Convinced she was floating on a volcanic flow, she parted her lips, her heart hammering. But instead of the crushing contact she expected from this physical man, he kept the touch light, skin feathering over skin. A whimper escaped her throat, offering proof that she needed something hard and fast. Bottom line, he'd imprisoned her, held her in place and consequently placed all control in his hands. She might try to straighten, try at least to run her tongue over his lips, but because he had her bent back and off balance, all she could do was strain, her desperation for what she wasn't quite sure naked.

"I don't play games," he all but growled. "I'm all about getting at the truth in everything. You have to be able to accept that."

"And if I don't?"

"You have no choice in this, Amy."

"How can you say—"

"Because if you walk away, you'll spend the rest of your life the way you are now—closed up, barely living."

She was hardly that right now. Couldn't he hear her heart thundering, feel her ever-growing heat, know how pliable and willing for sex she'd become? But even with her libido overloaded and her stomach knotted, his words left their impact. "I *am* living," she protested. "I make good money doing what I do. If I wanted, I could buy a house and I—"

"Why don't you want to?"

"None of your damn business."

"What's the matter, Amy? Afraid to face the truth about yourself?"

"You tell me, what's this so-called truth you believe you have to throw at me?"

Was that reluctance in his eyes? Was it possible he didn't want to answer her question? "You haven't bought a place because you know you'd run away from it."

No! Not true! Mostly not true. "My job keeps me out of town a lot. What's the point in having a lawn or flowers if I'm never there to enjoy them?"

"Maybe you'd stay home if there was someone there with you. A husband."

"What makes you think I'm not married?"

"I know."

He knew. Just like that, as if the condition was something to be ashamed of. "So? It's not a crime. You live alone, right?" She looked beyond his shoulder to the dark, serene surroundings.

To her surprise, he pulled her upright. And as soon as her feet were securely under her, he stepped back. When she started to reach for him, he shook his head. "I may decide it's necessary to tell you why I'm the only one living here, but that isn't important right now."

"Why not?" she asked to distract herself, at least a little, from the unwanted distance between them.

"Because I want right now to be about you."

"How are you going to do that?"

The corners of his mouth lifted, the gesture over so quickly that maybe she'd imagined it. Then, to her shock, he started unbuttoning his shirt. Wasn't it a *guy* thing for a man to seduce a woman by getting her naked so he could play with her body while maintaining a measure of control over the situation by remaining clothed? But as the gap between the sides of his shirt increased and his dark chest came into view, she was presented with a vivid example of the differences between the sexes.

He had no hesitancy about pulling off his shirt and tossing it onto a chair, no slowing his movements as he kicked out of his boots and bent over to remove his socks. When he straightened, his hands were already on his waistband. He wasn't asking permission to continue, wasn't studying her to judge her reaction. Instead, he was simply getting naked.

Run! What if he's a rapist?

A naked, barefoot rapist? Didn't make sense.

Competent fingers unfastened the metal button. Strong and sure fingers made short work of the silent zipper. He kept looking at her, his eyes accepting whatever he found in hers. His didn't challenge or test, didn't push her to the wall. Instead, they said that *this* was going to happen, and he knew she'd stand her ground.

She did, of course, her legs too weak to do more than support her suddenly great weight. And although she wasn't sure she could handle what she'd find, she dragged her eyes off his face and onto his waist and hips and from there to the newly revealed briefs-imprisoned cock.

There. The core and substance of him. What the whole male-female thing was about.

His movements seemed to switch to slow motion as he pushed his unwanted jeans down his hard-as-hell body, but maybe she was responsible for time's slowing. These moments mirrored what she'd experienced a couple of years ago when a truck had run a red light and plowed into the side of her sedan, and she'd had hours and hours in which to wait for the impact that had totaled her vehicle and fortunately deployed her airbag. They were also the same as what she'd survived the night her father had died.

Shaking off the destructive memories, she went back to watching and sweating and wanting.

When the jeans reached his knees, he stopped directing their movement. For a moment, the garment clung to him, then slid downward, exposing calves honed most likely by years spent on horseback. She needed them against hers, pressing and sheltering her body. Most of all, she needed them hammering his cock deep inside her.

Her hand somehow at her throat now, she gaped and tried to swallow while he stepped out of his jeans. Only his white, snug briefs remained.

Maybe he sensed her turmoil, because although his fingers were hooked over the elastic clinging to his hips, they were still. His belly was a hollow between his pelvic bones, the tan extending nearly to his navel, his legs pale in contrast to his upper body but nowhere as colorless as her breasts and buttocks. Winters at this altitude must call for coats and flannel shirts, but he stood as proof of warm summers with bare chests and backs. In her mind, she saw him swinging into a saddle and nudging his mount into a gallop, the wind caressing his naked upper body.

What about his cock? Did a running horse's straining power bring it to life, or did it take a woman for him to have an erection?

"What will it be, Amy? Stay and fuck or run?"

Run, a frightened part of her cried out. But if she fled this moment and this man, she'd be as good as dead, and she knew it. "Those are my only choices?" she asked, because she was still coming to terms with what she'd just learned about her needs.

"I thought you were going to, I don't know, get me on your shrink's couch or something. Tell me what the hell you believe is wrong with me and how to get over it."

"You already know what's wrong with you; you're just afraid to admit it."

"You're saying I'm flawed?"

"Not flawed. Tied in knots. Incapable of freeing yourself."

"How the hell would you know? What the hell are you talking about?"

"Stop throwing words at me. And at yourself. You live alone, work alone, sleep alone. It's time to face why that is."

Had he stripped the skin off her? Was that why she felt as if she were bleeding and couldn't swallow? Why he suddenly terrified her?

Wasn't nudity, or near nudity, supposed to make a person vulnerable? She sure as hell couldn't tell it by him, because although he hadn't closed so much as an inch of the distance between them, he'd somehow invaded her. Opened her pussy, softened and dampened it. Hardened her clit and made it scream to be touched. Licked. Nipped.

"Do it!" She jerked her head at his hands. "Just the hell finish what you started."

"And then what?"

4

_____

Amy didn't know whether to laugh or just stand there and gape, or rather continue gaping. One thing she'd learned—issue Tohon a challenge and he'd meet it head-on. After all, it hadn't taken him more than a couple seconds to get rid of his shorts and throw them in the general direction of his shirt. Far from looking ridiculous buck naked while she still sported every piece of her clothing, he looked right, absolutely right, while she was what, way overdressed?

Maybe he was designed to be naked. A committed nudist, he'd only forced himself into his outfit for the trip into Flagstaff. Now that he was back on his own turf, he'd reverted to a condition he was much more comfortable with.

Only she could hardly believe he went through life with a hard-on.

No, she was responsible for that.

She, Amy Patterson, responsible for a stranger's erection? The resultant sense of responsibility and power left her not knowing what to do with her hands or how to close her mouth, to say nothing of the delicious if overwhelming vibrations that threatened to take control of every inch of her body. Simply looking at him made her clench her fists and compelled her to press her legs together, and it had been nothing short of a miracle that she hadn't moistened her lips yet.

Shit, but the man was well hung!

"Are you afraid?" he asked. His arms hung at his sides, his elbows slightly bent as if ready to reach for her.

"Afraid? I'm hardly a virgin." *I just feel like one right now.*

"But you've never had a man do what I just did."

"How do you know?"

"I do. Tell me, what are you thinking?"

That I'm in over my head but I've never wanted anything more than I want you inside me. "What makes you think it's any of your business?" she threw at him.

"Don't play that game. The longer you run from yourself, the longer I'll stalk you."

Stalk. "What do you mean, run? I came out here, didn't I?"

"I'm not talking about today. This is about the way you live your life."

"So you keep saying," she snapped, her mood fashioned by what she was looking at. "You have an incredible body," she blurted.

His nod was half dismissal, half acceptance of a fact. He hadn't posed himself in any way. Neither had he tried to draw attention to his impressive cock, something he hardly needed to do. In fact, she'd swear that fucking and being fucked wasn't the first and foremost thing on his mind.

That insane thought had come because she didn't know what to make of anything that had happened since they'd met. Only a dead woman wouldn't note his straining cock or sense his sexual tension. He might sound in control, but his body couldn't hide the truth.

Oh, shit, he was coming toward her, closing in on her space, challenging her to stand her ground. Despite the pulse hammering in her temple, she took pride in doing that, and when he cupped his hand around her jaw and lifted her head, she found the courage to look up at him. At that moment, her body seemed to stop, to freeze, to maybe die. Then blood returned to her veins and strength to her muscles, and she returned to the here and now.

He kept staring at her, his gaze penetrating layer after layer, going deep. Finding places she'd locked away and thrown away the key for. *Don't!* she wanted to scream. *Don't make me go there and don't you, either!*

"You loved him," he said softly. "He was your life, your rock. He made you feel whole and safe, and when he died, it nearly killed you."

"What are you talking about? How can you possibly—"

"The pain of that loss is still with you. In many ways, you've never gone beyond losing him."

Him. There was only one *him.*

Suddenly more afraid than she'd been except that one time, she stumbled backward. Something pressed against the back of her thighs, stopping her. "Don't," she begged. "Just . . . don't."

"Why not, Amy? What are you afraid of?"

"Maybe I'm afraid of you!" she nearly shrieked. Suddenly she saw his nudity not as his strength but as his weakness. She could attack him and make him bleed, make him forget he'd said those insane things.

Except that regret and sorrow moved across his features in waves, and she nearly felt sorry for him. His limp arms now served as symbols of his helplessness. Yes, strength was etched in his muscles and bones and that magnificent dark cock, but those trappings did nothing to hide what he was feeling.

She was on the brink of begging him to tell her what was wrong when he went out of focus or something, his body changing in ways a human couldn't possibly change. It had to be a trick of the dying light, of course, but wasn't he slumping toward the floor, leaning forward until his hands were nearly on the carpet? At the same time, for a moment, she was absolutely positive that he was lengthening out, his face narrowing and becoming pointed, teeth turning into, what, fangs? His legs were larger now, the skin over muscle and bone loosening and growing hair. And a tail. Oh, shit, that couldn't be a tail!

"No!" The instinct for survival made her sprint for the fireplace and the metal tools she'd seen there. Turning her back on monster-man, she wrapped her fingers around a poker.

Then she spun around.

Tohon was back, tailless, standing erect, no short gray hair dusting his flesh. Eyes black and round again instead of oval.

"What?" Her throat closed around the word. Seconds passed before she could speak. "What happened?"

His nostrils flared, and it had to be her imagination, but he now seemed to be becoming part of his surroundings, more wood and leather than flesh and blood. "Something I'd hoped wouldn't," he said. "Usually I can make it stop, at least for a while." Gripping his cock, he jerked it as if trying to rip it off himself. "That's responsible." Staring down at himself, he took a deep, long breath. "You're responsible. I shouldn't have . . ."

"What?" she forced herself to ask. "Brought me here?"

"Yes."

"Then why did you?" *What are we talking about?*

"Because I'd be cheating you if I didn't offer you the chance to break free. I can deal . . . I know how to deal with what happens to me. I've accepted . . . I just didn't want it to take place so soon. And for you to see before I could prepare you."

How long was he going to speak in riddles? Equally important, would he ever relax his grip on his cock? More concerned for him than for herself now, she dropped the poker, pushed away from the fireplace, and strode toward him. The way he studied her was like a trapped animal, wary and watchful, refusing to surrender even though it knew there was no escape. But how could that be when he was so powerful?

Reaching out, she closed her fingers around his wrist and gently pulled his hand off himself. After lifting and turning his hand so his palm was toward her, she pressed her lips to the veins running up his forearm. He still overwhelmed her, frightened her with his knowledge of her and his changing body, but she wouldn't run. Not now.

"When . . . when you said what you did about some man's dying nearly killing me, you knew who you were talking about, didn't you?" she asked.

"Yes."

"How?"

He wasn't ready for the question, as evidenced by his slow blink and his fingers now around her wrists, holding her in place. She felt small and weak—and beyond alive.

"I'm Apache," he said.

"I know."

"It's more than that."

"Don't do this! I'm in no condition to play word games or try pulling something out of you."

"You're right," he said, his fingers easy and yet secure on her wrists. "You deserve more than I've given you. I just hope you can handle and accept—"

"Let me make that decision!"

"Have you ever heard of the Walapai?" He spoke with his nostrils flared and his eyes half closed. His fingers closed over her bones, the hold unbreakable. The room that had served as wonderful proof of his heritage and passion had again become his lair and she the creature he'd lured into it.

"The what? No, why?"

"Because that's where my roots and the truth about what I am begins. The Walapai were the first Apache, an ancient people who lived in harmony with their world and heard and heeded the spirits' wisdom. They understood as modern man never can that the land and sky are gods who must be worshipped. Rain, the sun, growing things, living creatures are all gifts from those gods, given to those who hear the earth's heartbeat. If man doesn't respect those gifts, he will be punished."

Too much, too damn much! "You don't believe that, do you?"

"Believe what?"

"What you just said. All right, I understand that ancient Native Americans were resourceful people when it came to making maximum use of their surroundings, but they didn't know about the world beyond what they could see. There was so much they didn't understand. It's understandable that they were in awe of their surroundings and determined to make them as safe as possible."

Speaking had exhausted her and opened her up even more to his impact. Seeking strength from him, she lifted her captured arms. He helped by guiding her hands around to the back of his neck, then released her wrists and wrapped his arms around her waist. She had no idea who was the first to lean into the other.

"I'm not going to respond to what you just said, not now," he told her. "I don't expect you to embrace my ancestors' beliefs. But although I don't want what nearly happened to me to take place, if *it* comes again, I'm not sure I can stop it."

He'd been pressing his pelvis, or more specifically his cock, against her, but now he rocked back while still holding on to her. "Whatever I become, don't be afraid of me. Promise me that. You won't be afraid."

"Of what?" *Lengthening out, legs becoming powerful, fangs revealed, turning from human into—* "I don't know what you're talking about."

His eyes took on that trapped look again. At the same time, she knew without a doubt that he was far from defeated—and was so turned on he was having trouble concentrating. The same was true for her; a tidal wave of sensations was piling up inside her, and she couldn't stay on top of them.

She loved having him naked! That's what everything boiled down to, didn't it? This man who any woman alive would want in her bed and over her body had brought her to his home before stripping off civilization's trappings and presenting his magnificent form to her.

"We're going to have sex," she said. "I don't know how the hell it got to this point, but it's going to happen."

"Unless you walk out that door."

Although he'd indicated the door they'd come in, she didn't bother looking at it. Didn't he know she was beyond backing out, beyond anything except satisfying a hunger so deep it gripped her soul? Determined to make him understand how desperately she needed their bodies to fuse, she let go of him, grabbed hold of her blouse, and yanked. Unfortunately, the buttons refused to easily give up their hold, forcing her to fumble with them one at a time until finally she exposed her bra.

The moment she did, she felt silly. What was she trying to prove, that she was the world's most desirable woman? Hardly. She wore a B-cup bra, just barely. Yes, her breasts were reasonably perky, but she was no eighteen-year-old hard body.

But she needed to offer him something.

The only thing a sex-craving man cared about.

He simply stared at her in that primal way of his, his gaze stripping her down until her nerve endings were rubbed raw and she'd become weightless. She longed to cover herself again, to slow down until she'd regained a measure of control over her emotions to say nothing of her pussy. But he must have known what she was going through, because he tugged her blouse out of her waistband before placing her hands around his neck again.

Then, oh, lordy, then his hands slid under the silk and his

fingers touched, just barely touched her spine. Shuddering, she willed herself to remain where she was, to simply feel and experience. To be.

Slowly, so incredibly wonderfully slowly, his fingers walked upward. She didn't know how to stop shaking, or if she wanted to. His breath was in her hair and on her upturned face, heat seeping into her temples and igniting the veins there. But his fingers, his magical fingers! They were everything. Life. Promise.

When he unfastened her bra, she could only sigh and wait and tremble. After pushing it up out of the way, he cupped her breasts in his callused palms, forcing her to hold on with every bit of strength she had. Somehow her fingers had moved from his neck to his shoulders, causing her to marvel at the power beneath his flesh. He spoke of things she didn't understand and looked deep inside her when that was the last thing she wanted, but she'd hold on and ride this current they were on, because his body promised sex. Sex that would blow off the top of her head.

"You make me feel alive." The naked admission drifted between them, her words seeming to hang in the air long after she'd said them.

He flicked his thumb over her right nipple. "You haven't felt like this before?"

"No," she fairly yelped. "I . . . don't do that again."

"Why not?" He treated her left nipple to the same assault, the same wonderful sensation.

Unable to come up with an argument, she dug her fingertips into his shoulders. If his stimulating her breasts had her thinking climax, how could she possibly hang on to sanity once he touched her pussy?

Or her clit, that remarkable nub with the ability to rock her out of her world. Bringing herself to climax during a self-session was more than a little unsettling, but she always soothed herself with reminders that she and she alone was in control of what happened.

It would be different with Tohon. Worlds different.

"You want what I have to offer," he told her as he spread his hands over her breasts, flattening them against her chest wall and forcing her to lock her knees to keep from being pushed off balance.

"I wouldn't have done this"—she looked down at her breasts—"if I didn't."

"But do you know what you're in for?"

Damn him for wanting to talk right now, especially asking the questions he was. "I have some experience, if that's what you're getting at."

"No, it isn't. I'm talking about some of the things I said at the beginning of this."

No, no! That wasn't what she wanted or needed. Determined to silence him, she released his shoulders so she could run her fingers down his arms. Although she was tempted to cover his hands with hers in silent encouragement of what he was doing to her breasts, making him feel as off balance as she did was more important. Everything.

He sucked in his breath the instant her searching fingers settled on his hips. It was his fault. He was the one who'd kicked things into overdrive by taking off his clothes. All she had to do was take advantage of his exposure, to touch—

Could she? Did she have the courage to cup her hands around his cock?

Intimate. Incredibly intimate. A message designed for one thing.

Putting off the moment and decision, she concentrated on sliding her hands over his buttocks. Beneath soft flesh lay yet more of the strength and power woven throughout him, a power and strength unlike any she'd ever encountered.

He was different, wilder and raw, basic. Primal.

And his hands fully and completely encompassed her breasts, closed them within his heat. That heat more than seeped from his palms and fingertips to her chest. Flames had already found that deeply hidden corridor leading to her core, flickering fire searing her inner tissues and forcing a moan.

Hating her damnable slacks, she thrust her pelvis at him. But instead of allowing the contact, he planted his hands on her hips, holding her in place. Furious, she dug her fingers into his buttocks. "What are you doing?" she demanded. "Don't you want—"

"I want. Oh, shit, I want. But first I need you to stand there and listen to your body while I take you someplace I don't believe you've been before."

Foreplay? Anxious as she was to scream and writhe while he flooded her with his cum, the idea of playing with each other's bodies sounded wonderful. "Just stand there? I don't know if I can."

"I need you to try. That's the only way I can be sure you can handle what else I now believe needs to happen to you today."

"What else?"

"Embracing life. Letting your heart out of its cage. Closing the door on your past."

Don't say that again! she nearly threw back at him. *Don't take me where I can't go!* But he'd promised her something she hadn't acknowledged she'd needed until today—he was the only man who could hand her that gift.

But was freedom from the past a gift? What if she couldn't handle everything it entailed? "Say whatever it is you're going to say. That way we'll have whatever the hell it is behind us." Trepidation stilled her voice but not her fingertips. Studying him through half-open eyes, she lifted his solid buttocks. A little reaching brought her fingers close, dangerously close, to his crack.

"You loved him with all your heart," he said, his voice strained.

"What?" Shocked, she cast around for a way out of this conversation, freedom from his words.

"The man you've spent more than half your life mourning."

"You promised! You said we weren't going there."

"No, I didn't. Listen to me, every time I touch you, I feel the pain running through you. Our having sex won't kill that pain, not down where it counts."

"How did you . . . what makes you believe there's—"

"I know a great deal about you, Amy. Not everything, but more than you want anyone to." He ground the heel of his hand into the small of her back as if trying to reach her womb.

Everything swirled around her, making her dizzy. In an instant, she'd gone from wanting to fuck as she'd never wanted before to needing to break free and run.

But could she survive being away from him?

Damn it, his words terrified her; that's what she needed to get a handle on. Order him to make some goddamn kind of sense! And then take them beyond the need for words.

"You . . . you're making a lot of assumptions about me." She made her voice as firm as she could. "What is it, you get off on a power trip?"

Although he didn't answer, she sensed his denial. Thinking while his hand was against her spine was nearly impossible. That had to be why she hadn't tried to break free and why her own hands continued their intimate assault.

He shifted position. Without knowing she was going to do something so damnably stupid and brave, she reached for his scrotum. But before she could capture his balls, he turned her around so her back was to him.

Freedom lay just beyond this room. A half-dozen steps would bring her to the door. She'd have to abandon her heels, but she'd run and run until he was no longer assaulting—

Too late.

He held her against his naked chest and wrapped his arms around her breasts, the strength of his grip leaving no doubt: He intended to keep her here. Fear flashed through her only to be lost in the awesomeness of what he intended. He'd trapped her arms at her sides, and his cock prodded her back.

"Let me go!"

"I can't."

Can't? What was he talking about?

She might have asked if he hadn't already unsnapped her slacks and wasn't tugging down on her zipper. His fingers so close to her core, his nails brushing her belly before gliding over her barely there panties, stilled her struggles. She even aided him in pushing her slacks off her hips by arching away from him. Then she fell back against his strength, his heat, eyes closed and mouth sagging.

There, those unbelievable fingers of his, skimming her skin. Fingertips on her belly, briefly held there, then sliding under flimsy and inadequate elastic. Her head sagging to the side, she spread her legs as far as the slacks, now clinging to her knees, allowed. On a level someplace between instinct and reason, she knew she was giving him permission to take her, to use her, to explore and maybe exploit, like trying to keep her legs under her left her incapable of questioning what she was doing or why.

She existed for him, lived for the relief and release of sex!

The exquisite brush of his flesh on her pubic hair sent a shiver through her. Even with her senses overloaded, she longed to tell him it was all too much, but silence was easier. And maybe all she was capable of.

Reaching around her body and down, he touched a forefinger to her drenched slit. That's all, just a touch. Throwing back her head, she hauled in as much air as her lungs could handle. *Do it, do it, please!*

His body trapped hers, turned it into his plaything. She'd never accepted the notion of giving up control; any man who tried the heavy-handed approach was sent on his way, but this was different somehow. Worlds different from anything she'd ever experienced.

His grip on her upper body tightened, but she barely noticed. Everything in her being was centered around her pussy and what Tohon was doing and about to do to it. If pushed, she might admit she existed nowhere except between her legs.

On one spot, one unbelievably hot spot!

Something between a moan and a sob escaped her throat the instant he caught her clit between his thumb and forefinger. A quick squeeze brought her onto her toes. "Oh, oh, oh," she managed, pressing the back of her head against his chest.

The pressure ended. Something, sanity maybe, began rolling over her. Then no more than a heartbeat later, he tapped her clit. She didn't care which finger or fingers he was using, how he'd known to turn her inside out like that, she didn't care about anything except liquid fire burrowing into her core. Her head started thrashing without her having anything to do with it. She struggled to free her arms, not to escape but so she could cling to him.

Holding her in place as if she were a wild bronc he was determined to tame, he pressed and tapped, sometimes closing his palm over her mons so he could shake it. Again and again he returned to her quivering nub, taking her to the edge, forcing her to stare down into some great and fevered chasm.

Animal sounds born of who or whatever she'd become tore at the air. Her legs gave out, leaving her to hang, twitching, in his grip. She was shattering, exploding, leaning out over some great deep canyon with her arms widespread and about to take flight.

More. Relentless. One moment his touch featherlike, the next harshly insisting she climax. *Do it!* his attack demanded.

Become a bitch in heat. Embrace what your body's capable of, now!

No, not now, not yet! Even as his fingers plundered her hole to be washed by her excitement, she fought the powerful need, because the moment she lost it, she'd become his toy, his slave, his possession. If he so willed it, he might keep the explosion going until she couldn't handle it. She'd beg and plead and melt, but maybe nothing she said or did or felt would stop him.

He'd win. Everything.

Her only salvation—even though every fiber in her wanted that hot explosion—was to fight it. Fight. Deny. Struggle. Tear her mind off his nail gliding over her outer tissues followed by rough masculine fingers plundering deep and deeper still.

"Let go!" he ordered, his mouth against her ear. "Why fight? You know how it's going to end."

"With . . . with you winning! No, damn it!" she shrieked as he took hold of her pussy lips. "No, stop it!"

"It's way too late for that, Amy," he told her, and tugged downward, drawing out the loose skin. "It was the moment we met."

"No!"

"Yes. We're going down this road—you because the only way the truth'll come out is by your defenses breaking down, me because I'm a bastard."

A bastard wouldn't bathe her clit in her own wet heat, wouldn't trace a light if possessive line around her outer lips, wouldn't lick her ear or nibble the side of her neck.

But he hadn't heeded her frenzied plea for him to stop, so what did that make him?

"Why? Why? Not so fast. Oh, shit, not so fast!"

"You don't want slow and you know it! My pace is the only way you're going to get past your damnable brain."

His hand had stilled while he was speaking. Granted, having

at least two fingers in her hardly brought rest and relief, but at least she'd been able to focus on his words. She was gathering herself, trying to, anyway, when he pulled free. Before she could adapt, powerful arms straightened her so her legs could bear her weight. His fingers yanking down on her slacks reminded her that they were still around her legs, preventing her from spreading any more than she already had.

Before she could decide if she had the courage to do that, he left the garment tangled around her ankles, slapping the insides of her thighs until she widened a few more inches.

Idiot. Stupid fool!

Too late. Before she could so much as send a new message to her legs, he again pulled her hard and tight and strong against his chest. Holding her in place with one hand, he slapped her mons. Startled, she fought to look back at him.

A second slap, this one farther between her legs and even more intimate. What had begun as shock morphed into plea-sure—more than pleasure. With a quiet sigh, she once more sagged in his hold, vision blurring, mind going no further than her sex. His assault on her cunt continued, one light, quick blow after another. *It* was happening, her system lifting and spread-ing at the same time everything tunneled down until only re-lease mattered.

"Do me," she whimpered. "Oh, shit, take me—let me—"

"Hush, Amy. I'm with you. I won't leave you."

Ever? Even as she silently asked the question, she knew she'd reached the point of no return. She was standing at the edge of a diving board now, arms outstretched, a bottomless pool below waiting to cradle her.

Screaming, she dove.

Her climax hit somewhere between the launch and the land-ing. Even as her thighs shook and heat exploded from pussy to throat, Tohon kept up his attack. Drumbeats of sensation on that sensitive and receptive part of her body drew out the over-the-top seconds.

Pure energy, fire and flame, she felt as if she were flying, sweet joy flooding her and sending fractured messages to her brain.

Live for this. Ride sensation. Float in heat. Die and embrace rebirth.

Her climaxes had never been like this, going on and on, showing no sign of ending. Her cunt clenched, released, clenched again, a wild animal determined to revel in its strength. But much as she embraced the ultimate release, she couldn't get enough air into her lungs. She was becoming exhausted, growing frightened. No breaks? No end? What if her heart couldn't take this?

"Please, please, please. No—oh, shit, no more."

Growling something unintelligible, he kept after her, pressing against her clit now, his possessive finger rolling back and forth, finding ever-deeper nerves and forcing the ultimate in pleasure-pain out of them.

No longer able to utter a sound, she dug her nails into his hips, weakly twisting in his grip. She cried and laughed at the same time, sweating, collapsing, ripping apart.

"How hard you are, how hot. This is the real you, Amy. No longer caged but free. Free to discover yourself as a woman."

"Can't . . . take . . . it!"

Whether he finally believed her or his cues had come from her limp and sweat-drenched yet shuddering body didn't matter. All she cared about was that after what felt like a lifetime, her body was no longer under attack. No longer being driven off the edge over and over again.

Her breath whistling, she leaned forward and with his help slumped to her knees on the carpet. She was aware of his hands massaging the back of her neck but couldn't tell him how wonderful that felt.

"Talk to me, Amy."

"I can't."

"Yes, you can. You have to."

"Why?"

"Because I need you to tell me about *him*."

5

She was naked. If asked, Amy would have been hard pressed to explain how that had happened. She had a vague memory of Tohon helping her out of her garments, but it hadn't been all his idea, far from it. Bottom line, as long as this fierce and wild man who'd taken over her world was naked, she wanted the same for herself.

At the moment, she was curled up on a corner of a leather couch, her ass sticking to the expensive furniture and Tohon with his still-erect cock sitting inches away.

Everything had been about her up till now, culminating with a climax that had left her drained, but even in her current state, she knew he deserved the same exquisite volcano. Her pussy was soaked and soft and swollen and more than ready to accommodate him. But maybe she'd close her lips around his organ and keep after him until he exploded in her mouth.

No, not yet. Not until she'd answered his question.

"My father." Hearing her wistful, little-girl-lost tone, she straightened a little and looked into Tohon's eyes. How beautiful they were! More than human somehow, wary and wise at the same time. "He died when I was thirteen."

Tohon cocked his head to the side. "How old was he?"

"Thirty-four. He'd been so young when I was born, barely out of his teens himself." Holding her gaze on Tohon had been a mistake, because it was taking so much out of her, but she'd lose something vital if she retreated into herself right now. "He had so much energy, more like a big brother than a father, and yet he embraced his role as a parent."

"You never sensed he resented the responsibility?"

How strange that Tohon had asked the one question that had defined her relationship with her father. "I asked him about that once, shortly before he died. He told me that I was the best thing that had ever happened to him. He hadn't expected that when he learned his then-girlfriend was pregnant. Mostly he'd been scared and resentful, but then he watched me being born and cut the cord and held me, and everything shifted. He, ah, he told me he'd never felt such overwhelming love." She blinked back tears. "When I was younger, I was too self-absorbed to wonder what becoming parents was like for my mother and father but—"

"How old was your mother when you were born?"

Just say the damn words. You can do this. "Twenty-five. She was older than my father."

"Old enough to put protection before passion?"

"What are you saying?"

"I'm not sure," he said, but his eyes revealed that his question had been calculated. "Just trying to understand all I can about the impact your dad's death had on you."

Why do you care? Why are we having this conversation? And most important, she reminded herself, how had he known she'd lost someone precious? Acknowledging that she was still a long way from being able to ask him, she wrapped her arms around her knees and tried not to look at his cock.

"I never asked my mother about that," she said, relieved that her tone was under control, almost. "My relationship with her was different from what my father and I had, more complex in many ways. Part of it, I now know, was that at thirteen I was just beginning to comprehend that the world existed beyond the end of my nose. My parents . . . I guess like most kids, my parents were the center of my existence. I believed they had all the answers, that they had their acts together and weren't besieged with the kinds of emotions I'd been hit with even before I reached my teens."

"All-knowing?"

"Kind of." How strange it was to be having this conversation with her body still recovering from what he'd put it through. They weren't finished with sex; how could they be when all the pleasure had been on her end? "Mom was less willing to allow me to take my lumps than Dad was. She and I were butting heads; I wanted her to untie the apron strings. Now that I've become an adult, I realize that every day is a learning process; no one ever has it all together."

"So you're saying you understand your parents better now than you did when you were living with them?"

He was trying to get at something, attempting to peel through the layers she'd worked so hard to construct around her heart, but although she was tempted to tear away the barriers, fear of what she'd find stopped her.

"What is this about?" she demanded. "Okay, so you're psychic or something. Is that what you were barely hinting at when you told me about your ancestors? You carry the genes necessary for looking into a person's past and seeing a traumatic event. But my *event* happened a long time ago. I've moved on. I don't want to rehash old territory."

"Of course you don't," he said, and stood. As he turned toward her, she could swear he was growing, taking up all the space in the room, and her world. "You've convinced yourself that it's safer that way. But you've never been in love, never trusted your heart to a man. That's no way to live."

"How can you say that? You don't know me!"

"Have you ever fully and freely given your heart to a man?"

Don't go there! "Let me worry about that."

"You're going to need to do a hell of a lot more than worry if you ever want to be whole."

She was whole, she was! She had a well-paying career, a paid-for car, and enough money to buy a house if she was so inclined. As for friends and lovers—

What friends?

What lovers?

"I want to go," she managed. "Either you take me back or I'm . . . where's your phone book? I'm calling a taxi."

"No." He planted himself in front of her with his arms folded and his legs spread, his demanding cock all but keeping her in place. "You're not leaving yet."

She should be alarmed, should be reaching for her purse with its small canister of pepper spray. And if not that, she needed to call his bluff. Only he wasn't bluffing. Determined to end his interrogation, she cast around for a way of distracting him, something that had served her in the past when men had wanted more than sex from her.

Sex. Of course.

Unfolding her legs, she slid off the couch and onto her knees in front of him. Doing so brought her nostrils near his cock and its heady male scent. Closing her mind to everything else, she concentrated on running her hands down his hips and from there to his thighs, not stopping until her fingers were on his calves.

His toes curled into the carpet, his leg muscles taut. Instead of taking him into her mouth as she'd intended, she turned her head to the side so she could rub her hair over his belly. She brought her nostrils even closer to his cock, drank in as much potent air as her lungs could hold, and blew out her breath, smiling and nodding when he gasped and took a backward step.

"What's wrong, Tohon? Not so easy when the tables are turned, is it?"

"Be . . . careful."

Although she abraded her knees a little, she scrambled after him. Sliding her hands upward, she grabbed hold of his buttocks and dug her fingertips into his flesh, holding him in place. Other than lacing his fingers through her hair, he did nothing, said nothing.

Battle of wills. That's what this moment had become, her pushing his limits while he did the same by presenting her with his magnificent nudity. His size and strength were reducing her to a primitive animal.

Only primal wasn't the only thing they had in common.

Fighting back her need for insight into what had truly brought them together, she kissed his navel. His harsh intake of breath encouraged her to run her lips lower. Avoiding his cock and balls, she concentrated on his upper thighs and hips, working him, hopefully challenging his sanity as he'd done to her a few minutes ago. She continued to fight, not just her physical response but her deeper considerations as well. Bottom line, she *wasn't* going to think about what he'd been trying to pull out of her, after all.

Looking down at her hair with its highlights and precision cut, Tohon fought to control his body. Hell, but she was making it hard! Nudity had never made him feel particularly vulnerable, but although she was equally naked, all he could think about was how deeply he'd exposed himself. And that she was exploiting that vulnerability.

Instinct had told him she didn't know much about the male beast, not from lack of opportunity but because she'd always kept her distance. And yet she possessed another instinct he hadn't considered, one that threatened to reduce him to pulsing need.

Had he been a damn fool to invite her into his home? His determination to bring her to life—just because who and what he was had given him insight into her secrets—didn't mean he had a right to open her old scars. Even more to the point, she was getting to him.

What did he mean *was*? She'd already probed through his layers and had targeted his sexuality, his essence, his destiny. He was a damn fool if he thought he'd win this round.

Dangerous. The word clawed at him. *Dangerous. On more levels than she could possibly know. More maybe than he could handle.*

But even as her soft-as-silk mouth glided over his flesh, he knew he'd stepped beyond danger and into the fire. He might dig his nails into his palms or bite the insides of his cheeks. He might grab her and force her away, but the damage had already been done.

It was happening. The accursed legacy that lived deep inside him was demanding freedom.

The moment when self-control became something laughable and frightening might not yet be upon him, but unless he ordered her out of his life, now, he'd change. Soon.

And when he did, she'd see.

Flee.

"Don't!" he insisted. Using his hold on her hair, he yanked her head upright. The moisture she'd deposited on his belly and groin started to cool, making him shiver.

"You want it," she threw back at him.

"Of course I do; I'm male." *Say something, anything. Stay here.* "But right now's supposed to be about you, not me."

"Why?" she demanded, her hands running up and down his legs.

"Because you're—"

"Don't say it again, just don't! All this crap about me being closed up emotionally or whatever you call it is absolute nonsense! And . . . and even if it isn't, it's my problem, not yours."

Human. Think human. "That's where you're wrong."

Her look told him she hadn't decided whether to haul off and hit him or bite a chunk out of his cock. But beneath her anger lay another emotion. This one spoke to the man he needed to reach and gave him focus.

"Maybe I've been going at this wrong," he told her, although he didn't for a moment regret forcing a climax out of her. The memory of her quivering body safely wrapped in his arms even as he made her crazy sustained him in ways he didn't understand. "Maybe we should be talking, nothing else." Prompted by her confused look, he released her hair so he could stroke her cheek. *So soft and feminine.* "But I don't do much of that. Most people, hell, most people don't want to get that close to me."

He regretted the words before they'd fully escaped, but there was no taking them back, no pretending he hadn't said them. Already he saw the change in her. She was no longer concentrating on herself but on him.

"Why not?"

Because those who know what I am fear me. "Not now. Soon." *Maybe.* "Right now I . . ."

Before he could finish, a familiar but unwanted force he called *the energy* nipped at his awareness with familiar teeth. A moment ago, she'd been his world, but until he'd regained control over his destiny, she didn't matter. His body taut and cold, he commanded the energy to leave him alone. Prayed even.

"Tohon, what is it?"

Fighting what he knew would eventually win, he blinked her into focus. There she was again, reality and warmth, something to focus on. Concern, compassion, and confusion warred for supremacy in her eyes, and he loved her for her emotions. Love wouldn't stay within him; it never did. But for now—

"Nothing." It took all his strength to get the lie out.

"Don't say that! You're so tense, I'm afraid you're going to shatter."

He couldn't help it, damn it! With every second, the energy was becoming more powerful. When it had first attacked, he'd been thirteen, a boy beginning the journey to adulthood with hormones coursing through his body. That afternoon, his father had gripped his hands and told him that what he'd always feared would happen to his oldest son was coming to pass. Because he'd seen his father trapped by the same great power, he'd known what the older man was talking about. On the brink of tears and hating his body, he'd forced himself to listen to his father's wisdom.

The curse and blessing would be part of him for as long as he lived.

"Tohon? Can you hear me?"

Darkness. Lightning building on the horizon. The smell of heat and death. Coming closer.

"Tohon!"

6

Amy hadn't been this afraid since her father's death. Back then, she'd been a child, in shock, helpless. Now, even though that same sense of helplessness threatened to overwhelm her, she refused to give in.

Tohon hadn't acknowledged her cry. His eyes were wide and staring but not looking at her. If he was having a seizure—

"I'm here," she said, dropping her voice to a low singsong. "You aren't alone. I won't leave you."

He gave no indication he'd heard, but unless she was mistaken, a little of the tension seeped out of him. Encouraged, she freed her hands and began stroking his chest. Sweat already coated his dark skin. "I'm here, here," she repeated. "You aren't alone."

Although she kept talking, she paid little attention to the words. Beneath her fingers, changes were taking place in him. She couldn't see anything; he remained the same physically fit, handsome man who'd made her body sing and scream. But it was as if something was happening to his core.

"Easy, easy," she chanted, her mouth now on his left nipple

and her words vibrating between them. "It's all right. Take deep breaths. Let it all out. If you can, tell me what you're feeling."

"The change. Happening."

Instead of pushing for an explanation she sensed he wasn't capable of giving, she concentrated on reaching him with her mouth and hands. With each gentle touch, a little more of that awful tension oozed from him until she took a chance on leaning back and looking at him. Maybe his eyes were coming back into focus.

"That's good, good. Nothing to worry about. Just a little short-circuiting of the system." Turning her head, she ran her tongue over his throat.

"I . . . don't . . . want . . . to . . . hurt . . . you."

Earlier he'd promised he wouldn't harm her. "I know you don't. No one wants to harm someone they lo—someone they care about." Swallowing back old pain, she continued. "But sometimes it happens."

Although she wasn't at all sure what she was doing was safe, she took his hands in hers and placed them on either side of her neck. Her pulse jumped, the sensation trickling down her body.

"Do you want to talk about it?" she asked softly. "I promise, no matter what you say, I won't leave you."

"I could stop you."

Was she just imagining it, or was he now pressing against her neck? "Why?" She forced the question. "Why would you want to keep me here if that's not where I want to be?"

Confusion warred with whatever else he was feeling, and for a moment she was taken back to a time and place when the emotions in her mother's eyes had nearly destroyed her. "I want . . . I wanted to help you," he muttered.

"I understand that." *Keep him talking, or something. Tear him away from whatever's going on inside him.* "This is an incredible place," she continued, reaching for words. "I don't know if I made that clear, but I love the house. How old is it?"

Giving no indication that he'd heard, he began stroking her neck. As he did, something lifted inside her—maybe the weight of concern and caution losing substance. No matter that she needed to put him first, his touch was getting to her, easing her. Turning her back into a woman.

"I have a two-bedroom condo," she said so she'd have something to focus on. "I spent an obscene amount on furniture, but now I'm not sure it's what I want. It sounds crazy, but I bought everything that was in this display set or whatever they call it." Something between a sigh and a sob rolled out of her, and she leaned into his right hand. "I didn't know what my style was; I still don't."

Much as she longed to close her eyes and drift in sensations, she kept her gaze on him. Maybe she'd only deluded herself into thinking she was pulling him back from whatever pit he'd been about to fall into, because there was no denying the darkness crawling over him. Insane as it seemed, she sensed he was going someplace familiar to him. He didn't want to return to that existence but was resigned to the inevitable.

"Stay with me, please," she begged. Taking his right hand, she guided it around to her throat and from there down to the valley between her breasts.

"I . . . want to."

He'd begun rocking a little as if trying to give his body something to do, but although she moved with him, humming in rhythm, the darkness surrounding him didn't lift. If she described her immaculate but sterile surroundings, would—

To hell with her condo!

"What is it?" The near hysteria in her voice startled her. "What's happening to you?"

Staring but not at her, he gripped her breast. Looking down at herself, she was shocked and yet not to note that his nails were lengthening and narrowing. *I don't want to hurt you*, he'd said.

Fighting the impulse to struggle, she stroked the back of his hand. It was becoming hairy.

"Listen to me!" she fairly yelled. "Hear my voice, damn it! Only mine. Not whatever's going on inside you."

There. Maybe. A lessening of the pressure on her breast.

"That's right. I'm getting through to you again, aren't I? Pay attention to every word I speak. You *have* to. Otherwise, hell, I don't know what I'm talking about." Short, rough hair grated against her finger pads. "Tohon, please, if you can, tell me what's happening. Whatever it is, I swear, I'm here for you."

"Too late." His eyes were wide and staring and unseeing, different in ways she couldn't comprehend. "My destiny . . ."

"All right, so this is about destiny. But why now—now when I want to give you what you gave me." Determined to make her point, she reached out and lightly cupped his cock. "What do you need, straight sex? Maybe you want me to play with you until—I'm not very good with my mouth, but I'll try. If that's what it takes, I'll try."

Once again he gave no indication he'd heard, but he stopped rocking. He remained tense, but she didn't believe he'd reached the point of breaking. Even his cock had changed a little. It was longer than her fingers remembered and maybe not quite as thick. If it continued morphing into something not truly human, could she continue holding it? Pushing aside the question, she concentrated on stroking, stroking, stroking.

"I've wondered," she muttered, "is a male climax the same as a woman's? Is there this delicious period when everything is all about pleasure and anticipation, when a man feels as if he's rolling around in wonder? Then the time comes when everything is beyond control."

Although he wasn't looking at her, she told herself he was hearing her words. And, thank goodness, she no longer feared he might start clawing at her breast.

"I love that part. Sometimes it scares the hell out of me, because I'm speeding down this hill, and whatever I'm on has no brakes. But I really don't care because the ride—hell, the ride's the greatest thing I ever do."

"There's no . . . stopping."

"That's right." She sounded almost giddy with relief simply because he'd spoken. "It's the same for you, then? A roller coaster."

Nothing. No reaction.

Now his silence nearly killed her. It wasn't fair. She'd worked so hard to save him from something she didn't understand, and he still wasn't back with her. Reluctantly leaving him to do whatever he might to her breast, she cradled his cock between both hands. As she did, her breast sent her powerful messages about the depth and range of sensation and the awesome weight of trust.

He wasn't the only one capable of exploring and maybe exploiting trust. She'd give as good as he did and in so doing, connect in ways they both needed. Because if she failed now, there'd be nothing between them.

Challenged in ways her career had never done, she arched her back, further exposing her breasts.

His *new* cock fascinated her. Enough of the old remained that she knew she was still holding Tohon, but the greater length and the short but thick hairs coating his scrotum spoke of the unknown.

"Earlier you mentioned the ancient Walapai Apache." Running the side of her thumb over his tip, she gathered a bead of moisture. "This thing that's happening to you is connected to them, isn't it? That's why you said what you did, so I'd be warned."

His breathing quick and ragged, he worked her captured breast in slow circles. "Answer me!" Shocked by her tone, she sought to calm herself by sucking on her thumb. His taste slid down her throat, making her wonder if she'd carry his essence in her forever. "I'm sorry. Maybe you can't. But please, at least try."

"The Walapai continue to live in me. And in the rest of my family."

He'd said something like that earlier, hadn't he? If only she could concentrate on words alone, but for that to happen, she'd have to stand on the other side of the world from him. "How can I learn about them?"

Before she could look around to see if he had a bookshelf, his cock's movement distracted her. At first she thought he was trying to free himself, but would he still be touching her the way he was if that was his intention? They were locked in a harsh embrace, him maybe a breath from drawing blood, her capable of inflicting damage on his most precious organ.

No, not damage! Never that.

Holding on to self-control with all her strength, she relaxed her grip so her fingers now glided lightly over him. After a moment, he shook his head and stared down at her hands and what he could see of his cock.

"We're going at this wrong," she told him. "What has it become, a power trip?" She indicated her aching, tingling breast. Were his nails continuing to lengthen? "I don't want it like this. Can you be gentle, Tohon?"

"Gentle?"

A single word and yet telling, proof that he was still human? "Flowers and soft music. Silk sheets." She nearly laughed at the insane notion. "All right, I don't expect you to have silk sheets. But you have a bed, don't you?"

His only response was to stare at her through eyes that had lengthened and sharpened. Even in the dimly lit room, she had no doubt he could see far more than she could.

"I'm talking about lovemaking. What you did to me was nothing short of incredible, and I want to show my gratitude, but not like this." Despite the cost, she made a show of releasing his cock and placing her arms at her sides. Her body throbbing with tension, she clenched her teeth. "You're hurting me." She again dropped her gaze to her breast.

Maybe he spoke. She wasn't sure because it sounded more like a growl than a word. Although she wasn't in pain, she'd hoped to get through to him with a white lie. Obviously it hadn't worked.

"Stop it," she ordered, turning to the side a bit in an effort to free herself. He responded by capturing her formerly free breast and gripping her nipple between his thumb and forefinger. Trapped. Caught. Imprisoned.

"Let go of me. Now." Near panic turned her voice high and thin.

He growled, only *growl* didn't adequately describe the sound. It was something between a rumble and a scream, deceptively quiet and yet potent. She glanced up at him only to close her eyes, because what she saw wasn't a human face, not entirely. It resembled a big cat.

"What have you done?" Unable to keep her hands at her sides, she gripped his forearms but didn't make the mistake of trying to fight his strength. Still, her nails made indentations in his flesh, his hairy flesh. "What am I, your idea of a . . . a sacrifice? Are you going to kill me?"

"Kill." The word rumbled out of him. "No."

"Then make me stop thinking you might. Look at what you're doing! Look."

He did, thank goodness, staring with those beautiful if frightening eyes of his at her captured breasts. His hold on her slackened, causing her to moan in relief. Then, suddenly wary again, she fell silent. Why wasn't he releasing her?

7

The answer came all too quickly. One moment they were on their knees and face-to-face. The next, he'd grabbed her around the waist and was pulling her down toward the carpet. Although she managed to throw out her arms, she wound up on all fours. When he released her waist, she tried to straighten but he spun her around so her back was to him. He now had an unobstructed view of her ass while she had to look back over her shoulder to see what he was doing.

More human, thank God, less beast! His flesh sleek and dark instead of disappearing beneath gray hair, eyes round and large and deep-set. She couldn't see his cock.

Doggy style.

He started stroking her flanks with long, smooth movements that reached far deeper than where he'd touched earlier. With each touch, she sank deeper into a zone filled with wind-music and the scent of wildflowers. Using his fingertips and palms, he covered her hips, buttocks, and thighs with heat and pressure. And when he slid closer so his cock rested against her crack, she lowered herself onto her forearms and let her head drop.

Her breasts dangled, pulling on her rib cage and increasing her awareness of herself as a sexual being.

A sound, her, moaning, growling a little. A moment later, a deeper growl echoed. Because it came from him, she pulled it into herself and trapped his sound deep inside her. Planting his widespread fingers over her hip bones, he leaned into her, letting her know he could easily keep her in place. When his cock glided over her crack, she opened her stance and lifted her buttocks.

Doggy style. Animal to animal.

Perhaps prompted by the thought, the image of a creature that was more animal than human on the brink of fucking her flooded her mind. But instead of being terrified, she buried herself in the fantasy. In her mind, she became virginal, new and innocent. The beast who'd brought her to her knees loomed over her, ready and able to claim her as his mate. Whether she wanted the union didn't matter; strength would win.

Yes, wonderful!

She longed for his strength, longed to be claimed. Even if it meant sustaining his greater weight and his teeth biting into the back of his neck, she'd accept what nature and instinct had determined. More than accept, she'd bring her own teeth to bear. If he drove her to the ground, she'd scratch and yowl, movement on both their parts turning sex into something frenzied.

As if in response to her fantasy, he cupped his hands over the join of belly and thighs and dragged her back toward him. Her mouth open and eyes unfocused, she spread her legs even more. His cock probed, seeking her pussy.

Before she could decide what she might do to ease his journey, he shifted his hands to the back of her shoulders and pushed down until her head rested on the carpet, her nipples brushing the short, thick fibers. Drawing back her lips, she hissed at him. If he wanted savage, she'd give him savage and in so doing, feed her own need.

There, his hands spread her buttocks. Part of her stood behind him watching as her anus and cunt were exposed. Instead of embarrassment and shame, she delighted in the primal.

"Do it!" she ordered. The carpet threatened to swallow her words, but it didn't matter because her body's message was inescapable. "Just the fuck take me!"

She fully expected him to spear her, to ram past her wet defenses and bury himself deep and sure, but he stopped with his cock head just touching her entrance.

"You're sure?" he asked.

I don't know anything. Can't you tell? "Yes," she said into the carpet. "Yes!"

Once more he released a sound that wasn't human, something that rolled up from deep inside him, part howl, part scream. Closing her eyes, she dove into imagination. He'd ceased to be a man. Fingers became claws, arms turned into front legs. Fangs dominated his features, and it took a moment to tear her attention off them long enough to study his eyes. No longer male. No longer human. Piercing and all-powerful, capable of finding the most elusive prey. And his muscles! Whether she surrendered or fought, the outcome would be the same—he'd have his way with her.

The way she wanted.

Because his hands no longer controlled her upper body, she rose up on her elbows and looked behind her. Night had somehow entered the room to lock them in darkness. She saw nothing and yet felt everything. Felt most of all the pressure on her sex lips.

A quick sting on her left buttock made her arch her spine. Belatedly she realized he'd slapped her there. Instead of becoming angry, she turned to the side as much as she dared without risking the loss of cock to cunt and reached behind her. Her searching nails found the back of his hand, and she scratched him. Because her elbow no longer supported her, she started to

sink to the floor, prompting her to release him. She was still re-
gaining her balance when he slapped her again. A heated tingle
spread out from the site of her *injury*.

Another sting. Followed by his nails gliding from her shoulders to her thighs. In her mind, she saw the thin, pale marks
he'd left in the wake of his brand of foreplay.

Marks. Yes, he was marking her.

Although she ached to do the same to him, as long as she remained in this position, she had no easy access to him. In telling
contrast, no part of her was out of his reach. She'd once seen a
video of a lion taking a lioness. The female had sunk to the
ground, head hanging and tilted to the side, a powerful animal
designed for killing reduced to helpless acceptance by the
strength of the male on top of her.

Was that her? Helpless? Accepting?

Before she could answer her question, Tohon leaned low
over her, forcing her to bear his weight just as the lion had
done. Reaching under her, he grabbed the breast he'd claimed
first earlier. At the same time, his cock slipped from its perch at
her entrance to slide along her labia. She felt him everywhere.

He'd fuck her when he wanted, when he'd turned her into
what he needed her to be.

And she'd love every moment of the taking.

Despite his greater size, she managed to rock back and forth
a little. He countered by increasing his hold on her breast, not
pinching but not gentle, either. Shared sweat sealed their bodies
together; her mouth hung open, moisture gathering at the corners. A more telling moisture oozed from her sex to bathe his
organ.

"Mine," he fairly growled. "For now, mine."

"Yes," she breathed more than spoke. She'd barely gotten
the word out when he all but collapsed on her. If most of his
weight wasn't on and over her thighs, she wouldn't have been
able to support him.

His other hand reached around, finding her dangling breast and capturing it as he'd done the first. With it filling his palm, he pressed upward as if trying to push it into her rib cage.

For several seconds, little mattered except trying to get enough air into her lungs. Then the crush of his body backed off enough that her muscles no longer trembled. He'd found a way to brace himself on his elbows while still holding on to her breasts.

"Mine," he repeated. "Mine."

This time she made no attempt to speak; the totality of his mastery was too much for words, for anything except acceptance.

And pleasure.

Stroking her breasts, his nails sometimes sent shock waves of sensation throughout her. His thighs and belly sealed to her, his breath on the back of her neck and crawling through her hair. And his cock, hot and hard, pressing on her nether lips.

She was still rocking, she realized, drooling now and making deep-throated whimpering sounds. His breath kept catching, and when he released it, there was little of the human beast to it.

She could keep doing this. Her body under his, his captive and his mate, nerves shrieking with an awful need that only sex could satisfy, refusing to beg, listening to his body and knowing he was coming closer to his own cliff.

Let him beg first! Let him spread her buttocks and lips and hammer into her. When he did, she would have won.

Won!

Only she didn't give a damn about who was the victor and who the vanquished. Or if there was a winner and a loser.

She simply needed him filling her. Sliding off into hot space.

Ah shit, he was straightening and taking his magical hands with him, leaving her breasts to sag in lonely neglect. For an instant, she hated him for abandoning her; then concern swept away that emotion.

What if the *spell* was coming over him again?

"Tohon?" Her throat felt rough. "Please, I—"

Ah shit, his fingers on her ass cheeks. Opening her up, running the side of a thumb from her puckered hole to her sex lips, letting her cheeks slide back together again but with his hand trapped between them. Barely thinking, she tightened her muscles there and squeezed his fingers.

She wondered if he'd ask if she was ready, waited for the words that would demonstrate he was a man and not an animal. But he already had his answer, didn't he?

When he leaned away, she made no attempt to look back at him, because night had fully claimed them; she couldn't see him, could only feel him. Only feel her need—and his.

Yes, oh, yes! His cock back at her opening again. No longer stopping but slipping in. An inch. Two. Lifting her upper body a little and arching her spine downward this time, working herself open. Welcoming him.

Large. Hard. Heated. Bearing no resemblance to the animal cock she'd held earlier. Fully human and becoming part of her.

Pushing back at him, she wiped her wet mouth against her upper arm. And although she couldn't see for the night, she closed her eyes. Her body felt sensitive in ways she had nothing to compare with. He'd left his marks on her just as she'd tried to do to him, but that was in the past. The present revolved around joined flesh.

Skewered. Speared.

Setting herself for attack, she lowered her head as the mating lioness had done. But unlike the lioness, she was no passive recipient of her mate's thrusts. If she didn't lock her limbs and balance her weight, he might knock her forward. As it was, each muscled drive pushed her forward a few inches until he again caught her at the base of her pelvis and held her in place. Still, they advanced and retreated as one until he planted his hands over her buttocks to keep her from moving back with him. As a result, she felt his cock dive hard and true inside her before sliding back. Not once did they lose contact. Not once did she mentally step back from the act of intercourse.

Rhythm. Heat gliding and building throughout her. Growling and growling again in response to the rumble rolling up from his throat.

Only one hand on her buttocks for support and control now. The other touching her here and everywhere, knuckles rolling over her ribs, reaching down and around so he could run his nails over her mons, tapping her breasts, burying a fingertip in her navel, caressing her flanks and lightly pinching her ass.

"Oh, shit, shit! Oh, my God."

"He isn't here, just me." That said, Tohon cupped his hand over her mons and shook it.

"No, no! I can't—"

"Yes, you can. Because you want."

Did she? If she could think, she might be able to answer. But nothing existed beyond her body and the powerful one looming over hers, the living spear that had turned them into a single entity.

Hot and weak, she fell into a space without definition. She half believed she'd passed out, but maybe she was trying to waken from the deepest sleep of her life. Only no dream had felt this real, and whatever clawed at her inner tissues let her know she was far from unconscious. Blood pooled in her temple to further muddy her thoughts, not that she cared. Not that she wanted to feel anything other than what she was.

Ripe. Yes, that's what she was, an all-encompassing ripe cunt.

He kept coming at her, pounding and pounding until she couldn't separate one thrust from the other. They were clawing up a mountain, working together and at cross purposes at the same time, two separate bodies fusing into one. She wanted to bite him, to bury her teeth in his flesh and taste his blood.

And if he opened his mouth and touched his teeth to her, instead of flinching, she'd remain in place so he could bite her, so her blood could run down his throat.

"Shit! Shit!" he fairly bellowed. With that, he slammed into her, knocking her forward. Once again her head was on the ground, her arms splayed outward and useless, all but broken.

He'd won, worn her down! And his cum—ah shit, yes, that was his seed filling her.

His hands glided along her sides, stroking her over and over again as if he owned her. Worshipped her.

Not a female in heat driven to the ground by a powerful male but a beast equal to the one on top of her. Screaming like the animal she'd become, she let go.

Climaxed. Died.

Found a reason to live in the dying.

8

Don't go there!

Someone wrapped their arms around Tohon, stopping his forward movement and bringing him back to earth. Still, conditioned by years of surrendering to the powerful inner force, he tried to shake off the grip. At the same time, his mind repeated its mantra—*Don't go there.*

"Tohon, wake up. You're having a bad dream."

That voice. He hadn't known it for long, and yet it was nearly as strong as the inner power. He would have opened his eyes if the inevitable journey into the future hadn't begun.

As had happened countless times, he floated on the wind, his speed picking up with every second. The world went by in a blur, and as always, he couldn't tell how many days had passed since the journey began. He'd long since stopped trying to determine where he was, but something about the strong and warm arms made him long for greater control.

"Wake up, please."

Distracted from the inevitable by her voice, he struggled to lift the dark curtain from the realm he'd once again been sucked into. But the force, the damnable unknown's grip on him only tightened.

He was heading into the unwanted future. Once more.

Seeing. Ah, no! Seeing.

"Tohon, Tohon, it's all right. You're here with me. Nothing bad's going to happen to you."

He already knew that because the *bad* that was sometimes a blessing never personally touched him. If only the tears of others didn't impact him!

The wind, tearing at him now, powering him into tomorrow or maybe next week, insisting he record what hadn't yet happened and carry that reality in his heart and voice. More than carry this burden, he had to spread it in that timeless way.

"Stop it!" Sharp nails dug into his upper arms. "Damn it, Tohon, snap out of it!"

What was that, daylight? No, he amended, morning hadn't yet arrived. The moon. It and her presence and words had freed him and killed the strong current. For now. If only he hadn't seen what he had.

No longer drifting but not yet convinced that he was in the bed the two of them had stumbled onto after their frenzied fucking, he blinked open his eyes and stared at what was real.

Her short hair was flat on one side with a lock falling forward to obscure her right eyebrow. A pillow crease marked her cheek. He was still on his side, but she'd sat up. One hand still gripped his arm; the other supported her upper body.

"Thank goodness." Her smile looked forced. "That must have been a killer nightmare. The way you were thrashing and protesting, you obviously didn't want to do something or go somewhere. I don't know. Do you think it would help to talk about it?"

Help? When his destiny had first manifested itself, he'd begged members of his family to tell him how to make it stop, but of course that hadn't happened. If those who were as intimately involved as he was had warned him not to ask for the impossible, how could he expect her to understand?

"Nightmare? Sorry. I can't remember ... are you sure ..." Disgusted with himself, he stopped the lie. Unfortunately, the way she looked at him told him he'd already gone too far.

"You might be the most complicated human being I've ever known, the most amazing," she said. "You don't happen to come from another planet, do you? That might explain some of your behavior."

Grateful as he was at her attempt to make light of things, he wasn't up to continuing the charade. "Lie down," he encouraged. "It's the middle of the night."

"A little after four going by your clock," she said. Stretching out beside him, she rested her head on his arm. One hand settled over his belly. "I, ah, I don't know if I'm up for a repeat of what happened earlier. I'm still recovering."

Belatedly, he realized he had a hard-on. Obviously she believed that meant he was interested in sex, but although his body was more than just interested, his mind, specifically the part of his brain that had succumbed to the *nightmare*, wasn't. Shaking off each mind-journey into the future took so much out of him, and if he didn't pit all his resources against the force, it was just a matter of time before it again captured him.

And when it did, he'd lose her.

"Go back to sleep," he said, exhausted by the effort the words took. "I didn't mean ..."

"Didn't mean to wake me? Sometimes the middle of the night's the best time to talk. No distractions, nothing except the person next to you."

Say something! Find a way to turn the conversation in another direction. But he didn't because he'd finally faced what he'd been trying to avoid since the moment he'd first seen her. Felt her tears. What a damnable fool he'd been to think they could have any kind of a relationship. It would end before he'd found a way to free her from her past, a past he scarcely comprehended.

"Why not, Tohon?" Her tone was no longer soft and gentle but sharp with an emotion he didn't want to venture near. "You've been trying to get me to open up, but you won't do the same, will you?"

"This isn't about me."

"Fuck you!" she snapped, sitting up again.

Before he knew what she had in mind, she'd stood and backed away from the bed. The half-moon made it possible for him to see her outline, just barely. In contrast, his memory easily painted in the details. Slender and small with almost girlish breasts and hips made for straddling him, she took pride in her reserved intellect. Only someone with the ability to see beneath that outer competence would find the unhealed scars.

Scars he lacked the skill to treat, after all.

"Still saying nothing, Tohon?" Her voice was stripped of its earlier sharpness. "Maybe you don't even understand why I'm angry."

"Why don't you tell me?"

"I intend to. You've been accusing me of building a barrier around my emotions, but you're doing the same. And when I throw that at you, you tell me that this . . . this whatever we're doing isn't about you."

A flash, familiar and overwhelming, warned him that the force she'd interrupted was trying to return. Desperate and determined to hold it at bay as long as possible, he slipped out of bed. Much as he wanted to embrace her, to lose his sanity in her body, he didn't try touching her. Maybe understanding, she took a single backward step.

Slow comprehension reminded him that she'd been the last to speak, but his mind refused to process what he should or dared say. The flash, the shaking of his entire body, struck again.

Come into the future, a voice as familiar as his own heartbeat commanded. *Do what you must. Let your cry serve as the warning.*

"No!" he growled. "Not now."

Yes, the force countered. *As always, yes.*

"Let me go! I can't . . ."

Yes, you can. You must.

"Why?" he begged. "By all that's holy, why?"

From where she stood, with her arms snaked around her naked middle, Amy cursed the darkness and his words. Tohon existed as the faintest of shadows. His tone revealed a great deal about his turmoil because of where he was standing, but she couldn't read his expression or see if he was changing form, again.

Not only did he outweigh her by many pounds but he was also far stronger. His words and tone left no doubt that he wasn't the man she'd thought she'd been talking to at the beginning. He wasn't even the man she'd recently had sex with.

Run! her instinct for survival screamed.

But because her body remembered the feel and wonder of him and because some of his essence remained inside her, she remained where she was. He'd fallen silent, thank goodness. The one-sided conversation he'd been having hadn't made any sense, and his pleas for freedom had shaken her deeply.

"I can't pretend to understand what's going on," she told him, deliberately keeping her voice low so he would have to work at concentrating on her. "Maybe you don't want me to try, but I don't think that's it." Pausing, she struggled for something else to say. "I think if you'd intended *this* to remain private, we wouldn't have wound up here. Instead of being determined to psychoanalyze me, you were determined that I see the real you. The maybe crazy you."

"What? No."

Unable to determine what he was thinking from his tone, she made what might be the bravest decision of her life. Killing the distance between them, she ran her fingers over his belly. He tensed and sucked in his breath.

Careful, don't allow yourself to be distracted, she warned herself. But with him this close, it was so damn hard. If she wrapped her arms around him, he might carry her back to his bed, and then nothing else would matter.

How seductive he was! How incredibly sexy!

"Are you saying you aren't crazy?" she asked, with her fingers now at his waist and their warmth blending. "I'm not so sure of that. Maybe if you told me what's behind—"

"I can't."

Why, damn it, why?

The moon, halfway to full and partly hidden by tree shadows, was calling to her. It was somewhere between silver and palest blue, more illusion than reality. In many respects, Tohon was like that, illusion.

Was that it? He was from another planet or time, an existence she couldn't comprehend?

Don't be ridiculous, her logical nature retorted.

And yet—

A sudden jolt of what felt like electricity shot from him to her, causing her to gasp and jerk her hand off his waist. "What was that?"

"The force."

How resigned he sounded, not defeated so much as accepting that nothing he might do or try would change the inevitable. "Tell me about this . . . force. Where does it come from?"

Try as she might to will a response from him, he didn't utter a word. He was a mass of tension, leaning away from her as if he was afraid he might shock her again. She sensed more of the movement, the changing she had earlier. Was he going to become something other than a man before her eyes? And if he did, would he remain in that form forever? Did the form include fangs and claws? The ability to kill her?

"Give me your hand."

To her surprise, he did, but although the contours were the same as she remembered, something had been altered. He lacked, what, warmth maybe. It was as if he was letting go of being a man and becoming something different. Something without humanity.

"Stay with me!" she ordered. Although she sounded shocked and even horrified, she concentrated on holding on to him. "I'm not going to let you go. Do you understand? No matter what you say or do, I'm not leaving." *Unless I believe you're going to kill me.*

Lifting his hand, she exhaled on his knuckles and then rubbed where she'd breathed. "Can you hear me?"

What was that, a nod? Whether it was or wasn't didn't matter, because she now knew with every fiber of her being that she couldn't desert this complex and tortured man. He'd fucked her as she'd never been fucked, and although her body would carry that imprint forever, that wasn't why she entertained no thoughts of running.

He'd broken through the barriers she'd spent so long erecting.

9

The wind became part of the night's mix and was pushing the trees about. Tohon's features were both steeped in darkness and lit with a strange silver-blue haze Amy tried to convince herself was caused by the moon. When the wind pushed the trees away, allowing the moonbeam to enter the room, she concentrated on making Tohon as real as possible. Unfortunately, his features slipped away, over and over again.

Because he was slipping off somewhere she couldn't reach?

"You . . . you asked me about my father's death." She hadn't known she was going to say the words until they rested in the air between them, but now that she'd broached the forbidden topic, she sensed it might be the only one capable of keeping him here. "I told you when he died, but I didn't say anything about how. You didn't ask."

His only response was a nod.

"Why not?" She deliberately posed the question.

"I . . . couldn't force the truth out of you. It had to come naturally."

Good, good. Keep talking. Or at least listening to me. "There was nothing natural about his death," she shot back, the old horror painting her tone.

"I didn't think so."

Too damn much night! What if she turned on a light? As soon as she'd considered the possibility, she rejected it, in part because she needed darkness to give her the courage to continue, in part because this way she couldn't see the changes in him, at least not all of them.

"He was murdered."

Until this moment, she'd been holding on to him. Now, however, he pulled out of her grasp only to close his fingers around her wrists and place her palms against his chest. "Where were you when it happened?" he asked after a silence during which her words swirled through her.

His question took her by surprise; the few people she'd told had invariably asked how, why, and by who. "In my bed. I . . . I'd been sleeping. The argument woke me up."

Covering her hands with his, he guided her palms over his pectoral muscles. The strength just below his surface flowed into her, but even without that, she'd come too far to back down. The truth needed to be told. And he had to hear it.

"My mother had been having an affair. I sensed that something was different about her. She wasn't as attentive to me as she'd been, but as a brand-new teen, I wasn't the easiest person in the world to be around. Dad's job kept him on the road a lot. He wasn't supposed to come home that night."

"A surprise that went terribly wrong."

"It didn't have to be!" The old wound in her heart opened. "*He* was there. In the bed my parents shared."

"Your father found them?"

Every inch of Tohon's body was tightly strung. His tendons and muscles felt on the brink of snapping. Much as she wanted to believe that what she was telling him was wholly responsible, she knew better. He was holding himself together, just barely.

"I didn't ask my mother; for months afterward, I couldn't speak to her. I went to live with my father's parents."

"At least you had them to turn to." His too-hot breath slid through her hair.

"The three of us grieved together." This was so damn hard, and necessary. "My bedroom was on the opposite side of the house from my parents'. The only time *he* came was when I was in bed. That's what makes me sick, one of the things, anyway. Knowing my mother was fucking her lover with me so near."

An ache in her left wrist told her she was pressing her hand against Tohon's chest, but although she didn't want to hurt him, she couldn't relax enough to stop. If only he'd envelop her in his embrace.

But would she be able to continue?

Eyes closed and swaying a little, she painted a detailed picture of what she'd seen when she reached the door to her parents' room. Her father lay crumpled on the cream carpet, his blood ruining it. She didn't learn until the trial that the bullet from the gun his grandfather had given him had struck his heart, killing him instantly. Her mother and her lover—even now she couldn't bring herself to call him by name—were naked. Her mother kept screaming, stopping only long enough to order her to leave.

In contrast, *he'd* endlessly repeated, "I didn't mean, didn't mean, didn't mean—" *He'd* dropped the gun she later learned the two men had fought over after her father loaded it and aimed it at *him.*

The killer had been convicted of manslaughter but had served less than a year. And although she now understood the legal nuances that had led to the verdict, when she'd heard it, her screams had been a twin of her mother's that nightmare night.

Her grieving teenage mind had closed down around a single fact—the person she loved most in life was dead, murdered, and the monster responsible would soon resume his life. She didn't care that her mother and *he* had barely spoken after that night. And for a long time she'd hated her mother.

"One night, one action, changed three lives and ended one," she finished. Emotionally spent, she rested her forehead against his shoulder. "The DA's office arranged counseling for me, but I couldn't talk to her; I couldn't. Every time I tried, I saw Dad's blood on the carpet."

"You haven't moved past that point, that night."

No, she nearly admitted. *I haven't.* But knowing he was speaking the truth and agreeing with him were two widely different things. She'd learned to function in the world by keeping her emotional distance. Her existence might be a lonely one, but at least she wasn't a drain on society. She paid her bills and provided a necessary service and supported three overseas orphans. Their pictures adorned her refrigerator.

"What about your mother?"

A sudden sense of betrayal stiffened her spine, causing her to try jerking free. Although he allowed her to back away a few inches, his hold left no doubt that she'd go no farther until he was ready. The damnable night settled like a cloak around him. Still, she imagined what he looked like. Not fully human. Not quite animal, yet.

"You'll have to ask her," she friendly replied.

"Because you don't know."

Was he blaming her for the distance between her and her mother? *She* was the innocent party in this, the victim. If he couldn't see that— "We talk, infrequently. There's this huge chasm between us."

"Has she tried to close the gap?"

Tohon was a hunk, a stud, complex and confusing and maybe dangerous. She didn't want him tearing into her layers!

But she'd known from the beginning that he'd try.

"In her own way." His body was giving off a new brand of

heat, denser and deeper than before. And although she couldn't see his eyes, she felt their awesome intensity. "Every time I feel her getting too close, I back off."

"Because you're afraid of what'll be said, or because you don't want anything or anyone jeopardizing your anger?"

One heartbeat she wanted to ram her fist down his throat so he couldn't speak. The next she stepped back from herself so she could study what the years and, yes, her anger had fashioned. "I don't know. I honestly don't know."

"Do you want things to change?"

Change. Becoming someone different. "I don't know."

"I think you do, Amy." He released her hands only to run his fingers into her hair at the temples. "For years I wanted to be anything but what I am. But it's different for me. I have no control over my destiny."

"Why not? Surely you—I don't understand."

Instead of acknowledging that she couldn't possibly stand in his shoes, he tilted her head upward. Certain he intended to kiss her, she settled her hands over his hips. Closer he came, that dense heat sliding past her layers, finding her heart.

Then, as she rose onto her toes in search of intimacy, tension again seized him. Determined to help him oppose his demons, she rocked forward until his cock pressed against her belly. "Whatever's happening to you, fight it! Fuck me. That's the only thing you have to think about tonight, fucking. The only thing you need to do."

No! His body slid off into a place and space she couldn't follow. Distancing himself despite her desperate hold.

"Stop it! Damn it, Tohon, stop it! Don't you—"

Something slammed into her forearms. Pain screamed, forcing her to release him. She was still trying to make sense of what had happened when he spun away. If it wasn't for the mix of agony and numbness radiating through her, she might have thrown herself at him.

Instead, all she could do was whimper as he bolted from the bedroom. By the time she started after him, he was in the living room, a shifting, fluid form heading for the front door. He didn't bother to shut it after him.

Gone.

No matter how many times she tried to make her peace with it, the abandonment hurt. Granted, he'd been gone for only a few minutes, but it might have been a lifetime. Her forearms still ached, not that it mattered. The door remained open.

Gone.

Logic—or rather what remained of the logic that had long sustained her—insisted she had nothing to fear from him. Granted, he'd left bruises, but his intention hadn't been to hurt her. Instead, he'd run toward something or someone whose draw was far stronger than hers could ever be.

He'd unlocked the protective wall she'd placed around her past and challenged her to face them and then leave them behind.

Then he'd returned to his life, his world.

She'd been sitting on the couch she'd shared with him earlier when she spotted a low shadow passing through the opening. Jumping to her feet, she tried to judge whether she could reach the fireplace poker before whatever had come inside stopped her. Then she realized the intruder was Tohon's dog. Remembering his fangs and growls, she picked up a throw pillow and held it to her breasts. The notion that she thought an armload of padding would protect her nearly made her laugh.

Besides, the dog showed no interest in her. Although it stayed just inside, its attention was on the outdoors. Its uneasy whine made her long to comfort it.

"Don't blame me because he's gone," she whispered. "I tried to make him stay."

A glance in her direction made her wonder if the dog was

blaming her for Tohon's disappearance, but maybe her own emotions were responsible for her sense of failure.

"You're good for him; I hope you understand that. Everyone, even someone as independent as Tohon, needs something living around. Someone or something who cares." *Who loves.*

This time the dog didn't bother acknowledging her. If anything, its interest in what lay outside increased. And although she hadn't quite convinced herself that she had nothing to fear from the large mutt, she started toward it. She'd covered maybe half the distance when the dog lifted its head and howled, a long, low, mournful cry.

It was answered by another howl from outside. No, not a howl. A scream. Inhuman. So loud she wondered if the entire county could hear. Echoing. Going on and on.

Her hand at her throat and her legs rubbery, she forced herself to stand next to the nearly waist-high dog. The mutt still didn't acknowledge her, but what caught her attention was that its hackles weren't raised.

A second scream.

No human throat could make that sound. What wild animal—

10

Only half aware of what she was doing, she stepped onto the front porch still clutching the pillow to her breasts. The half-moon offered a surreal white-blue cast that turned the land into something that belonged on another planet. Yes, there was Tohon's truck and beyond that the outline of a corral and the shadow of a barn and a handful of trees and a low hill, but the color, the amazing color had altered everything.

And the scream-howl! For the third time, it dominated her world.

Dropping the pillow, she rested her hand on the top of the dog's head and took comfort from the warmth she found. *What is that?* she ached to ask. "Tohon?" she managed. "Tohon, are you out there?"

If wanting something badly enough could make that something happen, he would be walking toward her right now, his body gliding in that beautiful way, smiling at her, reaching for her.

Instead, she spotted movement near the top of the hill.

Stifling a gasp, she clamped her hand over her mouth. Once

her heart started beating again, she was no longer sure movement had caught her attention. Maybe it was the shape.

Oh, hell, yes, the shape!

The *thing* reached the top of the hill, giving the moon the perfect opportunity to highlight its form. And to leave her with no doubt.

A big cat.

A puma.

Almost belatedly she realized she wasn't shocked or alarmed. Instead, a deep sense of acceptance slipped over her. After everything she'd experienced and seen tonight, how could the form be anything except a puma?

Massive.

Magnificent.

Even from this distance, she saw the powerful muscles, the lifting of the head, the stretching of the throat, the mouth with its great fangs opening.

Another scream. Harsh and hard and deeply, deeply lonely. A sound ripped unwanted from the creature's chest. She couldn't be sure but thought it lasted longer than the earlier ones. For what seemed like a lifetime, the wind carried it, sustained it, sent it out across the landscape.

The dog howled again, a resigned and relieved sound. And when it started toward the hill, she kept pace. Even realizing that the puma was heading toward them didn't stop her from doing what she needed to.

"Tohon," she said when maybe a hundred feet separated her from the beast. Although she stopped, the dog continued its slow approach until muzzle met muzzle. Judging by the size difference, she guessed the puma weighed over two hundred pounds. The moon still lent its cast to what she took to be a predominantly gray coat, but she couldn't make out the eye color.

"It's you, isn't it?" Saying the words brought a lump to her throat. An instant of disbelief was replaced by yet more acceptance. "Tohon."

Whatever message the dog wanted to pass on to the much larger animal must have been concluded because, its tail wagging a little, it lay down and rested its head on its front paws.

The puma remained alert but not tense. Its gaze was now on her. A gaze she knew all too well. Capable of reaching deep inside her and igniting a fire of need.

"Why didn't you tell me?" she asked.

I did. In my own way.

Sudden shock slammed into her. Stumbling backward, she clamped a hand over her throat. She'd fallen into a whirlpool; her world had been turned on end; nothing was right. "Don't do this! The way you've been messing with my mind—"

You didn't want your past brought into the open?

I want to wake up, in my own home, my own bed, my own— "The horrific sound you made. What the hell was that about?"

Nothing changed. She was still looking at a beyond-large puma. And yet there was something about his gaze. It was, she realized, a human quality that hadn't been there a moment ago.

Tohon, becoming human again? And when he did— "That cry," she repeated. "Everyone who lives within twenty miles of here must have heard it."

Not everyone. Just those who walk the old way.

Oh, shit, he was talking about the ancient Apache again, or more specifically those who carried Walapai blood.

I didn't want to send the message; I never do, he told her in his wordless way. *But the choice isn't mine.*

Get the hell out of here! she warned herself. *You don't want to get in any deeper than you already are.* "What are you talking about?"

Do you really want to know?

"I don't know, damn it! All right, all right, tell me."

I'm given visions of the future. Visions of death. It's my fate and task to pass them on so those who are about to die have time to prepare.

"You can't mean it."

I'd never lie to you.

Hating herself a little because her thoughts were for her alone, she nevertheless took note of the distance separating her from Tohon's truck. Had he left the keys in it? "Whose death?" she asked, stalling.

Chief Hobata.

"Who's that?"

You saw him today. He was the first to approach me.

Concentrating, she remembered the distinguished older Apache who'd briefly talked to Tohon. Chief Hobata had looked robust, and she'd been touched by the communication between the two men. It was as if they loved each other. "He's going to die soon?"

Yes.

"And it's your *job* to tell him?"

I just did.

With the unholy scream. "Does he know the cry was for him?"

Yes.

She could have asked how he could be so sure but sensed the answer lay in the timeless connection with the Walapai. "Your dreams or visions or whatever they are, do they show you exactly what's going to happen?"

Yes.

Speechless, she hugged herself. As she rubbed her arms, she knew the chill she was feeling came not from the cold but from what she'd just heard. Tohon had seen into her past, but most times his heritage gave him insight into the future, a future he dreaded.

One he was determined to share with her?

"I don't want this!" she fairly yelled.

I know.

She was barefoot. If she tried to run, she risked injuring the soles of her feet. In fact, she wasn't sure how she'd gotten out here intact. Just the same, the truck with its doors that locked called to her. Once in it, she'd be protected from Tohon and what he'd become tonight. Safe. Back in her world.

The dog stood, distracting her. A moment later she pulled her attention back to Tohon or the puma or whatever the hell the creature was. No wonder the dog had gotten to its feet. She would have done the same thing because the puma seemed to be flowing, floating, becoming less distinct.

It had to be the moon!

No, not the moon. The changes she'd seen in Tohon earlier were being reversed. Smooth as moonlight gliding on a quiet lake, the puma stood upright. The thick, short hairs covering it melted, revealing male flesh. Naked flesh. And the fangs were gone, replaced by a man's mouth.

A man's eyes.

A man's cock.

Watching her, Tohon reached for the dog. Man and animal spoke without words, fingers stroking a head, a tongue licking a callused hand. Love ran between them. Love and acceptance.

"Leave," he told her. "I know you want to."

Yes, his truck, her fingers starting the engine and shifting into gear, driving away. Leaving behind the incomprehensible, the threat to her heart and soul and maybe most of all to her hungry-for-him body. She didn't have to flee naked after all, because he'd let her know he wasn't going to stop her.

She'd be free.

Back in her world.

"I . . . one thing." Her throat seized, forcing her to swallow repeatedly. "I'm going to go see my mother. Talk about what I couldn't bring myself to before. I won't blame. I'll listen."

"So will she."

Although she sensed he was doing more than just telling her what she needed to hear, she didn't say anything. How could she when the dog was leaning against Tohon's naked side and she remembered when she did the same thing?

Don't go there. Go where you belong. Where things make sense.

"The key's in the ignition."

In her mind, she saw herself driving back into Flagstaff. She'd leave his pickup as close as possible to where it had been before, get into her rental, and return to her motel. On Monday morning, she'd go to the business that was paying for the audit and bury herself in financial records.

And when she was finished . . .

Just the thought of being surrounded by bank statements made her sick to her stomach. It wasn't the job she hated so much as everything it stood for, the adherence to protocol, the completeness of her report, her refusal to point fingers or sympathize if she found errors. She'd had clients refuse to believe her results, curse, complain about how hard it was to keep a company going, even cry. When those things happened, she'd nodded and handed them her bill.

Could she do that again?

Did she want to?

Or did she want to meet the children she supported, hold them, get to love them, laugh and cry with them?

Knowing with absolute certainty what her answer was, she blinked Tohon back into focus. As far as she could tell, he hadn't moved; neither had the dog. The moon still painted them with its unique color, but she now saw more than cool blue.

Yes, Tohon had his dog and his ranch and the horses but beyond that . . .

Comprehension deeper than any she'd ever experienced settled over her. Ignoring a bite of pain on her right instep from whatever she'd stepped on, she approached Tohon. She thought the dog might try stopping her, but it backed away, leaving her to look up at the naked man who'd fucked her as she'd never been fucked.

Although she could only guess at his reaction, she didn't hesitate from splaying her fingers over his hard chest. "It hurts, doesn't it?"

He didn't ask what she was talking about, and he didn't try to put distance between them. Instead, he wrapped an arm around her waist. With the other he started massaging her back. "You feel cold."

"You don't. Warm me, Tohon. Make me hot."

The moment the words were out, she cringed because they sounded melodramatic when she wanted to encourage and entice and seduce and be seduced. But first she had to finish what she started.

"I have some idea what your life's like," she tried. "My isolation has been self-imposed, a protective mechanism, while you're set apart by circumstances out of your control."

His silence didn't surprise her. Instead, it compelled her to continue. "I hope your family provides the support everyone needs, but that doesn't make isolation any easier to accept. It's as if you have this communicable disease. People are afraid they'll catch something fatal if they get too close."

"It isn't that simple."

"No, I'm sure it isn't." Much as she longed to kiss him in gratitude because he'd spoken, she knew where that would lead them, and until everything had been said . . . "They know you aren't deliberately bringing grief, but that doesn't blunt the impact of your news. They associate you with death, so they keep their distance."

"I don't blame them."

Maybe you should, she almost said, but bitterness would only make his burden harder to bear. "But you're still alone."

There it was, the sudden hardening of his body. Only this

time she wasn't afraid he'd change shape. "What? You don't want me saying that?"

"I didn't expect it."

"You haven't heard it before?"

He'd handed her telling silences before, but they'd never revealed so much. Half stumbling, half going by her heart, she'd happened upon something he'd never shared with anyone. For reasons rooted in the kind of man he was, he'd never told his family about his loneliness, and of course the Apache who made up his world were so wrapped up in their fear of what he represented that they didn't try looking at their shared world through his eyes.

Only she with the heart he'd penetrated and brought out of hiding did.

"What is it?" she asked as gently as possible. "Some macho code you live by that insists you be strong and independent?"

"No."

"Then what?"

"There's never been anyone I trusted with the truth."

Tears sprang free, but although she'd always cried in private, she felt no shame in letting him see her emotion. "I felt the same way. Tohon, look at what our emotional isolation has done. I've been only half alive while you—"

"I thought I was alive," he said, and kissed her forehead.

Thank you. "Thought? You no longer feel the same way?"

"Knowing you exist has changed a great deal. I'm still trying to sort it all out."

"So am I," she admitted, glad for a reason to smile. "Just discovering there's really such a thing as shapeshifting—are you done for now? No more getting down on all fours tonight?"

"I'm done."

She'd been looking at his broad and solid chest while talking. After licking her lips, she pressed her mouth against the tanned flesh. Maybe it was her imagination, but she thought she could feel his heart beating.

"Don't," he muttered. He didn't move.

"Why not?" She kept her lips on his skin.

"Because, any more and I won't let you leave."

"I'm not leaving, Tohon," she said as she sank to her knees. Taking hold of his cock, she ran her tongue over his tip. "We need each other too much."

In Ice

Crystal Jordan

Acknowledgments

First and foremost, this story is dedicated to Michal, best friend extraordinaire, the Mad Madam M, and the only girl I'd ever call my heterosexual life partner. Thanks for sticking by me even if this writing thing isn't something you always "get."

Much love and heartfelt thanks goes to my fellow smut peddlers, without whom I might never have gotten up the nerve to submit a book for publication. They are: Eden Bradley, Loribelle Hunt, R. G. Alexander, Dayna Hart, Jennifer McKenzie, Robin L. Rotham, Gemma Halliday, Gwen Hayes, and Lillian Feisty.

Kate Douglas and Lacy Danes deserve more gratitude than they know for taking the new girl at Aphrodisia under their wings and kindly answering every stupid newbie question.

Thank you to my editor at Kensington, whose name I couldn't pronounce until the day he called and said, "Hi, this is John Scognamiglio." I was in such shock that I don't remember much after that, but I'm really, really glad he made The Call. And thank you to Lucienne Diver, wunderkind agent, who held my hand through contracts and minor mental meltdowns.

Finally, this one is for Grams. I love you for always believing in me and kicking me to write that first story.

1

"Help me! Please . . . somebody help."

Jain's teeth chattered as she scanned the foreign landscape. Snow covered the rocky ground in a thick layer, and massive trees surrounded the clearing on all sides, hemming her in so she couldn't get her bearings. Night began to fall, and the temperature dropped rapidly. Crossing her arms over her breasts, she rubbed her numb hands over her biceps to try and stimulate circulation. God, she was so cold. Ice bit into her legs, scraping the skin away and leaving her feet raw and bleeding.

She'd been wandering around naked since her ship crashed, and her personal pod had released her from cryogenic freeze. Had anyone else made it out? The ship had held a full crew and one other passenger besides her. It had exploded in a fiery array of reds, yellows, and oranges, but she'd seen no one else from the ship. The roiling smoke had spun through the towering trees and into the afternoon sky in twists of black soot. Since no rescue party had responded to the crash, she assumed she'd landed in an uninhabited area.

"Hellooooo!" Her voice echoed over the frozen landscape.

With each moment that passed, she felt her strength draining, her ability to reason slipping away. She struggled to collect her wandering thoughts, to plan how to save herself. Fading in and out of consciousness, she wondered how much longer she could last without shelter. She had no idea what planet she was on. She should have landed on Aquatilis, where her brother worked as a marine geneticist, but Aquatilis was almost completely covered in water, and she was in the middle of a mountain range. Something had gone seriously wrong. There weren't supposed to be any other inhabitable planets in this solar system, but she could breathe and the gravity was *almost* normal. Where the hell was she?

Kesuk had seen the fiery explosion in the distance and had come to investigate. His sentries fanned out to surround the clearing. The feud with the Browns had just been settled, but it looked as though they wished to start again. He heaved a weary sigh, his paws crunching through the thick sheet of ice as he drew nearer the inferno. Would they never learn?

Their leaders smiled and bowed to his face while their warriors slaughtered his livestock and stole his women. He slid his tongue over his long fangs, enjoying the idea of catching them breaking the pact. His young daughter might enjoy a Brown slave. A low growl of pleasure rumbled through his chest at the thought. He hadn't started this feud, but he'd finish it.

Relishing the prospect of a good fight, he quickened his pace. Rolling his shoulders, he stretched into a lumbering run, his long strides eating the distance. Pricking his ears, he stayed alert for signs of an ambush.

"Help me."

The ragged cry sounded to his left, bringing him up short. His breath snorted clouds in the icy air as he waited to hear it again. Padding lightly, he crept between the trees, winding his way toward the origin of the noise.

A woman. A woman unlike any he'd ever seen. Naked, glorious, tiny, her short tufts of brown hair sleek against her skull. Her eyes drew him, greener than the leaves of a Sitka tree. He ran his tongue down a curved canine tooth, eyeing her softly curved form, the thatch of tight dark curls between her slim thighs. Perhaps it was not his daughter who would gain a slave this day. Her sudden appearance and odd coloring demanded he examine her more closely. His men would investigate the explosion and seek him out to report their findings. They knew their duty because he trained them well.

Foolish of her clan to allow her out alone. What was she doing in the borderlands? Her skin was too pale to be a Black or a Brown. He sighed in regret as he drew near. Perhaps she was addled; such birth defects or misfortunes were known to happen. She wandered through the snow, her broken gait and dazed expression making it obvious she would freeze to death. And soon. He raised his nose to the wind, trying to catch her scent. She wasn't of his clan, that much he knew, but she was on his land.

She belonged to him.

2

She dreamed of a polar bear. Massive and frightening, it blurred and shifted, somehow turning into the most beautiful man she'd ever seen. Unfortunately, the man was also frightening. His white-blond hair glinted in the wavering sunlight while his coal-black eyes tracked her like a predator after prey. She squirmed under his gaze, uncertain how to proceed.

Neither of them wore any clothes, and they stood in a great green forest. He towered over her, forcing her to tilt her head back to maintain eye contact as he drew closer. Without warning, he thrust a huge hand into her hair and drew her forward, slanting his mouth over hers, muffling her weak protest against his lips. Hot excitement spun through her, dampening her pussy, making it clench with want. Her breath rushed out, panting against his lips as their kisses grew more urgent. His heavy masculine scent caressed her nose. She couldn't explain her fierce reaction, but she didn't want to, was content to follow his lead.

He forced her back into a snowbank, his big body heating her front as he came down on top of her. Her legs parted to accommodate him, and she gripped his shoulders to pull him closer. She wanted him. She wanted him now. Her fingers slid down his smooth chest, flicking over his flat nipples. He reciprocated by closing his mouth over the tip of her breast and drawing on it strongly. She moaned, sucking in frigid air as her body raged with unbearable heat. Her fingers tangled in his pale hair. The dense, silky texture was unlike anything she'd ever felt before.

Spreading wet kisses up her chest, he bit the side of her neck. She jumped at the sharp sensation, and then tilted her jaw to allow him greater access. The head of his cock rubbed against her pussy lips, probing for entrance. Lifting her hips, she forced him into her. Her slick sex stretched to admit his huge length, making her moan as he thrust deeper and harder, again and again. She wrapped her legs around him, moving with him, their combined body heat melting the cold snow. Hot pleasure came in rolling waves, building—

She jerked awake, still shivering with unspent desire. Panting for breath, she waited for her heart to stop pounding. The dream repeated in her mind. She frowned. She'd never fantasized anything like that before. Not ever. She'd always controlled the sexual encounters with her ex-husband, however unsatisfying those encounters had been for both of them.

Putting thoughts of her sad love life aside, she focused on her surroundings. Gray-striped pelts lined a massive bed, cocooning her in warmth. A fire crackled in a stone hearth, reflecting light in a round room. Leaning forward and twisting her head around, she saw the only entrance was an arched wooden door right next to her bed. The entire room looked like something out of a medieval holostory, except the walls were smooth and curved with laser precision. She squeezed her eyes shut, trying to blink away the remnants of her dream. Where was she now? Pinching herself hard, she winced. Definitely awake. Well, this was a far better scenario than the last time she'd been conscious, where she'd dropped into hypothermia. At least she was warm and sheltered. Lethargy weighted her limbs. She must have been given painkillers of some sort, because her feet ached a little, but not as much as they should. When she tried wiggling her toes, she found they were too swollen to move. Tugging the huge pelt up, she saw that someone had wrapped them in neat bandages.

The sweet, high-pitched sound of a child's giggle pierced the quiet as a little head poked up from the foot of her bed. Maybe six years old, the girl was paler than a moonbeam, her dark gaze dancing with merry laughter.

"You're awake." An odd accent spiced the child's voice, but she was speaking Earthan Standard. Curiouser and curiouser.

She decided to gather as much information as she could from the only human she'd seen since she landed on this planet. "Hello. Where am I?"

"Sea Den."

"Seaden?" She raked her memory for a city called Seaden. Nothing came to her.

"What's your name?"

"I'm Miki. Who are you?"

"Miki, that's a pretty name. My name is Jain Roberts."

"My brother's name is Nukilik."

"And how old is Nukilik?"

"We're both seven."

"Seven! That's very grown up."

Miki nodded, sending her cloud of hair flying. Her smile showed an adorable gap in her front teeth.

Jain found herself smiling back. "And what about your parents? What are their names?"

"Mama's dead. And Papa's name is—"

"Lord Kesuk." A sub-bass voice boomed from the door. "That's enough, Miki. You know you're not supposed to be in here. Go find your nurse."

Miki's little face scrunched up in consternation. "I forgot, Papa."

"We'll discuss that later. Go on." Disapproval laced his deep tone.

Miki scurried away, pausing at the door to give Jain a jaunty little wave good-bye.

Jain tucked the furs under her armpits and attempted to sit up, not wanting to meet the man flat on her back. After a few moments, she admitted defeat. She didn't have the strength to rise. The bed dipped and a large hand settled between her shoulder blades, supporting her with ease, while another hand brought a cup of steaming liquid to her mouth. Her stomach growled, distracting her as she realized she was starving. She cupped her hands around the mug he offered and sipped at the hot liquid.

"Oooh, that's good." It tasted like some kind of spicy chicken stew. She turned to thank Miki's father and came nose to nose with the man from her dream. *Her very explicit dream.* Her heart skipped a beat before racing ahead at a gallop when she realized he was naked to the waist. He wore gray leather pants and laced moccasins, but his chest was bare and as smooth as she'd imagined. His hair was damp, but she'd bet when it dried it was the same silver-blond she recalled. Her mouth felt suddenly dry; she drank more of the broth to stall a moment so she could collect herself before speaking. "Th-thank you."

"You are welcome." His gaze dropped to her lips as he spoke, his hand burning against the bare skin of her back.

She flushed under his scrutiny, smoothing her hand across the pelts, fully aware that she was naked. "What is this place?"

His eyes narrowed, assessing her. "You are not addled."

"Well, I may have hit my head in the crash, but I think I'm all right now." Had he just insinuated that she was stupid? Not knowing where she was made her geographically challenged, damn it, not moronic. It wasn't as though she'd crashed the spaceship. She was just a passenger, not the damn pilot. Who the hell was he to call her stupid? So, fine, he was huge and intimidating and gorgeous, but that didn't make him some kind of super genius. She really didn't need to deal with some rude jackass today. Things were already bad enough without any help from him. She squelched her anger as she always did, pulling back from feeling too much. She pasted on a bright smile. "Were you the one who rescued me?"

"I did." Rising, he folded massive arms, triceps standing out in relief. He shifted, raised an eyebrow, and seemed to be waiting for something.

"Um . . . thank you?" She gritted her teeth over the sentence, hating even the slightest admission that she was incapable. She hated that she'd needed saving at all. She could take care of herself when things went according to her meticulous plans.

He grunted. "What clan are you from, and how did you come to my land?"

"I don't understand."

"Don't toy with me, little bear." He stalked closer to the bed, looming over her.

She shrank back into the pillows. "I . . . I'm not from a *clan*. Am I in Scotland?" Relief sang through her. This explained everything. Her spacecraft had landed back on Earth. Someone could tell her why her ship had crashed and if anyone else had survived. Clans, indeed. "I was on my way to Aquatilis."

He snarled, his upper lip curling in disgust. "The fish people."

Assuming he must be one of the purists so adamant about not mixing human genes with animal, she sighed. This would be an ugly argument. She put on her best lecturing teacher face. "It's necessary for the survival of humanity to adapt to the conditions of other planets before the sun supernovas. Gene-splicing is the best way to make that happen."

Shock flashed across his face for a moment, followed by swift calculation. "You are Earthan?"

"Of course I'm Earthan. What else would I be?"

He leaned against the footboard, staring at her in complete disbelief. It was the most human expression she'd seen on his face since he'd walked in the door. "You left Earth before the sun died? That was a ship that exploded?"

"Yes, of course it—wait, what do you mean *before the sun died?* Scientists say it will be around for at least another hundred years." *What the hell was going on here?*

"No, our loremasters teach that the sun died too soon. All but the humans on the four experimental planets perished. That was nearly five hundred Turns ago." He watched her closely, waiting for her reaction, something akin to awe in his dark eyes.

Shock and doubt roared through her. Her ears buzzed, making her sway. "That isn't funny."

"It is not a jest, little bear."

"This is a joke. A horrible joke. It isn't funny! I don't know what kind of sick game you're playing, but I want my brother. Right now, do you hear me? *Right now.*"

He clamped his hands over her shoulders and shook her in short little jolts. Then he wrapped his fingers around her jaw, forcing her to meet his steady gaze. "Calm yourself."

"Five *hundred* years . . . no, that can't be. I'm supposed to meet my brother on Aquatilis. He works there. He . . . he's my only family. The only one I have left. Please . . . please, tell me it's a mistake." She tried to jerk from his grasp, but he was too strong. Hot tears flooded her eyes, and she choked to fight them back. She couldn't cry in front of this emotionless man who'd just ripped her whole life away with a single sentence.

He released her, stroking the skin along her jaw. "I'm not sure how it's possible, but it is true."

"It's not. I won't believe it." Irrational, unreasonable rage pounded through her, made her glare at him. She knew this wasn't his fault, but he was the only one here to blame. Everything was spinning out of control, and that couldn't happen. This was unacceptable.

A stoic sigh escaped his lips. He bent and gathered her furs tight around her and scooped her off the bed, lifting her as if she were a small child.

"What do you think you're doing? Don't touch me." She wriggled to get down.

"Be still," he snapped. "I'm hardly going to molest you. Invalids and simpletons do not arouse me."

"I am *not* a simpleton." She tugged her left arm free of the pelts and wrapped it around his neck.

"Then stop acting the part. We have a long way to walk, and you cannot travel the distance on your own."

She glowered at him but remained still. Where the hell was he taking her? Why couldn't he just *tell* her what was going on? She fisted her fingers in the furs. Anger simmered through her at one more thing slipping away from her control. She hated that he was right. She couldn't get far by herself, but she wouldn't give him the satisfaction of admitting it.

He chuckled. "Stubborn little bear."

"I'm not a bear. I'm full human."

With each of his strides, her left breast brushed against his chest. Though she wasn't cold, goose bumps shivered over her skin. The friction of each brush of her naked shoulder against his smooth chest seemed exaggerated. Excitement twisted through her, heating her blood until her heart pounded. Her nipples peaked and she was grateful for the camouflage of the thick furs. She tried to control her breathing, but his scent filtered in with every breath. She fought the urge to bury her nose against his neck and breathe deeply. Yeah, that would go over well. Actually, it might and that in itself could be a problem. He rolled his shoulder, and her arm slid across his skin. Oh, God. Just that small movement was enough to make her hyperaware of every inch of her body pressed against his hard muscles.

"Never think for a moment that I don't remember you are unique. You are nothing like my people."

Whispering erupted up and down the cave corridor as they walked through an intricate system of tunnels until she had no idea how far they'd gone. Pale-featured people with dark eyes stared at her from wide rooms and stone hallways. She shrank into Kesuk's chest, avoiding eye contact, feeling their gazes on her as they passed. Shafts of light pierced the gloom from small openings overhead no wider than her fist. Glass capped the holes and made the light reflect and spread.

A bend in the corridor showed an opening so narrow Kesuk had to turn sideways to get through it. The cold slammed into her like a wall of ice once they cleared the protection of the cave. She quickly pulled her arm back inside the pelts, snuggling up against him for warmth. How did he manage to go shirtless? He didn't even seem to notice the frigid wind buffeting them. A guard stood on either side of the entrance. They nodded to Kesuk but stared at her until he grunted at them; then they snapped to attention and resumed scanning the landscape.

"What are they looking for?"

"Predators and enemies." They crested a rise, and Kesuk spun them in a slow circle. "Look around you."

"Predators?" she squeaked. "What kind of predators?" This place got *worse*? She swiveled her head around, trying to see anything dangerous. Jagged mountain peaks covered in snow and a type of tree she'd never seen before soared toward the brilliant blue sky. These trees weren't firs or spruce or any other kind of evergreen she knew of, but they were a rich leafy green against the pure white snow. How was that even possible? It looked like something from an Amazonian rainforest. In the middle of Antarctica.

Nothing but a light breeze seemed to be moving, so she started to relax. They were safe. Then Kesuk's whole body tensed, and his nostrils flared as he raised his nose to sniff the air. A quick glance back at the guards had them standing at alert on either side of Kesuk, spears in their hands.

"What's happening?" She turned back to look at Kesuk.

"An enemy."

"Who—"

"Shh."

She scanned the tree line in vain, searching for the enemy he spoke of. Straining her eyes, she still couldn't see anything but trees, rocks, and snow. Unease fluttered in her belly.

Suddenly, a large black figure broke through the underbrush. "It's a black bear!" she cried.

"Yes, it's a Black." Kesuk's lips pulled back in a small snarl.

"Is it dangerous?" She flicked her gaze between Kesuk and the enormous bear lumbering toward them through the thick snowbanks.

When the bear reared up on its hind legs and roared, she squeaked and tried to climb Kesuk. Her arm slid back around his neck in a stranglehold.

"Easy, little bear," he soothed, his gaze never leaving the bear.

A horrific sucking noise sounded as the bear seemed to shrink, his bones snapping and retracting, the hair disappearing from his legs until a huge, dark-skinned man stood before them. *A very nude man.* She choked, still squeezing the life out of Kesuk, unable to believe what she'd just seen. A shapeshifting bear! There were only supposed to be fish-shifters on Aquatilis. No experiments had been conducted with large predators.

The stranger's black eyes gleamed with avarice as they swept over her, lingering on her bare arm and the upper curve of her breast. She retracted her limb into the pelts, trying to cover as much skin as possible. This man was dangerous, that much she knew, and Kesuk didn't seem to like him. He swaggered forward, his gaze never leaving her.

"That's far enough. What news from Meadow Den?" Kesuk's deep growl sounded even lower than usual.

"So the rumor is true, then? A *real* human."

"She crashed on *my* land."

"Does she have a name?"

"*Mine.*" Kesuk's voice was flat and brooked no argument.

The dark man grinned, his teeth flashing in an ugly yellow line as he took another step forward. His penis twitched and rose into a huge erection as he leered at her. "I'd offer an exchange. Three of yours for her."

An exchange? The man was trying to *buy* her? Three of Kesuk's what? What did they barter with here? Oh, God, he wouldn't give her to the disgusting man, would he? Her stomach executed a slow pitch and roll. After all, what did she know about her rescuer? Feeling light-headed, she started to gag a little, horrified by what the black bear might do to her. Rape at the very least. After he was done with her, would he pass her off to his men? She swallowed hard. If he had even half as many followers as she'd seen in the caves—she cut herself off, ruthlessly suppressing her panic. She couldn't even let herself think it.

Kesuk's arms tightened around her, and she turned to his shoulder, pressing her forehead against his collarbone, struggling to pull air into her dry throat. She was going to vomit; she just knew it.

"She is not for barter." Kesuk growled low, his chest vibrating with the sound. She looked up in time to see enormous fangs begin to slide out of his mouth. Kesuk was a bear, too? Realization hit her right between the eyes.

He was the polar bear in her dream.

Whipping her head around, she saw that the bear had come even closer. She froze, refusing to cower because she had nowhere to go.

"Five of your people for the little tasty."

An inhuman roar exploded from Kesuk, his fangs fully emerging, long, curved, and deadly. Clenching her teeth, she fisted her hands in the pelts to keep from screaming.

"Get off my land, Black. I have no more use for you."

Kesuk's guards raised their spears and began circling the man. He snorted at them but backed away, folding over onto all fours and shifting into his bear form as he ran. She shivered at the sickening noise the change made.

After the black bear left, Kesuk shifted her in his arms. "Believe me now, Jain Roberts? Is this the planet you knew? Is this the water world you intended to land on? Are we the advanced people you lived among all your life?" His questions hammered at her disbelief. She'd used his physical presence as a distraction before, but *this* . . . this she couldn't deny. This wasn't Earth. This wasn't Aquatilis, and she'd seen nothing so far to indicate the type of technology she was used to. And the black bear she'd just witnessed change shouldn't even exist. At least not yet, not in her time.

"Take me back to my room," she whispered, squeezing her eyes shut to block out the bright snowy-white day, so at odds with the black empty void yawning inside of her.

She held herself together during the interminable walk back to her round chamber, focusing on *not* thinking about what had happened to everyone she knew. How terrified they all must have been when the sun supernovaed too soon, the horrible deaths they'd faced. Kesuk deposited her in the wide bed, tucking the soft pelts around her. Everything that had happened since the crash hit her in one relentless wave after another. She couldn't take it all in, and the truth overwhelmed her. She twisted away from him. Jesus, she hated losing control in front of people. Burying her face in the furs, she tried to stifle the sobs she couldn't stop.

"I'm sorry." His hand cupped the back of her head, stroking her hair gently.

"Please, leave me alone for a while."

"I will return soon. We have much to discuss."

He moved away from the bed, leaving her cold and bereft. She didn't know what to do, what to think. Never intending to return to Earth, she'd left everything behind to join her brother on the Aquatilis colony. Pressure built in her chest, choking her. Tears leaked from her eyes, and she let herself sob into the blankets. Her brother, her only family, gone. All the people on board her ship, including her brother's colleague Sera Gibbons. She hadn't known any of them well, but they would have at least been with her now. And Sera, well, they might have become friends. A million possibilities spun away into nothingness. Everything and everyone she knew was dead, killed by nature and time. She was five hundred years from where she started. Loss and grief tore at her. She could cry forever and never be rid of it.

"Imnek." Kesuk nodded a greeting to the guard outside Jain's door as he passed, his stride eating the distance between him and the mouth of Sea Den.

The woman was a distraction he didn't need right now. Or ever. She attracted him too much. He'd come close to ripping the Black's throat out for daring to want her. She belonged to *him,* and no Black was going to take her from him. He shook his head. No. No, she was only here temporarily, so he couldn't get attached to her. She couldn't matter enough to make him lose control. He had his people to care for and protect. Losing control in front of an enemy was not a luxury he could afford.

He was master of himself and everything within Sea Den. She'd know that soon enough. She was a temporary distraction.

Nothing more. A feral grin pulled at his lips. Perhaps she could serve as a very pleasurable temporary distraction. When she recovered her strength, he could think of many things to do with that pretty little body of hers. He had to keep in mind that she would only be here until he could hand the last Earthan over to the next trading vessel.

A *real* Earthan. Unaltered, unable to morph between human and animal form. Such a thing was unheard of on any of the four inhabited planets. Humans were extinct. He shook his head in astonishment, struggling to bend his mind around the explanation. Earth itself had faded almost into myth among his people. It wasn't until the weretigers' spaceship landed three Turns ago that they'd known settlements on other planets still existed. In fact, the weretiger king, Amir Varad, was scheduled to return before Thaw to exchange trade goods on his way to Aquatilis. That was only three weeks away. He respected Varad; perhaps the weretiger could offer some insight on how the woman could have been floating in space for centuries and be perfectly functioning after a crash landing.

A million questions raced through his mind as he calculated possibilities and probabilities. What had happened to make her ship go off course? Why had they never made it to Aquatilis? What was the likelihood that she'd land on the *one* planet in this solar system besides the fish world able to sustain life?

"Papa!"

Miki's small voice echoed along the corridor as she scurried after him, unable to keep up with his longer stride. An Arctic bear cub, Nukilik, trotted alongside her. Affection and pride squeezed his heart when he saw them. Miki puffed up beside him and collapsed against his legs with dramatic exhaustion.

Kesuk grinned down at her. "Yes?"

"Are you going sea swimming? Can we come? Please, Papa?" Miki's dark eyes widened, and she folded her hands together to plead with him. Nukilik nodded in agreement, bumping his shoulder up against Kesuk's other leg.

Please, Papa?

The cub's shaky telepathy was improving daily. Another fierce wave of pride hit Kesuk's chest, followed by an endless need to protect his young against all threats. He would not lose them to predators as he had lost their mother. Lingering pain echoed in his heart at the thought of Maruska. Their daughter looked so much like her. She would have loved to see their cubs grow.

"You can come, but stay near me at all times. Nukilik, go get four more guards to accompany us while Miki and I change."

Yes, my lord. The cub gave an exaggerated bow of his long neck before scurrying off.

"Scamp."

"Ready, Papa?" Miki tugged on his boot lacings.

He scooped her up and flipped her into the air, catching her over his shoulder while she squealed in delight. "Ready."

He set her down and watched while she changed into Arctic bear form, her little body stooping onto all fours, pulling in as white fur spread down her arms and legs. Her nose turned black and elongated into a snouted point. She bowed her head, her neck stretching in to the long slim line characteristic of his species. Tiny curved ears popped from the top of her widened skull. Though he'd done it himself countless times, the sound of changing forms had always bothered him, the strange suction and snapping pop of bone and cartilage as the body reformed made his skin crawl.

She shook from head to claws, wagging her tuft of a tail so vigorously it shook her whole back end. Tumbling forward in a wild display of acrobatics, she landed with a splay-legged thump in front of him. He ruffled the fur on her head.

Let's go, Papa! Hurry, hurry.

"All right, youngling. Patience." In a moment, he'd assumed his own bear form, flexing his claws against the cave floor. His cub pranced on her paws ahead of him down the corridor, turning back to watch his progress every few steps, her black eyes shining with excitement. At the last fork in the tunnel to the sea entrance, they met with Nukilik and the four requested guards, two in human form and two in bear.

"My lord." The soldiers dipped their heads in salute.

He swung in next to the front guard, who glanced sideways several times before speaking.

Amir Varad comes soon.

Kesuk grunted. *The weretigers will land before Thaw, yes. The human would make an excellent bargaining chip.*

Kesuk's hackles rose, and he had to rein himself in from snapping at the other bear. What was *wrong* with him today? The soldier was right, was he not? Isn't that what he should use her for? He'd saved her. She couldn't stay here. The weretigers would want her and would pay a great sum to have her. He snarled even thinking of it, stalking down the twisting tunnels until he reached the icy wading pool that opened out into the frozen ocean.

Several hunters passed them on their way in to the warm fires of the upper caverns, their fishing lines full of the day's catch. Miki plunged into the pool with her usual reckless enthusiasm while Nukilik preferred to wade in and test the water first. He'd worried for them since Maruska had died, but they'd adjusted well during the last two Turns. He was the one who'd struggled to move on. An unmated leader was looked upon unfavorably, a sign of instability in the clan.

A tilt of his muzzle signaled the two guards in human form to keep watch at the sea entrance while the two in bear form scouted out into the open water, wary of orcas. Shaking away his concerns, Kesuk slid in after his cubs, making sure they stayed above water, enjoying the rare time he had to devote to them.

Before he could stop himself, he wondered how the woman was faring. He licked his lips, anticipation building in his gut as he thought of seeing her again. The slim lines of her pale body were burned into his mind, and he wanted to stroke his hands over her, burying his cock inside of her again and again until they were both spent. He sighed. Unfortunately, there were a few things she needed to know before they could begin to explore the attraction between them. He doubted she would take it well when he explained the new position she had found for herself by crashing on his land.

3

"I'm sorry I lost it earlier." Jain blurted out an apology to Kesuk as soon as he made it through the doorway, her cheeks flushing hotly. She had blubbered all over the man, and he hadn't even turned a hair, just tucked her in like a child. She was furious with herself for the lapse.

"What did you lose?"

Did she have to spell it out for him? Her face heated further. "I'm sorry I cried in front of you."

He raised a brow. "Are you sorry you cried or just that you cried in front of me?"

"Both." She glanced away, not meeting his eyes. "I'm just sorry. Can we talk about something else?"

"If you wish."

"What was that man going to trade me for? Five of something?"

"Five of my people they've taken as slaves."

"Slaves! That's awful. Barbaric."

He growled, his eyes narrowing. "Beware of passing judgment, little bear. Slavery is common practice here for those captured in raids or battles."

"You have slaves?" Something in his face made her swallow hard. Damn. She'd just insulted the big, scary man who'd saved her bacon and kept her from black bear rapists.

He returned a tight smile. "We need to discuss what to do with you now. I saved you, so your life is now mine, according to the customs of the Bear Clans."

Her eyes popped wide in shock. He thought he *owned* her? She bristled. No one, but *no one,* controlled her. "I don't live by those laws."

"You do now."

"So you saved me and I have to serve you forever?"

He shook his head. "No, slavery is not permanent. You work until your debt to me is paid."

"And who decides when my debt is paid?"

"I do."

She scoffed. "Oh, that's fair."

A deep growl rumbled up from his chest. His eyes flashed as he leaned close, getting right into her face, their noses almost touching. "You are not of the Bear, so I will forgive that insult. Once. Do not make the mistake again, and do not *ever* question my honor. You will be released when your debt is paid."

She bobbed her head in a nod, fear and adrenaline making her heart race. The man was enormous and he had fangs. He could kill her with both hands behind his back. She licked her parched lips and cleared her throat. "And where will I go then? As you said, I'm not a Bear; I have no clan to return to. From what I've experienced so far, I doubt I would survive on this planet without protection."

"There are far greater dangers than rival clans and the cold. We will negotiate your position here when the time comes, little bear. Rest now."

"Wait. Please. How will I work off my debt? I can't cook or sew or do anything domestic. We had machines to do that for us in my time. I taught history to children on Earth." She struggled upward again, and the furs slipped down, baring her breasts. Squeaking, she hauled the covers back up while he watched, his gaze lingering on the edge of the pelt. A hot blush flooded her cheeks again, but she set her jaw and ignored her embarrassment. After the incident with the black bear, she wasn't taking any chances. "I assume the work won't include *servicing* any of the men on this planet."

A dimple tucked into his cheek as his white teeth flashed. "That isn't work, little bear. That's pure pleasure."

Her mouth opened and closed, but no sound came out. Her mind replayed the dream she'd had of them together. Pleasure didn't even begin to describe it. She couldn't help but wonder if he was as good in real life as she imagined. Squeezing her legs together, she tried to quell the sudden ache between them. She'd just met him; how could he do this to her?

"Perhaps you need a demonstration."

His gaze heated and he leaned toward her, his lips touching hers. She caressed his jaw as her mouth moved under his. His hands caught hers, forcing them behind her back, holding them so she couldn't move. He tilted his head to deepen the kiss, sliding his tongue along her bottom lip.

"Open for me."

Obeying, she stroked his tongue with her own. Goose bumps erupted over her flesh, and her heart rate kicked into warp speed. Her skin felt too hot and too tight. Wetness flooded her sex, made her moan and press closer to him. She tugged at her arms, wanting to touch him, but he shifted her wrists into one big hand, using the other to thrust the furs down. His fingertips closed over her breast, his rough skin abrading her nipple.

"Oh, God." Her breath rushed in and out; she couldn't suck

in enough oxygen to satisfy her lungs. She arched into his caress, pushing her breasts forward.

Nothing had ever felt this good. His steely hold almost made it better for her. *Sexier.* It was wrong to be so turned on by this, but she couldn't remember why just now. A low rumble sounded in his throat as he swooped down to capture her nipple in his teeth, worrying the peaked flesh. He flicked his tongue over the tip, exciting her further, making her cry out.

A light knock sounded on the door. "Lord Kesuk."

Kesuk jerked back, panting hard as he stood and tugged the cover up over her chest. He stalked to the door and flung it open to glare at the intruder. "Imnek."

A gangly young man stood beyond the threshold, his gaze darting from Kesuk's glower to Jain's flushed face and back again. Shifting nervously under Kesuk's glare, he cleared his throat.

"Speak, boy," Kesuk demanded.

Snapping his gaze away from Jain, Imnek focused on the hulking man in front of him. "M-my lord. The weretigers have landed and will visit High Den before traveling to Sea Den."

"Hmph. Leave us." Kesuk shut the door in the boy's face.

Jain cleared her throat, struggling to come to grips with what just happened. No man had ever made her want so much, so quickly. Not even her husband. Just thinking about Kesuk made her body throb; having him near pushed her past anything she'd ever experienced. All the feelings rushing through her scared her to death. Feelings weren't logical, weren't controllable. She needed to step back and *think,* and she couldn't do that with him touching her and confusing her. When he swung to face her, his gaze hard with lust, she grasped at the first thing she could think of to distract him. "Um . . . weretigers?"

"Yes."

"They landed? They have a spaceship?"

Hope fluttered in her chest. There was technology some-where. Not everywhere was like this, where they had slaves and bartered with human lives and kissed people without ask-ing. She pressed her tingling lips together. The man had actually held her down to kiss her! Her sex clenched at the mere thought of what he'd done. She shook herself. She was not excited about some backwoods barbarian sticking his tongue down her throat. She *was not.*

"Yes."

"And . . . ?" Could she have another word please? She wanted to know about the other wereanimals. Was he allowed to tell her more? Did he even know? Maybe the weretigers were better. Maybe she could go with them.

"And they will trade with the Browns before they come here."

"Browns? Not the Blacks?"

"No. Meadow Den is too remote; they will meet with the Blacks in the borderlands."

"I see." Only she didn't see. Browns? Borderlands? "So, where do the weretigers live?"

"Vesperi."

"Is that a planet? Or is it a country on a planet?"

"A planet in a neighboring solar system."

"Are there any other people in *this* solar system?"

"Aquatilis."

Realization slapped her straight in the face. Oh, shit. She knew what planet she was on now. Icy dread slid down her spine. Only one other planet in Aquatilis's solar system could support human life, and she didn't even want to remember the stories about what happened to the humans who settled there—*here.* She shuddered, her stomach roiling because she had to ask and she really didn't want to. This should not have happened. She should be safe on Aquatilis five hundred years ago. Licking her lips, she forced the question out. "This . . . this is Alysius, isn't it?"

Please say no. Please say no. Please say no. For once, she actually wanted to be dead wrong.

"Yes."

Again with the one-word answers. She wanted to shake him. "Yes?"

His eyebrow hiked up. "Yes, this is Sea Den on Alysius. Home of the Arctic Bear Clan. I am Lord Kesuk, leader of the clan. Are there any more questions?"

She shook her head, mute. Entire settlements had been wiped out on this planet, the first ever to be colonized. Large animals had attacked and killed the unprepared settlers. When they'd founded the colony on Aquatilis, they'd abandoned the failed attempt on Alysius until they could develop a way to eradicate the animals without damaging the planet's ecosystem. Colonization had still been in its infancy when she left Earth. "In my time, scientists said adapting to Aquatilis and becoming merpeople would prove easier for humans than staying on this planet."

He sucked his teeth at the mention of merpeople. "It takes a predator to kill a predator. The first bear-shifters settled here just before the sun failed. We had to learn to survive with the means at our disposal. Or die with those who came before us."

"My brother said—"

"You journeyed to Aquatilis to join him, yes? What of the rest of your family?" He switched topics, turning the focus on her. She hated that. She didn't like to talk about herself or her past. Especially not her family.

"They were dead. After my divorce—"

He interrupted again. "What is *dee*-vorce?"

"My husband and I—"

"You are *mated*?" His eyes narrowed, his shoulders tensing.

A frisson of panic slipped up her spine, sweat breaking out on her forehead. It was the same look he'd worn before he mentioned his precious honor. What had she said? She raked her mind for what she might have done to piss him off now. "Divorce is when you get *un*mated."

"There is no unmating. Mating is for life."

She threw her hands up. "Fine, then. I'm a widow. He's been dead half a millennium. Oh, *darn.* Happy now?"

He growled but made no further response.

"Anyway. My husband and I divorced, and I was at loose ends, so I decided to stay with the one family member I had left. Aquatilis colony was looking for teachers for the growing merchildren, and I hoped my brother and I would become closer if I moved near."

Now, why had she said that? He didn't need to know that "distant" was a good way to describe her relationship with her family. She'd been the misfit non-genius in her logical, rational, scientific family. She sighed, her mood darkening. Any opportunity she had to try developing a relationship with her brother was gone now, and she ached for the loss. Her eyes smarted, but she resolutely pushed the tears away. There was nothing she could do about it. She shouldn't cry over something that never was.

"Your marriage was unhappy?"

"To put it mildly."

"He beat you?" Kesuk's fangs popped out, his face reddening.

"No!"

He relaxed a little, fangs retracting.

How could she say this in a nice way? "He just didn't want me."

"Fool. Who would not want you?" He snorted.

There was a loaded question. "Um. Well, he wanted other women."

And there came the fangs again. "He was unfaithful to you, *his mate?* Did the man have *no* honor?"

"Look, buddy. Honor wasn't a big deal back then. Neither was infidelity, really. I just got tired of dealing with it, so I bitched at him and he left me for his girlfriend. We divorced. End of story." And end of discussion. She didn't want to talk about this. Time to go back to her questions about Alysius.

His eyes lost focus for a moment, and his head cocked to the side as though he were listening to something. How powerful was a bear's hearing? She didn't know.

When his gaze sharpened and fixed on her, she shivered under his stare. If just a look did that to her, she didn't stand a chance if he touched her again. That terrified her. She controlled everything about her life, and he was not the kind of man to let her run things. That much she knew already. And he thought she was a *slave.* Nothing about him should turn her on. He was pushy, peremptory, and rude.

"I am needed elsewhere. I will return later."

She opened her mouth to ask another question, but he issued a sharp nod, then turned and left the room, leaving her mouth flapping over an outraged response.

"Well, I was just dismissed, huh?" She stuck her tongue out at the now-closed door.

Yep. Defintely rude, crude, and socially unacceptable. At least in her society. So why the hell had she stared at his tight ass in those leather pants while he walked away from her?

She sighed, wondering where he'd needed to go. Whether she liked it or not, she was bored and lonely without him.

4

Jain's eyes narrowed as she lay in that big bed of hers. Her pretty mouth tightened into a scowl of annoyance. Tension stiffened Kesuk's shoulders. He'd had enough to deal with in the two days since he'd seen her without coaxing her out of an ill humor. He considered her for a moment before deciding she needed a reminder of who was in charge here.

"Would you like to see more of your new home, slave?" He asked it just to tease her. He couldn't help himself. His little bear reacted so well. Remembering the indignant look on her face when he'd left to handle an altercation between two soldiers had made him laugh, and he resisted the smile that pulled at his lips now. Preparing for the weretigers' arrival had consumed his every waking moment the last few days, but he'd found himself thinking of her far too much. So, here he was, taking the first opportunity he had to come to her.

"Can I have some clothes first?" She shifted, tucking the covers tight to her chest.

"You have no clothes?"

She smacked a hand down on the fur pelts. "Nope. Completely naked here."

"Are you, now?" A slow grin spread over his face, and he let his gaze slide down the soft curves of her body outlined by the pelts.

His cock twitched as he recalled the first sight of her naked in the snow. It was all he could do not to slide his hand to his leathers to readjust the uncomfortable fit. Her breath caught as her eyes locked with his. She felt this, too; he knew it.

Blushing, she looked away and licked her lips. He cut off a groan. Surely she knew what that did to a man. He wanted that little pink tongue caressing his cock.

Her gaze flicked back to him. "Don't look at me like that."

"Like what?" He let his desire for her show, so there was no mistake, just to see how she'd respond. It was only a matter of time until he had her. It had been a very long time since any woman presented any challenge. For the duration of her stay here, she would be his.

"Like *that.*"

His grin widened, and he ran his tongue down his canine tooth.

"Like you want to undress me."

"You are already undressed."

"That's entirely beside the point."

He approached the bed and watched her breathing speed up as he neared. Her gaze flicked over him, cheeks flushed. Good, he made her nervous. An excellent place to start. As he reached out to touch her, her pupils expanded, staring at his hard dick straining the fastenings of his pants.

"If you wish me to stop looking at you as though I want you naked, then do not look as though you want me to undress you."

"I'm not." Her voice was breathless, her gaze riveted on his cock.

"Stop."

"What?" She looked up at him, naked hunger on her face.

"We go." He bent and scooped her up before he talked himself into burying himself between her legs and staying for a full Turn. She was well enough to suffer from boredom, but not well enough to walk. If she couldn't walk, she was too weak for the hard sex he had in mind. He schooled himself to patience, knowing he would have her slim legs wrapped around his waist soon enough. Or around his face. He banished that thought before he made it impossible to walk correctly.

Her small form fitted against his chest, her cheek on his shoulder, her short dark hair tickling his skin. The sweet smell of her filled his nose. He breathed in, enjoying the experience of being this close to her.

"Where are we going?" Her arm slid around his neck.

Eyes closed for a moment, he savored the feel of her fingers splayed across his shoulder, her other hand pressed to his chest, stroking over his nipple. His breath hissed out. She would drive him to madness. His cock rode the seam of his leathers as he walked out of her chamber and out into the main corridor.

"Is everyone here always naked?" Her wide green eyes followed the progress of a soldier who'd obviously just assumed his human form.

Kesuk growled to hurry the guard on his way, not liking the way his little bear stared at the other man.

Glancing down at her, he answered her question with a shrug. "Not always, but our clothing does not come with us when we shift."

She blushed, glancing into a side cave at an equally nude woman before turning away. "We had laws in my time about indecent exposure."

"Indecent? Nudity is a natural thing, little bear." He frowned. The advanced past had been so provincial?

"Ooooh." Her grip tightened around his neck when she

spied what lay beyond the end of the tunnel. He gritted his teeth as her breasts moved against his chest, nothing but the edge of a fur keeping her soft flesh from pressing against his.

Dripstone rose from the floor and spiked down from the ceiling, creating a circular stone paddock. Only his ancestors had been able to carve with such precision. They'd lost so much in the centuries since settlement. The little one in his arms brought that home to him more forcefully than anything had since the weretigers landed on Alysius.

"Stalactites and stalagmites. I saw them in the Carlsbad Caverns when I was a child. These are huge compared to those."

"Dripstone. It is created by dripping water." He jerked his chin to indicate the droplets of water falling from the tips of the stone.

"What is this place? And why are some of the areas laser cut and the rest natural?" Her wave encompassed the cavern and the dripstone.

"Whatever was expedient. This area needed to be large for the herds."

"Herds?"

They cleared the upper tunnel, and noise from the paddock rose to an overwhelming cacophony. From this position, they overlooked the wide valley of stone separated into paddocks by carved barriers. Loud bawling of cattle and sheep in large grassy fields echoed around them. Sunlight streamed through thousands of covered light shafts in the cavern roof. Men and women roamed the herds, checking the health of young calves, rounding up the sheep for shearing.

Jain leaned forward as he backed away from the precipice, trying to look at everything at once. A sweet smile spread over her lips when she got a better view of the herdsmen. When she stopped trying to keep a stranglehold on every detail, she let herself enjoy life. He could help her in that area. She might even thank him.

"Where are we going next?"

She turned that wondrous smile on him, and he almost missed a step. The woman was beautiful. All the women on this planet had dark eyes and were tall with sleek muscular bodies. Not Jain. Perhaps it was her childlike size that made him feel protective. Even that excuse sounded flimsy to him, because he'd never thought of her as a child. Since the moment he'd seen her, he'd wanted her, and he always got what he wanted.

"We go to sup in the main cavern."

He wound his way through the twisting tunnels with an ease born of long practice, the smells of cooking food calling to him.

She sighed. "I'll never find my way back."

He grinned. "Reach into my back pocket."

Her eyes widened, snapping up to his face. "What?"

"My back pocket, little bear. The left one."

Her hand slipped from his shoulder down his back, smoothed over his bare skin, bumped the top of his leathers before curling into his pocket. His breath hissed out as her fingers moved over his ass, rubbing against him as she searched the pocket.

Keeping his tone innocent, he shrugged. "Oh, did I say left? I meant right. Try the other pocket."

"You did that on purpose!" She slapped his chest.

"Perhaps. The right pocket, little bear. Go on." Teasing her meant teasing himself, and he wanted to take her against the tunnel wall. Right now. He usually had more control than this when dealing with women. Frowning, he shook himself. He was no randy boy intent on mating with anything that moved.

Dipping her hand down, she tugged a folded sheet of parchment from his leathers. She smoothed it out against his shoulder. "It's a map."

"Yes."

Her smile was back and was the first thing his people saw as they walked into the wide cavern. All noise fizzled to a slow stop. She tensed, going rigid in his arms when she noticed they were the center of attention. She looked up at him in distress.

"Shh, little bear. They are simply curious about you. It will fade the more you are around them."

Her lips tightened and she said nothing, her chin jerking down in a small nod. She tugged up the furs self-consciously. He hadn't the heart to tell her they'd all seen her naked the day he brought her in from the snow. It had taken many people many hours to get her warm again, to save her fingers and toes from frostbite.

"Jain!" Miki waved from the head table, bouncing in her chair, a huge smile splitting her face. Her nurse saved her cup from tipping over as Miki's waving got a bit too enthusiastic.

Jain smiled back at Kesuk's daughter and returned a small wiggle of her fingers.

"Where is Nukilik?" Kesuk directed his question at the nurse as he settled Jain into the chair to the left of his.

"He decided to break his fast with the guards in the lower caverns."

"Ah." He smiled, remembering that he had done the same as a boy, eager to learn the ways of warriors.

"Have you met Nukilik?" The nurse turned a kind smile on Jain, and Kesuk blessed her for her open warmth. He had chosen well when he made her caretaker for his cubs.

"I've only met Miki and Kesuk. Oh, and my guard, Imnek, when I tried to leave my room." Jain turned an accusing glare on Kesuk.

"It was for your own protection."

"Sure it was, but then I am a *slave* here, aren't I?" Anger made Jain's brilliant green eyes almost incandescent.

He leaned close to speak in her ear. "Yes, and as such, you are under my protection. The caves can be dangerous, little bear. Your insistence on independence does not erase the need for caution."

She wrinkled her pert nose at him and turned away to speak to Miki's nurse.

He chuckled, sorry he'd missed young Imnek trying to keep her in her room as he'd ordered. As he had said, it was for her own protection. She wasn't yet well, and even with his map, she could easily become lost in the caverns. Some of the caves were no longer in use, and it would take a while to track her, especially if she fell and hurt herself. Refocusing on the women at his table, he caught a lively conversation about Earthan versus Bear Clan politics.

"It's too much." Jain folded her arms and glared at the stubborn man across from her. As usual, Kesuk remained cool and collected. It made her want to kick him. Why couldn't she ever hold on to her calm when he was around? He'd invited himself into her room again, and Imnek had just let him in. This was why messing with the boss was never a good plan; they did whatever they wanted and didn't ask for permission.

"What is?"

"What? This! All this." Her hands flapped to encompass the room, which was now overburdened with more clothes than she could ever wear.

Kesuk shrugged. "You said you needed clothing."

"I just wanted an outfit."

"You have been outfitted."

She sighed, knowing she wouldn't win this one. Settling back into the padding of her large chair, she toyed with the cord that belted her leather pants. Kesuk leaned back into the cushions of the matching chair that sat opposite hers. A crackling fire lit the handsome planes of his face. "Thank you. It's more than I need."

"If you need anything else, ask in the kitchens and they will give you whatever you require."

"I'm used to providing for myself. Working for what I

have." She shifted under his stare. Why had she even admitted that?

"You are not yet well enough to work. Give yourself some time. You nearly died, little bear. You look lovely in that."

Pleasure warmed her, and she brought herself up short. His approval shouldn't matter this much to her. She shouldn't care about this man. He was dangerous to her peace of mind, her hard-won calm. When the weretigers came, she was leaving. She needed to remember that. She shrugged, brushing a negligent hand down her bottle-green wool tunic. It matched her eyes. "Thanks."

He casually waved in a serving woman who brought a tray of food. The woman smiled at Jain and she grinned back. Her name was . . . Bel? "Thank you for bringing me dinner."

"Supper," Bel corrected gently. "We call it supper here."

"Supper." Jain nodded in acknowledgment. She noticed the tray Bel set down held more food than she could eat in a week. She raised her eyebrow, meeting Kesuk's gaze as Bel left the room. "Inviting yourself to dinner?"

He lounged in his chair, handing her a mug of mulled ale, serving up plates for both of them. "You don't really want to dine alone."

She didn't, but it irritated her that he said it. "You know me so well."

"I wish to."

Something about the position of his body or the hot, hard expression on his face made her recall her dream. "Kesuk, the day we met . . ."

"Yes?"

Hot blood singed her cheeks, and she knew her face had gone bright red. Smooth, Jain. Very smooth. "Did we . . . did you . . . what exactly happened after you found me?"

"You don't remember, Jain?" A wicked grin spread over his face, belying the innocent tone.

A shiver slid up her spine at the sound of her name on his lips. "I was naked—"

"Indeed." The grin grew wider, his eyes twinkling at her.

"—and freezing to death. I don't remember much of anything." Unless the dream was real, and then she remembered too much.

His tongue slid down a canine tooth, a sign that she already knew meant he intended to tease her. Here it came.

"It was such a deeply moving experience for both of us, little bear. I'm crushed." Clapping his hands over his heart, he actually batted his eyes at her.

"Oh, brother." She rolled her eyes.

"I'm *not* your brother."

No kidding. As if she'd have those kind of fantasies about her brother. "I just . . . tell me what happened. Please?"

He tilted his head and considered her for a moment, sipping from his mug. "My guards and I saw the explosion and came to investigate. I found you naked and freezing in the snow. When I changed, you fainted."

"You were in your bear form?"

"Yes."

"I saw you change?"

He shrugged. "I believe so. You were not coherent, little bear. A bit longer out there and you would have died."

So it had been a dream. *A very lusty dream.* She flushed, recalling how vivid the texture of his skin and hair had felt.

His gaze swept her face, and his voice became silky. "Why do you ask?"

She cleared her throat, blushing so hard her face tingled. "No reason."

"Come now, you don't expect me to believe that, do you?"

"I had a dream," she mumbled into her cup while she took a quick sip.

His eyes gleamed. "A sexy dream?"

"Maybe." She stared at her lap, not daring to look up.

"Tell me."

"I can't do that!"

"You can. Tell me, little bear. Did it make you moan?" His eyes locked with hers, heated, a little smile playing over his lips.

"Yes," she whispered.

"Was I inside you?"

Nodding, she squeezed her eyes tightly shut, as the fantasy played out in her mind. Her thighs clenched together as she tried to contain the wet heat building between them.

A small choking sound came from Kesuk, and she opened her eyes to find the fire in his gaze matched the flames in her body.

"Come here." His voice was low, demanding. Its rough edge slid over her skin like velvet.

She stood, her cup falling from her numb fingers. She walked to him as if it was the most natural thing in the world. No thought, nothing. Just reaction to this man, this moment. When she reached his chair, his hands rose to her waist. He pulled her into his lap, and her legs straddled his thighs. The muscles in his legs flexed, spreading her farther, pressing her against his straining erection. She gasped, rolling her hips to increase the contact. Sweet pleasure arced through her body. Nothing had ever felt this amazing. And he wasn't even inside her yet.

His lips touched hers, a gentle brush. She opened her mouth on his, darting her tongue out to slide over his lower lip. He tightened his grip on her waist, pulling her against his cock, grinding their pelvises together.

She moaned into his mouth, the sound waking her from her daze. She pulled back, panting. "Kesuk."

"I love my name on your lips, little bear."

"We shouldn't." Her fingers gripped the arms of his chair, her hips moving backward. "It's too soon. We just met. We have to be rational."

His hand stayed her motion, not letting her escape, but not forcing her closer, either. "Passion and reason don't often mix, Jain. And this is passion."

Taking her fingers, he guided them to his hard cock, cupping them to stroke his length. She closed her fingers around him, taking over the motion, fondling his dick through his leather pants.

He groaned, dropping his head back against the chair as he pressed himself into her caress. "Little bear, the things you do to me."

She wanted more, needed it. Throwing a lifetime of caution aside, she traced her hand over the lacings of his pants, using nimble fingers to untie them. His cock sprang free into her hand, the head glistening with pre-cum.

"Stroke me, little bear. I love your hands on me."

"You do?" Her gaze flicked to his handsome face.

"Oh, yes."

"Touch me, too."

"Where did I touch you in your fantasy, Jain?" His eyes were hard, glittering with unmasked lust.

Could she tell him? Maybe if she started small. "My hair."

"Like this?" His strong fingers slipped into her hair, massaging her scalp, sending tingles over her skin.

"Yes."

"Where else?"

"Everywhere," she whispered.

Sliding his hand down from her hair, he circled her nipple through her tunic. "Here?"

She froze at the sensation of his hand on her, hot pleasure storming through her. Nodding, she leaned forward, her nipples peaking into tight crests.

"Where else?"

Blood rushed to her face, her breath panting out. "B-between my legs." Just the thought of him touching her there made her thighs quiver.

"I like this dream." His other hand slipped low, cupping her sex, moving his hand against her tight leather pants.

"I do, too."

She caught her lower lip between her teeth and arched forward to meet his stroking, still fondling his cock. Her hand slid up the shaft and then curved over the head as she rotated her palm over the bulbous crest. She wanted to put her mouth on him, feel the slide of his long shaft between her lips as she sucked him. She licked her lips, staring at his cock; anticipation rolled through her in waves as his hands teased her pussy and nipple.

A soft growl sounded from his chest. "Keep looking at me like that and our night will be over far too quickly."

"I want to suck you." She looked him in the eye.

He groaned and laughed at the same time. "Little bear, you're killing me."

"Please."

"Later, I promise. Later."

She nodded, scraping a nail over the tiny opening of his cock. He pulled in a sharp breath, arching into her hand. He clamped his fingers around her wrist, removing himself from her grasp.

"Take your tunic off," he ordered.

Arms crossing over her body, she grasped the edges of her top and pulled it over her head in one swift motion, baring her small breasts to him. He dipped forward, catching a nipple in his mouth and sucking hard while his fingers tugged at the laces on her pants. She jerked back, standing to shove her pants off. She couldn't wait, didn't want to wait. Her pussy wept. She wanted that thick cock moving inside of her, wanted him more than she'd ever wanted any man in her life.

"Ah, Jain. Come here." While she stood, he jerked his shirt off, tearing his pants completely open.

Stepping forward, she swung her leg over his lap and mounted him in one smooth motion. He pulled her in, his hands guiding her hips forward until her wet vagina hovered directly over the head of his penis. Then he pushed down, forcing her to take all of him. She balanced her hands on his shoulders and sank down on him, feeling him embed so deep in her he touched her womb. God, he was big. She squirmed, just to enjoy the friction.

"You're so deep."

"Yes." He grunted, beginning to work her on his cock, lifting, lowering.

She squeezed her knees into his flanks, rising to ride him. Their plunging dance moved faster and faster, skin slapping together loudly.

It felt so good, so amazing, so *right* that for a moment it scared her. Her movements faltered as she tried to focus on something else, to not have this white-hot pleasure matter so much. He shouldn't be able to do this to her; she shouldn't *let* him do it to her. Staring at the chair behind his head, she concentrated on history lessons she used to teach her classes on Earth. Yes, now the pleasure was not so close, so deep. Now she could think.

He froze, pulling her tight against his pelvis, stilling their movements.

She blinked, focused on his eyes. "Why did you stop?"

"Why did you? One moment you were with me, the next you were gone."

A guilty blush washed into her cheeks. "Gone? You're still inside of me."

Cocking an eyebrow, he didn't bother to contradict her. "Do you want me to stop?"

Did she? Would it make it easier? "No," she whispered. "Don't stop."

"Kiss me."

Leaning forward, she pressed her lips to his, light caresses of warm flesh. His tongue swept out to lick her bottom lip before pressing into her mouth.

"Mmmm." She leaned closer until her breasts brushed his chest, rubbing her nipples back and forth over his skin. The feel of his flesh against hers was amazing, and she sank again into the intense visceral pleasure of his touch. His hands stroked up her back, tugged on her hair. She tilted her head back, and he nipped at her throat. Winding her fingers through his thick hair, she pressed him close.

Shoving her away, he knelt on the plush fur rug, lowering her and spreading her legs wide, a hand pressing each thigh to the floor. She flushed, her hands lifting to cover her exposed breasts.

"That's right, little bear. Fondle them for me."

"Kesuk . . ."

He smiled, his hot dark gaze sliding over her body, focusing between her legs. Bracing his forearms on either side of her hips, he lowered his shoulders between her spread thighs. His tongue parted the lips of her pussy, slipping over her labia before flicking her clit.

"Kesuk!" She fought to keep her fingers from burying themselves in his hair, from tugging him closer.

Do you know how good you taste, Jain?

She pressed her hand to her forehead, gasping as his voice echoed in her mind. "What? How?"

His tongue circled her clit with deliberate slowness before he drew it between his lips, suckling her wet flesh.

One of the many benefits your generation left behind. Don't you like it?

"Yes."

Play with your nipples for me. Show me what you like.

Panting, she relaxed her hands to cup her breasts, lifting

them high before letting them bounce back. She circled her finger-tips around the areolae, made them pucker into tight nubs.

This is a great deal of sweetness, little bear. Do you think it rational? Using that wicked tongue, he lapped at her juices, sucking her swollen lips between his teeth.

"Kesuk."

Perhaps if I made it easier for you, more controlled.

"What do you mean?" Her hips strained toward his mouth, pushing her toward orgasm, not caring what answer he gave. Her eyes squeezed closed. She was so close; any moment now she would—

He pulled back and her eyes popped open. "Hey . . ."

One hand reached for the slim cord that had belted her pants closed. He turned back to her, licking her cream from his lips with obvious relish. She blushed, glancing away. He clasped her wrists in his right hand and with a quick twist, tied the cord around them. "Hey!"

"Relax, little bear. You will enjoy this."

She jerked at her wrists as he tied the other end of the cord around the heavy leg of her chair. "I don't—"

"Have you not enjoyed everything else I have shown you?"

"Yes, but—"

Then you will love this. He maneuvered back between her thighs, his broad shoulders forcing her legs wide as he resumed the ministrations of his mouth and tongue on her hot flesh, sucking hard on her clit.

Her back bowed at the abrupt change in sensation, wrists pulling hard on the cord as she struggled to move against him. "Kesuk, I want—"

Shh . . . let go.

She whimpered, tugging at her hands. "I can't let go of any-thing. I'm tied up."

Her pussy flooded with more moisture from saying the words out loud. She shouldn't like this so much. Tears pressed against her lashes as her thighs burned and her sex pulsed with want.

You don't have to control anything, to be rational or reasonable. Just feel how good this is.

It *was* good. The panic from before reared up again, but she couldn't back away from it this time; she was bound. And free to do nothing but feel. Oh, God, it was so good, so hot. She twisted against the bindings, chafing her wrists, the heat building higher, hotter than ever. Spiraling down into intense need again, she couldn't fight it this time, didn't want to. She gave herself over to it. Tingles washed over her skin. *She felt.* She felt the softness of his hair brushing the insides of her thighs, the bite of his fingers into her flesh as he held her open for his mouth, the sharp nip of his teeth on her clitoris, the wetness of his tongue deep in her pussy. She screamed, jerking on the cord, needing this, *him,* right here, right now. Loving what he was doing to her, for her. It had never been this good before.

Yes, Jain. Let go for me.

He growled against her pussy, the vibrations making her sob. She was so close she could feel herself teetering on the edge of orgasm. "*Please,* Kesuk."

Lunging up, he braced his arms on either side of her torso, holding himself above her as he buried his huge cock into her quivering pussy. She wanted to rub her hands over the flexing muscles of his chest, feel the sinew shift under her fingers, but the bindings held fast when she pulled. His hard thrusts pushed her forward, the soft fur rug sliding against her back as they moved. The feel of the fur and his silky hot flesh pushed her closer, higher. She arched her back, rubbing herself against his chest and the rug.

"Kiss me," she demanded. Her hand met with the chair leg she was bound to, and she curled her fingers around the wood, the sharp carvings biting into her palms. The slight pain was just one more sensation piling on top of all the others.

He slanted his lips hard over hers, his kiss almost punishing. His dick worked inside her, shoving deep. Her body bowed under the building waves of pleasure washing through her. It felt so amazing, so hot. They were wild, biting at each other's lips. His fingers clenched hard around her thighs, jerking her farther open so she couldn't control the depth of his thrusts. The slapping sound of flesh on flesh turned her on. He manipulated her clit with his fingertips, flicking it in time with his pounding thrusts.

"Kesuk!"

It was more than enough to push her over into orgasm. Her pussy tightened on his cock as she came. Their eyes locked, and she gasped as the midnight irises of his eyes bled all the way to the corners, turning the entire orb coal black. His back bowed hard, hunching forward as he rammed into her, then froze. He threw his head back, his fangs sliding out as he roared his orgasm, his hips pounding forward in short jerking thrusts.

He collapsed onto his elbows, careful not to crush her. His forehead rested against hers as they panted hard. The *snap* and *pop* of the roaring fire sounded loud to her ears, and she noticed they'd crashed into the table, spilling their drinks onto the fur rug. That was a mess she didn't want to explain to Bel. Shoving himself up to balance on his hands, Kesuk pulled out from her pussy. The slide of his cock made her moan. Tugging her wrists free from the cord, he rubbed the circulation back into her fingers. His arms slipped beneath her shoulders, and he lifted her against his chest. Her head fell into the crook of his shoulder, and her eyes drifted shut. He dumped her on the bed, and she bounced, her eyes popping wide. Spinning away, he walked stark naked to her door.

She crossed her arms over her bare breasts. What the hell had happened? Hadn't he enjoyed it as much as her? He was leaving, so apparently not. Humiliation crawled over her skin. "Kesuk?"

She hated that her voice wobbled on his name. Just when she thought she had a handle on the situation, he did something to confuse the hell out of her again.

He paused, the open door in his hand.

"Is everything okay?"

Why was she even asking? She shouldn't care. She didn't even like him. Did she? No. Of course not. Then why had she slept with him? Everything was confusing and out of control again, so she hugged herself tighter and tried to pull back, shutting down the emotions, trying to remain calm and logical like her parents and husband had always insisted. Ten deep breaths and she'd forced herself back to cool composure.

"Everything is fine."

"Okay. Sure. Thanks for having dinner with me."

Dinner, right. They hadn't even eaten. She told herself it didn't hurt at all that he never looked back, shutting the door behind him with a final *thunk*. Crawling under the coverlet, she tugged it up to her chin, curled into a tight ball, and escaped into tear-stained sleep.

5

After leaving Jain, Kesuk plunged into the icy sea to cool his blood. He sucked in a breath as the freezing water met with his semi-erect penis. The water swirled around his chest as he walked deeper, hoping the frigid temperature would cool his ardor. He couldn't believe he'd lost control over the woman and almost shifted while still inside her. He hadn't lost control during sex since . . . ever.

What would have happened if he had changed inside of her? Such a thing was not practiced among his people. Jain was a tiny woman; hurting her would be too easy. A good lover, a good man, a good *leader* should be able to maintain control at all times. Tonight he had failed in that.

He still wanted her. The woman was addicting. Her smooth, soft skin and Sitka-green eyes drove him mad. Touching her had been a bad idea. He needed to stay away from her until the weretigers took her off his hands.

He rolled his shoulders, trying to work out the tension.

My lord?

Flaring his nostrils, he caught the scent of Jain's young guard as his large white bulk maneuvered down the tunnel and into the sea entrance. "Imnek."

My rotation is complete, my lord. You wished for my nightly report on the Earthan. The Arctic bear dipped his head in salute, not meeting his eyes. Imnek had been standing outside Jain's door all night; the young guard knew what had happened. Kesuk's respect for the boy increased that he would do his duty even though he'd have to deal with his lord's sour disposition.

He returned the nod. "Report."

She is bored and needs stimulus. We need to set her to a task.

"She tried to escape you, I've heard."

The bear shifted from paw to paw. *She . . . may have tried, but I handled the situation, my lord.*

"When I ask you to report on her activities, I expect a complete report. Am I understood?" Irritation whipped through him, and he knew he spoke unfairly to the boy, but his reaction to the human had him rattled. He attempted to rein in his ill humor without much success.

Yes, my lord.

"Is there anything else you'd like to tell me?"

A long pause ensued where the young guard obviously raked his mind for any small detail he'd missed. *She is beautiful, and all the clansmen stare at her.*

Kesuk growled, slapped the surface of the water, his jaw clenching. They would dare to ogle her?

Imnek hurried on. *I believe she is unaccustomed to and uncomfortable with male attention. Or nudity.*

Impressed with the boy's sense of observation, Kesuk found himself nodding in approval. "Well done. Report again tomorrow."

The young bear straightened, snapped a crisp nod, and turned in the direction from which he had come.

"But, Imnek? I expect to be apprised of *all* her movements."

Very good, my lord. Bowing again, Imnek left, his claws scraping against the stone floor as he went.

Digging his toes in the soft sandy bottom of the pool, Kesuk considered the situation. He couldn't let anyone else deal with her. She was his problem, and he wouldn't push her off onto anyone else. Especially any of his men. They might get ideas about sampling her sweetness, and he had to protect her.

Tonight was a mistake he wouldn't repeat. He simply had to maintain control and do his duty. Touching her again was not an option.

But now that he'd thrust inside her, not even the cold water could dull his lust for her slim body. His cock twitched in fevered memory and he groaned. This did not bode well.

"I can walk by myself." Jain's irritated voice echoed down the long corridor. Kesuk had insisted on continuing her tour of the caves, but she didn't have to be nice about it.

She hated being carried and not having any say about where she went or how fast she got there. After what had happened the last time she'd been helpless in his arms, she didn't want to repeat the experience.

Or maybe she did, but without the part where he dumped her into bed and ran like hell. Her luck with men was holding strong. Damn.

Heaving a long-suffering sigh, Kesuk set her down and steadied her until she gained her balance. Her feet were encased in supple leather boots, double-layered in fur for cushioning. Her long dress fluttered down to cover her legs. The gown was almost medieval in cut and style, with a tight bodice and belled sleeves, only it was made from butter-soft leather and lined in the same gray striped fur that covered her bed.

"This is the main entrance of Sea Den."

The tunnel twisted down at a sharp angle to a wide mouth.

It overlooked a breathtaking view of a frozen ocean. Sentries stood on either side of the entrance, and she nodded to them in greeting. They stared at her for a moment before nodding back. She walked quickly to escape their stares and nearly stepped off the edge of a cliff. Kesuk reached out and caught her before she went over.

"Oh, my God!" She clung to the arm he wrapped around her waist, her heart pounding. Her limbs started to shake from the close call, and she slumped back against him.

"Careful, little bear. It's dangerous."

"Why is the main entrance so hard to get to?"

"To keep out enemies and predators."

A huge black and white whale leapt from the ocean beyond the ice shelf. She gasped. "A killer whale!"

"An orca."

"Oh, that's what we called them on Earth, too. How did they get here?" She turned and grinned up at him.

"Our ancestors brought them. Sea life is abundant here; the water makes them safe from the predators. The land animals have had a harder time surviving. As have we."

"Why didn't they have merpeople here, then?"

"They may have intended to. The sun died before anything more than the basic settlements were in place." He shrugged, his shoulder moving against her back.

She shivered as an icy blast of wind scoured the sea cliff. Glancing up, she noticed a narrow path winding far up the rock face. Snow spun in whirling gusts from the sheared-off edge of the mountain. He lifted the edges of his cloak and drew them around her. She snuggled back into his warmth.

"Is the entire planet covered in ice?"

"No, but the high reaches are the areas least inhabited by predators, so the clans settled here. The original Earthans were in the southern hemisphere. Dangerous there."

"How many other dens are there?"

"Two. One for the Browns—High Den—and one for the Blacks—Meadow Den."

"Are they near here?"

"The Arctic lands form a large triangle. The Brown lands border us to the south, the Blacks to the north. Their lands extend beyond ours into the mountains and eventually meet."

"Do they like each other?"

"No more than we like them. The Browns don't coexist well with anyone, and the Blacks are thieves and scavengers who'd pick the bones of their dead."

"That's disgusting."

"Indeed."

An icy blast of wind whipped the cloak around them. "Well, are there seasons in the high reaches or is it always cold?"

"Cold? This is warm. Thaw is only a few weeks away."

"Warmer weather. Oh, thank God."

"Thaw is when the predators venture north to hunt."

She didn't want to ask. "Hunt what?"

"Us."

"There's always a catch." She sighed.

His chest rumbled in a quiet laugh.

"How do you survive?"

"Hibernation begins at Thaw and lasts during the summer. We stay in the den until the first snowfall."

"We can't leave at all?"

"Hunting-and-gathering parties go out to collect food stores, but no one else. It is too dangerous."

Then she should put in her request before Thaw came. "Where'd my ship crash?"

"Southwest of here." He tensed against her back.

She twisted to look him in the eye. "I want to see it."

He sighed. "Jain."

"Please, Kesuk."

"It's nothing but a charred hull. You were the only sur-
vivor."

"I know, but—"

"My warriors scouted the area thoroughly after I returned
with you. No one could be found."

"I believe you, but I need some closure. It's important to me.
I . . . I didn't know anyone on board really well, but they were
the last humans like me." She laid a hand along his jaw.

He sighed, his dark eyes showing resigned affection. "As
you wish."

"Thank you." She placed a soft kiss on his lips.

He went rigid against her for a moment, then groaned and
tilted her jaw up to deepen their contact. She sucked his tongue
as it pushed past her lips.

Thank me properly, slave. His growl echoed in her mind.

Spinning quickly, he swept her into his arms, fingers quickly
working her long skirt up around her hips. The cold air hit her
naked skin, and she shivered as he cupped the backs of her
thighs and drew her legs around his waist. He freed himself
from his pants in a few seconds. Her back hit the cliff wall as he
shoved his hard cock deep inside her.

"Yes!" The abruptness of his thrust made her back bow at
the intense pleasure-pain, her pussy stretching to the limit. She
dug her nails into his shoulders as she wrapped her legs tight
around him, clamping her knees on his flanks to ride him.
Needing to touch his skin, she slid her hands under his shirt,
splaying her fingers on the flexing muscles of his back.

You dreamed of us in the snow, did you not?

He scooped a handful of snow from the rocks beside them,
rubbing it against the back of her thigh. She gasped and arched
in shock, the cold making her hotter for him, her moisture coating his cock with each push. He rotated his hips as he plunged
into her, deepening his thrust, changing his rhythm. She stayed

with him, their mouths fused, tongues dueling. She sucked his bottom lip into her mouth, bit down, and scraped the soft flesh as she pulled back. He groaned and dipped his tongue back into her mouth. The coppery taste of his blood excited her more, spurring her on. Her nails bit into his back, raking over his flesh. He grunted, his hips slamming harder into hers. His hand pulled back and slapped her thigh. She peaked into orgasm, fisting hard around his cock, milking him.

He filled his hands with her ass, pulling the cheeks apart. He stimulated her anus with a finger before pushing in.

She drew in a sharp breath. "Kesuk!"

Chuckling, he buried his finger in her ass again and again, rocking her on his cock. He worked in a second finger, and the sensation was more than she could take. She was so full, so hot. Grinding against his dick and fingers, her pussy clenched tight before she shuddered again, coming hard and fast.

He pulled his cock from her soaking pussy, lifting her higher on the wall. His fingers spread her ass cheeks farther.

"Oh, God." She moaned into his mouth as the head of his penis pressed against her hole.

He sank in deeply, one slow inch at a time. She gasped, her ass flexing around him. Too full. It was too much. She wanted more. Using his shoulders for leverage, she lifted off his cock, letting gravity sink him back in. He groaned, burying his face in her neck.

He thrust deep and hard, moving them at a punishing speed, their ragged breath and slap of skin on skin echoing off the cliffs. He slid a hand over her hip and between them, working her clit with a finger. She cried out, the sensation more than she could take. When he sank his teeth into her neck, she again convulsed into hot orgasm. Moments later, he groaned his own completion, pumping hot fluid inside of her.

She panted, her forehead resting against his shoulder as she came down from the high. The pleasured fog that settled over her mind gradually receded as her heartbeat slowed and her muscles relaxed. What had he done to her? She had *never* had sex in public before. Embarrassed heat raced through her when she remembered the way she'd cried out. Then a horrifying thought occurred to her.

"What about the guards?"

"Hmm?" He licked a lazy line from her neck along her collarbone, making her shiver as the cold touched her wet skin.

"The guards. They must have heard us. I'm so humiliated."

"I told them to withdraw when we first came out. Did you not notice them leave?" He pulled back to frown at her.

"No. Telling them to leave is just as bad. They're going to know what we did."

"Would you have preferred they stayed nearby and heard us? I prefer my sex a bit more private than that. If you have other ideas . . ." A wicked grin spread over his handsome face.

"No! Jesus, Kesuk. That's gross."

He shook his head. "Half the time, I don't understand the way your mind works, and the other half I am certain I don't want to. Why are we talking about my soldiers?"

"Let me down. I can walk on my own."

He snorted. "Where have I heard that before?"

"I have no idea. You must have a nasty habit of hauling people around."

She moaned at the slow slide of his flesh inside of hers as he pulled his cock out. God, he still had a semi. She gave serious consideration to shoving him up against the mountain and going at it again, but then she really might not be able to walk on her own. Wouldn't that just give him all kinds of ammunition for carrying her around everywhere? *Nope, not happening.*

She turned toward the cave, ignoring the throb of want in her wet pussy and the sight of his cock disappearing inside his pants as he fastened the fly.

6

A week after Jain arrived, Miki came to fetch her for her first day of "slave" duty. She blushed at the thought of what had happened the last time Kesuk her called her that.

Kesuk confused her. Her violent reaction to him was completely out of character, and being with him made her do things she shouldn't. Like have sex on the side of a mountain. Wanting him this much made no sense. It was too intense for her to control, and it wasn't logical at all.

"Here we are." A flourish of Miki's tiny hand ushered her into a large room filled with children of all ages, half of them naked.

She shook her head. She'd never get used to this comfort with nudity, though Kesuk did his level best to keep her naked as often as possible. Sighing, she pushed thoughts of him aside.

"Where are we?"

"The lesson room."

"Lesson room?"

"Yes." Miki nodded, a smile creasing her lips. "Papa says you're our new loremistress. Our old one died last Thaw."

"Loremistress? I'm your new teacher?"

Miki bobbed her little head as she leaned in to whisper, "Don't tell, but I think you're much nicer than her. Or the loremaster before her. They were both *old.*"

Compressing her lips to keep the smile from breaking through, Jain wagged a finger at the girl. "Now, Miki, that's not nice."

"But it is true." A young male voice spoke from her elbow. She glanced down and found a smaller version of Kesuk looking up at her, complete with serious expression.

"You must be Nukilik."

"Yes. Miki and I are to help you settle in today."

"Well, lead on, kind sir."

Nukilik's forehead wrinkled as though he wasn't sure if she was teasing or not. Then he stepped forward and introduced her to the rest of the rambunctious group. The class immediately fired off a wild cacophony of questions about Earth. They wanted to know where she had lived and what were *mi-cro-waves* and how old she was. The day slipped away in organized chaos as she finally assumed a role she knew—teacher.

The next day, five adults attended her class. Then ten. Then twelve. Soon she had a constant audience slipping silently in and out of the back of the lesson room. The adults' endless curiosity about her matched the children's. They surrounded her at mealtimes and in hallways. These were the kind of eager students she'd have given her left arm for on Earth.

Miki and Nukilik were her constant companions, followed by Imnek, who she'd already surmised Kesuk had sent to watch her. Even when he wasn't there, he controlled her. It wasn't as annoying as it used to be. Maybe *half* as annoying. And a little endearing that he cared. Even though it was obvious he didn't *want* to care. She kept that little bit of knowledge to herself, glad she wasn't the only one struggling with whatever was happening between them.

The days and nights slid by. Though she would never admit

it to Kesuk, she was adjusting to this new lifestyle with greater ease than she could ever have imagined. She hoped the weretigers were as welcoming as the Arctic Bear Clan. Over a week after her first class, she was at dinner, surrounded by the usual motley crew of adults with questions, when Miki tugged on her sleeve.

"Yes?" Jain asked, grinning down at the girl.

"I have something for you." Miki smiled shyly, an expression Jain had never seen on her face.

"That's so sweet. I love presents." Please, God, don't let it be anything live or slimy.

Miki tugged Jain's hand into her lap and dumped a small pile of something into her palm. Jain lifted her hand and found a dozen tiny round shells. They looked like a cross between a tiny conch shell and a sand dollar from Earth. All of them were perfect.

"Oh, Miki. They're so pretty. The best present *ever.*" And they were. Jain didn't remember the last time anyone had given her an unpractical, just-because present. Her family had thought holidays too foolish and sentimental, and her husband hadn't cared enough to bother. She hugged Miki tight and started to tear up, but she managed to blink back the emotion, burying the happiness along with the hurt the way she always did. Tucking the shells into her pocket, she cleared her throat and straightened, resuming her meal.

After dinner, Jain and Kesuk returned to her room. She expected him to pull her into his arms and make her scream for hours. She shivered, a little grin playing over her lips. He made just as much noise as she did when they had sex.

Instead, he sat down on the bed, his fingers splayed on his spread knees. His expression was unusually serious. "Since you came here, you act as though you're living someone else's life. As though all this is temporary and you intend to wake up soon. You pull back when circumstances become too real, when you feel too much. You did it when we loved the first time and again tonight with Miki."

Crap. He'd noticed that? She sighed. "That's how I was raised, Kesuk."

"Hiding from life won't make it stop moving forward without you."

"Like time did."

He snorted. "An unfortunate comparison, but yes."

His hands curved around her waist, lifting her astride his lap. The position brought her eye to eye with him, and nothing had ever felt this intimate. This *right.*

She jerked back, denying herself and him. "I shouldn't want you this much. Ever since I came here, everything's been jumbled up and confused. I didn't used to be like this. I never doubted who I was or what my purpose was. Everything was clear—what I should do, who I should be with, where I should go. It was all planned, all logical. My life made *sense.*"

"That was the way of your world, your people. Everything ordered and in its place. Life is not about planning every moment. Joy comes in the spontaneity of life, Jain. It doesn't have to make sense. Sometimes people die when they shouldn't. They also love where they shouldn't. Those are things you cannot decide."

"I enjoyed my life before," she insisted.

"Such rigidity is not a good thing in one as young as you."

"I'm over five hundred years older than you."

He cocked a thick blond brow and folded his arms.

"All right, fine. I'm still not that young. And I'm not rigid; I'm logical."

"No, your family was logical, perhaps. Your mate. But not you. You pretend to be logical, because you think you should, because it's safer to believe you're in control. Deny yourself all you want, but I see the passionate woman in you. I've held that woman in my arms, clawing my back, screaming my name in ecstasy."

She squeezed her eyes closed, shutting out the image he painted. He was right. She always pulled back when emotions got too deep. Her family had been scientists, eminently logical. Nothing emotional was acceptable. Since her husband left her for another woman and her parents had died, her emotions had been locked in ice, frozen and untouchable. Was that who she really was? Who she really wanted to be?

She sighed. "I'm sorry, Kesuk."

"Do not be sorry; be here."

"I want to be." And she did, so much. She wanted to be where she mattered, where she was safe to *feel.*

"If you want it, then you'll do it." He pulled her tighter to his pelvis until she felt his hard cock.

"That simple, huh?" Arching an eyebrow, she smirked down at him.

"Some things are. Like this." He slipped a hand between her legs, rubbing her through her leather pants.

Pleasure swirled through her, but she twisted her leg to avoid the touch. If he wanted to bring up personal issues, she had a thing or two to say to him as well. Maybe they should just get this all out in the open. She wasn't the only one here with flaws, damn it.

"And then there's *you.*"

"Me? I have done nothing." He cocked an eyebrow, wary of what she might say. Women were unpredictable. A man never knew what strange things ran through their minds or what would pop out of their mouths.

"Ha! You're Mr. Fix-It. You have to fix everyone and everything. Let's forget about me and my control issues for a second. You also keep your soldiers from fighting *and* insist on handling every last detail of the preparations for the weretigers' arrival. You need to try delegating some things. Let the rest of us work it out for ourselves. Trust your people. Trust me. We won't end up killed by predators."

Her hands planted on her hips, which still straddled his thighs. They should be loving now. How had his evening's plans gone so awry?

He narrowed his eyes. "You would prefer I'd left you dying in the snow?"

She snorted at him. "Don't be deliberately dense. I'm not saying we don't need you or your help *at all;* I'm saying we can do some of it ourselves. You don't have to be all things to all people, Kesuk. You have advisors and soldiers. Let them do their jobs. They're competent, or you wouldn't have put them in those positions in the first place. Am I right?"

"Yes." He didn't like the direction of her questioning.

"I'm guessing this micromanagement started after your wife died. You used to listen to your councilors, used to let your lieutenants make some executive decisions about their men."

"I was younger then." Why was he defending himself? She *wasn't* right. Was she?

"And now you know everything and don't need anyone?"

"I did not say that."

"But that's what your actions say to your people every day."

"That—"

"Everyone else is allowed to be human, Kesuk. Me, your family, your men, but not you. You have to be perfect. Why is that?"

He slid his tongue over his teeth. Perhaps now was a good time for a distraction. "It was a human between your legs last night, was it not?"

She ignored him. "You see your wife's death as your failure. Now you keep everyone at arm's length so you never get hurt again. Miki and Nukilik are your only exceptions."

Anger flashed through him. "Are you finished pretending you know me?"

She flinched. "I didn't realize I was pretending."

"You've known me only a few weeks, yet you've uncovered everything that's wrong with me. How miraculous."

Face flaming, her eyes sparked with anger and challenge. "And you're any better? You constantly tell me how wrong I am, how I need to let go and feel. Sometimes it takes an outside opinion to see what's really going on."

He snarled, his fingers tightening on her hips. He did not wish to consider this. "You have no idea what you are talking about."

"If I'm wrong, I'm wrong. It wouldn't be the first time I misjudged a man. Don't dismiss what I said because it's uncomfortable to think about. Deep down, you know I'm right." She poked a finger into his chest.

A knock on the door interrupted his retort. He growled. Typical.

"Come," he snapped, holding Jain still when she tried getting up from his lap.

Imnek opened the door, glancing at them once before fixing his eyes on the far wall. "My lord, the weretigers have crossed the border into our land."

Jain's lips tightened. She thought he'd run off to fetch the weretigers himself. And she'd be right. He sucked his teeth in self-disgust.

"Take a contingent of guards and escort our guests to Sea Den."

"Me, my lord?" The boy's eyes popped wide, his voice rising an octave.

"You are qualified, are you not?"

He snapped upright. "Yes, my lord!"

"Go, then." He turned back to Jain, smirking. "There, you see? Delegation."

She lifted her chin and folded her arms, which plumped her breasts. His hand twitched as he fought to keep from peeling away her clothes and filling his palms with her soft flesh. "Uh-huh. Make a habit of it."

Growling, he gave in to impulse and pulled her closer to him, crushing her lips under his, ending the argument the best way he knew how. He closed a hand over her breast, making her moan into his mouth. She responded to him every time. He loved that about her. His cock hardened to painful stiffness, and his free hand cupped her ass, lifting her so he could rub himself against the juncture of her thighs.

"Papa?" Miki's wavery voice sounded from outside the room.

"Every time. Every *single* time." He groaned and laid his forehead against hers.

"I seem to recall at least one time on the side of a mountain . . ." Those exotic green eyes tilted up at the corners as she grinned.

She licked her lips, her eyes dropping to his mouth. He stroked the breast he still held, plucked at the nipple. Gasping, she leaned into him.

"Jain?" The door latch rattled as Miki struggled to get in. "Please, let me in."

The ragged edge of Miki's little voice alerted him. A nightmare. She hadn't had one in over a Turn. He set Jain on the bed and opened the door, stooping to gather Miki up to his chest. She buried her head in his shoulder, already sobbing, her thin arms clinging to his neck.

"Sweetie, what's wrong?" Jain reached over and smoothed Miki's hair, obviously distressed by his daughter's tears.

"I h-had a bad dream. Can I s-stay here with y-you, Jain?"

"Of course."

Kesuk groaned, mourning the loss of a night in Jain's bed. A father's duty was never done. Miki leaned away from him and held out her arms for Jain. His eyebrows rose. That was new. Miki never sought out anyone but him when she had a night terror.

His surprise was echoed by the look on Jain's face as she

tucked Miki into her arms. She rocked the girl, swaying from side to side with each step as she walked to the bed. Tucking Miki under the furs, Jain crawled in next to her, snuggling close. Kesuk shifted, feeling awkward and unnecessary. Jain looked up, patting the bed in invitation. Walking across the room, he banked the fire until the room was lit in a soft glow and joined them.

Jain hugged Miki closer, resting her chin on top of the girl's head. "What was your nightmare about?"

"Mama."

"Oh?"

"About when she left."

"It's all right to miss her."

"Papa says we don't need to because we'll see her in the next life."

Jain seemed to consider that, to consider his beliefs before answering. "Remembering the way you loved her in this life isn't bad. Even if you get to see her again."

Kesuk smiled down at his daughter, propping himself up on an elbow. "You will see her again, Miki. Don't ever doubt it."

"I won't, Papa."

"Go to sleep now." He tucked the covers under her chin, and she closed her eyes.

"I love you."

"I love you, too." Kissing her forehead, he petted her hair until her chest rose and fell in a slow, even rhythm.

"She's not allowed to grieve?" Jain asked.

He turned the question on her because he knew his response would only make her bring up his need to control everything. "Do you allow yourself to grieve? Truly?"

She didn't speak for a long moment, and when she did, she changed the topic rather than answer him. "How did your wife die?"

Her soft words washed over him in the darkness, and he

closed his eyes against the ugly memory, the guilt of his failure. The woman was right about that, the failure, the guilt. "There was a raid."

"And she was taken as a slave?"

"No." He couldn't speak of this to anyone. He never had before.

A small hand cupped the side of his face, stroked his cheek. "Tell me."

"The Blacks overran a hunting party. It was normal; it happens all the time. We attack them; they attack us. Slaves are the commodity of choice. Trading them is how we get the things we need. Deer and bison stay to higher elevations; fish are in the sea. We use the exchange of people to get goods. Simple. Easy."

"But not that time."

He swallowed hard. "No. Not that time."

"What went wrong?"

"During the raid, predators attacked, too. My mate was with the hunters and she . . . she was taken by the predators."

The memories washed over him in relentless waves. After his warriors told him Maruska was gone, he'd hunted for her for hours, tracking the pack of predators until he finally found her body. She'd been mangled and half-sunk in an icy stream, her blood making the water run pink. He'd roared out his grief, the pain more than he could contain. Then he'd taken her in his arms and rocked her, knowing he was too late to protect her. She was gone.

His breath shuddered out as he allowed himself to recall his failure. He couldn't bear to suffer such loss again. He would never leave himself or his clan so vulnerable. Hunting parties now went out with an entire contingent of guards. No women or children ventured out alone. Ever. He accompanied as many expeditions as he could manage. It was his duty to protect his people. He would not fail again.

Jain's soft hand stroked over his cheek, pulling him from his reverie. He shook away his gloom, turning to face her. She withdrew her hand, settled her chin in her upturned palm. "Hi. Where did you go?"

I'm right here.

"You loved her."

Fierce guilt hit him again, threatened to strangle him. "I did."

"I'm so sorry, Kesuk."

"Yes." He made his voice abrupt, hoping she would let this subject go. He did not wish to speak of it.

"What was she like?"

He sighed. Maruska. What had she been like? He was ashamed to admit he could no longer see her face in his mind, but he remembered the life they'd shared. He summed it up as succinctly as possible. "She was the exact opposite of you."

Jain gasped, a small sound of pain. "I understand. Good night."

She slid down to curve around Miki, closing her eyes. He winced, realizing how what he'd said would be taken by his current lover. Foolish.

Our marriage was arranged by my father. We were raised together, respected each other's strengths. Love grew from that respect, slowly and over time. She was . . . boisterous and wild.

"Nothing like me."

"Don't assume that is a bad thing. My mate is dead. I don't wish to replace her with a pale imitation." He reached to slip his fingers through Jain's hair, the dark silken length sliding between his fingers. She tilted her cheek to lean into his palm, opening her eyes to meet his gaze.

You are a beautiful woman, Jain.

She huffed a laugh, looking away. "Right."

"What's this? Look at me, little bear." He frowned when she didn't comply, tilting her chin so he could see her expression.

Her jaw flexed in his hand, but she didn't try to pull away. "You don't have to say those things to me, Kesuk. I know what I look like. You don't have to lie."

He swallowed his anger at that, stroked his thumb along her jaw. "Questioning my honor again, Jain?"

"No!" She glanced down at the sleeping Miki and whispered, "No."

"Why would I bother to lie?"

She shrugged, looking anywhere but at him. "I don't know."

Something deeper lay here. "Who made you doubt?"

"I'm just not pretty, okay? I've always known it. Besides, beauty is not as important as intelligence."

He heard the echo of someone else in her voice. "Hmm . . . your family told you this? Or your mate?"

"Both. He, my husband, and I grew up together. He was part of my family."

He suspected her husband had been far more a part of her family than she had. "They were proud of you?"

"No, I . . ." She shook her head. "They were very busy. We didn't spend much time together. They worked on projects and experiments."

"They sound frigid."

"Their work was very important." Her voice came out stiff, controlled.

"Did they not love you? Tell you they approved of your accomplishments?"

She scoffed. "I'm just a teacher. My brother and husband were the scientists."

This explained so much about her—her need to control everything in a world that wasn't safe. Anger burned in his gut, the muscles ticking in his clenched jaw. He wanted to go back in time and pummel the unfeeling parents who had abandoned the vulnerable young Jain. He growled at the mere thought of her mate, a man who should have made up for a lifetime of no love. Made her see she was beautiful and wanted. He would never permit Miki to mate with such a man.

"Here we have no scientists. Loremasters are valued. They carry our history into the future."

"Things here are backward of what I know."

"Different is not bad, Jain. You will adjust." What was he saying? She was leaving when the weretigers arrived. He sighed, pushing that knowledge away. Best not to deal with it tonight.

"Do I have a choice? Everything here happens to me. I have no say in it."

"Controlling everything is not the answer, either, Jain."

"Controlling nothing is irresponsible. I'm going to sleep now. Good night, Kesuk." Her voice was prim and antagonizing.

Sighing, he fought the urge to throttle the stubborn wench. Yes, entirely the opposite of his easygoing mate. Too bad he'd developed a soft spot for recalcitrant women.

He dipped his head to meet her gaze. *You are beautiful, Jain. I would not say it if I did not mean it.*

"I know." She shook her head and closed her eyes again, sighing.

In time, she would come to see he was right. Unfortunately, with the arrival of the weretigers, their time together would soon draw to a close. He hated to miss seeing her passionate nature come full bloom. He didn't allow himself to consider that some other man might get to enjoy her after she left Alysius. She deserved what happiness she could find. Chest tight with an emotion he had no business feeling, he reached out to slide a tender hand down her soft midnight hair, reveling in the silky feel of her soft cheek. He lay for a long while, watching her chest rise and fall in sleep before he tucked the furs tighter around her and his daughter. The two most precious females in his life.

7

At sunrise the next morning, Miki dragged Jain along on a hunting-and-gathering party. She was curious to see more of the planet. With her clothes on this time. They bundled in warm cloaks and slung gray striped leather satchels across their shoulders. Everything was striped here. She made a mental note to ask Kesuk why at dinner this evening.

That thought brought her up short. This outing was also a convenient way to escape Kesuk. He hadn't been in bed when she woke up this morning, and he hadn't bothered to leave a note about where he'd gone so early. She didn't really want to see him after they'd shredded each other last night. She'd said more than she should have about her family history. Her heart gave a painful squeeze. What an awful mess.

Miki thrust her hand into Jain's and pulled her as fast as her little legs could go. "Jain! Come on, we must keep up."

"All right, I'm coming. Hold your horses." At least spending time with Miki was guaranteed to lift her dark mood.

"We need to stay with the guards. There are predators at Thaw."

"Have you ever seen one of the predators?" She swallowed, glancing around, grateful for the full contingent of Kesuk's huge guards.

"Yes, but I've never seen a horse. What is it? Why do you have to hold it?"

Squeezing the girl's hand, Jain laughed. "It's an expression that means *don't be impatient.*"

Miki wrinkled her pert little nose. "I don't think I like horses."

Soon they were spread out in a small clearing, chattering, laughing, Miki showing Jain how to pick fresh berries.

"This one. It's the very best one this Turn." Miki held up a tiny plum-colored berry between her fingers before popping it into her mouth and chewing with exaggerated delight. She'd declared the same thing about almost every fruit she'd picked.

"If you don't stop eating the very best ones, how will anyone know you found any at all?"

Miki grinned. "I'll tell them. Oh, but *this* one. It's the very b—"

A high-pitched scream of animal pain rent the air, raising chills down Jain's arms. Her head whipped around to see one of the guards go down in spray of crimson blood and gore on the white snow. A huge gray tiger-striped animal pounced on his chest, fangs bared. It was vaguely the shape of an Earthan wolf but nearly the same size as Kesuk in his bear form.

Jain gasped. "Oh, God."

"Come, Jain, back to the caves. They hunt in packs!" Again, Miki grasped Jain's hand tight, pulling hard.

Women and children ran and screamed, dumping their satchels and changing into bear form to run faster.

"Go, Miki!" Jain ran behind the girl, making sure she kept up as they followed the line of Arctic bears. Adrenaline sang in her veins. Her heart pounded as her arms and legs pumped hard, kicking up snow behind her. Roaring sounded from the clearing they'd left behind.

They skidded through loose gravel alongside the steep ravine that led to the back entrance of Sea Den. Suddenly, Miki lost her footing and dropped over the side.

"Miki!" Jain dove for the girl, catching her hand and keeping her from falling to the rocks below. Miki's wide, frightened eyes locked with hers as her desperate grip tightened. Her dark irises disappeared as the black spread to touch the corners of her eyes.

"Don't let go!" Miki's nose turned black and started to elongate, her breath panting out. She grew heavier by the second as she started to shift forms.

"I won't, honey. But I can't hold you if you change into a bear, okay? I've got you. It's okay," she soothed.

Miki whimpered, but her nose resumed its human shape. "Okay. Okay. Can you pull me up?"

"Yeah." Jain grunted and shimmied backward over the gravel. Small rocks scraped the skin on her stomach as her short tunic rode up. She wrapped her free hand around a protruding rock, ignoring the bite into her bare flesh, because it kept her from sliding into the ravine. Miki hefted her torso over the lip of the crevasse, and then curled up her knee to hoist herself the rest of the way. She flopped over on her back, panting.

"Come on, sweetie. We need to hurry." Jain pushed onto her knees, intending to pull the two of them to their feet.

Miki sat up, sniffing the air before her gaze focused over Jain's shoulder. "*Get down.*"

Jain hit the ground, hunching over Miki as a hulking dark shape flew over their heads and down the side of the ravine. The predator scrabbled for purchase, growling and leaping for the top. Its loud baying would bring more if they hunted together. Where the hell were all their guards?

Jain hauled Miki into her arms, sprinting for the nearest tree with low limbs. It was a young sapling, but it looked like it could hold them. If the predators were like the wolves on Earth, they wouldn't be able to climb a tree. *She hoped.*

The predator topped the edge of the ravine and hurtled toward them at astonishing speed. Oh, God.

She shoved Miki onto the lowest branch. "Climb up!"

After Miki hefted herself up to the next branch, Jain jumped to catch her elbows over the branch. She'd always been awful at chin-ups in school. Her booted toes kicked into the tree trunk, giving her purchase so she could haul her left knee up. Something snapped around her right ankle, yanking her back, her chin scraping on the bark. She caught the branch with her hands, and it bowed under the combined weight of her and the predator.

"Jain!" Miki shrieked.

Jain screamed, panicking as the predator's teeth bit into the tough leather of her boot with crushing force. She swung wildly, fighting to hold on to the branch. Looking over her shoulder, she could see the evil thing's yellow eyes. Drawing her free foot back, she aimed for the tip of its snout. She connected, hard.

The predator yowled and dropped her foot, shaking its head madly. Adrenaline pumped through her veins as she hauled herself back up onto the branch. She sobbed for air, bouncing on her good foot and forcing herself to climb up and up, away from the predator.

"K-keep going, Miki. High as you can."

"Are you all right?"

"Yes. Just c-climb, sweetie." Jain pulled herself as high as she could before the slim branches began bowing under her weight. That put her only about thirty feet above the ground, and the little tree shook as the predator hurled itself at the base. She straddled a branch and tugged Miki down in front of her, wrapping her arms around the trunk to secure them in place. Bark bit into her fingers, and the branch chafed her inner thighs. The pungent aroma of tree sap filled the air as leaves and twigs broke away.

A second predator joined the first, circling the tree, baying eerily. The hairs stood up on the back of Jain's neck, and she prayed harder than she ever had before. *Please, let the guards be all right and on their way to help. Please let Kesuk come.* Her ankle throbbed, and she squeezed her eyes shut, not wanting to watch as the predators hurled their combined weight against the slender trunk. The budding leaves shivered at each impact.

A deep roar sounded in the distance. More must be coming. What the hell was she *doing* here? She didn't want to be mauled and eaten by some freakish wolf-tiger beastie. She bit back a sob, pulling air in through her nose to calm her erratic breathing, coughing as she sucked pollen into her airway.

"Make them go away, Jain." Miki whimpered, her tiny fingers forming claws to dig into the tree. Jain couldn't think of a single comforting thing to say, so she just hugged her close and held on for dear life. They weren't getting her out of this tree until they knocked the damn thing over.

The roaring came closer, almost upon them. She turned her head in the direction of the clearing, watching to see how many predators would come. Instead, a massive Arctic bear broke through the line of trees, followed by four more. It let out a bellowing roar, leaping forward with claws extended and fangs bared, galloping for the nearest predator. The two met with a loud crunch of bone and sinew, two huge animals locked in combat.

"Kesuk," Jain breathed. The two rolled away, and she strained to see what was going on, careful not to lose her balance.

Terrifying growls, squeals, and grunts exploded from the two fighters. They reared back on hind legs to slash at each with tooth and claw. The predator slammed Kesuk over, and they spun sideways through the snow before crashing into the base of the tree. Jain squashed Miki against the tree as the wild swaying started to crack the trunk. The whole tree began to give way as half the roots tore from the ground. The two hit the slim tree again and again, the impact of fangs on flesh audible as they ripped into each other.

As quickly as it had begun, it stopped. Everything was silent.

"Papa!" Miki tried to dive down, but Jain held her still.

Groaning, Kesuk heaved away from the still predator. Blood matted his white fur. He shook hard from head to tail before approaching the foot of the tree. The predator's fleeing pack mate was easily overtaken by the other bears and dragged to the ground. Jain looked away; she didn't want to see any more.

Come down now. It's safe. Kesuk's thoughts echoed in her mind.

She eased her cramped grip on the trunk and scooted back to let a straining Miki down first. The girl made short work of the climb down, landing on her father's back and chattering about how she hadn't been scared and how exciting it was and how Jain had saved her from the big, bad predators.

Jain followed more slowly, the ache in her ankle becoming more pronounced. Adrenaline still pumped through her system, making her hands and legs shake. She reached the lowest branch and bent to grasp it, lowering herself to dangle a foot from the ground. Bracing herself for the pain, she dropped down. Gasping as her ankle nearly buckled, she stumbled back against the trunk.

Jain?

"I'm fine." She straightened, laying a hand on the dense fur on Kesuk's back while his now human and very naked warriors gathered their silver-and-black striped kill. Well, at least she knew now why almost everything they wore was striped.

Shaking that inane thought away, she turned toward Sea Den and began the long slow walk back, careful to pick her way through the rocks and gravel so she didn't worsen her ankle by twisting it. A large young bear pulled alongside her, nudging her hand with his nose until she used his shoulder for balance. She suspected it was Imnek but couldn't be sure and didn't ask, because she was so focused on getting back in one piece. Miki, now in her bear form, gamboled ahead of them, pouncing into snowdrifts.

Steam rose from the large tub, the heated water lapping around Jain's thighs and buttocks as she lowered herself into her bath. A low moan slid from her lips at the sensuous delight of the water on her skin. The stiffness eased from her calf and ankle, and she flexed the joint. Sighing, she leaned back against the rim and tried to relax.

The fear she'd felt this afternoon was not something she'd soon forget. How had these people survived so long with those *things* hunting them? Why had they settled this planet if they hadn't been able to eradicate such a threat? Back on Earth, she'd heard reports of whole settlements being wiped away without a trace. Now she understood why.

She tapped restlessly against the sides of the tub, water sloshing as she shifted. Sighing, she gave up trying to relax and attempted to leverage herself out of the tub. She was still too keyed up from the adrenaline rush. She was still half in, half out of the water when the door slammed back against the wall, making her jump.

Kesuk stood there naked, having just shifted. His eyes were still black from corner to corner, and something wild and dangerous lurked in his gaze. Her stomach fluttered, breath speeding with anticipation. Sharp desire rushed through her, peaking her nipples, dampening her pussy, readying her for penetration.

He kicked the door shut behind him with one foot as he advanced across the room. "I won't be gentle."

"I don't want you to." No, she wanted him fast and hard, to burn off the terror she'd experienced today. Knowing what he needed, what she needed, she lifted her arms in invitation.

Never hesitating, he scooped her out of the tub, dripping water all over the floor. She ignored the mess, thrusting her fingers into his hair, pulling his lips to hers. They bit and nipped at each other, and she dragged her teeth hard over his bottom lip.

Setting her on the edge of her side table, he lifted her knees, pushing between her thighs. "Lean back," he rasped.

She reclined on her hands, widened her legs for him, arching hard as he jerked her pussy lips apart to thrust into her. He started a fast, deep rhythm, pumping into her hot channel.

They fell on each other with a desperation she'd never expected. Beads of bathwater rolled down her arms and legs, making her slide on the table. Her head rested against the wall, her neck tensing as she moved with his thrusts. Tears gathered at the corners of her eyes, slipped unchecked down her cheeks, the emotions of the day pushing forward until she couldn't contain them anymore.

He was hitting her just right, and she was screaming, the sound too loud to her ears, but she didn't care anymore. Her fingers wrapped around the edge of the polished wood table, and she pressed her pelvis up to meet his hard thrusts. He pulled her knees higher on his hips, pistoning deep, faster and faster.

"I'm coming!" Her hips froze midair, legs tensing as her pussy spasmed around his cock. His thrusts became deep and wild as they raced each other to orgasm, their eyes locked, riding the storm together.

His fangs slid out and he roared as he came, his head thrown back, the muscles of his neck and shoulder tensing. His hands clamped on her ass, pulling her closer, pressing his cock as deep inside her as she could handle. Then he sighed, relaxing, his forehead dropping to rest on her chest.

The drag of his hot flesh in hers as he slid out of her made her pussy clench on his dick. He groaned, thrust against her cervix hard, and pushed her into an aftershock of orgasm. She shuddered, clinging to his shoulders. Backing away, he slid an arm under her legs, lifting her against his chest. A few steps and he laid her across the bed, settling beside her.

He feathered his fingers down her legs, making her shiver at the light touch. She eased her thighs apart a little, hoping to encourage further exploration. His fingers circled her injured ankle, and she flinched from the touch. She could walk on it, but it was bruised.

"Did I hurt you before?" Concern creased his forehead as he examined her leg.

"No. It's just sore. Really." He wasn't going to stop for the night, was he? He'd never stopped at one orgasm before. She felt cheated.

"Hmm . . . I think you need to keep this ankle elevated." He flashed a wicked little grin, and her heart turned over. God, she adored being around him. Just in these small moments between them. How he teased her and made her laugh. Maybe even when he made her mad. Even when she wanted to kick his ass, she knew he cared. Her problems mattered to him. She had a very short list of people in her life she could say that about. Plus, sex with him was the best she'd ever had. She smiled back at him. Nope, she couldn't forget the great sex.

Still grinning, he propped her legs on his shoulders and kissed his way down her good leg to swirl his tongue under her knee. She moaned, surprised that was such a sensitive area. He nipped the soft flesh, and an echoing fire flashed between her legs. As always, she was hot for him within two seconds. She didn't think she'd ever get used to it.

"Put your hands above your head."

"Yes, *master.*" She smirked, but stretched her arms up, locking her hand over her wrist.

"I see you're learning your place here."

She opened her mouth to argue, but when he shifted suddenly, pressing his cock deep into her wet pussy, all that emerged from her throat was a low moan.

He grasped her thighs, controlling her movements, pumping so slowly she wanted to scream. The angle was amazing. It was so tight. Rolling his hips, he increased the friction, slipping one hand down to flit over her swollen clitoris.

She strained upward, her hand tight on her wrist. "Please let me touch you, Kesuk. Please, I want—"

Begging, little bear? I like that. Do it again.

"Please." Her hips bucked, but his hand moved from her clit to press down on her belly, staying her movements, making her sob in frustration. "Go faster, deeper, *something.*"

Chuckling, he resumed his lazy circling of her wet flesh, pushing into her, pulling away. She clamped her pussy on his cock, squeezing tight with each thrust until he groaned. Grinning, she watched his control slip. His breath hissed and his fangs slid out.

"Jain," he growled.

"Yes?" She kept her tone as sweet and innocent as she could, but she knew her wide grin gave her away.

His next thrust slapped against her and she gasped. Hot pleasure rolled through her. Her thighs flexed to meet his next push. He slapped her ass, the shock thrusting her into orgasm.

"Kesuk!"

But he wasn't listening. He'd lost all control. His eyes were solid black, and he pounded roughly into her, consumed by his own needs. He threw back his head and roared his finish, filling her with his hot seed.

He collapsed beside her, panting. He turned her on her side and then buried his face in her hair, each breath fluttering the short strands. His arms tightened around her, pulling her back against his chest, cradling her to him.

She fought the sudden tears pressing against her lids because she felt . . . safe. Right here on this barbaric, backward planet with this uncivilized man.

"I thought I'd lost you. That I failed you." His harsh whisper seemed to echo in the chamber. "You and Miki. I thought . . ." He swallowed, shook his head, and stopped speaking.

"You didn't." She turned to face him, laid a hand on his cheek, smoothing her fingers over his strong jaw.

"I could have. In a few more moments—" He leaned his forehead against hers, shuddering, his breathing ragged.

Stroking his shoulder, she tried to comfort him. "It didn't happen. You can't control everything, remember?"

He chuckled. "My own words used against me."

"Used *for* you. You were right." Her fingers slipped into his hair.

"Truly? Say it again, little bear. My ears must be deceiving me."

"Shut up!" She laughed, bucking away from him.

Planting his palm in the middle of her back, he arched her torso toward him, dipping to suck her nipple.

"Ah!" Clenching her fingers in his hair, she pulled him closer.

He bit and released her nipple, just rough enough to make her moan, pulling as much of her small breast into his mouth as he could. His stubble scraped at the soft underside. She hooked her leg over his thigh, opening herself to his thick dick.

A crisp knock interrupted them, and they both groaned.

"If it's one of my soldiers, he'll be on night duty for a full Turn." Kesuk reared up, his still-hard cock bouncing in the air.

A sleek man with dramatic black-striped auburn hair walked in without waiting for permission. His kohl-rimmed gaze took in the entire situation, including Jain's blushing cheeks. Everything about the man was golden, including his skin, his eyes, and the thick loop in his ear. What appeared to be faded henna tattoos curved in stripes over his forearms.

Kesuk gave a warning growl before jerking the pelts over Jain. "You have a great deal of nerve coming in here, cat king."

"The correct term is *Amir,* and felines are known for their arrogance. I am no exception." The golden man favored her with a charming smile. His pupils were slitted like a cat's. Fascinating.

Forgetting to be embarrassed, she held out her hand. "Hello. I'm Jain."

"So you're the lovely woman who's caused such a fuss. I am the Amir Varad Mohan." Ignoring Kesuk, he swept her hand to his lips.

"Are you really a cat king? They were just considering gene-splicing experiments with Siberian tigers when I left Earth."

"Yes, tigers were successfully spliced. The king of the jungle, as it were."

"That was lions."

"I don't see any lions left. They abandoned the throne." His golden eyes twinkled in good humor, and she liked him immediately.

Kesuk padded naked to his own room, Varad on his heels.

"My apologies for interrupting, Lord Kesuk. I wished to warn you—"

"Warn me? Of what?"

"The Aquatilian ambassador accompanied me on this voyage. He awaits us in your main hall."

A growl rose in Kesuk's throat. "He should have remained on the ship. He has no business here."

"He wants to collect the humans."

He frowned, shooting a quick glance at the other man. "The humans? There is only one."

"No, there is a second. She was at High Den."

"What did you have to trade to get her?" Browns were notorious in their wily dealings, so much so that he was amazed they had parted with the other human at all. Especially if she was as attractive as Jain.

"Nothing. They thanked me for taking her. She is not as . . . amiable as your human."

"Mine?" He missed a step, the blow hitting him hard. *Jain.* He braced an arm against the wall, trying to catch his breath. A hard hand closed over his shoulder.

"I am sorry, my friend."

Kesuk shook Varad off. "I'm fine. I knew this day would come. I planned to send her with you when you came."

"Not everything goes according to plan. Keep her if you wish. Unless my instincts deceive me, the lady would remain if you ask."

"No. She is not suited for this world." If he said the words enough, he would believe them. He had to. It was his duty to do what was best for those under his protection. Look how close he had come to losing her this day. He shook his head. He couldn't keep her, and she would be safer hidden under the oceans of Aquatilis.

"Kesuk—"

"I will join you shortly. I must dress."

8

Jain pulled the soft dove-gray tunic over her head. It fluttered around her thighs, almost brushing her knee-high charcoal boots. Wanting to look good for Kesuk and his guests, she forked her fingers through her short hair. The side slits on her tunic exposed tight striped leather pants with every step she took. She hurried to the main hall, limping a little on her stiff ankle.

Before she'd even entered the room, a loud feminine voice demanded, "I don't want to be patient. I want to see her now. I want to make sure she hasn't been mistreated."

She knew that voice. Breaking into an uneven jog, she rounded the last corner.

"She has not been mistreated." Anger laced Kesuk's deep voice, his prickly honor at question.

"Dr. Gibbons? *Sera?*" Jain asked, stunned to see someone from her ship.

"Jain!" A huge smile lit the young scientist's face.

"Where did you . . . *how* did you . . . the ship exploded. No one else got out but me. I waited and waited and no one else was there."

"My cryogenic pod was thrown from the ship. The ship probably started breaking up when we entered the atmosphere. I was thrown clear of the crash somewhere in the mountains and ended up with a bunch of smelly bear-shifters . . . You're hurt." Sera abruptly changed topics as her gaze took in Jain's limp. She turned an accusing glare on Kesuk. He growled in return, his irritation plain.

"I had an accident, Sera. It wasn't Kesuk's fault. He saved me from hypothermia." *No need to mention the predators.*

Jain stepped up onto the dais that held the main table and Kesuk's large chair. She stood next to him, placing a hand on his shoulder. Bare-chested, he wore tight leather breeches and a long, sleeveless leather cape with a huge fur collar, making him appear even more massive than he already was. A hammered silver circlet hugged his muscled bicep. Some symbol of his rank in the clan? She'd never seen him wear it before. He lounged in the chair, his leg hooked negligently over the arm, chin propped in his hand. She fought a grin as she realized he was playing the barbarian they thought him to be.

Sera sniffed, scanning the large hall with obvious distaste. Jain stiffened, wanting to defend this place. She loved it here. She loved the people—exuberant Miki, contained Nukilik, controlled Kesuk. *Kesuk.* She tried to be rational, to see Sea Den through Sera's eyes. Large, scrubbed bare stone floors, decorated skins on the walls, trestle tables. It lacked the technology she was used to, but the roaring fire and groups of chatting people made it homey and welcoming.

She wanted to stay.

"You're coming with us, Jain."

Sera's voice broke through Jain's reverie. "What?"

"We'll be on Aquatilis in three weeks. They came to get us."

"They?" She swiveled around, seeing Varad and another man behind him. The stranger's pale skin set off the sheet of inky hair that hung straight to the middle of his back. Almost as white as Kesuk, he had deep turquoise eyes and a high fore-head. He also had an air of perpetual blasé boredom.

The man had a small flat nose, and his nostrils flared in obvi-ous distaste as he took in the main hall of Sea Den. Then he turned to Jain and executed a neat bow. "Ambassador Hahn of Aquatilis at your service, Dr. . . ."

"Oh, I'm not a scientist. My brother was. I'm a school-teacher. And, please, call me Jain."

Disappointment flashed in his turquoise eyes, but he recov-ered quickly. "How charming. You may call me Bretton, of course."

Memory kicked in and her history knowledge popped up. "Sirius Hahn was the founder of the Aquatilian colony. Is he your ancestor?"

"The very same." A wide genuine smile curved his lips. Bretton was a handsome man when he wasn't wearing a conde-scending look. "Aquatilis will embrace a woman with so fine a knowledge of our past. I'm sure we can arrange for more . . . comfortable lodging than the Alysians offered you."

"I somehow doubt Aquatilis could compare." Jain grinned, remembering the feel of soft pelts under her back as Kesuk pounded inside her. A private smile lit Kesuk's face as he glanced up at her, letting his gaze slide down her body.

Bretton's lip curled. "Unlike the barbarians, we still have use of most of the technology from your time. It will be much more to your liking."

Kesuk's gaze flashed with resentment. When he smiled, he let his fangs show. "It is unfortunate that our calls for aid from your *advanced* people resulted in nothing. Our loremasters teach that while we were struggling to survive, your *technology* was worthless because you never came. How un-neighborly."

The ambassador flushed, taking a small step back. "Yes, well. We had our own problems when no supplies were deliv-ered from Earth. Our life-support systems were failing, and half our population was still made up of unaltered humans. You understand our dilemma."

"Oh, yes. I understand perfectly."

A cold silence settled over the group as old bitterness played out between Kesuk and Bretton. Jain took a breath. "As far as I can tell, every one of the colonized planets have done what they must to survive. For Aquatilis, that meant preserving the technology that runs your life-support systems in the underwater city. For Alysians, it meant learning to cope with being hunted by predators." Flexing her sore ankle, she shivered at the ugly memory.

Varad stepped forward. "An excellent assessment. I'm sure you would be fascinated to know about the adaptation the weredragons have made on their desert world."

"*Dragons?*" Sera and Jain echoed together.

Sera's brow furrowed. "That's not feasible. All the other shifter species were created from splicing human genes with known animals. Dragons are a myth."

"These are not." Varad shrugged.

"I want to see." Academic zeal lit Sera's eyes. This was the kind of puzzle the woman lived for.

"We have several Harenan diplomats stationed on Aquatilis. You'll see them soon." Bretton's nasal accent cut across their conversation. He smiled at Sera, and she all but melted in a puddle at his feet. Oh, dear. Sera was the youngest scientist to be recruited to Aquatilis, and only then because of her precocious genius. She had no social skills or experience with men. How unfortunate that her first crush would be on such a techno-snob.

Jain rolled her eyes and sighed. She probably fawned just as much when Kesuk smiled at her.

Kesuk rose from his chair and bent to Jain's ear. "We must speak, little bear." He held out his hand, and she placed her fingers in his proffered palm. He drew her away from the group as they discussed the vagaries of dragons and led her down the hall to her chamber.

She knew what this was about. What he was going to say. Panic exploded in her belly. *No.*

His big hands closed over her shoulders, and she leaned back into his warmth. His forehead rested against the back of her head.

"I don't want to go." The words burst from her.

Tears pressed against her lids. How could she leave this place now? She loved it here. They needed her for what she could teach them. She was valued, free to be herself as she never had been before. No expectation of rigid logic. If Bretton was anything to go by, she doubted that would be the case on Aquatilis.

"You cannot stay." Kesuk's hands tightened on her shoulders.

She closed her eyes over the pain. Her voice grew softer. "Why?"

"It is not safe here."

"It's not safe anywhere. Even technology malfunctions. How else did I end up here? Now?"

He sighed, his breath tickling the back of her neck. "Jain—"

"Safety isn't a good enough reason. What else do you have?"

"I don't want you here. This is my Den. You must go."

He didn't want her to stay? Pain hit her square in the chest, squeezed her heart in an iron grip. She searched for something, *anything* to change his mind. "But . . . but, my debt isn't paid. I'm still your sla—"

"You risked your life to save my cub. Your debt is repaid. I release you."

She turned to face him, pulling out of his arms. "I only did what anyone would have done."

"That is not so. Anyone not in my clan would have left her for dead."

"That's horrible and barbar—" She cut herself off, the look on his face freezing her blood. "Oh, Kesuk, that's not what I—"

"No. Perhaps you are right. You will be more suited to the *civility* of Aquatilis." He spun on a heel and strode from the room, never once looking back.

Her breath choked on a sob. "Kesuk."

Light-headed, she leaned against the bed, her body tingling with shock. She felt as though a part of her had been ripped away. *He wanted her gone.*

Well, she sure as hell didn't want to stay where she wasn't wanted. She began to pack, stuffing her clothes and belongings randomly into a satchel. Her hands shook so badly, Miki's shells slipped through her fingers and scattered across the floor.

"Damn."

She gathered up the shells, crawling halfway under the bed to retrieve a few strays. The only man to ever make her feel didn't even want to be on the same planet with her. Her breath rattled past parched lips as she tried to swallow the huge lump in her throat. She pressed her forehead against the cool stone floor, trying to push away her emotions like she used to. She tried to make it matter as little as her husband leaving her. She couldn't.

Someone knocked on the door. "Jain?"

"I'll be out in a minute, Sera."

"What are you doing under there?" Footsteps tapped across the floor.

"I dropped Miki's shells." Where were they? She searched, frantic to find them all. She couldn't leave them. She just couldn't. They were her present. Her breath sobbed out, stirring the dust.

"There are plenty of shells out here. Just leave them."

"No! I have to bring them all. I *have* to." Tears burned her lids, and she clamped a desperate hand over her mouth to stifle her sudden sobs.

"Okay . . . okay . . . I'll help you." Sera's usually impatient voice was kind and soothing.

"I can do it myself. I can—" They were her *present*. The only connection she'd have to Kesuk and his family after she left. Her hand closed over the last tiny shell. She sighed, an inordinate amount of relief singing through her. A tear leaked down her cheek. "I have it now."

She swiped at her eyes, sniffling as she shimmied out from under the bed, dragging a few stray dust bunnies with her. Standing, she brushed off her clothes and turned to slide the shells into her bag, avoiding eye contact with the other woman.

"It's better that we're leaving, Jain. We were supposed to go to Aquatilis in the first place."

"I know." She cleared her throat. She'd dealt with difficult situations before. She could handle this. She didn't have a choice. If Kesuk didn't want her to stay, then that was it. End of story.

The big bed was empty without Kesuk. Cold. Jain squeezed her eyes shut, willing sleep to come. Wavering dawn sunshine filtered through the small light shafts in her ceiling. *He hadn't come to her.* She swung her legs over the side of the bed, standing. If he wouldn't come to her, then she would go to him. She deserved one more time in his arms, damn it.

She realized she was stark naked and had no idea where his room was. He had always stayed with her. Stumped, she sat back down. Looking around, she tried to remember where she'd put the map he'd given her when she'd first arrived. Maybe his chambers were labeled. On her knees, she rummaged through her pack, trying to find something that felt like parchment.

Her door swung open.

She froze. She didn't even need to look to know it was him. "Kesuk."

He didn't say a word. In two strides he was on her, scooping her into his arms. She clung to his neck, wrapping her legs around his waist. Thank God he was already naked. She could definitely develop a distinct liking for nudity. *If only she had more time.* She shoved the thought away, focused on enjoying this time with Kesuk. Her last time.

Stroking his hands over her back, he seemed to relish the feel of her skin, burying his face in her neck to breathe deeply. Surprised that he wanted to go slow, she tightened her legs to press closer to him.

"Kesuk, I—"

The time for words has passed, little bear. Be with me tonight.

"Yes." The answer was simple, plain. She'd take what she could get before she had to leave. One night. One time. One moment. If that's all there was, she'd let go and enjoy it. He'd broken down all her barriers, and she was done pretending he hadn't. She wanted him.

His mouth covered hers, his tongue twining with hers in a slow, deep kiss. Walking blindly, he lowered her to the bed. The furs felt soft against her back as he settled on top of her. The tip of his dick rubbed against her wet pussy lips. Arching up, she waited for the hard thrust that would bury his cock deep within her. It didn't come. Instead, he moved backward, spreading soft kisses over her jaw and neck. She gasped when he nipped her earlobe, the sting causing hot moisture to pool between her spread thighs.

"Please."

Shh.

He pressed his lips to the base of her neck, and his teeth raked over her collarbone. She buried her fingers into his dense, silky hair, loving the texture of it, tugging sharply to speed his progress. Not wanting to wait, she wriggled her hips, pushed the head of his cock into her vagina. He sucked her nipple deep into his mouth, drawing hard on the tip.

Frantic, she bucked against him, her heart pounding hard. She couldn't wait. She needed him now. She clamped her legs tight around his hips, pulling him down as she arched up. He groaned, his cock sinking into her, setting a slow, steady, maddening rhythm. Twisting beneath him, she tried to urge him on.

"Kesuk, *please.*" She cupped his cheeks between her hands,

forced him to look at her. "I want you. No one can make me feel the way you do. Only you. Now, *hurry up.*"

Surprise flashed across his face and he laughed, a cocky grin playing over his lips. *Like this?*

Three quick hard strokes filled her to the limit. "Yes."

Her hands closed over his ass, pulling him closer, deeper. He quickened his pace, taking her hard, just like she liked it. His masculine scent filled her nose as she sobbed for breath. She clung to him as he rode her, locked together, driving toward orgasm. A few more moments and she would go over, but she held it off, fighting to draw the pleasure out.

He froze, his eyes going all black, his hips jerking in fast plunging strokes as he came inside of her. Groaning into her mouth, he sucked her lower lip between his teeth.

Jain. I . . . Jain.

His thought echoed in her mind, connecting her to him as she shuddered hard, pussy clenching around his dick, her nails biting into his back, her legs tight around his waist.

"Kesuk," she whispered.

Dawn broke and lit the small skylights in her room, the beams gilding his pale skin in a golden glow as they held each other tight, not wanting this last moment to pass. He pressed his forehead to hers, his unsteady breath caressing her face.

Then he rolled off her, taking his warmth with him. He rose gracefully from the bed, his large body beautiful in the morning light. "I will leave you to your final preparations."

She swallowed and crossed her arms over her breasts. "You're not even going to see me off?"

His long fingers clenched on the wood doorframe. His voice grated out. "No. I . . . can't. Imnek will escort you."

Hot tears flooded her eyes, and she tilted her head back, trying to hold them in. "Okay," she whispered. What else could she say? It was over. Finished.

"I'm sorry, little bear."

A soft laugh caught on a sob at his use of her nickname. God, she would miss that.

He finally looked at her, glancing back over his shoulder, a sad smile playing on his lips. "You wanted me to delegate."

"Just . . . go." She made herself watch the door close behind him.

9

A thin layer of ice crunched under Jain's heavy boots. She walked with Sera, Bretton, and Varad toward the weretiger ship. A huge number of Kesuk's guards accompanied them. He seemed to have emptied out the entire Den for their escort. After her last jaunt outside, she wasn't complaining, but it seemed overkill to send this many to protect them. Her steps dragged. They'd been walking for hours, but it seemed the shortest journey of her life. Everything inside of her wanted to turn around and run back, but instead she pressed forward.

"I have some theories."

Jain sucked her cheeks in to stifle a laugh. How many times had she heard that phrase when Sera was working with her brother? Her heart squeezed at the bittersweet memory of her emotionally distant brother. It hurt so much that even the possibility of growing closer had died with him.

Jain gave Sera a sad smile. "Theories about what?"

"About why we never made it to Aquatilis, of course." Sera rolled her eyes as though she couldn't believe Jain wasn't keeping up with her line of thought.

"Tell me." Jain wasn't sure she'd understand half of what Sera said, but she'd listen. *Anything* to help her not think of Kesuk.

"I would like to hear this as well." Bretton walked a few paces behind them, his hands clasped behind his back.

Sera blushed and swallowed hard. "Um . . . well, it's simple really . . . we, um, we . . . it's possible the hyperdrive failed when we were down-jumping, and my postulation is that we came out of lightspeed too quickly and actually ended up in the neighboring solar system, still traveling toward our destination, but slowly. Then we were caught in the orbit of Alysius for centuries, those on board sustained by the life-support systems in our individual cryogenic pods."

"Why wasn't the crew alert to the problem?" Varad matched stride with Jain on the right.

"Our ship was strictly a supply berth. Jain and I were the only passengers. On supply ships, it was procedure for the crew to enter cryogenic freeze shortly after the jump to lightspeed, and the system would automatically wake them at the end of the standard jump. Ours was not standard, so the crew never woke up. However, it *is* possible—"

"So, why did we crash? Why didn't we remain in orbit forever?" Jain interrupted Sera's academic rambling.

A frown puckered the other woman's face. "Well . . . I don't know exactly."

"You're here now; that's all that matters." Bretton smiled at Sera.

Jain actually thought the good doctor might swoon. She fought her fifth eye roll of the day. Her gaze met Varad's, and he coughed into his palm to hide his laugh.

"What's Aquatilis like?" Sera grinned back at the ambassador.

"It's wonderful, much better than this. Atlantis is a beacon of lights you can see for miles. We have acres of botanical gardens inside the city proper with dozens of shops to choose from. Saltwater silk would look phenomenal with your lovely hair, Doctor." Bretton's nose wrinkled at the thick fur cape Sera wore now. *Jain's* cape.

Jain's hands balled into fists as she tried to rein in her anger. Bretton had been here only a few weeks; he didn't know anything about these people. She brushed aside the fact that she'd been on Alysius only a few days longer than he had. It had been, what? Three weeks? That was all? It felt like forever. And yet, it had passed far too quickly.

Sera smiled. "I can't wait. I hate it here. It's like something out of a backward caveman holostory."

"Not everyone here is like the Browns." Jain bit her tongue. Damn, she should learn to keep her mouth shut.

Their guards grunted in agreement.

"Look at this place." Bretton waved his elegant hand to indicate their uninhabited surroundings.

"It's beautiful. Just because it's not like *your* planet doesn't mean there's anything wrong with it. You're awfully rude for someone who's supposed to be a representative of your people, *Ambassador* Hahn." Jain didn't bother hiding her disdain.

Bretton flushed, whether from anger or embarrassment, Jain didn't know or care. The snob could go sleep with a predator for all she cared. They'd be the perfect match, and she didn't give a damn that she was being unfair to the Aquatilian.

"If you like it here so much, why are you leaving?" Varad's casual question knocked the wind out of her anger.

"Kesuk . . . doesn't want me." Jain's voice sounded stilted, even to her own ears.

God, it hurt to even say it, let alone feel it. He didn't *want* her.

Varad folded his hands behind his back. "Hmm . . . that's funny."

"I'm not amused." She shot him a dirty look. Had she thought

Varad was the polite one? Well, chalk that one up to another wrong assessment of a male.

"I meant, Lady Jain, that your Lord Kesuk—"

"He's not mine." She clamped her eyes closed, determined not to cry. Not now, not in front of all these people. Striving for her old calm, she opened eyes that were still misty with tears. Damn Kesuk for making her feel and then throwing her away.

"As I was saying, Lord Kesuk did not act like a man who didn't want you."

"That *is* funny because he's the one making me leave. So what did he act like, hmm?" Her voice was so sweet it was acidic.

"Like a man doing his duty and cutting his heart out in the process. Like a *good* man with the misfortune to be in love." Varad's mouth kicked up in a memory only he could see.

"You speak like someone with experience." Jain's mind raced. Could it be true? Kesuk was making her leave as a duty? He loved her?

"I am mated."

She blinked, paying only half a mind to the conversation. Her heart fluttered wildly in her chest. Kesuk *loved* her. Stupid man. Stupid, wonderful man with his stupid, ridiculous honor. She smiled at Varad, a huge blinding smile.

Varad blinked, looked away, and muttered again, "I am mated."

The spaceship came into view, a huge monolithic silver blemish on the pristine forest landscape. Seeing it, Jain made an immediate decision, no thinking, no planning.

"I'm staying."

"Excuse me?" Bretton looked stunned.

"You can't be serious," Sera exclaimed.

Jain took a deep breath, and the heavy weight that had been crushing her chest lifted. "I'm staying. I hope you all have a nice trip."

Varad threw back his head and laughed, the rich sound bouncing off the surrounding mountains. He caught her hands in his. "Oh, my lady. Remember the look on his face when he first sees you. You must describe it for me in detail when I return next turn."

"Only if you bring your mate with you so I can meet her."

"Done." Varad kissed each of her hands.

"My lord would not appreciate your actions," Imnek growled. Surprised, Jain glanced at the guard who'd stayed within three steps of her the whole journey.

At first she thought Imnek meant encouraging her to stay, but he didn't even look at her. Instead he stared pointedly at Jain's hands tucked in Varad's grip. Varad stepped away from her, bowing to Imnek. "I trust you will see her safely back to Sea Den."

"Her protection is *my* duty." He glared at the weretiger.

Jain didn't even want to figure out what kind of manly undercurrents were going on here. She was just glad no one was going to make her get on the ship.

"You should come with me. You'll be living in the Dark Ages here." Sera frowned at Jain from the bottom of the pallet loaded with all the trade goods. As the men started loading supplies onto the Vesperi ship, Jain crawled on top and pilfered through the bags until she found hers.

Jain hefted her pack, hopping down into the slushy Thaw snow. The men were growing impatient, watching them work it out. "I love him."

"You could love someone on Aquatilis. That's where we were supposed to go in the first place. And even Varad says it's not as backward as here."

She arched a brow. "That doesn't sound like Varad."

"Not in so many words, but that's basically what he said." Sera folded her arms and tilted her jaw.

Jain sighed. "Things have changed."

"No kidding."

"I meant things have changed with me. Maybe you can walk away from love and find something else that will make you happy. Maybe all you need is your work and your machines, but I need Kesuk and I'm staying."

Sera's eyebrows rose until they almost met her hairline. "You are different."

"I just said that."

"Yes, but you would *never* have said anything like that before. Or told off Bretton. It was always yes, Dad, yes, Brother, yes, Husband."

"*Yes, Sera.*"

Sera snorted, then sobered. "You're sure you'll be okay?"

"As sure as I can be."

"Good luck." Sera leaned in and offered a tentative hug, awkward with affection.

Jain squeezed her tight, popping a kiss on her cheek. "You, too."

"We'll see each other again," Sera whispered in her ear. Then she bolted up the ramp and into the ship.

Waving until the door sealed closed, Jain turned to Imnek, grinning. "Ready?"

"Lord Kesuk is going to kill me."

She looped her hand through his arm. "Well, he wanted you to make more executive decisions. Congratulations, you've succeeded."

Imnek just groaned in response.

It was for the best. It was for her own good. Kesuk stalked to her room, flung the door open, and stomped inside. His gaze swept the room. He could still smell her. Smell the lingering scent of their sex. He dragged in a deep breath, knowing he'd need to remember every detail in the future, when the pain had subsided. It had been that way with Maruska. Someday, he would cherish his time with Jain. Someday the pain would fade. Now he felt as though a dull blade had ripped his heart out.

He'd been so careful. Not to need her. Not to get attached to her. Not to love her. He wasn't strong enough to lose two women he loved in one lifetime. Nothing had ever hit him as hard as she had. Feelings had developed gradually with his mate. But with Jain? His world had tilted on its axis when she crashed into it. Going back to the cold man he had been before Jain wasn't appealing. Duty was a poor substitute; he knew that now. He'd had Jain to point it out. Passion he could handle, control. But love? He sighed, laid a hand on the untidy furs, imagining he could still feel the warmth of her body on them. The warmth of her smile, her touch.

"Papa?"

He straightened, turning toward the small voice. Miki and Nukilik stood in the doorway, tears streaking their faces. "Yes?"

He waved them forward and they ran in to hug his legs. "Where did Jain go?"

"She left for Aquatilis. Did she not say farewell?" Surely Jain would never have done such a thing. She adored his cubs, of that he had no doubt.

"She said she had to leave. When will she be back? Next Turn with Amir Varad?" Nukilik's steady eyes gazed up at him, waiting for him to say the right thing. He wished he knew the answers for them.

"That's a very long time to wait, Papa. We'll be so much older then. What if she doesn't recognize us?"

"She's not coming back."

"Not coming back? Why not?" Nukilik's forehead furrowed.

Miki dug her fingers into the top of Kesuk's boot. "She'll miss us very much. She loves us. She said so before she left. She said we weren't to forget."

"Then you're not to forget." He stroked back Miki's soft

hair. He took a deep breath, sat on the edge of Jain's bed, and pulled a child onto each leg. "Jain was supposed to go to Aquatilis. She needs to be there."

"She didn't like Ambassador Hahn. I could tell. She likes us, so she should have stayed here." Nukilik nodded at that logic. Simple. Reasonable. Fair. The boy would grow into an excellent clan leader someday.

"She has to come back. We love her and she loves us," Miki sobbed, her fingers clenching in the laces on his shirt. He hugged her close, knowing nothing but time would ease her grief.

The distant roar of the weretigers' spaceship flying over Sea Den shook the ground under his feet. The dull ache in his chest intensified to a sharp, blinding pain. He closed his eyes, swallowing. Jain was gone. It was well and truly over now. He felt . . . empty.

Jain found Kesuk lying in her bed, the covers still mussed from their lovemaking, his arms folded behind his head, staring at the curved ceiling.

"I couldn't do it."

Jerking upright, he twisted to stare at her. He blinked, his expression blank for a moment. "You're supposed to be on the ship."

"I couldn't leave. I was there, ready to board and do what you wanted, what you thought was best. Hell, what was *logical,* but I just . . . couldn't do it." Spreading her hands, she shrugged.

"I told you I didn't want you here."

"You lied."

He blinked. "What?"

"You lied. I understand; you were trying to do the right thing. I really do get it."

He rolled to the edge of the bed, his booted feet landing on the fur rug. "You won't be able to leave for another Turn."

"Yes, that ship has sailed." She grinned, starting to enjoy his confusion. It was about damn time she had the upper hand in something.

"Jain . . ." He trailed off, at an obvious loss for words.

"I'm staying. I already decided and there's nothing you can do about it. Be angry if you want, but I'm still here. You won't stay mad long, though. You want to know why?"

"Why?"

"Because you love me."

He choked.

"That's right, you love me. It took me a while to figure it out, but now it all makes sense. You try to make me happier with myself, more comfortable in my own skin. You worry about me all the time. You sent a whole legion of soldiers to guard me today. Did you really think we needed that many? You saved me from the snow, treat me with respect even when you're being a bossy jerk, and you get angry when people try to hurt me."

"I would do the same for anyone under my protection."

"Maybe, but you didn't have to bring me under your protection in the first place. The Blacks wanted to buy me, so you could have gotten rid of me if you wanted to. You didn't want to. You wanted to keep me."

"Blacks are scavengers. I wouldn't—"

"We can argue about this all night long if you want, because I'm here for another year, so we have plenty of time. Or we can occupy ourselves with something more entertaining. . . ." She smiled at him and unbuttoned her heavy fur-lined jacket. Her tunic quickly followed, and his gaze locked on her bare breasts. She bounced on her toes a little to make them jiggle for him, their tips peaking tight.

He sucked in a hissing breath. "Jain—"

"Touch me." She leaned forward so he could do what she wanted.

His hand lifted to stroke down the slope of her breast, fingers plucking at her nipples. Using his other palm to cup her ass, he pulled her forward and buried his face between her breasts. He breathed deeply, nudged her soft flesh with his nose, and slid his tongue up to swirl around the crest before sucking it deep into his mouth, pulling back to worry the very tip of her hard nipple between his teeth.

She caught her breath, rising on tiptoe to get closer to that wicked mouth. She moaned deeply, fisting her hands in his hair. She loved the silky feel of it.

He sucked a deep breath, let go of her nipple, and rested his chin on her chest. "I did the right thing."

"You did. So did I." She stroked his hair, tears gathering in her eyes.

"Kiss me."

A wicked grin played over her lips, and she dropped to her knees between his spread thighs. She slid a fingernail up the seam of his pants toward his cock. It strained against the leather as she traced the lacings to the top and tugged the strings open. "As you wish. You didn't get to have me as your slave very long. Maybe I should make it up to you?"

"Ah, little bear. I do love how your mind works."

His heavy dick slipped free, and she wrapped her fingers tight around the base and stroked to the tip. Rotating her hand around the head of his cock, she licked a bead of pre-cum from the tip. She sucked the whole head in, her lips slipping down to the shaft as her hands worked his flesh up and down, slow at first, then faster and faster.

He groaned, his fingers slipping into her short hair, using his grip to pump her mouth as if it were a pussy. His cock touched the back of her throat. "Hmmm," she hummed around his dick, looking into his eyes so she knew he saw her envelop his cock in her mouth.

"Jain!" Panting hard, his hands slid under her arms, lifting her off the floor and away from his cock. He rolled them onto

298 / Crystal Jordan

the bed and jerked at the lacings on her pants, which tangled tight.

She laughed. "Hey, I wasn't finished yet."

"I very nearly was."

"That was kind of the point."

He growled in frustration, ripping her pants open, the tough leather snapping under his strength. "Lift your ass."

She obeyed, leveraging her hips up to help him slide her pants down, trusting him to take her where she needed to go. He had her naked in a few seconds and rolled her to her hands and knees. He slid his fingers between her pussy lips, stroking her clit. She moaned, pushing back into his hand. He pressed down on the small of her back, arching her ass up.

The head of his cock pushed at her opening and then slid hard and deep into her pussy. She dropped down, pressing her face to the covers, gasping at his deep penetration. His hand reached around to stroke her clit in time with his slapping thrusts.

"I can't—"

"You can." He rotated his hips, grinding her in a different rhythm.

"Kesuk . . ."

"Straighten up," he ordered. His hands pulled up on her rib cage until her back pressed to his chest.

One of his hands resumed stroking her pussy. The other fondled her breasts.

She reached back to tug on his hair, twisting her head around to pull his mouth to hers. His lips captured hers, stroking his tongue into her mouth. Their tongues rubbed, stroked, dueled as their bodies moved together in hard, pounding rhythm.

Blood sang through her veins, pumping her heart fast. She rubbed her ass against his pelvis, bouncing on his hard cock. He broke from her mouth, his teeth moving to her shoulder and biting down.

"Kesuk." She clawed his strong thighs, which flexed to pump into her hot pussy. Her juices made a slapping noise as they coated his dick.

He pressed down on her clit, rode her on it with his thrusts, pinching her nipple hard.

"I'm coming! Kesuk, I'm coming!" She twisted under the lash of pleasure, her pussy spasming hard. Her heart pounded so hard she could feel the beats just under her skin, her whole body flushing. Oh, God.

"Yes." He pounded with short, jerky strokes, his breath harsh against her neck. Stiffening, he froze, shuddering his orgasm.

Gasping hard, they collapsed onto their sides. He wrapped his arms around her, cradling her back against his chest, burying his nose in her hair, breathing deeply.

She rubbed her hand over his forearms in lazy circles. "I was right. That was definitely more fun than arguing."

He grunted, his arms tightening. "You had your chance to go. I let you. Now you're mine."

"And you're mine. Forever." She sighed, snuggling back against him, content.

"Forever."

"I love you, Kesuk."

"I know."

"*I know?* That's all I get?" She clawed his arm in retaliation.

He chuckled. "I love you, too. Now kiss me."

His cock rose between the cleft of her ass, and she gasped in surprise, pushing her hips against his hardening flesh.

"Again?"

"Forever."

Turn the page
and Lydia Parks
will have you
ADDICTED!

On sale now from Aphrodisia!

1

_____

Jake Brand tipped his chair back on two legs, wrapped his hand around a glass of whiskey, and took in the sights as if he had all the time in the world. In a way, he did. At least, in the foreseeable future, he had a decent shot at eternity.

The young blonde leaning over a table, shaking her backside in his direction, was another matter. In a few short years, her firm breasts would start to sag and her tight ass would droop. If she were lucky, some lonely trucker would offer her his life savings and a ranch-style home in the outskirts of Albuquerque before that happened.

But tonight, Jake planned to entertain the sweet young thing in exchange for dinner.

"You sure are taking your time with that drink," the blonde said, frowning at the five-dollar bill on his table.

Jake plucked a folded fifty from his shirt pocket and dropped it on top of the five. "I've got nothing but time, darlin'."

The young woman's eyes widened and her red, full lips stretched into a greedy smile. She snatched the bill from the table and stuffed it into the back pocket of her denim miniskirt.

She winked at him. "I'll be back for you in just a minute."

"I'll be right here," he said, grinning. He watched her hurry to the bar, toss her towel under it, and whisper something to the bartender.

The burly redheaded bartender glanced over at Jake and nodded, and the blonde started back for Jake's table, swinging her hips as she tapped out the background song's rhythm with her high heels. He liked the way the shoes made her legs look a mile long. The thought of those legs wrapped around him caused a pleasant reaction, and he moved to adjust his tightening jeans.

She didn't stop at his table, but continued forward until she stood straddling his thighs, her hands locked behind his neck as she swayed back and forth in time with the music. "My name's Candy," she said, her voice soft in his ear. "You like candy, don't you?"

"Hmm," he said, inhaling her scent, weeding out vanilla shampoo, cheap perfume, stale cigarettes, whiskey fumes, and sweat. Yes, he definitely had the right dinner partner. "I can eat candy all night long."

"Oh, baby," she whispered, "You make me hot."

He chuckled at the insincerity of her words. Undoubtedly, few of her many customers cared if she meant them or not, and he didn't, either. Before the night was over, he'd get the truth from her, and she'd be more than just *hot*.

Jake ran the tips of his fingers up the backs of her exposed thighs.

She stepped back to frown down at him. "No touching. That's house rules."

He grinned again, enjoying the way her simple emotions played across her face.

He lowered his voice a notch. "I could bring you to a quivering climax without touching you, but it wouldn't be nearly as much fun."

One corner of her mouth curled up in cynical amusement. "You think so?"

"I know so." Jake used the Touch to retrace the paths of his fingers with his thoughts, remembering the warmth, the smoothness, the soft hairs on her upper thighs.

"*Hey.*" She took another step back and stared into his eyes.

Jake pushed a simple concept into her simple mind. *Pleasure like you've never known.*

She swallowed hard, hesitated, and then moved forward to straddle his thighs again. He could smell her excitement as she sat on his legs and wrapped her arms around his shoulders. "I don't know how you did that," she said softly. "And I don't really care. You wanna go in the back room?"

"I think we should go up to my room."

She nodded, then turned her head to kiss him. Her warm breath caressed his skin before her lips met his, and he closed his eyes to enjoy the heated tenderness of her mouth. Her tongue slid across his lips, moving precariously close to the razor-sharp points of his teeth. Jake let a groan escape as he enjoyed the way her heat enveloped his growing erection, in spite of the clothes between them.

Candy ended the kiss and stood, drawing Jake after her with her small hand in his, leading him upstairs. The noise of the saloon-turned-strip joint faded below them as they climbed, leaving only a bass vibration in its wake.

"Which room?"

He nodded toward the door at the end of the small hallway. "Six."

"The best." She raised one eyebrow. "You rich or something?"

"Something."

"Oh, I see." She tossed her head, sending her blond waves into a dance around her shoulders. Candy knew exactly how attractive she was. "So, you're a man of mystery. Your name isn't *John*, is it?"

"No, it's Jake." He withdrew the key from his pocket, unlocked the door and pushed it open, then stepped aside as his young visitor entered. She didn't look around; she'd seen the room before.

"Jake." She turned in the middle of the room and smiled as she surveyed him from head to toe. "You know your fifty bucks don't buy you much. You want a blow job, or straight sex?"

Jake laughed then. "How do you know I'm not a peace officer?"

"A cop?" Candy grinned. "I know cops. Half the force comes in here after their shift. You're different, but you ain't no cop."

He nodded as he crossed the room and sat on the foot of the bed. "You're right about that. I'm different."

Candy tugged at the hem of her shirt, her head cocked seductively. "For twenty more, I take off my clothes just for you, baby."

Jake pulled off his boots and dropped them onto the floor. "I've got a better idea. How about a wager?"

The young woman straightened and narrowed her eyes. "You tryin' to tell me you ain't got no more money?"

He withdrew a hundred from his pocket and dropped it onto the bed. When she reached for it, he covered her hand with his own. "Not so fast there, sweet thing. Don't you want to hear my proposal?"

"*Proposal?*"

"For a wager."

Candy withdrew her hand slowly, then folded her arms across her chest. "I'm listening."

Jake stretched out on his side, studying the girl. "How long have you been at this?"

"At what?"

"Hooking."

Candy frowned. "You ain't some kind of preacher or something, are you? If you think you're gonna convert me—"

Jake silenced her by raising one hand. "You've got me all wrong, sweetheart. I'm definitely not a preacher."

She waited, her hands now on her hips.

"I'm willing to bet you one hundred dollars that I can bring you to a screaming climax in the next half hour."

Her eyebrows shot up and then she burst out laughing.

Jake watched her, enjoying her amusement.

"Right," she said between guffaws. "A *screaming* climax?"

He nodded.

When she managed to regain control of herself, she dropped down onto the edge of the bed, extending her hand. "You're on, Jake."

He took her hand in his, enjoying the warmth. Then he sat up and raised her hand to his lips.

"But you gotta wear a rubber."

Jake looked into her blue eyes. "Do I?"

Candy nodded. "Safe sex or no sex, that's how I stay alive."

"I promise we will run no risk of infecting you with anything."

Jake rose and drew Candy up to stand in front of him. Watching her face, he ran his palms slowly up her sides, peeling her shirt off over her head.

She stared at him with calm resolve, but goose bumps rose on her skin where he'd touched her. "Your hands are cold," she said.

"You'll just have to warm them up for me, darlin'."

He unsnapped her skirt and pushed it off in the same manner, sliding his palms over her rounded buttocks and down the backs of her thighs. As she stood before him in her high heels, he stepped back to drink in the sight of her.

Her breasts were full and firm, with large, dark areolae. As he studied them, her nipples puckered, and he knew she liked to be watched.

Her waist, narrow with youth, led his gaze down to her partially shaved pubic mound, the line of dark brown hair giving away her true color.

Then there were those legs. Damn, they were long.

"Oh, yeah," he said, aloud but to himself. "This will be fun."

Jake stepped closer and eased his hands down from her shoulders to her breasts, memorizing the shape and warmth of them, twisting the nipples playfully before moving on to her waist and then her ass. *Nice.* He nuzzled her neck to get more of her scent, then pressed his lips to the top of her shoulder. The sound of her heart beating drowned out the hum of the room's air conditioner, and he let himself enjoy it for a few moments before turning back to the task at hand.

He moved his mouth to hers, covering her lips with his own as he eased one hand into her soft blond hair. His other hand he slid down her back to the smallest point and pulled her gently to him.

Her hands rose to his chest for balance.

He opened her mouth then, and ran his tongue around hers, catching the taste of whiskey and tobacco, as he moved his hand around her hip and eased it between her legs. Her swollen vulva parted for his fingers as he slid them back and forth, hinting at entering her, stirring her juices.

Her hands flattened against his chest.

Jake eased one finger deeper, stroking her clit, and her fingers curled. She drew on his tongue, and he continued to stroke, enjoying the way her hot little bud swelled.

Candy tore her mouth from his. "You said . . . a *screaming* climax."

"Yes, I did," he said, his mouth near her ear.

Her hips began to rock to the rhythm of his hand, and she gripped the front of his shirt in her fists. "Damn, you're good," she said, "but I don't scream for no man."

Jake chuckled as he slid his hand out from between her thighs. "Good, darlin', 'cause I don't want this to be too easy."

Candy rubbed against the front of his bulging pants. "Even if I ain't screaming, you don't have to stop."

"Don't worry, sweet thing, I'm not about to stop." He reached down with both hands, cradled her ass, and lifted her from the floor.

She wrapped her legs around his hips and her arms around his neck.

Jake carried her to the bed and eased her down as he kissed her. The girl knew how to kiss, and he felt his erection hardening to the point of discomfort. He unbuttoned his pants to relieve some of the pressure, then he withdrew from her.

Her eyes blazed as she looked up at him, partly with passion and partly from whiskey, no doubt.

Jake parted her legs, knelt at the edge of the bed, and kissed the insides of her thighs as he drew her to his mouth.

Her cunt was hot, salty, and wet, and he slowly licked the length of her, savoring the taste. Her legs opened more in response, and her ass tightened. He continued with long, slow laps as he listened to her suck air between her teeth, and he enjoyed her quickening heartbeat. Not long now, and he'd have her ready, sweetened, primed for him.

Jake pushed his tongue between her cunt lips and lashed at her clit, then drew it carefully between his teeth and sucked.

Candy's back arched, and she moaned as she neared an orgasm.

He moved away, nibbling at her thighs.

She grunted in frustration and he smiled.

Closing his eyes, Jake pushed his thoughts out then, moving the Touch up the length of her body like a hundred butterfly wings, caressing every part of her at once, flitting across her nipples and stomach, as he slid his fingers into her cunt.

Her hips rose up off the bed and she cried out in joy. "Oh . . . God . . . that's good," she said between panted breaths.

She clamped down on his fingers and flooded them with her juices as he moved in and out of her, traveling across her damp skin with his thoughts, feeling the conditioned air blow across her breasts, finding her pulse in a hundred spots at once.

His burgeoning cock emerged from the front of his pants as he enjoyed Candy, pulling her to the edge of her resistance, then pushing her away.

She cooed, and then groaned, and then growled with disappointment.

Continuing the Touch, Jake rose and removed his clothes. He loved the feel of heated flesh against his own when he drank. Letting the Touch drift lower now, he stretched out on top of Candy and kissed her neck, her jaw, and her shoulders.

She wriggled under him as the treatment intensified. His thoughts rolled over her cunt, then dipped in and out.

"Fuck me," she said, digging her fingers into his back. "Please. I'm on fire."

"Yes," he whispered, easing his cock between her legs.

She thrust up into him, taking him into her all at once, and he almost lost her.

"Oh, no, you don't," he said, drawing back.

She locked her legs around him before he could withdraw.

"Good lord, get on with it."

Jake glanced over his shoulder, surprised to find Thomas Skidmore standing beside the bed, pale hands fisted on his narrow hips.

"Go away," Jake said.

"Why do you insist on doing it this way?" Skidmore waved dramatically with one arm, his style mimicking the British theater of years gone by. "I've never known anyone who felt they had to get permission. You are strange, dear boy."

Jake returned his attention to Candy, rocking against her in time with her growing need. She hadn't noticed the intrusion.

"Just hurry. We have places to go." Skidmore closed the door behind him as he left.

"Oh, God," she said, louder now. "Don't stop. Fuck me. Harder."

Jake turned his head to speak softly into her ear. "I need more than your cunt, sweet thing. I need your blood."

He felt her tense as fear crept into her fevered excitement.

"I won't hurt you," he said. "We'll come together."

After a moment of hesitation, she turned her head, offering her neck to him as she writhed in anticipation, her hands fisted against his back.

Jake pressed his lips to her neck, thrilling to the pulse rising and falling beneath the surface. He let loose of the reins then, thrusting into her sizzling cunt as his cock hardened to steel, pushing deeper, needing release nearly as much as he needed to feed.

His fangs lengthened, and he opened his mouth. Trying to hold back, savoring the anticipation, he smelled her approaching climax. Yes, she was ready.

Jake pressed his fangs into her neck and she screamed. He closed his eyes as her orgasm flooded him, first biting down on his pulsing cock, then flowing through his veins and exploding in his brain. He drew hard as he pumped his seed into her, letting her fill him with need, fulfillment, dreams, wants, desires.

He knew her arousal as she danced for hungry eyes, her smug disgust as sweaty men humped her for money, her euphoria as she lay alone at night with a vibrating orgasm rolling through her narcotic haze. And he felt her ecstasy as his own. She came again as he thrust harder, longer, until he'd taken all he could, and given all he had.

Jake held his mouth to her neck for a moment to stop the flow, then moved it away and slowed his thrusts to nice, easy strokes.

Her grip changed to a shaky hold on his shoulders, and her cries softened to weak groans.

He stilled, then withdrew and rolled onto his back to enjoy the sensations of nerves popping and firing through his entire system, waking from a long sleep. After more than a century and a half, he still loved the vibration, especially when sweetened with orgasms.

"You win."

Jake turned his head to find Candy lying with her eyes closed and her arms at her sides, her body glistening with a fine sheen of sweat. Already, the small wounds on her neck were nearly healed, and her heart rate had begun to slow.

He grinned.

If not for Skidmore waiting impatiently outside somewhere, Jake might have spent a few more hours with his little morsel. But the old man was right; they had places to go.

After getting dressed, he dropped the bill onto Candy's bare stomach, then leaned over and kissed her soundly.

She hadn't moved much, and smiled up at him. "You come back anytime, Jake."

He winked at her, then tossed the room key onto the bed beside her before leaving his dinner guest and the air conditioner's buzz behind.

Downstairs, he found the tall, thin vampire in an out-of-place purple velvet suit, standing in the shadows near the door, and Jake made his way through the maze of tables, young strippers, and horny old men.

"It's about time," Skidmore said, wrinkling his nose with disapproval.

"Some things shouldn't be rushed." Jake picked up his black felt Stetson from a hook by the door and slipped it on as he stepped into the New Mexico night. Warm, clean air swept over him as if he were no more than another jackrabbit making his way across the desert, and a star-filled sky opened above as Jake strolled across the parking lot to the convertible parked near the exit.

"Will you please get a move on?" Skidmore hurried ahead, hopping effortlessly into the passenger's seat. "I refuse to spend another day trapped in the boot of this wretched beast. It'll take at least four hours to get to the mine, and that's thirty minutes more than we have."

"Don't sweat it," Jake said, trying not to get annoyed with his fellow traveler. Skidmore tended to get on his nerves after a month or two of whining. "We'll be there in three."

Jake started the Impala and pulled out onto the narrow highway, turning north. With no one else around, he easily pushed the car to ninety and they roared through the darkness.

"Oh, I nearly forgot to tell you what I heard," Skidmore said.

It was a lie; the older vampire never forgot anything. Jake waited, but Skidmore just smiled.

"What?"

"A very special friend of yours will be at the meeting. If we get there early enough, perhaps you'll have time to get reacquainted."

"Katie?" Jake glanced over at his companion, whose face seemed to glow in the starlight.

Skidmore grinned and ignored his question.

CPSIA information can be obtained at www.ICGtesting.com
Printed in the USA
LVOW06s1627230713

344256LV00004B/333/P